DRAGON'S BLOOD

Book 1 of the Blood of the Covenants Series

Leah E. Welker

Lightbound Media

Library of Congress Control Number: 2024937881

Print ISBN: 9781964174013

Ebook ISBN: 9781964174006

First Edition

CONTENTS

To Mom and Dad, for everything.

Lead, Kindly Light, amidst th'encircling gloom,
Lead Thou me on!
The night is dark, and I am far from home,
Lead Thou me on!

John Henry Newman

KEY TERMS & TRANSLATIONS

Races

draká ("druh-KAH"): the original "dragons."
amá ("ah-MAH"): human(s); the sentient inhabitants of Earth.
dramá ("druh-MAH"): the race that emerged from the combination of draká and humans.

Blood Manifestations

drakón ("drah-KOHN"): dramá chosen to have far greater magic and gain a drakáform.
amón ("ah-MOHN"): dramá who are not chosen, yet still have the Blood of the Covenants and cannot accurately be called "human."

Distances

Rough equivalents
ild: inch.
foot: literal translation.
erd: yard (only a couple dramá feet).

ald: 100 dramá feet.

eld: half an English Imperial mile.

elden: an English Imperial mile.

Time

dek: Roughly 1 minute, made of 56 moments.

deken: Roughly 1 hour, made of 56 dek.

day: 28 deken.

PROLOGUE

KAVARIAN

KAVARIAN SUNFILLED, DRAKÓN KING of the Six Realms, was dying.

One would not know it from looking at him as he strode down the sandstone halls of the Temple of Flame. Though he had seen over one hundred and forty summers, that was not an unusual lifespan for a drakón. Standing straight and tall at seven-and-a-half feet, he towered over all the amón and most of the drakón priests. As he acknowledged their greetings with brusque nods, his golden eyes were sharp and clear and his smile as warm as ever. His stride was brisk and strong, carrying him with steady purpose through the web of tunnels carved into the desert rock.

Though there were no obvious signs of his condition, Kavarian knew it to be true. Even if he could not feel the chill coming over the flameheart inside his chest, even if he hadn't experienced a slow decline in his power, he knew his end was coming—for the Tree had told him it would.

He had been anticipating this day for twenty revolutions of his home world, Ythra, around Kaldrir, their precious sun. Despite his readiness to depart for most of those twenty years, there was still the matter of the ones who would be left behind. For a few of them, there could never be enough time to prepare, no words to be said to reconcile them to the necessity, no salve to be given to heal their wounds.

Kavarian, having lost and grieved so deeply himself, knew that truth all too well. That was why he was here, seeking a way to ease the pain of his son.

He reached one of the seven entrances to the Temple Heart within a handful of dek. Good. He had timed this visit to be after the dawn ceremonies had ended and most of the supplicants had left, but before the newcomers would arrive for the next. As King, he could politely dismiss any lingerers to speak to the Tree alone, but the more people who saw him requesting a private audience, the more people who would wonder why he had.

Kavarian had made a point of requesting private audiences with the Tree frequently for that very reason: so that each time was worth no more notice to the common person than an idle remark. This latest bit of gossip would spread through Crownhold within the deken, though it would not make more than a passing impression on anyone's mind, save perhaps on that of one person only.

His son, Koriben, would know at once why his father had gone to see the Tree that morning, and for the few deken it would take the young man to track Kavarian down, the King knew Koriben would allow himself to hope. Though his son should know better by now, that was the way Koriben was.

Kavarian could not bear to crush that precious hope. That was why it had been so long since he had come here. Several weeks now, at least. Not since Kavarian had told his son about his condition.

The King sighed as he stopped just before the Gate of First Light: right now, only an enormous and elaborately carved arch with deep, scorched cavities set into the walls and floor. He lingered one moment to wistfully run his large, calloused hand over the smooth stone tongues of flame carved into the wall before entering the Temple Heart.

The chamber was immense. All who entered for the first time gawked at the size of it. Large enough that a dozen transformed drakón could fit inside, the borders of the round room seemed to almost fade into the distance, as did the domed ceiling hundreds of feet above Kavarian's head. In the center of that dome was a vast hole, perhaps several hundred feet wide and circular, apart from the cracks that radiated outward from the center portion like rays of the sun. At this early hour, the desert light was mild. At noon, it would become so scorching, amón would hardly be able to bear being in the Heart chamber, and even drakón would be uncomfortable.

But the Heart's size and dome were nothing compared to the chamber's occupant at its center: the Tree of Flame.

She was a Tree of epic proportions. Her roots alone, even at their furthest extent above the ground, were larger than Kavarian's humanform, and they spread through most of the entire length of the chamber in every direction before sinking fully into the rock. The Tree's height stretched all the way to the dome's ceiling, and Her branches spread their lengths to form their own covering. Her perpetually burning leaves eagerly drunk in every drop of sunlight. Her mighty trunk would have taken scores of humanform arms linked hand to hand to circumscribe—if such proximity could have been advisable, for tongues of fire continually licked at Her sides. Though the flames caused Her no harm, they were real and not possible for even a drakón in humanform to withstand for long.

As Kavarian entered the Heart, he collected the stares of almost all the lingerers from the dawn ceremonies, and then the whispers began. Kavarian outwardly ignored them, though he sighed as he tallied a dozen worshipers that would be soon scattering back to Crownhold to spread the word of his audience with the Tree. To add to the unfortunate nature of his witnesses, he thought he spotted one of Koriben's friends and former classmates—an orange-headed Brightflare.

Kavarian went straight to the High Priestess, who stood at the stone dais that had been constructed over the tree's roots. By then, the aged drakón, dressed in humble gold-dyed robes, had spotted the King coming and was patiently waiting for him.

"My King," she said with a deferential nod.

"Mother Tivien," Kavarian acknowledged with a deep nod in return. At a little over two hundred years of age, Tivien was the oldest member of the Sunfilled Clan, and thus she was owed nearly as much deference as Kavarian himself. "How went the Dawn Welcoming?"

"Good, good," Tivien said with a cheerful chuckle. "It will be a bright, clear day. You picked a good one to come, my boy."

Kavarian gave the warmest smile he could manage. "I tried to."

"I suppose you would like a private audience, then?" the High Priestess said genially, yet her faded golden eyes were sharp with intelligence. She knew Kavarian too well by now to think this was a mere courtesy visit.

"Indeed, Mother. If it is no trouble."

The High Priestess waved dismissively. "No trouble at all. These hatchling priests could use the rest, anyhow."

"Not you, of course," Kavarian said with a straight face.

"Of course not." Tivien winked as she turned to the center of the dais.

There lay the shallow pit with the ritual fire, freshly lit from the Tree's own flame that dawn and smelling of earthy incense and burned leaves offered by the worshipers. The High Priestess raised her hand over the flame, and the fire flared higher for a moment with a flash of brilliant gold: the signal for everyone else but the King to depart. In case anyone had missed the flare (which was hard to imagine, since all eyes had been on him since he had entered), all the fires in the torches around the perimeter wall turned the same even color of gold. Finally, all the gold-clad priests on duty began going to each gathered group to kindly ask them to take their leave.

The priests had little to do, as some of the lingerers had left upon seeing Kavarian. Most had made their way to the Gate of First Light even before the signal, though they cast curious glances all the while. The King was glad that none of those glances held any concern—for him or for themselves. He was also grateful that he had made a habit of consulting the Tree often. Her wisdom alone made the effort worth it, but now it had the much-needed benefit of masking the direness of his current need.

"May the Tree grant the wisdom you require, and may you have the strength to heed Her," Tivien said as she turned back to him, face now sober. Her words were traditional, but her tone echoed the tenor of his thoughts too closely to be a coincidence.

"So may it be," Kavarian said quietly.

Tivien clasped his arm in a surprisingly firm grip for her frail-looking hands, faded gold eyes burning as they met his for a moment, and then she turned and walked down the marble steps without another word. Kavarian itched to help her down, but he knew she would refuse his hand if he offered it. Still, it comforted him to see an amón priestess waiting at the bottom of the steps for her. When Tivien reached her, they began walking arm in arm to the gate together.

They were the last two to cross the threshold. As soon as the High Priestess did so, she turned back and raised a hand to the King. He soberly raised his in reply.

Immediately, all seven of the gates around the Heart's perimeter erupted into roaring flames, closing off access to as well as sight or hearing of what lay within.

Kavarian turned back to the ritual flame with a sigh, partly of relief, partly of a heaviness he could not seem to shake. He had little hope that his audience with the Tree would go as Koriben hoped it would. But for his son's sake, he had to try.

He held his own hand over the flame now and closed his eyes in reverence.

"My Lady of the Flame," he murmured. "I, Kavarian, whom you appointed to be a King over your children for a season, come before you seeking an audience, for I require your wisdom."

He waited for one breath, then two, inhaling the smoke and incense. Then....

"Speak, Kavarian. I am here."

The King opened his eyes in mild surprise and a flicker of unease. He could not remember if the Tree had ever answered him so immediately.

The Tree was not a tame creature who always came whenever called. She was their guide, their protector—their Mother in spirit if not in flesh—but as such, She chose when She appeared to Her children. Even Her anointed Monarch, who by Her own command was to come to Her often for counsel, could not always expect to be granted an audience. Even if She came, it was often after a period of humble meditation to prepare his mind to receive Her.

Which meant either Kavarian was already prepared or the matter She had to speak of with him was too urgent to wait.

Or both.

The Tree's avatar stood across the firepit. She had appeared to him in many forms: often that of his great-aunt and former Queen Ethris, but sometimes as a beautiful young woman with light brown skin and dark brown hair and eyes, whom he could not remember having ever seen, or a little girl he had once met soon after becoming King who had died of darkfever despite his and the healers' best efforts. Other times, She appeared as a being of coal and flame, with embers for eyes and flowing ash for hair, and only the tongues of fire flicking around Her legs and torso for clothing.

The latter was the form She was taking now, and the sight gave Kavarian another flicker of unease. Each form had a purpose, carrying a subliminal message that set the tone for their conversation. She appeared as the girl when She wanted to remind Kavarian he could only do so much, that all life was in the Creators' hands. She appeared as Ethris when he needed confirmation of what he already knew he should do—which seemed to be often. And She appeared as the young woman when counseling him about his son and Heir. That was the form he had expected to see, if the Tree had granted him an audience at all.

She only took *this* raw and elemental form when they spoke of the gravest of subjects. His already weakened flameheart chilled for a moment in dread.

"My Lady," Kavarian said with the deepest of nods, so deferential that his torso bent to follow. Dramá—proud and egalitarian—bowed to no one, not even their Monarch. No one but their Tree.

"*Speak*," She repeated softly, Her voice crackling like embers and hissing like falling ash.

"My Lady, it has begun," the King said quietly.

"*You feel it, do you not?*" She said, putting one hand over Her chest, where a heart—had She been a mortal creature—would have rested.

"Indeed," Kavarian said heavily.

Her voice was not accusatory or scolding. It was mild, merely recounting the facts of the matter. "*I told you this would come to pass if you were to have an Heir. You agreed to pay the price. As did your mate.*"

"You did, and I do not recant my oath or regret my choice. No matter...." He swallowed, and when he spoke again, his voice was low and rasping. "No matter what it has cost since. We did what had to be done. For our son. For our people.

To redeem ourselves of the blood our ancestors spilled in breaking the Second Covenant."

"*Then why do you come to Me with regret in your heart?*"

The Tree knew why. She always knew the hearts and minds of Her children. Like a patient mother, She asked the questions that needed to be asked to bring out the words that needed to be said.

Kavarian took in a ragged breath. "I come before you with regret not for myself but for my son. Koriben."

"*You told him,*" the Tree said.

"Yes. And he is taking the news...poorly."

"*As you always knew he would. What else could you have expected?*"

"I expected him to have more time!" Kavarian burst out. Then flinched, bowing in apology. "Forgive me, my Lady. I did not mean...."

His voice broke, and his eyes pled as they met Her unreadable embers. "Please, my Lady. Does it have to be *now*? I was sixty summers before Ethris gave the crown to me. Koriben has only seen just over nineteen. He is still so young. Just a boy."

"*Yet a boy he will always remain, as long as he may happily linger under the shadow of your wing,*" the Tree murmured, words soft as pillows of ash. Strands of Her gray, particle-formed hair floated around Her face, obscuring Her burning eyes for brief seconds.

"He isn't ready!" Kavarian protested.

The Tree's eyes flared hotter for a moment, and Her next words crackled. "*We will* make *him ready. As he must* be *ready, before the times of darkness I foretold to you before. And as long as you live, he will never be ready.*"

"Please," Kavarian pled with all the agony of his soul. "I do not ask for myself, but for him. If it were just my suffering to consider, I would think nothing of it. You know how weary I have become, especially after you took my beloved back to You and the Creators. But *his* pain.... He is my *son*. And I am all he has left."

"*He is your son, yes. But I told you when I gave you a child that he would belong to more than just you and your mate—that the time to redeem the Covenants was at hand.*"

Kavarian bowed his head in defeat. "Yes, I know. And that my son would be the one to restore them."

"*He will be one of them,*" the Tree corrected softly.

Kavarian looked up, startled. It was the Tree's first mention of another. For too many years and for too many long, sleepless nights, Kavarian had agonized over how his son would bear such a burden alone.

"What?"

"*You should know by now that the Covenants cannot be restored by one alone, Kavarian,*" the Tree said softly, the flame in Her voice whispering like a flickering candle in a draft. "*There is another prepared. I have shown her to you many times, and yet you have not seen. You have heard her voice on countless days give you counsel and yet not understood.*"

For a moment, the ritual fire between them roared higher, increasing its warmth tenfold. Then, as if in waves of heat over sunbaked stone, Kavarian saw the form of the brown-haired young woman overlay the Tree's elemental form. For the one second when her face appeared over the Tree's, the young woman was smiling at him, kindly brown eyes comforting.

Then the illusion vanished, and the ritual fire lowered to its previous level. Yet Kavarian could hardly breathe for the sudden hope that was growing inside him. He had always wondered why the Tree had chosen that form, a form he could never remember having seen, when all others he had recognized as the influential women of his past.

At last, his long-held hope was confirmed: this woman was *not* of his past or even of *his* future....

"*Yes, Kavarian,*" the Tree said. "*Your son will not have you at his side. But he will not be alone.*"

Tears stung the King's eyes as he bowed his head in acceptance. When he spoke, his voice was rough with emotion. "Then that is enough."

The Tree cast Her eyes at one of the gates, ember eyes flaring. She let out a sigh that sent Her ash-tendril hair swirling around Her head. "*For you, perhaps. Your son will be more difficult to convince.*"

Then, in a booming voice that carried across the Heart, She declared, "*Enter, Koriben, son of Kavarian, Heir to the King I have chosen.*"

Kavarian turned in shock to see the young man stepping through the flames of the Gate of First Light. Koriben's burning golden eyes, so like his own, went immediately to the King and Tree on the dais, his normally open and buoyant face now hard and determined. He swiftly strode to them with a firm step, the set of his jaw making it clear to Kavarian that he would not be told to leave. Rarely had the King ever seen such defiance from his dutiful son, and it was nearly as startling and troubling as his interruption of the King's private audience with the Tree.

"How?" Kavarian demanded. He had expected to have a deken or two at least before Koriben caught wind of Kavarian's visit—long enough for the visit to be over. Instead, it had been mere dek, and here Koriben was.

"Kor," Koriben said tersely.

That was explanation enough. Kavarian nodded impassively at the mention of his son's leftwing, Korinth. This was not the first time the King had had reason to suspect that the prodigal Starkissed had already developed a network of informants to nearly rival that of the King's own leftwing. If the need for Koriben and his wings to be prepared to govern had been any less critical, Kavarian would have acted much sooner to stop an initiative that bordered on ambition. As it was, this further sign of *Korinth's* readiness for his own role was as troubling as it was comforting.

"Did you think of what kind of panic it will cause once word spreads that you rushed in to interrupt us?" Kavarian said sternly as Koriben climbed the steps to join them.

Koriben's eyes flashed with uncharacteristic hardness. "You know what would cause a greater panic? Your death."

Kavarian was further taken aback by his son's behavior. The King could not remember the last time Koriben had spoken to him this way. But no irritation arose; instead, the King was struck with how similar they looked, now that Koriben was reaching physical adulthood. It was like looking in the mirror now. That clench to his son's jaw was his own when Kavarian faced a task he would not be moved from. For the first time, Kavarian realized their eyes were nearly level now. His son must have grown yet again. How could Kavarian not have noticed?

Koriben sighed, softening a tad after Kavarian's long silence. "Don't worry, Avva, I *did* think about it. I came directly to the Gate of First Light. Nobody knows I'm here except you and the Tree."

By then, the Heir seemed to have regained at least some of his manners, because he turned to the Tree's avatar and bowed even more deeply than usual, perhaps to make up for his rudeness. "My Lady. I am deeply grateful to You for allowing me entrance."

"*As you should be, boy,*" the Tree said with a mildness that mixed with steel. "*Even when you are King, I will not take kindly to pounding on My gates. I only allowed you entrance because it was I who wished to speak with you.*"

"I understand," Koriben said as he straightened. "Dare I hope, then, that means You will finally grant my request?"

"*Your* request?" Kavarian said with a raised eyebrow.

"Avva, I admire and respect you," Koriben said shortly. "If I ever become half the King you are, it'll be a torched miracle. But I know I can't expect *you* to advocate for yourself. As soon as I heard you'd gone to see the Tree, I knew you'd ask Her for more time but you would accept whatever refusal She gave you. Am I wrong?"

Kavarian's only response was to keep his eyebrow raised.

"I thought so," Koriben huffed. Fortunately, he smoothed his expression to something more deferential before turning back to the Tree.

"Please, my Lady. All my offers from before still stand. If You will spare my father's life, I will do anything You ask. Even give up my own."

"Koriben—" Kavarian began.

Koriben near-shouted as he turned back to him. "If you and Avvi had to pledge your very *lives* to give me mine, then why can't I pledge mine to Her to give you back yours?!"

"That isn't for you to decide—"

"Then was it *yours*?" Koriben raged. "If you'd asked me before I came into this world, I would have said *no*."

Kavarian took a step back. No childish tantrum, no adolescent angst had come even close to the mature anger and grief and betrayal he could see in his son's burning eyes now. Not even when Kavarian had told him the true reason for his mother's death five years ago.

Koriben closed his eyes and put his hand to his forehead, struggling with himself for a few moments. When he spoke, his breath was more even, and his voice was quiet but still far from calm.

"Did you ever consider what *I* would think of the cost? That perhaps the price was too great? Maybe *you* didn't think it was, but you don't see yourself for what you are. You never have. But if my life required those of the best two souls of our time, then *I* say it was too great. How do you think that makes *me* feel about the worth of my own?"

"Koriben," Kavarian breathed, reaching out for his son, but Koriben flinched away. Kavarian's flameheart felt like it was tearing itself in two. He was at a loss for what to do to ease the pain inside his boy now—the boy who was, before his eyes, being forced to become a man.

The Tree's words echoed in Kavarian's mind. *We will* make *him ready.*

He had never thought the Tree to be cruel. Hard, when She had to be. She had millions of children to care for and balance the interests of, across six worlds, no less. Her knowledge and memory so far surpassed their own that there was no comparison between their intelligences. What seemed cruelty to a single mortal was always kindness for the eternal good of all.

Or so Kavarian had always believed. Yet, for the first time, the King felt a flicker of doubt. He had been so certain in his decision, as had Nyethra. When they had come to Her asking why an Heir had not been born to anyone in the Sunfilled Clan after so many decades of Kavarian's rule, the Tree had explained to them the necessity of their sacrifice so clearly, so gently. She had left the choice entirely up to them. After much thought and discussion, the King and Queen had felt the rightness of their choice to their bones. The time for their redemption had come, and if it required their lives, then so be it.

He had not anticipated this degree of suffering for the one they would bring into the world.

Perhaps Nyethra had. She had been the one most troubled about their son as he grew, though she always told Kavarian she would make the same decision again. Kavarian had thought he had taken on the burden of that worry once she was gone, but still he had not foreseen the full extent of his pain.

The Tree would have. Nothing came as a surprise to Her: She saw all and anticipated all. Yet the Tree had asked that sacrifice of them—of all three of them.

For the first time, Kavarian wondered if that made Her cruel.

"*Koriben,*" the Tree murmured, voice as soft as drifting ash. "*All parents give of their own lives to their children, to see that life goes on.*"

"Yes," Koriben rasped, not lifting his gaze from the ritual fire. "But mine did in a far more literal sense. And that is a burden I cannot bear."

He looked up, his eyes hard with determination as he met the ember ones of the Tree. He held out his hand, palm up, over the ritual fire. "And so my offer stands, my Lady. Is there *any* way, anything that I can do that will allow you to spare the life of the one I still have left?"

Kavarian's throat was too tight to speak; besides, Koriben would not want to hear his words. So he silently pleaded with the Tree with all the fervor of his soul. *Please. For his sake, just give me a bit more time. Give him* something *to bring hope back into his heart again.*

There was a long moment of silence. Kavarian nearly cried out from the pain of watching Koriben's hand slowly fall and his head bow in despair.

"*You will do anything I ask?*"

Both of them started and looked back at the Tree. Kavarian heard Koriben's breath quicken. His golden eyes sparked with something the King had not seen there in too many weeks.

"*Anything at all?*" She asked solemnly.

"Yes!" Koriben breathed, taking a step closer to the ritual fire that put the tip of his boot at the edge of the pit. "Anything. Please! If there is something that I can do, anything at all, *please* tell me!"

The Tree looked between Her King and Her Heir. When She spoke to Koriben, Her words were simple, but they burned like hot coals. *"There is one chance. It is slight. It will be difficult. And dangerous. It will tax you to your very core. And it will take much of the precious time you have left with your father, requiring you to travel far and wide while he remains here. But there is...one chance."*

"I'll do it," Koriben said. "I swear it. Name it, and it's done."

"Koriben," Kavarian cautioned, heart clenching with a different sort of anxiousness now.

Koriben's eyes flashed to him for one moment. "You made your choice, Father. This one is mine."

Kavarian had to suppress a flinch. Koriben never called him by the formal name of *father*, not even in public. Always, it was the tender, boyish *avva*.

The Tree nodded, coal eyes increasing in intensity for one moment. *"Indeed. It is."*

Cruel? Perhaps.

But it was time Kavarian shouldered more of the agony for his own choices. If this dangerous assignment was what Koriben needed to be spared the suffering Kavarian was only just beginning to understand lay in wait for him, or if this was the Tree's way to prepare Koriben for that suffering should it still come to pass...

...so may it be.

Chapter One

SACRIFICE

Sarah

On the sweltering July evening that would change my life forever, winding up as a blood sacrifice was *not* on my to-do list.

Trust me, I was running through the list in my head as I waded through our Pennsylvanian neighborhood creek looking for my baby sister's beloved macaroni-and-bead necklace, which she had dropped when Rachel and I were watching the littles play in the stream earlier.

When it came time to bring them inside to clean up and get dinner ready, Abby was still desperately looking for it, and she threw an absolute hissy fit about leaving it behind, saying something about the "tree lady" (whoever the heck that was) saying it was important. So I, being the wuss that *I* was, told her I would look for it, and Rachel took them back inside.

Wading through a creek looking for a five-year-old's necklace, half the components of which could be disintegrating in that very moment, had most certainly not been on that to-do list either, and it was now looking like it would be a long night. I still had dinner to make, though with any luck, Rachel was starting that for me. Though I doubted she would do the dishes afterward; finish, sort, and fold the laundry; clean up the messes in the kitchen from lunch and the forthcoming dinner; and put the littles to bed.

My phone in my back pocket vibrated. I pulled out the old model with the cracked screen and looked at the caller ID. And groaned.

I hit the answer button and snapped, "What?"

Rachel said, "Sheesh, no need to bite on first hello."

"Oh, I think I do. Let me guess. You're *not* starting dinner. You're about to ask me if you can ditch me to go off to the mall or the movies with that latest boyfriend of yours."

"First off, ouch. There's no need to put it so harshly. I'm not 'ditching' you. After all, I brought the littles back and cleaned them up, didn't I? Now they're happily running amok—sand and mud free—through the house for you. Second, we're going to the rock-climbing place: far more B.A. Third, he's not my boyfriend."

"Yet," I said, rolling my eyes even though my older sister couldn't see.

There wasn't a boy alive who had resisted Rachel once she set her smoky eye on them.

"True," Rachel said smugly. Then her voice got sweet. "Come on, Sarah. It's my night *off*. I have only so many nights off left before the semester starts again."

So do I, I thought with a growing pit of dread in my stomach.

Except this would be my first semester of college, and in a very uncharacteristic move for me, I hadn't fully decided where I was going, and the time to make that final decision was running out.

Oh, I'd gotten acceptances aplenty. But the gratification had worn off quickly in the face of being forced to choose my destiny. The hardest choice of all: stay local, like Rachel had...or leave. Pack my bags, get on a plane or in an even more beat-up car than the one Rachel and I shared now, and leave it all behind.

To play it safe, I accepted the offer of a local four-year university by their May deadline, but doubts still plagued me.

Staying local had all the usual advantages of lower tuition and living at home, but living at home had its own costs. Particularly, the needs of my large, busy family and two hectic, in-demand parents. I couldn't see those costs decreasing.

If anything, they had increased with Mom and Dad taking on more responsibility at work; Michael moved out and married, with his own toddler to worry about now; and Rachel taking on less and less for her own, less noble reasons. And if anything had been drilled into me about college by now, it was that it would be hard, harder than high school, even though I'd taken almost all advanced classes by my senior year. I was only just now, in the middle of summer, catching my breath. I couldn't *imagine* trying to juggle a part-time job, an even harder course load, and increasing family demands on my time and energy.

As I waded through that creek, I was tempted more than ever to just *go*. Even Mom and Dad were encouraging about that, saying it might not be too late for me to change my mind, or to transfer somewhere else after my first year. They said they would rebalance somehow to cover the gaping hole of responsibility I would leave behind. They were proud of the schools I'd gotten into. Not Ivy League (I hadn't even dared mess with those), but good schools. Better than Rachel had managed, who hadn't even bothered with applications and just gone to the community college, and seemed perfectly content to stay there, an undeclared major, even though she'd just finished her second year.

The most aggravating part of Rachel's blasé attitude about her education was that I knew she would get whatever job she finally set her mind on *anyway*. Because she was Rachel.

Who, right now, was working her magic on me.

"Pleeeeease, Sarah? My most amazing, brilliant, faithful sister? I'll buy you a book if you'll take over tonight. Isn't that author you like coming out with a new one soon?"

"Alright, fine!" I huffed, caving. Not just because of the bribe—I could never seem to say no to her, or to any family member, and I hated that.

I bent over to fish around for something shiny, but it just turned out to be a mica-laced rock, smelling of mud and minerals.

"Go. Leave me and have fun. But could you ask David if he could start dinner?"

My options for backup meal preparers were limited tonight, seeing as Mom was out of town at a conference and Dad was teaching night classes this summer. Even Lizzy was at dance practice. Which was why Rachel was *supposed* to be helping me with the littles. That left David, the next oldest kid after me.

"It's not his night to cook," Rachel said. "You know he'll—"

"Just tell him to put a pizza in or something. *You* can put a pizza in or something."

"We don't have any left. I just checked."

Figures. She had probably hoped it would add sweetness to the abandonment deal if she could at least throw something in the oven.

I gritted my teeth. "Could you please *nicely* ask David if he could at least *start* a meal for me? I'd take peanut butter and jelly at this point. The littles will be hungry soon."

"He's playing that new video game he just got. You know he'll just—"

"Rachel, I am wading through *mud* right now, looking for Abby's silly necklace. Do you want to be doing this instead, or do you want to brave David's petty wrath to deliver a message and then be on your merry way?"

"Fine," she huffed. "I'll deliver the message. But you know what you're going to find when you get back, and that's zilch."

I know, I thought as I squeezed my eyes shut. *I know.*

A breeze started blowing hard through the trees. I opened my eyes and looked up in surprise, but the sky was still clear, not a cloud in sight. Still, that wind felt nice, drying the sweat that the humid summer evening had worked up over my body and made my clothes cling unpleasantly.

Rachel's voice brightened at my silence, which she correctly interpreted as giving up on even the David plan. "Thanks, Sarah. I'll make this up to you, promise."

She would, somehow. She wasn't a monster. It was just...I was done. So done.

"Yeah, whatever," I said, anger dying in the face of that exhaustion. "Go have fun."

"Will do! Love you, byeeeee."

The call disconnected.

I sighed. Before I put the phone away, I set a five-minute timer.

I had to be able to look Abby in her adorable, watery eyes and tell her I had *tried,* and tried hard. So I would give this fruitless search another good five minutes...and then I would go in and take care of my family. Like I always did.

That was one of the hardest parts about the thought of leaving. Mom and Dad said they would manage without me. But...how?

I was too self-aware not to admit that there was an even deeper fear tangled up in all the others. My family was my world. We had moved so much that we'd *had* to bond together, just to even have friends, have normalcy, have something that always stayed the same, something you could count on. Their bonds around me were as needed as they were becoming suffocating. I wasn't sure what would happen if I cut myself adrift. Just the thought filled me with terror, both for them and for me.

Without my family...without who I was to them...who was I?

That wind was kicking up now, making the tops of the trees sway. The scent it carried was crisp, much more like the cold clarity of winter than the heavy richness of summer. Dead leaves, stirred up from the mulch of the forest floor, were spinning in the eddies. The sunhat hanging by its cord around my neck flapped wildly at my back, my tiny side purse swung like a pendulum, and my sneakers sitting on the bank fell over, getting sand on the socks I'd stuffed inside them.

Worried now, I glanced at the sky again as I waded over to and grabbed the sneakers, but the sky was still clear. I hadn't heard of a tornado ever hitting this area, but then, we'd only lived here a year, and there was a first time for everything. Still, if this was a tornado in the making, shouldn't there be *some* clouds?

The wind was now officially cold. I had thought that my cooling skin was just my sweat evaporating, but now I was certain that with every passing second, the wind was plunging in temperature. Goosebumps were breaking out everywhere over all my exposed skin—which was a lot of skin, considering I was in a white tee and jean shorts.

Timer or not, I decided my search was now at an end. I'd done my best, but the necklace was gone for good, and I would just have to endure Abby's disappointment. It was far better for me to be with them to keep them safe from any pending natural disaster than for Abby to have it back.

Just when I was about to step out of the stream and onto the sandy bank...it froze.

Instantly.

All the way down to its half-foot depth. I knew that all too well, because my feet were encased in ice. I couldn't budge them.

I'd heard of snap freezes before, but this...was something else. Chills ran down my spine, and that wasn't just from the frigid prison my feet were now in.

Vainly, I tried to jerk them free, but all I did was throw myself dangerously off balance. If I had fallen in that moment, I would have probably broken both my ankles. Horribly.

It was almost fortunate that in that very moment, I felt a sinking crack beneath me, as if my weight had broken through more fragile ice beneath, even though that was impossible. There was nothing below me but muddy, sandy dirt.... Right?

Then I fell.

Straight down.

Into darkness.

MY HEAD *HURT* WHEN I woke up, and my mouth tasted like dirt. As I blinked my eyes open, the world still spun.

But something about that world was off.

That giant, squat, living-granite face with the blue fires for eyes leaning over me, for instance.

"Holy cow!" I shrieked, flinching away from it, no matter how much the movement sent further stabs of pain through my skull.

I braced my arms in front of me, uselessly, because the stoney, moss-and-vine covered ogre thing just grinned, grabbed one of those arms, and—nearly wrenching my arm out of its socket—lifted me up so that my feet dangled at least a yard off the ground.

A frantic glance around showed me that I was surrounded by these stoney, unfriendly looking, ten-foot giants. Behind *them*, a thick, luscious jungle towered around me from all sides. Unseen creatures hooted and hollered, exotic birds flitted through the thick canopy, enormous purple trombone-like flowers dripped glowing gold liquid, and the air I was gasping in was rich, humid, and cloying.

Assuming all this was real, that I hadn't hit my head or wasn't dead or hallucinating, I...was not in Kansas anymore. I wasn't even in *Pennsylvania* anymore. And these were no friendly munchkins who greeted me.

They spoke to each other in grinding, stoney voices that made me flinch. Now, I was *trying* to not be rock-ist or anything, but I found it difficult to imagine that their hard expressions, blazing eyes, and harsh tones were...benevolent.

"Er, would you mind putting me down, please?" I asked, with little hope. But I had to try. My arm was in agony, and I was afraid that at any moment, the socket would pop.

My phone's timer went off.

The ogre holding me shook me, gargling some rock nonsense, and I cried out in pain. With my other hand, I frantically pulled out the phone to turn off the timer.

Before I could even hit the stop button, another ogre grabbed the phone from me—scraping my fingers painfully as it did so—and crushed it in its fist. I stared as perhaps my last hope for salvation spilled from the ogre's hand as so many useless shards of glass, plastic, and electronics.

Sure, maybe the phone wouldn't even *work* here. It wasn't even a nice phone; I'd been saving up for a new one for a while now. But it was the disheartening principle of the thing.

The only good thing in that moment, if you could call it that, was that my captor used its other hand to grab me by the waist instead, pinning my other arm and letting go of the one it had been holding, probably seconds from doing serious damage. I still hissed in pain as that abused arm fell limply against its stone fingers.

So, I had one arm free now. To defend myself against half a dozen ten-foot stone ogres. Fantastic.

As I thought through my options, the ogres seemed to be verbally doing the same. Not long after, they came to a consensus and began marching through the trees. With me in tow. Helpless, as far as I was aware, to do anything about that.

My captor's giant fingers around me were literally rock solid, and when I tried wiggling, it grunted something nasty sounding at me and tightened its grip. I froze, not daring to push it to tighten further. I was already finding it hard to breathe. If I made it mad, I was sure it could crush me nearly as easily as its comrade had my phone.

After only a minute or two of marching, we broke through the jungle and came into an enormous clearing, larger than a football field. The sun shone down with mocking innocence on its dirt, moss, and rock expanse and on the crude stone table in the center, which the ogres were heading straight for.

Wait, I thought with dawning horror.

Was I going to be for *dinner*? Were they not even going to have the decency to *kill* and *cook* me first? I couldn't see any sign of a fire or other element of meal preparation in sight. Just that enormous stone table, made with four boulders for legs and a large, flat stone for an uneven, unlevel surface.

Anxiety at my situation skyrocketed to downright terror. My heart felt like it was going to explode, my body sweated from more than just the sweltering jungle heat. I was almost surprised the ogre didn't drop me from how slick I was becoming.

How had it all come to this? How had I plunged straight from my neighborhood creek in Pennsylvania, where my worst problem was the fact that I had so many chores to do, I'd be doing them until I collapsed into bed? I took it back, I took it all back. I would do the dishes from now until eternity if I would just *wake up.*

But the nightmare didn't end. In fact, it only got worse.

The ogre dumped me on the table. Vertical, so I fell on my back with an impact that sent a blaze of pain through my already sensitive head, stunning me. That was fine with the ogres, because the others began tying me down, wrapping thick vines around me and under the table again and again, until I couldn't budge, even though I soon recovered enough to try.

What did they need to do *this* for? Weren't they just going to tear me limb from limb? Wrapping my entire body except my head and upper chest would make that rather difficult. Not that I was complaining about a change in plans, mind you....

Until I saw one of them bring out a knife.

It was the epitome of a stone-age weapon: a large, flat rock that had been chiseled into a narrowing, pointed tip. But its shape and the way the ogre gripped its "handle" were unmistakable.

So was the way the others all gathered around, almost ceremoniously. And started chanting, repeating the same grinding, nails-on-chalkboard words as the others, in unison.

Just as quickly as before, my mind flipped the script.

Now, I was new here. I couldn't understand what they were saying. But from the way the biggest ogre was holding the knife over my torso with both rocky hands....

I was almost one-hundred-percent certain that this was a sacrifice.

If I'd ever taken the chance to contemplate how my life would end, I would have never pictured this.

The ogre raised its serrated stone dagger with both hands above my chest and finished its garbling chanting with one final triumphant proclamation, so loudly that I was caught in the spray of spittle. If they hadn't tied me on my back to the crude *altar* (not table), I might have rolled over to puke from revulsion. But my last lingering instincts of self-preservation and the frozen apathy of fear combined to keep the burning bile from rising further than my throat.

Besides, my mind was a little more occupied by the terrifying silence that ensued as the ogre paused ominously and its gathered comrades waited with bated breath and *literally* burning eyes for the dagger to plunge into my heart.

My very last thought was of bewildered loss. *Who is going to tuck Abby in tonight?*

And then....

A roar.

A deafening, ears-ringing, bone-chilling, muscle-jellifying roar that I could never, in my deepest, darkest nightmares have ever imagined. It was like a *Tyrannosaurus rex* had stolen a megaphone and somehow held it up to its mouth with its tiny arm and gave the loudest, most bestial bellow of its life.

For one tenth of a second, the ogres froze. Their blue flame-eyes barely had time to widen and turn purple at the edges before *IT* was upon us.

I saw only a blur of a maw so big it filled my entire field of vision and teeth longer than baseball bats—curved, ivory, deadly canine baseball bats—before the knife-wielding ogre priest was gone with a screech as grating as steel nails scraping a granite boulder. From the way the screech rapidly faded, I assumed it had been tossed and was flying away from us at what would have been a lethal height and velocity for any human.

I couldn't ponder the ogre priest's fate beyond that. I was much more occupied with my own. Because not a second later, I was staring at the scaly gold underside of the *Thing*.

Which was at least a story above me, and so massive I could see nothing else. All I got was the impression of a horizontal mass with four giant oak-sized legs from the curvature of its giant musculature, which looked taut and powerfully lean in proportion to its size. As it turned, I glimpsed a long, supple tail as thick as a small car and as devastating as a battering ram, and once I saw outspread, shimmering webbed wings as large as galleon sails.

Screeches began filling the air as the *Thing* agilely twisted its girth above me. If I'd been capable of more thought than abject terror, I might have noted the oddity of how it never moved from its position over me, no matter how it had to turn, shift, or twist to counter whatever insane resistance the ogres were putting up for losing their prize to the much bigger and deadlier predator.

If I *had* noticed, I would have assumed that the *Thing* was determined to keep me for itself. Which would have led me to question why a single human female would have been appealing enough to steal and then guard so determinedly. To a *Thing* so big, every step caused a tremor, I would have been just a morsel.

But my brain wasn't capable of such detached philosophizing now. The only thought it had the capacity to support was thinking of how to get *away*.

I yanked at my bonds, expecting to feel their implacable resistance once again. But there was none. My arms and legs thrashed freely across the rough stone. I had been so frozen with terror that I hadn't even realized that at some point between the roar and now, the ropes had simply...fallen off me, crude but tight knots undone.

That oddity was enough to register in my brain, but I didn't take the time to guess why. I pushed myself up so quickly my head spun.

Just at that moment, I realized the screeching had stopped, and as I looked around, I saw the last of the ogres were fleeing into the woods. The *Thing* above me growled, a rumbling sound I felt as much as heard, being just beneath the enormous chest where it originated. Then it roared after them in a threat universally understood at the primordial level what it would do to them if they dared come back.

Then it stepped back and away from me with a care that I might have noted in different circumstances. Instead, all I saw was the blessedly clear and scale-free sky and shadowy trees ahead.

I didn't even think. I was already pushing off the altar and hitting the ground feet-first and sprinting before conscious thought caught up to me, heedless of how my bare feet bled from running on that rocky, mossy ground. I just ran.

Then I heard an astonishing thing.

I'd heard many astonishing things since stumbling into this nightmare. Guttural garbles coming from stone-like ogres with flames for eyes. Also, creepy chanting and terrified screeching from the same. That roar, which I would never, *ever* forget even if I lived to be a hundred. I would hear it as I lay dying, as if the sound had infiltrated every cell in my body to welcome me to the end.

Perhaps this new sound was so remarkable because it should have been unremarkable, and it was the stark familiarity in an unfamiliar and monstrous world that made it seem like the most unbelievable thing I had heard thus far.

It was a human shout.

I didn't recognize the male voice. I didn't understand the word he shouted. Even so, it was so astonishing that it pierced my haze of panic and made me stumble in my headlong sprint. For one split second, I hesitated.

Was another human about to be the *Thing's* lunch? Or had he come to help me escape? Because *escape* was the only possibility for a human now, unless that human happened to have a tank or some missiles.

That second of hesitation was all the human needed to catch up to me, because in the next moment, something slammed into my waist, and I was flying forward.

But I didn't hit the ground. Instead, I crashed into my tackler, who, through some feat of agility, had simultaneously grabbed me and twisted us in midair to take the brunt of our fall. My breath was still knocked out of me for a second from hitting his hard chest, but the ground would have been harder.

"What—was that—for?" I huffed, using my arms on either side of his face to push myself up. I had another split second of costly hesitation when our eyes met. His were a color I had never seen before: an astonishingly vibrant gold that seemed to be...glowing. Almost as bizarrely, the color perfectly matched his longish hair and short beard.

"*Adelak,*" he said urgently. "*Dedran es ethankil.*"

I didn't understand a word, but then again, that wasn't surprising. I had already been ninety-nine percent sure I wasn't in Pennsylvania anymore, and his Babel talk pushed my certainty to one hundred. Thing was, though, I didn't have time to waste surmising even that much because *there was a dragon about to eat us.*

That was when I admitted to myself that I knew what the *Thing* was.

Naming it didn't make it any less deadly, and in fact made it about twice as terrifying, if that was even possible.

I scrambled to get off my tackler, but though he let me get onto my hands and knees to put some distance between us, he continued to hold on to my waist while shooting off more words I couldn't comprehend.

"What...are you...doing?!" I panted in pure panic. "There's a—"

That's when I finally could twist enough to look behind us at our impending doom.

To see nothing and no one in the clearing but us.

I was so astonished, I nearly fell on him again. I looked around frantically, and the man let me go to do so. I sat back on my heels, fingers of one hand against the ground as I twisted and turned, but I could see no sign of the behemoth that had no doubt been baring down on us for the kill not a second before.

"Where—where—where—" I said, until realized I was repeating the same word like a broken record and bit my tongue to make myself stop.

"*Adelak,*" the man insisted, his voice turned soothing as he too sat up. I realized I was still crouched over his legs. I fell sideways onto my rear, partly to get off him, partly because I could do nothing else but sit there in numb shock.

"Where did it go?"

I stared, for a lack of anything else, at the altar where I'd come inches from being a human sacrifice and nearly as close to being in a dragon's belly, if only by proximity. But I was reevaluating the past few minutes in a bewildering blur, rewriting the script again. I'd been certain the dragon had intended to....

Well, actually, I had no way of knowing *what* the dragon had intended to do. And that was almost as disturbing as its sudden disappearance.

"*Nema?*" the man said, a questioning rise to the end of his speech. That is, if a vocal rise had the same meaning to him as it did to me.

When I glanced at him in a daze, his expression seemed to match the lilt in his voice: eyes open and searching, head tilted toward me.

"The...." I swallowed, finding it hard to force the word through my throat. "The dragon."

I didn't know why I was bothering. If I couldn't understand him, he sure as heck wouldn't understand me.

And yet, comprehension dawned on his face. "*Drakón?*" he asked. The *A* was lower, the *G* turned hard into a *K*, the low *O* fully vocalized—but it was unmistakably similar.

"Yes!" I said, pointing across the empty clearing. "*Tell* me I'm not crazy and that a...*drakón* was just there."

He hesitated, looking at me as if not sure I was serious.

I groaned and put my head in my hands, which were still trembling from shock. "I'm crazy, aren't I? Must have lost it there near the end in just sheer terror, I guess."

I raised my head, eyes falling on the altar. "But then...what scared away those...other things? The ogres, or whatever they're called?"

I couldn't have imagined those too, could I? No—my wrists and ankles were still raw from the ropes they'd tied there. I could still smell their acrid stench in the clearing, lingering in the back of my nostrils....

"*Ahglen.*"

"What?" I asked blankly, looking back at him.

He pointed at the altar with a dark, hard look. "*Ther suther ep '*ahglen.'"

The emphasis on the word the second time finally helped me understand. "The ogres are called *ahglen*?" I asked.

It was only when he nodded that it hit me.

"Wait one freakin' sec—*you can understand me?*"

A faint chuckle escaped his lips, and he nodded.

"How?" I demanded. "If you can understand me, why do you keep replying in *your* language?"

Once again, he hesitated. But this time it appeared less because he was evaluating how serious I was and more because he could not think how to explain.

"Never mind, then," I huffed, getting to my feet.

I wanted to keep sitting. Actually, what I wanted was to lie on my back and stare at the sky until my shaking stopped, my sweat dried, and the world turned back to normal. But that didn't seem like a smart idea with...ahglen somewhere in these woods. And, if I wasn't crazy, a dragon.

How could I have imagined that *roar*?

"*Eklan dres oden?*" he asked hastily, getting to his own feet.

Then I was staring up—way up—at him.

Goodness. I'd known from being so up close and personal with him that he was rather...large. And I did *not* mean in the heavyset way. Every inch of him that I could discern underneath his loose golden shirt and pants appeared to be thick, hard muscle. Every...ninety inches or so of him.

I then felt every inch of my five-foot-six. For the first time, a bit of nervousness started creeping in. Surprising that it had taken this long, considering this guy had just tackled me. Maybe it was our shared humanity, but even as we were falling, I never once considered that the man might mean me harm; I had no idea why he'd done it and still didn't, in fact. But I'd subconsciously assumed good intent.

I still did, seeing the clear earnestness in his golden eyes look back at me. But it was hard looking up at that seven-and-a-half feet of viking-esque beard and muscle and not feel a twinge of my comparative helplessness. Plus...all that...*gold*. His hair, his eyes, his clothing.... It was a bit more overwhelming standing up. Maybe it was the way the setting sun could now strike his face over the angle of the treetops, making him into something a bit less mortal and a bit more godlike than was suited for comfort.

I'd stand behind him if the ahglen came back, though. Somehow, I got the feeling that he could take them.

I realized from the puzzlement going over his features that I was still staring and looked away.

My eyes fell on the altar again. Hard for them not to, what with it being the only feature of significance in this clearing. I shuddered, rubbing my arms. Goosebumps were reappearing there from the chill of the drying sweat on my skin.

"What drove them away?" I asked, not expecting an answer. "If not a dragon?"

The man hesitated long enough that I looked back—all the way up—at him. If our facial expressions meant anything remotely similar, he was looking a bit...reluctant.

"What?" I asked.

He ran a hand through his hair. Which tussled those metallic, shoulder-length locks in a distracting way for me. "*Yeth drakón.*"

"I know," I said, sighing at how short a distance this one-sided understanding was going to take us. "You already made it clear that I hallucinated the dragon."

He was shaking his head grimly before I even finished. "Yeth *drakón*," he said, emphasizing the first word this time, and pointing at the altar as he did so.

I puzzled it out for a second before my heart began hammering in understanding. "There *was* a dragon?" I asked, nervous. I glanced around the clearing, but it still was not in sight.

Just when a certain lovable Disney kid's movie about an *invisible* dragon was entering my thoughts, the man sighed again. This time, he pointed to himself.

"*Ani eh'drakón,*" he said slowly, gently, as if to avoid startling me.

I stared at him, uncomprehending.

He huffed in frustration and folded his arms as he stared out into the clearing, as if trying to find something there to use to communicate with me.

"*Drakón,*" he began again, pointing beyond the altar.

"Right, I'm with you that far," I said. "I saw that part for myself. And heard it—loud and clear. What I don't get is where it *went*. You'd think I would have noticed a thing that size taking...."

I trailed off, because as soon as I said the word *went*, his eyes lit up with an idea, and his pointing finger began tracing a line from the altar toward...us.

Ending pointing back at himself.

Again.

Ani eh'drakón, he'd said. While pointing to himself.

I stared. And swallowed. Even though it felt like no saliva was left in my mouth to go down.

"You...*are* the dragon?" I rasped.

He nodded slowly but firmly.

I couldn't help it: I took an unconscious step back. I didn't regret it, even when I saw him wince.

"*Adelak,*" he said quickly, hands spread out by his sides peaceably, palms toward me. The same word he'd said several times after chasing me down. Though I didn't understand it still, his gesture and expression were unmistakable.

He meant me no harm.

"How?" I choked. "How...can you be...."

He shrugged helplessly. I realized that perhaps that had been an unanswerable question, the kind that had no answer, even for philosophers speaking in the same language for hours, much less in our case. After all, I could have asked "Why am I human?" and there would have been nothing for him to say in reply.

As I stared at his tentative, all-too-human expression, I tried to banish my unease. But that *roar*.... That enormous mass of scale and sinew, that unstoppable force of death and destruction....

Even given his imposing presence as a human, my weary mind just didn't seem up to reconciling the two halves of the whole in my head.

I cleared my throat. "So...sorry, but just for clarity's sake, I have to ask: you don't...mean me harm?"

He sighed and shook his head. "*Adelak. Ani droden makethwella.*"

I believed him. With the openness of those eyes...I found it hard not to. That didn't mean my primordial instincts quieted all at once, but...I found my heart rate beginning to slow.

"Great," I said faintly. "Great. Um.... Glad we had this talk."

In fact, it was a good thing that we'd cleared that up by then, because just at that moment, I heard yet another sound that I'd never heard before.

A powerful rushing in the distance, as if a great wind were sweeping through the trees toward us. Accompanied by a heavy *whump...whump...whump....*

On any other day, I might have had no clue what was coming. With dragons on the mind, well....

I am proud to say that when I looked toward the sound, though my face probably went white—judging from the sharp look the man cast me—I did *not* run for cover. Or scream. Or even flinch.

OK...I might have flinched. Just a tad.

"*Edlen,*" he said soothingly. But he stepped between me and the rushing, thumping sound.

That ratcheted my heart rate to a whole new level. Because if I found it difficult to believe that this human version of a dragon meant me no harm, then I was going to have a heck of a time keeping it together with this new, very dragonlike addition. If even *he* didn't entirely trust the newcomer....

The *whumps* made their presence felt; I could feel the ebb and flow of gusts of air first. Then, as the sound increased to almost a dull, hissing roar, I felt the air pressure in my eardrums with each beat.

Then the dragon appeared over the treetops, soaring low and fast.

Seeing the immensity of that apex predator coming straight for me, all my survival instincts kicked into the highest gear. I'll admit it: if the man had not reached behind him in that moment and grabbed my upper arm in a loose hold, I might have bolted.

I doubted *anyone* seeing their second dragon would not have done the same.

At least I bit back the whimper that threatened to escape as the violet dragon soared into the clearing a second later. With two mighty backward wing flaps that sent blindingly powerful gusts of air, it hit the ground with its hind legs and settled elegantly onto all fours a second later.

Then...it was gone. Just like that—poof. Granted, I'd been huddling behind the golden man and not paying close attention, but I hadn't thought it necessary to. How *hard* could it be to keep track of a beast the size of a super jet?

I had only *just* learned not five minutes ago that dragons could become something quite different, but I'd had the longest and most harrowing fifteen minutes of my entire life, and my mind and body were wrecked from the first adrenaline crash and needing to ramp up for another.

Worldviews take longer than five minutes to adjust.

A second after the dragon disappeared, I realized my mistake as soon as I heard a human female swearing.

Foreign language or not, I was positive most of the words she was throwing at us like daggers were swears. And those daggers were coming closer. I peeked around the golden man and nearly flinched again.

Lithe, with the effortless grace of a cat. Fiercely beautiful with high cheekbones, a pointed chin, perfect eyebrows only marred by one small scar, and white teeth that flashed menacingly as she continued swearing. Olive skin. Long, slightly kinky, bound dark violet hair with matching eyes still glowing. Violet plate armor tightly covering every inch of her below the chin, including her long neck. And, of course, she must have been over six feet tall.

I didn't know if I had ever seen a more intimidating young woman. My sole comfort was that it appeared her furious gaze was fixed not on me but on the golden man in front of me.

Or...it was until she caught sight of me peering around him. Halfway in between where she'd landed and us, she froze in both mid-step and mid-curse.

She took me in with wide eyes for one moment. Then those eyes narrowed as they made their way back to the man.

He winced. I didn't blame him. Those eyes promised death.

Then I did perhaps the most courageous thing I had ever done.

This man...dragon...person had just saved my life. I wasn't sure why, but I believed him when he said it was with good intentions. If he had violated some kind of dragon code by doing so, I didn't think it fair that he be sentenced for it while I huddled behind him.

So, since his grip on me had gone slack, I slipped out from his grasp—ignoring his muttered protest—and stepped in front of him. I did my best to lift my chin and square my shoulders. I'll admit, though: meeting her glowing violet eyes with her dragon form fresh on my mind took a heroic effort.

"It's not his fault," I said, proud that there was only the slightest tremor in my voice. "I'm not sure what he did wrong, but I'd be dead right now if it wasn't for him. So...if he's to be punished, then I should be the one to take the punishment."

She stared at me for a moment, as if she couldn't quite believe what she was hearing. Then she looked at the man just behind me—not a hard feat with both able to look over my head—and arched one eyebrow.

This time, when she spoke, her tone was much more on the dry than lethal side she asked the man a pointed question. He replied steadily, with no hint of anxiety or guilt in his voice.

Sheepishly, I got the feeling that I *might* have overestimated the level of trouble we had been in. That feeling appeared to be confirmed when the young woman rolled her eyes; I was pretty sure from the casual hand on her hip and her air of pure annoyance that the eye roll meant the same thing to me as it did to them.

My heartbeat slowed to a pace that was not quite normal but much closer to self-consciousness than fear.

The young woman strode the remaining distance to us while she and the man traded questions and answers. Meanwhile, he moved to my side, so they were no longer talking over my head. She still glared at him, but now I recognized the glares as not meaning *literal* harm, and his expression was merely chagrined as he took his scolding. I hazarded a guess that far from wanting to kill him, she had been worried about him—that he had been reckless in either taking off on his own or trying to tackle an entire tribe of ahglen solo, or maybe both.

I wasn't sure why either would be a problem; he'd managed them easily, and I couldn't imagine anything that would have posed a challenge for him in dragon form—and few in his current one. But that was probably my dried-up imagination failing me. If a fierce young woman like her had been worried, then things could have gone differently.

Although I shuddered to think how.

The young woman's gaze fell back on me for a moment, and she asked me a pointed question. All I could do was stare at her helplessly before the man interceded, probably explaining my lack of understanding. She demanded something, he shrugged in reply.

When she looked back at me, she said something that sounded different from the way they'd been speaking before. I got the fleeting impression of a more lilting, almost melodic cadence. Then I realized she'd most likely been trying a different language on me.

"Still don't understand that one," I said.

She scowled and spoke again. This time, her words were much more clipped and guttural.

I just shook my head. "Nope, sorry."

The man spoke this time, trying a different language again: one that sounded like Latin, which I'd taken as my language credit in high school. I shook my head again. "Nope."

The young woman threw up her hands and barked something at the man. He frowned severely at her and gestured to me as he replied. The young woman spread her hands and said something emphatically, and she too gestured at me.

I sighed, feeling the second adrenaline crash of the day draining the rest of my patience. I put a hand to my forehead, feeling even more of a headache coming on. "Look, guys, I know there's not much you can do about it, but it's getting annoying for you to be talking about me like this as if I'm not right here."

The man looked at me and grimaced. "*Ahdrah.*"

I was fairly sure that meant "sorry." The young woman huffed, not looking the least bit sorry as she glared at him.

He groaned, but the way his shoulders sank seemed to indicate giving in somehow. He looked at his friend imploringly, but she only smirked and then gestured to me with both hands and a comment that I swear sounded like, *You're the one who saved her. She's* your *problem.*

He sighed but didn't argue. Then he looked at me hesitantly.

"Look, I don't mean to be a bother," I said. "I'm grateful for your help and all that. But I should get home. If...that's possible I guess.... I don't suppose you two have ever heard of a place called Pennsylvania?"

As I had expected, both just stared at me. I sighed, shoulders drooping. "I...didn't think so. Seeing on the planet *I'm* from, there aren't dragons or ogres or ahglen or whatnot."

The young woman said something dryly, and I was glad I couldn't understand her, because I guessed from the man's glare at her it wasn't complimentary.

I tried to ignore her and asked the man, "Do you have *any* idea how I could have gotten here? I was just wading in a creek in my world, and...."

I swallowed. "Then something...weird happened. Everything got windy and cold, and I fell through *ice*, and by the time I woke up, I was...here."

From the grim look in his eyes, I saw he *did* have some idea, even before his nod. Even the young woman's expression sobered, and they exchanged meaningful looks.

I swallowed. "Do you have any idea how I can get *back*?"

He hesitated, looking at the young woman. She just looked back at him, folded her arms, and shrugged. Then she unfolded one arm to point at the fading light and said something firm.

My heart sank. "I'm assuming that means you need to go soon."

She looked back at me with an eyebrow arched in surprise, but the man chuckled at her and said something that sounded teasing. She scowled at him and snapped something back.

The man ignored her and looked back at me. And sighed. Then began rolling up one of his sleeves with a grimace.

"Uh, what's going on?" I asked, eyeing him.

The young woman snorted, but at his glare, she seemed to take pity on either him or me and made herself useful. With her most serious expression yet, she pointed to me and then made a beak shape and mimed talking by opening and closing the "mouth." Then she cupped her hand behind her own ear, made her eyes demonstratively wide, and nodded with slow emphasis. Then she looked expectantly at me.

"Uh...." I said. "You're saying that you can understand what I'm saying?" She nodded.

"*Ka avain drakón,*" the man told me with an inclined head. Then, for emphasis, repeated, "*Drakón, hem?*"

Drakón—dragon.

"Right," I said, remembering. "You two can understand me because you're *dragons.*"

Because that's logical, I thought but wasn't rude enough to say out loud. Besides, I understood all the rules of reality had changed.

He nodded, giving a quick, tense smile at my effort.

"I still don't understand what this has to do with...." I said, looking at his now bare forearm. Heavily muscled, of course, but hairless. Not a single freckle, either. Just smooth, pale skin.

The woman waved her hand to get my attention again. Once she had it, she pointed to her own mouth and opened and closed it to mime talking. Then she pointed to me, frowned, and made a slashing motion while shaking her head: a clear negative.

"But I can't understand what *you* say," I repeated back to her.

I tried to hide my impatience to know where this was going. If they had to go soon and leave me in this jungle to find my way back home, I'd prefer they started figuring out a way to *help* me rather than state the obvious.

She nodded. Then she pointed at the man and handed him one of the daggers at her waist, hilt first.

As if that were his cue to take up the explanation, he took the dagger and looked at me to make sure I was watching. Then, with perfect equanimity, as if he did this every day, he pricked his pointer finger with the dagger.

I stared, trying to wrap my head around why he'd done that. Was he trying to show how sharp the dagger was? But *why*?

He held his finger out to me, inviting me to look. Swallowing, but glad the sight of blood didn't bother me, I took a step closer and looked.

And stared.

His blood...was the same color as his eyes and hair. It was...*gold*.

"*Yven drakón,*" he said.

I looked up at him, eyes wide. "Dragon blood?"

"*Yven drakónani,*" he clarified.

I frowned as I puzzled what the meaning could be. "*Your* dragon blood?"

"*Hem,*" he said with a nod. Again, that tense smile of approval.

I looked at the woman, at her violet hair and eyes. "But yours...would look different?"

"*Hem.*" She pointed to that drop of blood. Then to her ear and her mouth. Then waited expectantly.

I looked between her and that drop of blood several times, trying to put all the pieces together.

They could understand me because they were dragons. I couldn't understand them...because, well, I wasn't. *This* was dragon blood, which they had thought was important to show me, because....

"It's your blood, isn't it?" I looked up at the man. "Something in your *blood* makes you able to understand me."

"*Hem!*" he said with a wide smile.

"I still don't understand," I said with a frown. "*Why* are you telling me all this? How does that help me?"

"*He'yven ythresha ve sevyen,*" he said patiently.

When no comprehension dawned on my face, he sighed. Then he reached toward me with the finger trailing a bit of blood—trying not to startle me, eyes locked on mine for permission.

"Wait, what are you doing?" I asked nervously, backing up a step.

The young woman threw up her hands again and grumbled, clearly nearing the end of her patience. The man spared a glance at her and said something sharp that made her scowl, but she folded her arms and fell silent. He looked back at me with a grimace of apology. Then he reached up with the bleeding finger and tapped his own ear.

I reached up to touch my ear. Could a dab of his blood, however magical, *really* give me the same understanding that he had? He seemed convinced it could, or at least wanted to try.

I trusted him, but I was still apprehensive. Yes, it was just a drop or two. Yes, it looked thick, gold, and metallic and nothing like human blood. But it was still *blood*.

Yet what other choice did I have?

"OK," I whispered.

He moved his hand again, raising it to the ear I'd exposed by tucking my dark hair behind it. He lightly brushed his fingertip down the outer edge with the faintest of touches.

It was still enough to send a shiver down my spine. Maybe it was the surprisingly warm blood—almost hot enough to be uncomfortable—lingering on my ear. Or the tingles that shot over the entire surface and into my ear canal in one quick flash. It couldn't have been the way he leaned in close, eyes tight with concentration, as if *willing* the blood to do something.

"What...happens now?" I asked nervously, avoiding his gaze.

Then he spoke. And when he did, my heart gave a thud and my eyes shot to his again. "What was that?"

He said the same words again—for the third time now, since they were the same ones he'd said after I'd asked, "How does that help me?"

"*He'yven ythresha ve sevyen.*"

I still heard them in his language. But now, after three times—especially after the two since he'd touched my ear with his blood, I *understood*. That's what he had been trying to tell me.

The blood will help you understand.

My jaw dropped. "It...it did! Holy cow, but...it did. It took me a bit, but I understood that."

He grinned and leaned back.

"*How?*" I asked, dumbfounded. I touched my ear, but the blood must have already dried. I didn't so much as feel crustiness. "It's just *blood*."

"*Yven a'drakón,*" he reminded me. It took effort, but I understood that too. It helped that I somewhat knew the words already: *Dragon blood.*

So not just *any* old blood. Dragon blood. Which, apparently, was so darn *magical* that it could impart its language abilities on me with just one swipe of the stuff in the right place. I could take nothing for granted anymore.

The young woman said something fast and hard, pointing at the darkening sky. She spoke too quickly for me to keep up, but I could guess her meaning: time was short.

The man muttered something to her, but he raised the dagger to his bare arm in a businesslike manner.

"Wait, what are you doing *now*?" I said.

"*Et sa kalthen?*" he asked with a raised eyebrow. The amount of effort it took for me to puzzle out the meaning—like turning the dials into just the right positions on an antique radio—proved his point.

Was that enough?

I grimaced. "No, but...are you seriously going to...to *cut* yourself right now to make up the difference?"

He shrugged, as if that were nothing. "*Hem.*"

I stared at him. "Are you *sure* you want to do that?"

"Aaagh!" the young woman said, throwing up her hands.

I didn't need a translation for that.

She turned on her heel and began marching toward the woods. She shouted something over her shoulder while drawing a claymore that had been strapped to her back and looked far too large for any normal person to wield.

I looked at the man in mild alarm. He just shrugged and sighed, not appearing concerned. "*Ad'a ythren,*" he said. *She'll be back.*

"Sorry," I said with an apologetic grimace. "I know I'm dragging this out, but it's all so...foreign to me. Using blood as a tool like this.... Especially if it means hurting you."

He nodded. "*Kalla,*" he said, holding out his finger. *Look.*

I looked down at it, wondering what I was supposed to be seeing. Then frowned as I realized that was perhaps the point. "Wait one second—isn't this the finger you pricked? Where's the blood? Or scab?"

"*Wyrshen,*" he said with a smile. *Gone.*

"Yeah, I see that," I said. "Where did it *go*?"

He chuckled. Then he pricked his finger again with the tip of the dagger and held it out to me. "*Edrin.*" *Watch.*

I watched, then stared as he wiped the bead of blood away with his thumb to reveal the tiny hole, which disappeared not a second later. He wiped the blood trail off on his pant leg and showed me his perfectly whole finger once again.

My eyes went wide. "No way. You can heal *that* fast?"

"*Hem,*" he said with a chuckle.

I looked at his forearm. I was getting an inkling how such smooth perfection was possible. "How fast would your arm heal?"

He shrugged. "*E'dek ev resh.*"

I still didn't understand what a *dek* was, but I got the vaguest sense that it wasn't long.

"It wouldn't scar?" I wanted to be sure I wasn't asking something unreasonable of him before I gave him the go ahead.

He shook his head. "*Ahn.*" He raised an eyebrow and inclined his head pointedly at his arm, as if to say that if what he was about to do scarred, he'd be covered in scars by now.

I frowned. "This *really* isn't a big deal to you, is it?"

He shook his head again with a small smile. "*Ahn.*"

"OK," I said as I let out a breath. "If that's the case, and you really want to do this...."

"*Hem,*" he said firmly.

"Alright, then," I said, steeling myself. As if *I* were the one about to be cut open. "Go ahead."

Without further ado, he calmly raised the knife and cut a neat line across the inside of his forearm. Thick golden blood congealed in the crevice of parted skin, so hot it steamed in the air. My stomach turned a bit, especially when I caught the faintest whiff of something pleasantly pungent, almost like a spice; the way it appealed to me was the exact opposite of comforting. Revulsion was the proper reaction. What did the lack thereof say about me?

I wanted to look away or to step back, but I fixed my eyes on the wound. This was for my sake. I wouldn't take that for granted by looking away, no matter how uncomfortable I made myself.

He swiped his finger down the line of blood, collecting enough to paint a good portion of his finger gold. Then he raised his finger and looked at me questioningly for final confirmation. I swallowed and nodded, turning to show him my other ear while tucking my hair behind it.

This time, he covered my ear in blood, moving his finger back to his arm several times as if his wound were a palette and his finger a brush. The hot tingles that were shooting from my ear into my skull were enough to make me close my eyes within seconds from the effort it took to hold still.

Just when I thought I couldn't take it anymore, he moved back to the first ear he'd touched, painting it entirely over. I distracted myself from the sensation by imagining how strange my blood-painted ears would look once he was done. Good thing Mom had convinced me to let my hair grow so long, down to nearly my waist, so it could conceal them.

"How long will this last?" I asked, searching for another distraction.

He stepped back and examined his handiwork on both ears. "A sevenday, perhaps. Maybe a bit more. It's always hard to tell."

It took me a whole second to realize that his meaning came through so quickly and clearly, he might as well have been speaking English to me.

"Holy cow," I breathed.

I answered his questioning look. "The difference. Goodness, it's like...I had cotton in my ears before or something, but now...I don't even have to think about it to understand you. I just *do*."

"Then it's working as it should," he said with satisfaction. "Good. Because that's Yvera returning from her scouting, and she's not going to wait for us to leave any longer."

I turned and saw the violet-haired young woman striding back to us. I noted enviously how much ground she could cover with those long legs of hers. She would *dominate* the competition in track....

I made myself focus on my priorities. "Oh," I said, trying not to sound nervous. "Good. Um, I guess that means you can give me directions on how to get home and be on your way."

"You don't honestly think it's safe for you to wander around this jungle with a whole rogue tribe of ahglen after your blood, do you?" he asked, folding his arms. "I went through all that trouble to explain to you that I'll get you the help you need, but you're going to have to come with us first and wait until morning. Even *I* shouldn't be out here at night, which is why Yvera is so anxious to get me back."

"*Oh.*" The relief felt like a mountain was being lifted off my shoulders. I trembled with it. "Thank you. I was not looking forward to...."

"Ending up right back where you started?" he asked with a crooked smile and dark eyes, inclining his head toward the center of the clearing. And the altar there.

"Speaking of which, we should smash that before we leave, Ben," Yvera said briskly as she reached us.

"Right," the man said grimly.

I was stuck on his name. "Ben?" I asked.

I had a tough time believing such an imposing man had such a run-of-the-mill name as "Ben."

"Short for 'Koriben,' actually, but hardly anyone except my elders calls me that," he said with a crooked smile, as if inviting me in on a joke. "You can just call me Ben."

It was the unexpected comradeship in his eyes that made it dawn on me. The beard had thrown me off, but....

"Wait, how old *are* you?"

Yvera snorted and Ben laughed. "Not much older than you, I imagine. Twenty summers."

"*I'm* twenty-one," Yvera said smugly, as if that made a whole lot of difference.

I tried not to stare. *Twenty*.... Just two years older than me? He couldn't be....

Granted, I did not know how long a year lasted on this planet, but still.... *He* thought we were close to the same age. He thought we were...peers.

"And your name?" Ben prompted, interrupting my muddled thoughts.

"Oh. Sorry," I said, feeling heat rising in my cheeks for no good reason. "Sarah."

"Sarah," he repeated with a brilliant smile, as if he could no longer contain the excitement he was inexplicably feeling. "You won't be able to appreciate the full gravity of this until we've explained, so just trust me for now when I say it is a rare honor to meet you."

My blush deepened. I didn't know what to say in reply, but Yvera's impatience saved me.

"Yeah, yeah," Yvera said. "Daylight is wasting, remember? Now that she can understand us and knows we're not kidnapping her, can we *go* now?"

Ben sighed but didn't argue. "Are you carrying her or am I?"

I noted with interest that his arm had already scabbed up, and I could almost see the ridges sinking as I watched.

Yvera snorted. "Like I said: you found her, so she's *your* responsibility. Besides, I need my full range of motion in case your dallying gets us ambushed."

"Is that...likely?" I asked, trying not to sound worried.

"Not if we leave now, no," Ben assured me. "Yvera is...my bodyguard, basically. It's her job to be paranoid."

That raised quite a few questions for me, none the least of which was why *he* needed a bodyguard, but Yvera shoved him and said, "Less talking, more changing. Go on. Shoo. I'll get her onto you, we smash that altar, then we're out of here."

"Be nice to her, Yv," Ben said sternly, but he turned and started walking away.

"'*Be nice to her*,'" Yvera mocked pettily. "Who does he think he is? The King?"

"I heard that!" Ben called over his shoulder.

"Uh, *is* he a king?" I whispered to her.

"What? Pshh, no," Yvera said condescendingly.

"Oh, good," I said with a sigh of relief as I watched Ben's retreating figure.

The thought of having someone *that* important bleed for my sake had twisted my insides. Plus, I knew so few people in this world; I'd felt a pang to think that the first person I'd ever met was the one I'd never see again once he inevitably passed me off to someone else.

Because I was watching this time, I saw Ben fall forward, and in a bewildering and nausea-inducing few seconds, his form shifted and stretched and expanded and surged in all directions, until not a handful of moments later, I was staring at a golden, scaled behemoth that occupied a good fourth of the enormous clearing, one so large that he had to turn carefully in place to keep his giant tail and roof-sized wings from scraping the trees as he did.

Had Yvera been as large? I was almost certain she hadn't. I couldn't imagine any creature being bigger. Or more...magnificent.

Yes, now that the worst of my terror was over, I could admit it: he was the most awe-inspiring creature I had ever seen. At the end of a very exhausting, world-changing half hour, the sight of him was enough to make me unsteady for a reason other than but not unlike fear.

Awe in its extremity feels the same.

"Nah," Yvera said casually as the dragon completed his rotation and fixed us under his golden, serpentine gaze. His neck frills and two sets of thick, spiral horns fanned around his head more majestically than any mane or crown. "He's only the Heir."

CHAPTER TWO

DISCRETION

KORIBEN

WE HAD LITTLE DAYLIGHT left by the time we were aloft, so I pushed us as hard as I thought it was safe, given the Earthren's obvious newness to flying.

Her weight was next to nothing on my drakáback, so I had to focus on the sensation of her there to make sure she was stable. I didn't have any sensation in the spine she clung to, but I guessed her legs were pressing into my sides with all her might. I felt terrible that there wasn't much I could do to make things easier for the poor girl.

Sarah, I reminded myself. She had a name now. I was glad she'd brought up introductions before we took off; otherwise I might have forgotten and would have had to keep thinking of her the whole flight back as *the Earthren*.

An *Earthren*, though! I almost wriggled in midair with the force of the excitement I'd been trying to contain this entire time. Avva was not going to believe this. *I* could hardly believe it.

As hard as it was to contain myself, she was the reason I had to keep my body straight and my wingbeats steady. I reminded myself of her inexperience and lack of equipment every time I got the itch to spin through the air. I wished I'd had the chance to grab a saddle, but as it was, I was glad I'd set off for the wildgate as quickly as I had.

Otherwise, she might not have survived.

The thought of what those torched ahglen had come so close to doing made heat build in my stomach for more reason than one. Using magic that dark and twisted was one thing. Blood taken unwillingly was punishable by death, even if the victim survived the ritual. Sacrificing the life of a sentient being on top of that was monstrousness of an unspeakable degree. But to sacrifice *her*....

Had they *any* idea what they had nearly done? They couldn't have, but even so, I'd see them hunted and burned to molten heaps for it. I'd have done the service *myself*, immediately, if I hadn't needed to remain with the Earth—with Sarah to make sure none of them snuck back to retake her.

In fact, that's why I'd run her down so rudely, back in the clearing. I hadn't expected her to bolt like that, and I'd panicked. Losing her in the jungle—where I would have had to pursue her on foot or been inhibited in my drakáform—that close to sunset would have been disastrous. Fates even worse than the one the ahglen had intended for her awaited her there. After all, the ahglen had been monstrous...but stupid. Other monsters might not have been so blind to what they had on their hands should she have put herself in them.

I didn't let myself linger in those kinds of thoughts. They weren't conducive to my goal of flying as steadily as possible to Elspeth Hold. Besides, even my alternating fury and excitement couldn't keep my flameheart from dimming inside of me as the sun sunk beyond the horizon: a chilling reminder that our time was short.

We were fortunate all three of Ykran's moons were on display tonight to varying degrees, casting their soft radiance over us. The energy they gave wasn't much, but it was enough to keep us aloft if we were conservative, and we were almost there. I could see the lights of the mountain hold ahead already.

You've been rather quiet, Yvera said, interrupting my thoughts. Her inner voice was teasing, but I could tell that underneath, she was still irritated with me for surging ahead of her earlier.

Are you surprised? I answered mildly.

I reminded myself that she had every right to be annoyed, and what was more, she could get me in a lot of trouble for it if she wanted to. I was going to have to be on my best behavior for a while to keep her mouth shut. And she knew it.

I've quite a lot to think about, I added.

Yes, but I'd expected you to be doing acrobatics by now.

Blast. She knew me too well. Case in point why I probably shouldn't have assigned my best friend to be my primary bodyguard, especially since that friend was Yvera. Avva had warned me she'd be trouble, and he was right.

If you hadn't noticed, I have an inexperienced amá on my back—who doesn't even have a saddle. You're *the one who insisted I carry her, remember?*

Oh, come on, she teased. *Let it out, just a little. She can hold on for just* one—

No, I said, harder than I meant to. I softened my tone. *Yvera, think how you would feel in her position. She must be terrified right now.*

She certainly looks tense, Yvera said dryly. *So stiff I could use her as a toothpick right now.*

Yvera!

Oh, come on, *Ben, don't tell me you're not getting tired of all this trembling nonsense. The girl is more delicate than a fogblossom. Seriously, how did amá ever stand a chance against us?*

For the sake of the cooperation that I would desperately need from Yvera in about ten dek if I didn't want to be grounded from now until the solstice, I bit back the correction that I would have normally given: *We are as amá as we are draká.*

Yvera had always overlooked that detail in our history. She stubbornly failed some classes because of it. It made sense, I supposed. She'd always related to her draká side more than her amá one, no matter how dual our natures were.

However, one other thing silenced my normal textbook correction. Until six years ago, I'd fully believed what I'd been taught. The balance, after all, was the key to the Covenants—to our very survival. As the next living vessel of that balance, I had never wanted to contemplate the alternative. But now....

Now certainty had been replaced with a deep-seated fear.

As well as Yvera knew me, she had no clue how much cause I had to be glad that there was an Earthren on my back right now. One that I was *not* going to endanger or alienate by indulging in a few youthful spurts of jubilance.

Especially now that it was dark, as Yvera well knew. So why was she being so pushy about this?

That did, however, remind me of a few things that we needed to get straight before arriving, and the lights of the hold were getting brighter.

Yvera, I began.

Yeah, yeah, I know, she said. *You don't want me mentioning how you left me in the dust to get to that wildgate opening. You know what that's going to cost you, don't you?*

You are the best, most amazing, most fearsome, most deadly of all my elites, I said, trying to sound sincere.

Well, she was. I had been justified in making her my rightwing—no one, not even Avva, had questioned my decision. Publicly, that is. Privately, Avva had warned me beforehand that she'd cause me just as much trouble as she was worth, but he still left the final decision up to me.

But being forced to say so out loud in so many words didn't make me sound like I meant it.

And?

And I would be dead a thousand times over without you.

Only a slight exaggeration.

Aaand?

Yvera, I can't say I'm sorry for what I did, because that would be a lie, I said with care. *She would be* dead *now if I hadn't, and even you should have some inkling of what that would have meant.*

But you didn't know she was there, she said hotly. *You just felt the gate—*

Yvera, we're almost there, I said, trying to keep anxiousness from my voice. I wasn't a naughty child trying to avoid a just punishment. I had good reasons—*especially* now—to not have my freedom curtailed. But the elders who would urge Avva to administer consequences for my recklessness would not—could not—know them.

Fine, I'll go along for now, she growled. I heard the rumble and caught the whiff of smoke on the wind. *But you're going to hear it from me later.*

You can rail into me all you like once we're alone again, I promised.

Oh, I will.

And...there's one more thing. I inwardly winced. This part would not go over well either. Yvera was terrible at keeping secrets, and keeping two at once was going to be a challenge she was entirely unmotivated to tackle.

What? she asked suspiciously.

Please, please, for the love of the Flame, can you try *to avoid mentioning that the girl is an Earthren?*

Oh, she said. *Uh. Sure.*

Sure? I asked in surprise.

Uh, yeah. Um—if you promise to tell me why.

Now I *knew* something was up. She seldom cared to know the "why." Those troublesome details she was happy to leave to me or Kor. She wasn't unintelligent; she was simply very...focused. The "why" was far less important to her than the "what," which was *her* realm of expertise.

She'd made up that requirement on the spot just to make it seem like she wasn't giving in too easily. Which meant she didn't care about what I was asking her to do or what I would tell her as payment. I'd still tell her the truth; I just wouldn't have to tell her much.

I was relieved, but I also wondered: what had she *expected* me to ask her to do? Clearly there had been something. Something she found distasteful enough that she'd agreed a bit too hastily when asked something else.

Fine, I said, hopefully doing a better job than she had at feigning reluctance.

Alright then, she snipped, recovering her irritation. *You know there's not much point, though, right? They're going to figure it out the moment she opens her mouth. And you're going to tell your father, anyway.*

I'm going to tell him, I assured her. *Just not* anyone else. *And anyone else who hears her will just assume she's speaking Vardak or something.*

My native tongue, Drona, was the primary language of the Six Realms, but plenty of other dialects and full-fledged languages had developed among the clans since their founding and dispersing to their own worlds. Vardak was infamous for having one of the fewest native speakers and belonged to this Realm besides.

But why? Yvera asked, sounding genuinely intent now. Or maybe she was just turning up the irritation. It was hard to tell with her sometimes.

I sighed at having to explain something like this to her. Kor would have gotten it immediately. Then again, "indiscreet" was how Avva had succinctly described her.

Because there's no reason to start the mass excitement that her arrival is going to cause—not yet. It's going to get out, and soon, yes. But we need to handle this carefully.

Whatever, Yvera said, losing patience with the duplicity of the idea, as I'd known she would.

There. Not much truth at all. Barely even scraping the surface. That was also the *good* thing about Yvera. Kor would be much, much harder to handle.

I inwardly groaned. I was already tired from night flying, and I had so many people to go through before I could get some sleep: the Elspeth elders, who would expect a full report in private and wouldn't be easy to fool into thinking Yvera had been with me the entire time; possibly a healer if they insisted on getting me checked; then Yvera (unless she lost patience with waiting her turn to chew me out and went to bed); then, if I was lucky, I could push off Kor until the morning (but the longer I did, the longer he'd have to plan his interrogation technique); after that, if I had the energy and she was still awake, I should check on how Sarah was settling in; and last but most important, Avva, who would want my report on this development, no matter the time of night.

There were implications only he and I could know about, and permissions I needed to get from him to go where I needed to go and do what I needed to do to pursue the miracle we'd been given, and I already knew he was not going to be pleased with my plan.

It was going to be a long night.

Chapter Three

ARRIVAL

Sarah

DRAGON FLYING IS NOT all that it's cracked up to be, let me tell you. At least not for someone so utterly unprepared as I was.

One: No saddle. Only sitting wedged as tightly as I could be between two of the golden dragon's spine spikes and holding onto the one in front of me with all my might.

Two: The height. Which I tried hard to forget by always looking pretty much straight ahead. About two-thirds of the time, his Godzilla-sized neck and head blocked out everything else, but I still got a stomach-churning view with every downbeat of his wings, which brought his shoulders up higher than his neck and me with them, offering me a brief but still-too-long panoramic picture of the darkening jungle. I might have been able to appreciate the beauty of it...if I'd been less obsessed with holding on. Yvera hadn't been comforting when she'd told me that if I was careful, I *probably* wouldn't fall to my death.

I was sixty-five percent sure she was joking, but I wasn't about to take those odds. Also, I was beginning to not like her.

Three: The cold. This one was the most surprising to me but shouldn't have been, seeing as it made perfect sense if you thought about it. Even if the air hundreds of feet above ground wasn't cooler than just above the sweltering jungle, night had fallen as we flew. Between our speed and the dragons' mighty wings striking a constant beat, I was buffeted on all sides by bone-chilling wind. Only the heat radiating from the dragon underneath me kept me from being worried about hypothermia, but the hot-cold contrast wasn't comfortable, either.

Four: The homesickness. Now that I was *somewhat* safe, I had time to worry about the littles, wondering how they were faring with Rachel gone. David was still at home, so he would probably keep them from burning the house down, even as occupied as he was, but I still fretted.

What would they all think and feel when they discovered I was gone?

The drudgery that the rest of my evening at home would have been now seemed warm and comforting. Blissful even. Being able to give Abby a big hug, or ruffle the twins' hair and see them squirm but grin all the same. In cajoling David away from his video game for long enough to eat dinner with us and hearing him regale me and the twins with the details while Abby sagely expressed her disgust. Dad asking about my day after he got home, no matter how tired he must be himself, and seeing his smile of gratitude at all I'd done. Texting Mom goodnight after crawling into bed and getting a dozen emojis and expressions of comfort and support back.

Routine. Home. Family. Right now, the thought of it all was like a distant campfire in the dark, promising warmth but too far to reach.

Why had I ever wanted to leave it all behind?

Perhaps if darkness hadn't marred the view or if I'd felt more comfortable looking around, I might have been able to occupy myself better. As it was, once I'd gotten the hang of hanging on, I had little more to distract myself from my homesickness than the thousands of questions bumping around in my skull.

There were the obvious, of course: Where were we going? What would they do with me once we got there? Would I get a place to sleep? (*Do dragons sleep? Please tell me they sleep—or at least know humans need sleep.*) Would I get a shower first? What would come in the morning? What would Ben's "help" look like? Would he help me personally or hand me off?

Then came the less obvious questions, shrapnel from the bombshell that Yvera had so casually dropped just when I had no time to ask any of them. Coincidence? I thought not.

He's only the Heir.

Well, what the heck did *that* mean? Did that mean he was the *prince*? Of *what*, may I ask? The dragons? Or...humans who turned into dragons. Or dragons who turned into humans. What even *were* they?

Again, what did that make *him?* The prince of *all* dragons? Or just a good chunk of them? Or was this a medieval "monarch" in which pretty much any lord with enough land could give himself the title of king? Did Yvera's word, *Vereth*, even mean the same thing as *king* did to me?

Yet whatever magic on my ears and in my mind now that was translating for me gave me *King*. Not *chief* or *lord* or *governor* or any other half a dozen words for rulers that I could think of, none of which felt right. Only *King*. Somehow, I *felt* the capital K in there.

Ben hadn't struck me as the kind of pretentious prince who would be too important to bother with interrupting a sacrificial ritual, tackling the girl he'd just saved to keep her from running off into the jungle to get herself captured again, and slicing open his arm to paint her ears in his blood just to make her understand he was *trying* to help her.

Yet Yvera had called him the *Heir*. Again, with a capital H.

I was so confused.

And tired. And cold. And done—just done. I wanted to go home. To close my eyes and just believe that all of this was a dream that would fade moments after I woke up.

Then, oddly, the image of the first time I saw Ben—the human Ben—popped into my mind. I had been too terrified and bewildered at the time to comprehend the awkwardness of the position we'd been in, and I felt a belated heat build in my cheeks as I remembered the sight of him underneath me.

Yet my main thought was that if all of this had been a dream, I would have never met him.

The golden dragon banked his wings and descended, and when I looked down, I realized that I'd been too wrapped up in my own thoughts to see before that the darkness ahead was broken up by many bright lights scattered up and down what looked like a mountain. He and Yvera were angling for an enormous circle carved into and two-thirds up the side, brightly lit and clearly meant for landing.

I clutched the spike and clenched with my legs with all my might as we soared in, but the height of the landing pad meant he and Yvera could coast onto its surface, so the landing was surprisingly smooth. Ben *did* seem to take more care with his touchdown than Yvera did; it took him a few moments longer, and he crouched deeper as he did so, perhaps dispersing more of the impact—I had no idea how landing worked, so I could only guess.

Both humans and a bewildering number of dragons—OK, *two*, but that was double the amount I had ever seen up to that point—approached as soon as he did so. One was a midnight blue; the other was an emerald. The blue was smaller than Yvera, the emerald bigger, but I noted that both were smaller than Ben.

I'd expected a chatter of voices, but all was silent for a few seconds as the humans and dragons approached. Then....

Yet another new sort of sound. It seemed to be my day for them, after all, so why not?

It was a *voice*. And yet it was not a voice—not one I heard out loud. It was a voice I *felt*, reverberating somewhere inside me; I would have said inside my head, but it caused a powerful stirring inside my chest, and how did that make sense? It was deep, too—powerful enough to make me quake—and echoing, as if it spoke in a vast chamber.

Koriben, she—the voice felt female, though it didn't have the normal characteristics of pitch to judge—intoned. *You had us worried. We were about to send out searchers.*

Apologies for troubling you, Elder Jaya, Ben said to the emerald dragon.

Even without the golden dragon's head bowing at the same time, I knew the voice belonged to Ben, but I didn't know how. His "silent" voice didn't sound exactly like his vocal one, and it was no louder by proximity to me, and yet somehow it still had the same *flavor* of him. It also seemed *younger* than Elder Jaya's voice, but not by sound but by having the...well, *essence* of youth.

We were waylaid by the opening of a wildgate, Ben continued as he raised his head. I noticed, though, that he kept it at a level below that of the emerald dragon, to whom he appeared to be looking. *I was obligated to investigate. Which was fortunate, because we discovered this young woman, Sarah, nearby*—Ben turned sideways to display me better, and I had to resist the urge to duck under the level of his wings—*about to be sacrificed by ahglen.*

A few humans gasped, and a third dragon—a large scarlet who had joined us moments before—hissed. All eyes, human and dragon, fell on me.

I stared helplessly back. Was I supposed to do something? Say something? All I could think of doing was giving a little wave, and that just seemed silly.

Fortunately, Ben plowed right on. *She has been through a great deal today and I am sure would be grateful if someone could take her to a room to rest here for the night. In the morning, Yvera, Kor, and I will ferry her to her destination.*

Of course, Jaya said in the same mild tone, unruffled by Ben's statements.

I can escort her, a new dragon-voice said. If I was any judge of where these thoughts were coming from, my guess was on the midnight blue. I felt a tiny burst of pride when the dragons turned their massive heads to him.

Yes, since I was fairly sure it wasn't Yvera, I'd had fifty-fifty odds by that point between the blue and the scarlet, but I needed that small win.

You will? Yvera said next, mental tone suspicious.

Of course, the blue said smoothly. *Since I have already settled in, I can help make her comfortable while the two of you speak to the elders about your much more eventful journey here.*

Excellent, Ben said, and from the narrowed look the violet dragon cast him, I guessed he'd anticipated Yvera had been about to say something and had cut her off on purpose. *Thank you, Kor. If you approve, Elder Jaya?*

Yes, of course, Jaya said, a note of amusement entering her mild voice.

Ben was already making his way over to the inside edge of the platform, the part carved into the mountain. There, built into the massive retaining wall, were platforms of varying heights with rungs leading down from them to the ground. I understood their purpose as soon as the golden dragon crouched next to one, putting me level with it.

Oh, this is so much nicer than getting up here, I thought in relief. *That* had involved a creative combination of climbing on top of the altar and relying on

Yvera to pull me up his leg; and that had been with Ben lying down as low to the ground as he could make himself.

Still, I was up high enough and there was just *enough* of a gap between the flatter part of Ben's back and the platform that it took me a moment to work up the willpower to let go of Ben's spike, get up, and make the uneven, slippery transition. I let out a breath of relief as soon as my feet were both squarely on the platform.

The golden dragon got up and turned his long neck around to gaze at me. I trusted Ben by now, but instincts aren't easily overruled when a predator that big gets his head in your space. His slitted golden eye alone was as large as my torso, and I could see my pale reflection in it. To my credit, I held my ground, but I saw my flinch reflected back at me.

Goodbye for now, Sarah. If I do not see you again until morning, sleep well.

"Thank you," I said unsteadily, swallowing.

As he turned away, he spoke again, and this time there was no echoing quality to his voice. I got the impression he was speaking only to me. *Don't worry. You're safe now. Although...watch out for Kor. He means well, but he can be a bit....*

Just then, Jaya called for Ben to follow her, which he did, passing out of sight through the great archway into the mountain. Whatever Kor *was*, I was going to find out for myself.

"You use the rungs to climb down," a voice called up to me in amusement.

I looked down over the rim of the platform to see a clean-shaven, brown-skinned young man with folded arms; short, curly, midnight-blue hair; and matching fine clothing smirking up at me.

I scowled at him. "I'm not stupid. I was getting to that part."

His mouth dropped in mock amazement. "So, she speaks! And in what a *fascinating* dialect of Vardak, too."

I flushed, feeling off-kilter, as if I'd been tricked.

"Hold your horses," I said, making my way to the rungs. "I'm coming down."

"Horses. *Amazing.* You're going to have to describe those to me in detail once you do."

"Wait, you don't have *horses* here?" I asked as I went from rung to rung.

"Not a one," he said with relish. "Since nothing comes to mind but a vague myth when you say the word. I'm eager to have you separate fact from fiction for me."

"Are...you joking?" I asked suspiciously. Fortunately, just then, I reached the floor and could turn around and scrutinize him.

"Oh, I assure you, I'm absolutely serious," he said.

I narrowed my eyes at him. "Then why are you grinning like that?"

"Because I can't believe my own eyes—or ears, for that matter," he said, grin widening. "I *honestly* can't believe it. Ben has *done* it. After all these centuries.... I owe Yvera an emerald, but I don't care one bit; I've never been happier to lose a bet in my life."

I just stared at him.

He shook his head and turned, beckoning me to follow. "But I'm being rude—I'm supposed to be showing you to a room. Long day, was it?"

"Yeah," I said dryly, falling in beside him as we walked toward the arch. "Stumbling into another world, nearly being sacrificed, being saved by giant monstrosities that shouldn't exist, and then being whisked through the freaking cold sky by said monstrosities does that to you."

Kor—it had to be him—laughed in delight. "Scorching Flame, you aren't *quite* as timid as you look, are you?"

Before I could retort, he put a finger to his lips.

"Better keep that part about another world to yourself for the moment," he said in a near-whisper. "Ben didn't mention it in front of everyone for a reason."

"What, he talked to you about it?" I asked, startled.

Kor shook his head. "Didn't have time to, didn't have to. I'd be a poor leftwing if I couldn't guess as much myself."

He winked at me.

"What's that?" I asked. But I was only half paying attention. The other half was trying not to gawk as we passed through the stone arch.

It was *massive*, big enough for three dragons to pass side by side, and beautifully carved and gilded. In the lights of the various huge crystals set around the rim of the landing circle, it shimmered. And that was just the beginning. The hall we passed into had rows of columns on either side carved into the shape of trees with the occasional golden crystal for a leaf, casting enough light down on us to make it feel like day, even though the arched ceiling must have been over fifty feet above us.

"What, a leftwing?" Kor said casually, as if the architectural marvel we were passing through were nothing. "Don't have a close enough equivalent, do you?"

"I guess not." I was still focused on looking around as much as I could without being obvious about it.

"Hmm. How to describe what I do...." he said thoughtfully. Then rolled his eyes. "I can't believe I'm going to do this by starting with *Yvera*, but you've met her, I presume? And learned what her role is?"

"Ben said that she's his...bodyguard?"

"His *primary* bodyguard, to be more precise," Kor said. "She's his rightwing, which makes her the person in charge of his safety. She's the head of his elite—that's the rest of his bodyguards, though Ben only bothers with them when he has to—and his adviser on all things martial. When Ben becomes King, she'll become the head of the Warflight."

I started paying more attention after that last sentence. The more I learned, the more questions I had. For example, what was a *warflight*? But I guessed that Kor loved to talk and that I could get him going down rabbit holes if I asked the wrong questions, and I was more concerned about another detail.

As casually as I could, I asked, "So Ben is a prince, then?"

Kor paused in what he'd been about to say and blinked. "Prince?"

For a second, I was as much at a loss to describe what a prince was as he had been to describe a leftwing. "A prince is a...son of a king—or queen," I hastily added. "A monarch at any rate."

"Fascinating," Kor said. "So you have a title for the sons of a Monarch? *Any* son is a 'prince'?"

"Well...yeah. Does that mean you *don't*?"

He shrugged. "Well, no. The Heir is the only Heir, unless he or she dies. Then the next eligible Sunfilled becomes the Heir. There's nothing significant about the Monarch's other children unless they become Heir. If the Monarch ever has any others. Being Sunfilled, they seldom have more than one or two at most."

"So, just so I've got this straight, Ben is the Heir," I said. "But *not* a prince."

Not sure how that made me feel any better. We were pretty much only discussing semantics at this point. But it did.

"Correct," Kor said. "He's the son of the current King *and* the Heir, but those two don't necessarily go together. The Tree chooses an Heir from among the rest of the Sunfilled Clan as frequently as not, especially if the Monarch's child turns out to be a spoiled brat. Can't have someone like that become the Monarch."

My head was spinning now, and I was too disoriented to know which direction to go next. Fortunately, Kor didn't need prompting to continue talking.

"Now, where were we? Gah, I can't believe we left off on *Yvera* still. Alright, you've got a general sense of what a rightwing does, yes?"

"A general sense," I said pointedly.

He waved a hand. "Good enough. She smashes what needs smashed—that's pretty much all *she* cares about, and all you need to know. I, on the other hand, have a much more complex, nuanced role. I have to defer to Yvera on martial things, but I advise Ben on and assist him with pretty much everything else. I'm his head scholar, counselor, ambassador, and collector of lesser-known information."

I stared at him. Then my eyes narrowed as the last piece of what Ben had been warning me about clicked into place. "You mean you're his spy."

Kor winced.

"No need to put it so crudely—or loudly," he whispered mournfully, perhaps because the foot traffic around us was increasing. I tried to pay careful attention to his words and not to the bewildering array of colors, clothing styles, and branching corridors.

Then he raised his voice but kept it at a low volume. "Besides, that takes a very narrow view of what I do for him. I find out what he needs to know, whether I need to cloister myself in a dark library for days on end or...elicit the information through more creative means. I'm also his representative in all political matters. When, Flame willing, he becomes King, I'll oversee his Grand Council and run everything that needs running if Ben can't or doesn't want to see to it himself. It's a complex and crucial role. A competent rightwing is good to keep people safe, but everyone knows the Realms would fall apart without a masterful leftwing."

"Not to mention a humble one, too," I said dryly as we began climbing a flight of stairs.

I noted with interest that smaller, human-sized steps were on either side of the passage, but giant, scraped, and gouged blocks formed steps in the center.

"But of course," Kor said with complete seriousness.

I raised an eyebrow at him, and he burst out laughing.

"Oh, I think I'll like *you*. You're so much more fun than Yvera. Yes, I know I'm not perfect, thank you very much. Fortunately, I should have plenty of years to grow into my role before I need to bear the full weight of it. Leftwings and rightwings are much more limited in their roles for Heirs. For now, suffice it to say that Yvera tries to keep Ben alive, I try to keep him out of trouble, and between the two of us, someday he'll become a King."

"Is that hard for you to do?" I asked, feeling a clench in my gut. Probably because any danger to Ben was a danger to me as long as I was around him.

"For *this* Heir?" Kor sighed dramatically. "You have no idea."

His voice lowered again, which was odd, because we'd turned off into a nearly empty corridor lined with doors.

"How shall I put this.... These aren't...the safest of times, and Ben is an unusually...*active* Heir. Normally, Heirs his age are still taking interesting classes, going on recreational hunts, attending feasts, dinners, and parties, and otherwise dragging out their last years of freedom. But Ben has never been interested in any of that, especially since graduating tertiary two years ago. He's put us through a hellwind of a year flying from this corner of the Six Realms to that, ostensibly to take a tour of the lands he'll one day rule."

Ostensibly?

The weighted hint hung in the air, more noticeable for how Kor fell silent to let it sink in. That, combined with what I'd learned about him so far, meant that he hadn't said a word more than he'd intended to, no matter what his careless chattiness implied.

He'd done more than drop hints, I realized. He'd freely given me details that no self-respecting, loyal prince's confidant would give—not one whose job at least partially revolved around information and secrecy.

"Why are you telling me all of this?" I asked, looking at him sidelong.

"*That* is the smartest question you've asked me yet," Kor said, his face and voice both sober for the first time. This time, his smile was grim, and his midnight-blue eyes flashed with a look that was both satisfied and dark. "You have no idea how relieved that sign of your intelligence makes me."

"Why?" I demanded.

"All in good time," Kor said enigmatically, stopping in front of a door. He grinned and folded his arms as he leaned against the side of it. "Besides, I thought you were tired."

I looked at the door. "So you're saying this is my room for the night?"

"It is indeed," he said, pointing to the clear gem in the center. "Touch that."

I glared at him sidelong.

He chuckled. "Intelligent *and* wary? Good. That will make it easier for Yvera and me to keep you alive."

He straightened and pointed to other doors in the hall. "See those? They're all for hold guests."

I looked around and saw many identical doors, some with clear gems, some with gems glowing an assortment of colors, with what seemed like the full range of the rainbow represented.

"The ones with glowing gems are claimed," Kor went on. "When the occupant first touches the crystal, that's them claiming the room for themselves. From then on, they're the only ones aside from the hold's guard who can open the door—until they tap the gem again to show they're leaving for good. Then the gem goes back to being dull and clear."

He waved his hand vaguely. "Mine is down there a few doors. When Ben and Yvera are done being grilled about their encounter with the ahglen, they'll make their way here and claim ones for themselves."

"Really?" I asked in surprise. "Ben's going to sleep here?"

Kor cocked his head at me, fascinated again. "This is the guest wing, and he's a guest. Where else would he sleep?"

"I don't know," I said. "I'm just surprised you don't have somewhere set apart for...important guests."

Kor chuckled. "It's this 'prince' thing again, isn't it? *Maybe* in this remote hold at the edge of civilization there's something that could be arranged for the *King*, but that would only be to accommodate his elite around him without having to reshuffle all these guests who were here first. But since Ben insists on traveling with just Yvera and me, this is what he gets. He *is* the Heir, but he's *just* the Heir, if that makes sense. The only thing special in his case will be that Yvera will touch his doorgem right after he does, to make sure she has access in an emergency. Even that's not that special. Friends or even couples wanting to sleep in separate rooms do the same thing all the time."

"Are they, Ben and Yvera?" I blurted out before I could think better of it, then trailed off with hot cheeks.

Kor laughed so hard he was wiping tears from his eyes before he could answer. "Oh, sorry. That just...if only you knew the history there.... The short answer is most definitely *no*, they are not a couple and never have been. As much as people have often thought otherwise."

Including Yvera? I wanted to ask but didn't.

"Yvera isn't consort material, and they both know that," Kor said, wiping the last tear away with a smirk. "And Ben's never seemed interested in flings. So, his relationship history can be summarized as *nonexistent*."

I hesitated. "Surely that's not...advisable."

I didn't know how dating and marriage worked here, especially for the Heir, but if this was a fair and open-minded society, Ben would be encouraged to...at least get to know a few people before settling down.

Kor gave a long-suffering sigh. "That's what *I've* always told him. But does he listen to me? No. I'm only his leftwing, after all, merely charged with making sure he's prepared to become King. No big deal. He has all the time in the world to find out what he wants in a partner—*later*. When he's not so *busy*."

I looked at him sidelong. Once again, that was far more information than I'd asked for. Information that was probably public knowledge given Ben was a public figure, but also, those were details that, if Kor were a good friend and careful adviser, he wouldn't have shared quite so freely with a stranger from another world.

What game was Kor playing? Particularly with *me*?

"Here I go again about my problems, when you're supposed to be getting some rest," he said, leaning against the wall to the side of the door again. He inclined his head to the gem. "Well? Go on then."

I didn't know why I still hesitated, but since I couldn't think of a good reason not to, I reached up and slowly touched the dull gem on the door in front of me.

The second I did, I felt a zap like static electricity—except a dozen times stronger—surge through my chest and into my finger. The lightning-fast sensation had shocked more than hurt, but it was still enough to make me say a four-letter word. I yanked my hand back and cradled it in my other one gingerly, but there didn't seem to be any damage.

When I looked up again, I watched in shock as brilliant light blossomed in the center of the gem like a multifaceted flower and grew until it filled the entire stone. For a moment, the gem shone almost too brightly to look at before fading to a duller—but still dazzling—white.

"Interesting," Kor said mildly, but his dark eyes were alight with the intensity of his scrutiny, and I knew for certain I'd been right to hesitate. There *had* been more to that simple touch than he'd pretended. Once again, he had tricked me into revealing something he'd wanted to know. The most irritating thing was, I still didn't know what either of those things he had learned from me *were*.

Just who had gleaned more from our short few minutes together? I thought I knew the answer, and it wasn't me.

I gritted my teeth. "You knew that was going to happen."

"No," he said, still in that mild tone as he looked away to examine the white crystal. "But I hoped something like it would. Once again, you exceeded my expectations. You've made me a very happy leftwing this evening, Sarah."

I straightened and took a step away from him. "I *don't* like being manipulated," I said coldly.

"Good," he said coolly, none of his former charm and lightheartedness visible now. "Very good. Because there *will* be many people who will try to manipulate you, and few of them will have yours and Ben's best interests at heart like I do. So, consider this my first bit of advice in this dangerous world: Trust those instincts of yours, Sarah. You have good ones. If you want to keep up with Ben, you need to start listening to them. Or an amá like you might not last long."

Without preamble, he shoved off the wall and started walking away. He called over his shoulder, "The lavatory is at the end of the hall, with showers and baths, too. They're communal, only separated by gender, so if you don't want company, then I'd suggest you get to it before the night rush. I'll see if I can scrounge up a change of clothes and send them to your room. Sleep well."

And just like that, he walked out of sight, hands in his pockets. Whistling.

I stood there in front of my door for a full minute, seething. I decided I'd changed my mind: Yvera was fine in my book. It was *Kor* I had to watch out for. And I would.

CHAPTER FOUR

CLEANSING

SARAH

A MINUTE OR SO after Kor left, a guest came down the hall and gave me a curious look, snapping me out of my stupor. I turned and pushed on my door—no handle, only a metal plate on the right-hand side.

I felt only a mild tingle from the plate—a sensation I might not have even noticed had I not been watching for one—and the door swung open. I slipped inside as quickly as I could and let the door swing shut behind me.

The room was surprisingly big. I'd expected a cramped, dorm-style space with only a bed and maybe a chair, but perhaps I'd underestimated this dragon-people's need for space. Sure, a dragon could never have *fit* in here, but from everything else I'd seen of their architecture, they liked to build big. That only made sense, seeing as everyone I'd met except Kor had seemed like a giant to me—and even Kor was still just about six feet.

It was also...homey.

The room was brightly lit by more of the glowing gems that I'd noticed were the primary source of illumination in this place; at least, I assumed thumbnail-sized lights set into the walls and ceiling, shining with warm daylight-like radiance, came from gemstones, and when I touched the closest one within arm's reach, I discovered I was right.

The stone walls of the mountain had been plastered over and painted a neutral but still warm cream, a couple tapestries of beautiful landscapes substituted for windows, and the ceiling arched overhead in beautiful curves that reminded me of castle interiors. The furniture was made of sturdy logs polished to a bright gleam, covered with cushions, and draped with furs. There was even a *firepit* in the sunken center of the room, with a coal-filled brazier that was already alight with a cheery and smokeless flame. I knew there couldn't be smoke because, though I saw a shaft in the center of the arched ceiling, the surrounding plaster didn't have a single smudge.

Also...who just left a fire burning in an unoccupied room? Or had that thing magically lit as soon as I claimed it?

I warily approached the fire as I examined the rest of the room.

The firepit was the central focus of the room, and the sides of the sunken level had a built-in bench that served as the single step down in two parts, and the rest was covered in furs of various shades and matching cushions.

At the far side of the room was a counter with a few high stools, what looked to me like a teakettle, and some canisters. To my left was a large desk with an equally large chair, again draped with a fur blanket. The desk had a few drawers underneath and a slanted writing easel on top. On the wall, just over the desk, was a set of four brackets, arranged as if to hold some oval picture. I hoped the picture was simply being replaced now and that the last occupant hadn't stolen it—and that I wouldn't be blamed for the crime.

I made a mental note to ask Kor—no, Ben was better—about it before we left as I looked to the right. Where, last but far from least in my weary mind, was the bed. Which, of course, looked bigger than a California king and was covered in a few giant furs. I stared at those for a moment. Had someone killed a few polar bears? Because those white furs were...massive.

I gave a tiny shudder.

The entire room had the air of thoughtful design and welcoming comfort without being excessive. I now understood why Kor thought these rooms were good enough for the Heir: they might not have the gilded extravagance that princes and presidents were accustomed to on Earth, but they were a whole lot better than most hotel rooms I'd stayed in and, in my mind, good enough for anyone.

Speaking of which, was all this luxury just...free? Kor hadn't led me to a desk to check in or told me about any sort of payment system. If a fee would be due, surely they all understood I had nothing to give, right? Even if they had taken American credit cards, I just realized that I had somehow lost not just my shoes but also my hat and purse in whatever magical fall had brought me here. I felt guilty about putting all of this on Ben's tab, but I didn't have any other choice, and surely as the Heir, he could afford it. I'd just have to remember to thank him.

Right then, my body reminded me that there were a few needs I had to take care of. I reluctantly turned away from my temporary sanctuary and returned to the hall. I felt a little anxious letting the door swing shut behind me, especially when I heard the click of a lock. I felt the absence of any key or pass card, so to be sure I could get back in, I put my hand on the door plate just to feel the charge of energy and the mechanism unlock again.

Then I turned and went in the direction Kor had pointed. Sure enough, at the end of that long hall, there were two doors, side by side.

I realized I had a problem: Kor had *not* told me which door to use. The doors were clearly marked in the center of each...with a rune that was meaningless to me. Not even the colors were helpful: both were painted in a neutral white, and even if they *had* been different, I doubted they would have been the stereotypical pink and blue.

As I nervously stared at the doors and contemplated my doom of potentially committing the greatest social faux pas by going in the wrong door, I heard a warm, friendly voice say behind me, "Need any help?"

I turned to see a tall, pretty young woman with medium-olive skin and emerald hair and eyes. She wore a loose emerald-green tunic, brown apron with various pockets, green pants, and soft leather slippers. Those eyes gazed at me with the warmest, kindest expression I'd seen on anyone but Ben since arriving here, and I instantly felt more at ease.

"Yes, thank you," I said fervently. "I'm...uh...new."

At the last minute, I remembered Kor's warning not to mention where I'd come from. Although what I was supposed to say instead, I had no clue. I silently begged her not to ask.

"You're that girl Ben and Yvera rescued, aren't you?" she asked, studying me with frank curiosity.

My cheeks grew warm at the hint of how quickly and widely word of me had spread. Now that all the danger was past, I felt the full embarrassment of being just another damsel in distress. But what else could I say? *I'd had it handled?*

That would have been delusional in the extreme.

"Yeah, pretty much," I admitted.

"Don't feel bad," she said with a chuckle. "*I* couldn't have scared away a whole tribe of ahglen on my own. Few of us—aside from Ben, of course—could. In fact, we all felt terrible when we heard. They've been giving this hold some trouble, but blood sacrifice...."

She shuddered. "The guard should have taken care of them before something like that could have happened. I hear Elder Jaya's going to send a hunt after them and apologize to you personally."

She grinned. "That is, if Ben doesn't sweep you away first. Rumor *also* has it he wants to leave first thing tomorrow and is taking you with him."

My blush increased, this time at the implication in her words. "He promised to help get me home."

"Right," she said with a wink. Before I could protest further, she walked past me and pushed open the door to the right.

"Come on," she said brightly, holding the door open. "Don't be shy. I'm sure you're ready to clean up after the day you've had."

"You have *no* idea," I said gratefully as I followed her inside.

I was also immediately grateful that I had some guidance, because what was the first thing I saw? A bench along the right wall carved from the stone, with uncovered seats set into the top at regular intervals. No privacy whatsoever. Lovely. At least I smelled none of the usual odors accompanying a pit toilet arrangement, so whatever they were doing to take care of the waste, it was effective. The wall was set far enough to the right that it wouldn't be visible to an outside observer if the door were open, but still....

Just so there could be no mistake of the seats' intended use, the young woman went over to bench and took care of her business, asking me questions all the while.

She soon caught on that keeping up a conversation and overcoming my self-consciousness to take care of my business in front of her was a bit too much for me to handle at once, so she let us both finish up before saying with some measure of amusement, "You *are* new, aren't you? What part of Vardak are you from?"

I blinked. Vardak? Something sounded familiar about the word, but I couldn't place it. I figured it was just best to play along with her assumption.

"Um...a very...different part."

"It must be," she said with a laugh. "And I thought *this* place was remote. Come on, I'll show you how things work here."

I followed her, relieved both with her offer and that the inevitable question about my origin had been handled so easily.

Who told her I was from "Vardak"? I thought. Then, the inevitable answer came to me. I was a newcomer to Ben's little group, but even I could guess who would have *already* spread just the right rumor to explain away my unusual circumstances.

Kor.

I resisted the urge to be grateful to him. For all I knew, Vardak was the hillbilly equivalent here, and Kor had taken the opportunity to "help" me by offering a mocking jab at the same time.

As I followed her down the hall, she asked, "So, what's your preference? Shower or bath? And do you like to steam?"

"Steam?" I asked eagerly. "Like a sauna?"

"That's a weird word for it, but, yeah," she said, chuckling.

I was at a loss. "Uh.... What do you usually do?"

She shook her head with a smile. "When I have the time? All three. Let's do that to make sure you know how."

"Do you *have* the time?" I asked. "If you don't—"

"Don't worry about it," she said with a flippant wave. "I wasn't looking forward to playing another dozen rounds of arkan before bed, anyway. You're a breath of something new."

Amid my fervent thanks, she showed me the showers, where I was particularly glad for her help, otherwise I never would have figured out the system of crystals set into the wall to control the flow and temperature of the water. Even, apparently, the level of oily soap, which was dispensed on command through the water itself. I was so grateful, I didn't even mind stripping and taking our showers right in front of each other—again, no privacy, but her utter lack of body consciousness was rubbing off on me. Even as I tried not to take a hit to my self-esteem at how perfectly toned and spotless her tall, Amazonian body was.

To add to my embarrassment, Svyer—I'd gathered her name by that point—fussed over me a little when she spotted some scrapes and bruising, especially on my bare feet.

"I'm surprised at Ben," she muttered as I tried not to go red under her scrutiny. "Since you clearly can't self-heal, he should have sent you to the healers instead of straight to a room. And he should have given you *shoes*."

"It's nothing they could have done anything about," I protested.

"Don't be silly," she said. "There would have been *someone* with enough spark left to heal this much. I don't know what the reserves are like where you're from, but this hold has plenty enough, so there's no need for you to be scrimpy. I'm assisting in the healing wing here for a few sevendays, so I should know."

"Oh," I said brilliantly. I reminded myself that this world's rules were different. Here, the people could do more than shapeshift. Ben had also done *magic* of some kind to make me able to understand him, and his self-inflicted cut had healed before my eyes, so there could very well be solutions to even a bruise.

"I can heal that in the steam room, if you want," Svyer offered. "I've still got some spark left, and the heat will help me a bit."

"It's nothing," I tried protesting, but that only seemed to make her mad. Before she could give the lecture I could see growing in her eyes, I relented.

The next room was the sauna, which we went into with only a towel wrap that had been hanging outside for the purpose. Once we sat down on the bench, Svyer put her hands on my shoulders with a professional air. Then her green eyes glowed with an inner light, and I felt an amazing *warmth* sink into me.

It was like...feeling warm hot chocolate go down my throat and warm up my belly on a chilly winter day. Except *all over* my body, taking away every ache and pain and melting me into a barely upright pile of flesh.

"Flame Above," she said under her breath, her glowing eyes open but unfocused. "From the state of you, you'd think you'd never gotten a professional healing in your life.... And...."

Then she trailed off, sightless eyes going wide. A few moments later, the glow in her eyes died, and the warm feeling retreated, but by then, I was sweating enough from the steam that it wasn't a significant loss. I sank back against the wall with the most contented sigh of my life.

"Thank you," I said. "That felt *amazing*."

Svyer bit her lip, looking troubled.

"What?" I asked with a sinking feeling.

"Sarah—that was your name, wasn't it?" she asked hesitantly.

"Yes," I said slowly.

The young woman's eyes darted to a couple of newcomers who entered the sauna. They sat on the opposite side of the room from us, well out of earshot. Or, at least beyond my range, but Svyer looked at me intently, and I heard her voice in my mind.

Her mental voice was gentle—not accusatory in the slightest—but there *was* a surprising undercurrent that took me a beat longer to identify: awe.

You're not from Vardak, are you?

I looked at her helplessly. I didn't know how to answer her back, either what to say or how to say it. I didn't know how to speak mind to mind as these dragon people did—or if I even could.

Kor had warned me not to say where I was from, but he hadn't told me *why* or how urgent it was to keep it a secret. She'd guessed at least part of the truth, anyway, and I didn't have the knowledge or skill to lie convincingly enough to erase whatever she'd just learned from healing my body.

My very...human body.

Suddenly, I understood why neither Kor nor Ben had sent me to a healer. If I'd been thinking properly, if I'd been as wary as Kor had tried to make me, I would have found some way to refuse her healing—no, I would have never undressed in front of her. I was just too different to expose myself in any sort of way.

Though surely this kind young woman could be trusted....

I met her gaze while giving the tiniest shake of my head. Then I whispered as quietly as I could, "Please don't tell anyone."

I won't, she promised earnestly. *But...does Ben know?*

This time, I nodded.

Good, Svyer said in relief, and she relaxed back against the wall. From the way she let it go, that seemed to have been the primary thing that had been bothering her.

She closed her eyes and breathed deeply, so I guessed it was time to simply relax. I did the same, letting the heavenly steam—scented with smells like pine, cedar, and incense—waft over my healed and loosened muscles as I tried to think of nothing at all.

Tried being the operative word, because this was the first time since stumbling into this world that I'd had the luxury of sitting around, safe and with nothing to do. Even on the flight back, the height and my whirling questions had partially distracted me. Now my thoughts could fully turn to my family.

What were they thinking right now? Had they noticed I was gone yet? Were they worried? What would they do when I never came home tonight?

My heart clenched and eyes squeezed shut. It felt wrong to be relaxing in a sauna like this. Shouldn't I be doing everything in my power to get home right now?

I then snorted at myself. Like what? Marching out of this place and back into the dark jungle, where the ahglen waited for me? Perhaps worse, if Yvera's urgency was anything to go by. Ben had said I needed to wait until morning, and that made sense on a practical level. I had no idea what kind of help I would need, but most likely it would require powerful and complex magic, and darkness probably wouldn't help.

Waiting was the only thing I *could* do now, and while I was waiting, I should take care of myself. That's what my family would want me to do. I would see them tomorrow morning and explain everything, and they would be glad to see that I wasn't any worse off for my brief adventure.

At least, that's what I kept trying to tell myself, but the entire time we sat there in silence, I inwardly squirmed with enough guilt that it threatened to tie knots back into my relaxed muscles.

Svyer got up. "Done?" she asked. I was relieved to see she didn't appear to resent me for my deception. In fact, her smile was softer, gentler now.

"Yes," I said.

"Then it's bath time," she said with relish.

The next room was the bathing room, with only two giant pools with sloped sides and benches for lounging, as quite a few women already were. There were even some children playing in the shallow parts or in their caretakers' laps. The air in the bathing room felt cold after the sauna, and I was sure it wasn't just my imagination from the steam emerging from one pool.

"That's the hot bath," Svyer said, pointing to the steaming pool. Then she pointed to the other. "And that's the cool one, depending on your mood and energy level."

I wasn't sure what that last bit meant, but "cool" didn't sound like what my muscles needed right now. Besides...I was a wimp when it came to cold water. Or cold in general. Winters were rough.

"Probably the hot?" I said. "Although...that looks really hot."

"Oh, it's not," Svyer said, then hesitated, biting her lip. "At least...I think it's not too hot...."

For the first time, a scowl crossed her face. I guessed she didn't like not knowing how to care for someone properly.

"Maybe just test it to be sure," she suggested.

I dipped a toe in, but though the water was a shocking temperature, I thought it was one I could get used to, so I mimicked the young woman by hanging my towel wrap on a nearby hook and came back to the pool.

Svyer just plopped herself down with a happy sigh, but I eased into the water inch by embarrassing inch, with a lot more curious onlookers than I thought was polite. Either I really was a strange sight, or these dragon people were a nosy bunch.

Don't worry about them, Svyer said, following the flickers of my gaze around the room. *They've probably all heard about you by now, so they're just curious. They don't mean any harm.*

"It's rude to stare," I muttered.

"Is it?" she asked curiously.

That took me aback. "Uh...isn't it?"

"But it's natural to feel curiosity, so what else are they going to do? Pretend you aren't there?"

"Yeees?" I said, but I dragged the word out like a question.

That made her laugh. "Well, here, *that* would be rude."

I was so floored by that statement that I had nothing to say in reply. By then, I had eased myself into the water up to my armpits, covering my chest, so I felt more comfortable.

I said, "If they're that curious, I'm surprised they aren't coming over to bother me with questions."

"Ah, but night cleansing is an exception," Svyer said as she lay back with her eyes closed. "It's the time of day to focus inward. They won't come over unless you indicate you want them to."

That made me feel better, so I took advantage of my newfound knowledge by examining the others in the room a bit more openly. I still made sure not to look at any one person for too long, lest they mistake that as an invitation.

I noticed something interesting. I'd thought that all the dragon people had hair and eyes as closely matched and unnaturally colored as Ben, Yvera, Kor, and Svyer did. I'd also thought they were all sculpted giants. Though there was one other young woman in the room who fit that description, I discovered the majority were much more normal looking.

Those women had the normal ranges of hair colors—mostly a dark brown in this case—and, from what I could tell at a distance, normal eye colors as well. Though they were all tall, none were as tall as Yvera and Svyer, and I wasn't even the shortest one in the room, not counting the kids. Though none of them were fatty, their bodies were also more natural-looking: spots and sagging chests and body hair and cellulite.

Our shared imperfection was comforting, since I'd begun to think I was doomed to develop an inferiority complex.

"What is it?" Svyer asked. I turned and saw her eyes cracked open as she gave me a lazy smile. I was struck by the thought of a cat curled up in a sunbeam. The hot water, now that I was used to it, felt nice, but it didn't seem to do the same thing for me as it was for a lot of the other women here; Svyer wasn't the only one with the same lazy, contented bliss about her.

I added another detail to the list of things I was learning about these dragon people: they liked warmth.

I hesitated, wondering if my question was offensive.

"Go ahead," she encouraged, sitting up a bit. Her eyes softened. Silently, she added, *You must feel so lost here. I want to help.*

My heart clenched with gratitude for this remarkably kind young woman. How else was I supposed to learn these things except by asking?

I leaned in closely. Even though the splashing and chatter around us probably masked our conversation, I didn't want anyone to wonder why I was so ignorant. She seemed to agree. When she leaned close enough that her ear was nearly at my lips, I whispered, "What's the difference?"

"What difference?" she whispered back.

"Between you and...most of them." I didn't want to gesture, so I settled for that vague description instead. When her eyes remained questioning, I tried again. "The ones who look more like me."

"Ah," she breathed, and nodded. "That. Yes, that's an important thing to know."

Her full pink lips pursed in thought for a moment. *Ben, Kor, Yvera, and I...we're all what we call drakón. And they...are human.*

I inhaled. "Like—"

She was already shaking her head, sympathy in her eyes. *No, not like you. They, too, have the Blood in them. It just doesn't manifest strongly enough to make them drakón.*

I nodded, realizing now that the word she used for "human," *amón*, had a different meaning than I had assumed. Not quite human. Still something *other*.

"Why are some...drakón, and others aren't?"

She shrugged, idly swirling the water with one long finger. *No one knows. We all have the Blood in us by now—there are no true humans left, not since....*

She trailed off with a troubled look and a quick sidelong glance at me.

You're the first in a very long time, she finished, but I got the impression she'd been intending to say something else.

That was an avenue to explore later. For now, the single revelation she'd given me was enough. My eyes widened and breath caught as I put the pieces together.

"*That's* why Ben doesn't want to tell everyone just yet."

She nodded, eyes still troubled. *Your presence here is...significant. You think people are staring now, but as soon as they find out....*

"Am I in danger?" I whispered—so quietly, I worried for a moment that she wouldn't have heard.

Her eyes widened in surprise. *No!*

Then she hesitated. *At least...not from us. Or...most of us. It's...complicated.*

She bit her lip in clear distress. *I'm not sure how much to explain right now.*

Which made me realize I was feeling pretty darn toasty by now, and I decided I'd better get out before I turned as red as a lobster.

"That's OK," I assured her as I climbed out. "I'm sure Ben will get around to it tomorrow."

Svyer hissed, and I glanced back at her in surprise. She was getting out of the water and ushering me to the towels. *Get that on,* she said urgently. *Quickly.*

I finally understood from the way she was shielding me from view with her...unwrinkled and unreddened body. Which was pretty much the opposite of mine right now.

Oh, I thought with a further flush to my cheeks. Another difference between me and them, apparently. From glances out of the corner of my eye as I hurriedly wrapped the towel around me, I saw that no one else, not even the "humans," were as pink as I was from the hot water.

Let's go, she said, silent voice still urgent even though outwardly she looked calm. I tried to mimic her expression as we strode out of the bathing room, stares following us. From the prickle on the back of my neck, I was almost certain that a few of those stares were more intent than they had been before.

Her shoulders relaxed a little when we entered the empty hall. She turned and looked me up and down, biting her lip. "Are you hurt?"

I shook my head. "No—this is natural...for me. But it's a good thing I didn't stay in there any longer. I'm pretty sure that water was hotter than the average jacuzzi."

She sighed. "Then don't even try the springs at Crownhold—those might scald you."

"I don't think that's going to be an issue," I said with a smile, attempting to lighten the mood. "Hopefully by this time tomorrow, I'll be back home."

She cast a troubled look at me that made my heart clench, but all she did was repeat, "Hopefully."

Until then, I hadn't had the time or inclination to consider whether delivering me home might be beyond Ben's ability, or perhaps I had been overawed with him from the start. He'd said he'd help me, so I'd naively assumed that would be enough. Now, the first sliver of doubt crept in.

I didn't ask her if she knew the odds of Ben being able to send me home.

I didn't want to know.

CHAPTER FIVE

ELIGIBILITY

KORIBEN

I SIGHED IN RELIEF when I walked out of the healing wing to see Yvera hadn't waited for me. Elder Jaya hadn't required me to get checked, but I'd decided it was my best chance of dodging my rightwing, and the gamble had paid off. Though I didn't doubt she'd pound on my door before she turned in to make me give her access, I might get a few uninterrupted deken of solitude before she did. Then, with a lot of luck, I could also avoid....

That had been wishful thinking, and I didn't even sigh when I saw Kor studying a plaque underneath some sculpture or another of some long-dead healer that had once served this hold, as if it were the most fascinating text he had ever read.

No one could wait so casually in plain sight to ambush someone as Kor could.

I'd known as soon as he had volunteered to see Sarah to a room that I wouldn't be able to escape him tonight. I knew he would figure out everything that *I* knew about her within seconds and then extract far more from the poor girl than I would have ever asked him to...at least, not so soon.

Or by using his usual methods. Kor had this fixed belief that if you wanted to get the truth from someone, you couldn't just *ask* them for it. There was something to that with many of the people he had to deal with as my leftwing, but Sarah was *not* one of those people, and I'd been anxious to leave her in his hands without any sort of preparation.

On the other hand, there was no one better to help me conceal the fact that she was an Earthren. As soon as he'd volunteered, I'd *also* known I could take that one worry off my mind. Kor would have ensured she spoke to no one, he would have escorted her straight to a room by the swiftest route, and he might have even warned her to not reveal her origin.

Now, if only he'd behaved himself....

Although from the smugness that came over him as he glanced at my approach, I doubted it.

"What did you do to her?" I asked suspiciously as I stopped in front of him.

He grinned. "Made her hate me, of course. You're welcome, by the way."

"Kor, we need her to *help* us," I hissed, but fortunately, no one was in the hall outside the healing wing at this deken.

"No, we need her to help *you*, and I'm quite sure she's willing to do that in spite of me. Maybe even because of me. After all, the worse *I* look, the better *you* look. See how that works?"

"You don't need to alienate her—for any reason," I said. "She's a good person, Kor."

Kor tsked. "I know. A tad *too* good, if you ask me. I'm going to need to harden her up, and that urgent task started tonight."

"I—agh!" I threw up my hands and started walking. There was no changing Kor's mind when he was set on something like this. He could be as stubborn as Yvera that way. I could try *ordering* him to be nice to Sarah, but ordering Kor was a tricky business. He would obey me, but only in the most technical sense. He would inevitably find a loophole in what I said and somehow do what he wanted anyway—maybe using even less appealing methods.

I trusted Kor. I'd known him for six years, and soon after we'd met, he saved my life, at great personal cost. He was good at heart, and I knew he was loyal to me and wholly dedicated to his role as my leftwing. That was part of the problem: if he weren't *so* dedicated, he might not have been so merciless.

I once again marveled at the contrast between my wings, and yet how neither of them was what they seemed.

People always thought Yvera was the one they had to watch out for. She was the one wearing the armor and carrying the claymore after all—the fiercest fighter and most skilled flyer of our peers. A rightwing had to be the best of the best, and she was rightly feared for holding the position as mine. What they didn't realize was that underneath her bristling exterior was an undeviating conscience and utter lack of guile.

When they looked at Kor, all they saw was a small, excitable, charming Starkissed scholar dressed in finery; even knowing he was a leftwing, very few people, even in Kor's clan, realized that was all a front, and what was inside was something...entirely different. Something frighteningly brilliant, sharply observant, always calculating, and utterly ruthless in performing his duty as he saw it.

The Realms had no idea how lucky they were that Kor was too small and weak to have been a warrior. I shuddered to think of having to duel *him* if he'd had a bit more size and strength.

So, Kor said with his inner voice. *What happened? The real version, not whatever story you fed Jaya.*

I sighed. There was no point in wasting energy in being mad at him. *I wondered why you were so willing to miss the interrogation. What makes you think I fed Jaya a story?*

Which had not been easy, and Jaya seemed to guess the one detail I had been trying to conceal, but without evidence and with Yvera backing me up, Jaya didn't have grounds for reporting me to Avva, and she didn't seem inclined to pursue it, anyway. I'd stacked all the odds against such a measure: I was physically fine; the ahglen had only put up a token resistance once they'd realized just who they were contending with; my only wound had been self-inflicted and was long gone by now, anyway; and if Jaya brought the matter to the King's attention, Avva would probably say I'd been justified in racing ahead to the wildgate. Gates *were* one of my primary responsibilities, after all. Especially unexpected, unstable ones like that one.

Because I know you, and I know Yvera, Kor said. *So, details. I can guess most of them, but....*

You like knowing you're right, I finished, rolling my eyes.

I told him. Not that there was all that much to tell, so I was finished by the time we reached the guest wing.

I scanned the corridor for a sign of Sarah and relaxed when she wasn't in sight. I also felt a twinge of disappointment—which I quickly silenced, as I did with every inclination I'd had toward a pretty girl for years now. It was a habit I was doubly grateful for now; it would prove useful while....

I noticed Kor smirking at me, and I realized I should have controlled myself even better. Of course he hadn't missed that one glance.

"She's probably back from her bath now," Kor said. "Since I see don't see the clothes or food I set in front of her door."

He pointed down the hall.

"Thank you for doing that," I said coolly, going to the first available room I saw and touching the doorgem. I didn't even notice the price of power it extracted to attune itself to me and only listened for the audible *click* of the mechanism before shoving the door open.

"Now, are you going to leave me in peace, or—" I began as I looked back.

Kor interrupted me, something intent in his expression now. "Don't you want to see which room is hers?"

"No."

"I think you should see which room is hers," Kor said in a tone that made it clear he wasn't just suggesting.

"Why?" I asked suspiciously.

He shrugged. "Lots of reasons. In case there's an emergency. In case you need to find her. Or walk her to breakfast tomorrow.... You know how I like to sleep in."

"We're all leaving at dawn," I said quietly. "Even you, since I don't want to come back for you. You can show me then."

Torch it, Ben, Kor snapped inside my head, which told me he was serious. *Go look at her door,* now. *Just trust me on this one.*

"Fine," I huffed, closing my door even though blessed rest beckoned.

I followed Kor irritably, intending to glance at Sarah's door and then march straight back to my room before she could catch me in front of it. But when Kor stopped and pointed, and my eyes followed....

My jaw dropped.

The gem in her door shone at me so benignly. Yet the truths it revealed were anything but ordinary.

There were many colors of gems on the doors of occupied rooms in this hall, reflecting the colors of the various clans each occupant belonged to, as did the hair, eyes, and scales of drakón. Quite a variety tonight for such a remote outpost, though the majority was unsurprisingly emerald Peace-growth, followed closely by violet Battleblood and scarlet Strongshield.

There were only two gems that glowed with *that* intensity of power. Mine...and hers.

Even mine was not that color.

No one's was.

"White," I whispered.

"Quite a brilliant white," Kor said, arms folded as he examined the gem. When he turned to look at me, his eyes said everything he wasn't saying out loud. "Interesting. Don't you think?"

I closed my jaw, pivoted, and strode back to my room. I was too shaken to stop Kor from following me inside, so I just let the door close behind him. It was probably better to get this conversation over with sooner rather than later, anyway.

"So," Kor said, leaning against the desk and allowing himself a wide grin now that we had privacy. "What do you think of her?"

"Kor," I said in a warning tone. Really, I was surprised he was trying to bring this up tonight. Normally he timed discussions he knew I wouldn't like more carefully. He must have been fit to burst.

He ignored me and plowed ahead. "Right, you hardly got to talk to her after she could finally understand you. Not much time to get an impression there. So, I'll just tell you what *I* think of her."

I could have stopped him there, and I was sorely tempted to. Especially since that freshly made bed beckoned me like it was my only friend in the world—the only one that didn't seem to demand something of me tonight, at any rate—and I still hadn't even called Avva yet to give my report.

But with Kor, it was better to let him get everything out and *then* tell him no. He was always baffled that you could possibly disagree with all the logic he'd just laid so perfectly before you, but having nothing else to say, he'd just go off somewhere to sulk and curse the stupidity of dramákind. Rather, since I was the only one he had to bother with these days, just *my* stupidity.

Kor held up a hand and started counting down fingers as he said each point. "Let's first get through the pluses you already know. She's Earthren, she's a good person—your words, remember?—and as you've just discovered, she's powerful *and* compatible with you. At least one would presume so. White is, after all, the reflection of all colors...."

He was referring to a nonsense relationship theory that said certain clan colors were fated to be more romantically "compatible" than others, and a laughably weighty factor was simply whether the soulcolors of the two dramá in question *matched.* Strange as it sounded, couples had broken up or never even formed because of "soul matching."

The Tree, the Temple, and the Crown had all firmly discounted the theory, but that hadn't stopped it from being a pervading influence—or a "kind" way to reject someone, or an excuse to fall back on if things didn't work out.

As romantically ridiculous as Kor could be (this discussion being a prime example), I knew better than to think Kor believed in soul matching himself. In this, his personal beliefs were irrelevant to him. As a proper leftwing, he was thinking only of how the *public* would perceive a match between us and was relishing at how soul matching could work in our favor, making his job that much easier.

He was right, unfortunately. Even I had to admit briefly to myself that my shade of gold would go with her shade of white perfectly. No one could have objected on that front, at least.

I dismissed the conclusion as not just ridiculous but also irrelevant.

"White," Kor continued with relish. "Simply fascinating. That was the Moontouched color, as you know, but it's incredible to see her soulcolor so undiluted by so many subsequent generations of amá blood. That makes me wonder if white is the soulcolor of amá themselves. Wouldn't *that* make a great paper! I'm going to have to do some research—and some tests if Sarah will let me.... Huh. Maybe I *should* have been nicer to her, after all...."

"Kor," I said testily when he paused for breath.

"Right, sorry, I'm just a bit excited, as I'm sure you are too," Kor said, taking a deep breath to calm himself. "But one topic at a time. Here are some things I noticed that you might not have had the chance to catch yet: she's not as timid as she looks—that's just all this overwhelming newness, I think. Push her, and she pushes back, alright, so she's got spine. She's intelligent—"

Despite my initial resolve, I couldn't take this anymore. "Kor, *stop.*"

"What?" he asked, nonplussed.

I pinched my nose. I'd been feeling a headache coming on (ironically, ever since leaving the healers), and this was not helping. "Just...stop. I know what you're doing, and I'm having none of it, you understand?"

"Oh, come *on*, Ben," Kor said, gesturing to me with both hands. "Even you can't be blind to the fact that the most eligible match for you has just *fallen* into your life. I couldn't have found a better girl for you if I'd been able to line up all the ones in the Six Realms—and trust me, *I've been making a list.*"

"Of course you have," I said with a sigh, going over to the kettle sitting on the counter while praying it was full already. To get rid of this headache without using my emergency reserves to heal myself, I was going to need a big mug of tsha.

Or maybe three.

Yes, thank the Flame it was. I poured leaves into the kettle, set the kettle on the spit hook over the fire, went back to the counter, and grabbed a mug while Kor went on in earnest.

"I'm not just talking about eligibility here, Ben. I'm talking about what is good for *you*, what will make *you* happy. And I'm telling you, she's it. As soon as you spend some time with her, you'll know what I mean. The potential is a bit buried right now, but I can see it. Give her time to adjust, to find her footing, and she's going to be so perfect for you it's ridiculous. Your father's going to love her."

This was the harder side of Kor's persuasive technique to dismiss, and he knew it, torch him: the "I'm only doing this because I care about you as a friend" card. Because what could I say to that? "Stop caring about me"?

I shoved the mug back, braced my hands on the counter, and took a deep breath, pleading with the Flame for calm. "Be that as it may, I can't risk alienating Sarah—as you're so determined to do. I need her help, not her...company."

"I feel like I'm talking to a five-summer when you get like this," Kor said, folding his arms. "Ben, those things aren't mutually exclusive."

"Well, they are to me," I retorted, straightening.

"No, now you're just giving excuses, as you always do. First, it was that none of the girls met this or that criteria. Then it was because you were too busy. Then, until yesterday, it was because you couldn't spend long enough in any one place because you were trying to chase down an Earthren for your father. Well, now you *have* one, and not only is she powerful enough to help you, but she's also—"

"I'm *not* interested in courtship right now, Kor," I said through gritted teeth. I walked away from the counter to the other side of the firepit to give myself some more space from him. "I've told you."

"Yes, but you still haven't told me why," he said with narrowed eyes. "You know you're going to want to marry eventually—"

"No, I don't," I snapped. And instantly regretted it when his eyes widened at that insight.

"I can't believe I'm hearing this. You're not intending to marry...*ever?*"

I exhaled. I'd slipped, so I might as well finish what I'd started. "No, I'm not. There's nothing in the law that says I have to. I don't *have* to have a consort or produce my own Heir. Any other Sunfilled can take my place."

Theoretically. Truth was, they had to be the right sort of person to be chosen, and that necessity made a scarce pool of Sunfilled even smaller. I could only think of a handful that I would be comfortable with becoming my Heir, but I wasn't about to mention that to give Kor more fodder.

"Yes, but...Ben...*why*?" Kor looked floored, and that wasn't an expression I saw very often on him. "I know you aren't *inclined* toward celibacy. Why do that to yourself? Especially when...you're a Sunfilled."

Having children was so difficult for a Sunfilled that society considered it a duty for every member of the clan to do so if possible. Because if there were no more Sunfilled....

That was the part that made me feel the worst about the decision I'd made years ago.

No...the worst part was Avva's quiet, mostly hidden disappointment as each summer since my sixteenth passed without me finding a daughter for him. I'd gathered a long time ago that he'd always wanted one, but after Avvi's death....

The only way Avva was going to have a daughter to dote on was if I presented him with one.

I would do anything for Avva. Anything...but that. I knew he understood, which was why he never, ever said anything about it. After all...how could he ask me to go through the same suffering he had after losing Avvi?

At least he was the one person I would never have to explain myself to. Kor would be another matter. I'd always known we'd have to have this conversation one day; after all, it was part of his job description to help me find a suitable match, given how important a consort was, for many reasons.

The possibility of the consort bearing an Heir was actually far down that list, given the unlikelihood of the Monarch's child being chosen, so my excuse in that regard was flimsy. No, a consort was desirable to the people for other reasons, foremost among them being that a consort was the clans' best chance for one of their *own* to share the crown. The consort was, in a sense, the *people's* Monarch, chosen not from the Sunfilled clan, not by the Tree, but by some other combination of fate, suitability, expediency, and affection. The people knew the consort was chosen as much by *them* as by the Monarch.

Because Kor had figured out my inclinations a long time ago, he'd taken that as all the directive he needed to find the right girl. Nothing I'd said up to this point had discouraged him, and probably nothing would unless I told him the truth in all its entirety.

But there were some secrets I couldn't entrust to even him. Even if I'd wanted to.

And yet, how to give him just enough truth to make him stop, at least for now?

He watched the conflict in my expression, and he sighed. "Alright, maybe this was a mistake to bring up this evening. I'll let this go for tonight, *and* I'll even promise to be nice to Sarah tomorrow, if you'll answer one question for me."

"What kind of question?" I asked suspiciously. But if it was going to be *that* easy to get rid of him tonight and guarantee his best behavior on such a crucial day...I was already sorely tempted.

"Just an academic curiosity—an indulgence, really. Only tangentially related to our discussion, I promise."

Alarm horns were trumpeting in my head, but I was *done* for tonight, so I foolishly ignored them. "Alright, fine. What is it?"

"Excellent," Kor said. Then, for dramatic effect, he went through the trouble of pulling out one of his small leather-bound notebooks and a pencil.

I began to feel nervous.

"Here's my question." He paused significantly, and I began to truly regret my decision. "When you first saw her, how did you feel?"

"Well, worried, obviously," I said in confusion. "And furious. Like I said, those ahglen were about to—"

"I guess I need to be more specific," Kor said dismissively. "When you first made *eye contact*, how did you feel? Any sensations to note? Particular energies? Did you notice any soulflare in her eyes?"

Suddenly, I understood what he was getting at, and I went still. And said nothing.

"Interesting," Kor said, noting something in his notebook. As if I *had* told him all he needed to know.

"Wait, Kor, it's not—you can't—you don't understand, I...."

I swallowed. I'd skimmed over this part when giving my account to him, and for good reason. I should have known better than to think he hadn't noticed.

"She ran from me while I was still in drakáform, and I panicked, so I ran after her in amáform and knocked her down. *That* was when we first made eye contact, and given the awkwardness of the circumstances, that isn't something to read into. I'm sorry, but your 'academic curiosity' will never be satisfied on this point, because the one chance you had to test your theory, there were extenuating factors."

"Noted," Kor said with a nod, and he indeed continued to write something studiously, but from the look in his eyes, I knew I hadn't fooled him in the slightest.

"Well, this has been a most enlightening conversation," Kor said, pushing off from the desk and heading to the door. "But I'm sure you're tired and need to report to the King at any rate, so I'll keep my end of the bargain and leave you to it."

"Thanks," I said between gritted teeth. "I'll expect you to keep your word *tomorrow* as well."

"Oh, don't worry about that," he said with a wink. "I'll be on my best behavior, as promised."

Somehow, I no longer found that comforting.

As soon as the door swung shut behind him, I collapsed face first into the bed. I couldn't fall asleep yet, obviously, but neither should I call Avva until I could manage a calm, controlled facade.

I cursed myself for being so naive. This was *Kor*, I was dealing with, after all. I, of all people, should have known better than to take his deal.

Now, without even saying a word, I had given him all the fodder he needed to *never* let this go.

Chapter Six

FEVER

Sarah

Svyer led me to a final room, which seemed to be a wind tunnel of some sort. Where all the warm air came from (beyond the wooden slats in the walls, of course) I had no idea, but I was almost completely dry and toasty warm by the time we were through. That brought us back to the shower room, so we'd completed some kind of loop.

I had to admire the system: dragon people (at some point, I was going to have to ask for the proper term for them as a whole, if some were drakón and some were amón) had clearly mastered the art of getting clean.

There, we reclaimed our clothes from the shelves where we'd left them and threw the towel wraps in a bin. Then Svyer led me to a final area that was familiar enough: a room full of counters and mirrors, ready to assist females in getting presentable.

Svyer let me borrow her brush (where she'd produced it from, I didn't know) and began braiding her hair while I worked through the knots in mine. I didn't know what kind of bristles those were, but they worked miracles in my long, damp, tangled hair.

"I'm going to make sure Ben gets you a full kit," Svyer said with a frown as she looked at my brushing efforts out of the corner of her eye while she continued her braid. Then she sighed. "Scratch that. *I* should just get the kit and charge him for it. Ben's nice and all that, but he's...."

"Male?" I finished with a grin.

"Exactly," she said with an answering grin, and we both laughed.

That felt...good. That there was something so universal as our shared femininity.

Just then, I brushed the hair past my ear, the touch of the bristles reminding me of Ben's gentle touch there earlier. When I pulled my hair back and looked at my ear in the mirror....

Svyer looked down in alarm at my quiet gasp. "What?"

I touched my ear. Then I put the brush down on the counter and uncovered the other one too. "The blood. It's...gone."

I bit my lip in worry. I hadn't thought about that when I'd gone to take a shower, and Kor hadn't warned me either. Obviously, I still understood Svyer, so the magic hadn't faded just yet, but would washing it off make it fade more quickly? Was Ben going to have to bleed for me that much sooner?

"Oh, right," Svyer whispered, casting a glance around the room. Either we'd taken longer than usual through each step or the others had skipped more steps, because the room was now full of women in the last stage of their night ablutions.

Ben had to put his blood on your ears to make you able to understand us, didn't he? she asked silently.

I stared back at her. "You didn't notice?" I said in a whisper.

What, the blood? No, of course not. It had faded by then.

When my blank expression didn't go away, she grimaced and elaborated. *The blood...it was used up in the ritual. It was never there for long to begin with.*

My eyes widened with understanding. *Different rules,* I kept reminding myself. But when would I learn what those rules *were*?

"So...." I whispered, face flushing. "I was worried about my ears being stained gold for nothing?"

Svyer laughed. *I guess so. Wouldn't* that *have caused a stir.*

Having gold-blood-stained ears while being accompanied by the golden dragon Heir.... Yes, I could see why that would cause a stir, alright. My flush increased.

I handed Svyer the brush when I was done, and to my surprise, she offered to braid my hair too.

My eyes stung for a moment as I thought of Rachel. As annoying as my older sister was sometimes, one way she redeemed herself was by doing my hair, since I didn't care enough to learn how to do it myself. Sometimes Rachel even applied a bit of makeup on the rare mornings she didn't sleep in as late as possible.

Those weekday preparations were hectic but also our greatest bonding time as sisters, the time when we got a chance to talk, complain, and laugh. To feel like we weren't so different after all. To everyone else, I was the smart one, she was the pretty one. Yet she herself never emphasized that difference between us while she was helping me. Making me feel pretty, as much as that was possible, was Rachel's way of showing she cared.

That reminder gave me a pang, but I blinked away the tears before Svyer could see them, and I accepted her offer.

Svyer did a beautiful job, twisting my brown hair around my head in an elaborate crown.

"You have such pretty hair," she complimented as she worked. "So long and thick, and such a nice shade."

I stared up at her in the mirror. "You like *my* hair?"

"Of course," she said with a chuckle. "Do you have any idea how *limiting* it is to have green hair? I don't dress this way entirely by choice. If I had hair as neutral and complimentary as yours...."

She sighed. "Imagine the possibilities."

"Is it possible to dye it?" I whispered.

She shook her head sadly. *Nothing holds. We're cursed forever with the color from the moment we are changed.*

Now I understood her longing. How...limiting indeed. I'd always felt so-so about my hair color, but I'd also known I could change it whenever I bothered to. Now I felt an unfamiliar surge of gratitude for it being...just the way it was. Bland, maybe, but also full of potential.

Then something she said struck me. "Changed?" I asked.

She nodded. *We're not born like this. We start out like everyone else. It's only when we're taken to our Tree when we're twelve summers that...we become drakón.*

"Tree?"

She looked down at me in surprise, which soon shifted to that troubled look again. *Maybe it's best if I leave that explanation to Ben.*

She said nothing else, and I didn't pry. My head was so bursting with new information already that I decided it was best to leave the matter be for now.

"Done!" she declared at last in satisfaction, stepping back to admire her handiwork.

"Beautiful," I complimented her, turning my head this way and that.

She winked. "Too bad Ben is probably going to turn in the first chance he gets."

I just laughed, so certain she couldn't be serious that I didn't even feel the need to blush. "He won't look twice at *me* while I'm standing next to *you*."

I honestly believed that, and because it was her, I could say it with goodwill.

She snorted in amusement as she started leading me away from the vanity room. "Unlikely."

"Why? You seem to know him pretty well."

She laughed. "Yes, rather *too* well. I'm the closest thing he'll ever have to a sister: I'm his cousin. On his mother's side, of course."

Of...course? I thought curiously. *Why would that just be assumed?*

To be honest, that line of inquiry was only a mental distraction from the surge of relief I felt. Which was ridiculous, really. I had no idea where it came from.

A few moments later, she was pushing open the bathroom door and leading us into the hall of guest rooms again.

"Wait, that's it?" I asked.

She looked at me questioningly. "Was there something else you needed?"

I thought about that for a moment as we walked. "I suppose...just brushing my teeth. Feels odd to go to bed without it, I guess. Do you do that here?"

"Brushing...teeth?" she asked in amusement. "Like hair? Why would you do that?"

Figures they would have perfect teeth, too, I thought.

"Because we unfortunate full humans get holes in our teeth if we don't."

"Ah, I see," she said, turning sympathetic. "That's not just a human problem, though. Amón do too if they don't rinse their mouths and see a healer often enough. But even if a hole grows, that's something a healer can fix easily."

"Oh," I said, blinking. "Um...good, I guess."

"Still, as a healer, I approve of you trying to do your part," she said with a wink. "I'll put the mouthwash tablets in your kit."

"Thanks," I said with a laugh.

"A toothpicker, too," she said to herself, eyes going distant. "You really are going to need *everything*, aren't you? I'd better get to the market before all the shops close...."

"I don't want to be a bother," I said. "Especially since *hopefully* I won't need any of it after tomorrow."

She absently waved away my protest. "Don't worry about it. Ben can always trade in anything you haven't used at the next hold. Now...which door is yours, so I know where to bring your things?"

"Uh...." I had a moment of panic as I scanned all the doors. Which looked the same to me, apart from the glowing gems. Were those the only markers we were expected to go by?

Then I spotted it: the bright, white gem glowing a few dozen feet away, and at its doorstep was Kor's promised food and a small pile of clothing—with a pair of slippers. I led her there hesitantly and pointed.

"I think...this one. I don't see any other gems like it, anyway."

When she didn't answer, I looked up at her—and was startled to see her wide eyes staring at the gem.

"No," she said faintly. "You wouldn't."

"What is it?" I asked, heart sinking.

She shook herself. "I'm...not sure," she said, biting her lip as she looked away.

Strange. She'd dodged some of my questions and said she wouldn't answer others, but for the first time, I got the impression that she'd outright lied.

Obviously, there was something *very* significant about how that gem had reacted to me. Kor had tricked me into touching it while he could watch, and now Svyer, the kindest soul I'd met here, had been shocked speechless and then refused to tell me why.

It's best you go in now, before anyone sees you, she said, looking back at me with sincere concern. *People will guess anyway, but...you don't want to outright confirm for everyone that this is your door.*

"You said I wasn't in danger," I reminded her in a whisper.

She glanced at the doorgem and then back at me, eyes anxious. *I wasn't thinking.... Well, this makes things a bit more complicated.*

She'd said they were complicated before. Now they were even more so?

You'll be fine, she insisted. *Ben will take care of you. You'll see. He knows far better than I do how to handle this.*

She bent down and picked up the clothing and tray and stacked them in my arms by turns.

"Well, at least that's one thing I don't have to take care of tonight," she said with a wan smile. "Go on, get some rest. You're safe tonight, at least, and you're in good hands. Remember that."

She walked away, then paused for a moment. "Oh, Sarah?"

I had to clear my throat to answer. "Yes?"

"Don't let Ben drag you away until I've given you a *proper* healing, you understand?" she said sternly.

I laughed tightly and nodded. "Understood."

"Good," she said, and turned and resumed walking.

My heart unclenched in my chest a bit as I watched her go. Other than that one lie, she had been sincere. Which meant, as far as she was aware, I was safe—for *tonight*.

Hopefully that would be enough.

I shifted the clothes and tray to one arm so I could push open my door. Once again, I felt that mild tingle as I touched the doorplate, and the mechanism unlocked, letting the door swing open.

I went inside and set my burdens down on the desk, thinking hard.

Getting home was going to be more complicated—and dangerous—than I thought. There was more going on here than having to wait a night before Ben could give me a lift. Monsters prowled outside this underground settlement, and even vaguer threats lurked in the shadows within.

No matter what I did, there would be risk. If I went with Ben, if I *trusted* Ben, then I had to brave both the external and internal threats, perhaps even increased by Ben's company; both Kor and Svyer had hinted by now that he wasn't the safest person to be hanging around.

If I stayed, I faced those internal threats alone, except maybe with Svyer. She seemed the type who would help me no matter what I decided. Yet Svyer admitted she didn't have the same capabilities as Ben did. Staying, or waiting for some safer escort (if I could even expect one) might decrease my odds of returning home, maybe even trap me here forever.

Might. Maybe. If. There were so many unknowns! So many questions these drakón hadn't answered yet. But with the way my day had gone, I felt like I had to make at least *some* kind of decision on what to do, before I let myself just be swept away again, doing whatever I was expected to do. I couldn't let myself procrastinate making yet another life-altering decision—and this one far more significant than deciding whether to leave home.

I longed to choose the safe choice yet again, to tell Ben I appreciated his offer, but I'd taken enough of his time. That was the practical choice on so many levels, none the least of which separating the two of us before I got the wrong idea in my head about him.

And yet...I pictured it, telling him goodbye, and....

I yanked my thoughts back to practical considerations, ignoring the pang in my chest.

Going with Ben had the greatest risk...but also the greatest chance of getting home. That was what mattered most, didn't it? Besides, for once in my life, it would be taking a *risk*. A leap.

It's what I want to do, I realized.

That's what decided me.

I was going to go with Ben...because I knew that was the risk I'd forever regret not taking.

QUIET KNOCKING JOLTED ME awake. I had a bewildering second in which I had no memory of where I was or why I was there, and then it all came rushing back.

I collapsed back into the bed and groaned. I'd had a terrible night's sleep. At first, it had just been the tossing and turning, trying to relax after Svyer's vague warnings and small bit of comfort. Then I was too hot and threw off the furs. Then I got too cold. Then I got a headache just from the sheer sleeplessness. When I'd finally drifted off to sleep....

Knocking.

At least it was a comfy bed....

A knock came again, still soft but persistent.

"Just a second," I mumbled loudly and sat up. I waited until the blood stopped rushing before pushing off the covers and getting up. I stumbled through the dark room until I got to the door.

Just as I was about to push it open, Svyer's anxiousness and Kor's bit of "advice" came back to me with a chilling effect that jolted me wide awake.

Trust those instincts of yours, Sarah.

I did not know what dangers existed for me in this world, but wasn't it common sense to not answer the door without knowing who was behind it?

"Who is it?" I asked, trying to sound casual.

"Sarah?" a male voice asked tentatively. "It's me, Ben."

It *sounded* like him, but how could I be sure? There were humans who could turn into dragons, for goodness's sake. What *else*, or *who* else, could they turn into?

Gah, Kor was going to make me paranoid!

Or...was that what he meant? He didn't say *suspect everything*. He'd said *trust your instincts*. What were my instincts telling me right now, underneath all that paranoia?

I took a calming breath, and then I just...felt for the right answer.

I began to...have a new sense—not a touch or a taste or a smell or anything like I'd ever experienced before. But I *felt* someone on the other side of the door.

And I knew that someone was Ben.

Just like that, the last of the fear left.

I pushed open the door just wide enough for my face, but now that was just from vanity. My braid was a mess, and my new clothes were rumpled and probably put on wrong to begin with.

Sure enough, I saw Ben standing there, looking adorably self-conscious and holding a tray of food. If my anxiety hadn't been dispelled already, that would have clinched it.

"Hey, sorry, I was dead asleep," I said with a yawn for emphasis. "What's up?"

"Sorry," he said with a wince. "I should have talked to you last night but.... Anyway, um...I brought you breakfast?"

He said that like it was a question as he held out the tray. Like it was a peace offering between us.

"Thanks," I said as I pushed the door open far enough to take it. I tried not to show any self-consciousness about my frumpy appearance. "But...why?"

Most especially, *Why you?*

Even though Kor had clarified that an Heir was treated a lot differently than a prince, it still made little sense for *him* to be fetching me food.

Then again...when I thought of either Yvera or Kor doing it for him....

Yeah, if it were going to be any one of those three, it would be him.

"Because we're going to be leaving soon," Ben said. "I know it's early, sorry, but I figured you'd forgive me, seeing as we're going to go look at the place where you emerged into this world. And start figuring out a way to send you home."

Hope surged in my chest as my fog-filled mind remembered what was on the agenda for today. "Really? Oh, thank you *so* much!"

Now his cheeks were growing red under that short golden beard. I couldn't understand how I had thought he was so much older than me before. "I'd promised you yesterday that I would help."

"I know, but thank you, thank you," I said. "I'll get ready to go and be out in just a sec, don't worry!"

"There's no need to rush," he said hastily as I began letting the door swing closed. At his words, I put my hip against it to hold it back. "You can take the time you need. Kor won't reach a functioning level for another half deken at least."

I stopped in place. "Uh...how long is a deken?"

"Um...."

"Never mind, we can go over time-telling later," I said. "I'll get ready and be out *soon*."

"That works," he said in relief. "See you *soon*."

I let the door swing shut, and as I set the tray on the desk, I realized I was smiling goofily for no good reason—more so than just the thought of going home warranted, at any rate. I smacked my cheeks to get the silly expression to come off and was only marginally successful as I began gathering up my own clothes to head to the bathroom.

When I opened the door and stuck my head into the hallway, Ben was nowhere in sight, which was a relief and a disappointment. Mostly relief, seeing as I was still a mess. Then I darted down the hall as fast as my aching body and pounding head would let me, feeling intensely glad that I'd figured out the bathroom situation *last* night while he had still been busy, and that I'd had Svyer to help me. Svyer, his cousin. Thank *goodness*.

For her help. Obviously.

I felt grimy after my sweaty night, but I decided to skip the shower and simply take care of business, change, and straighten up a bit. But as I was moving from the toilet area to the shower room—figuring the area by the cubbies was as good a place to change as any—my pounding headache reached a crescendo that made me stumble on the wet floor.

The world spun, and I...didn't...feel...so....

Staggering, I slipped on a wet patch, and my head hit the stone with a crack that sent a white-hot flash of pain through my already pounding skull.

Then—nothing.

Chapter Seven

HEALED

Sarah

Voices intruded on the blessed nothingness, both low and anxious. Familiar voices, though they weren't anyone in my family. Why were they in my bedroom? Why wouldn't they just let me *sleep*?

"—more than a quarter deken in the hot bath," a young woman was saying passionately. "You *have* to take better care of her than this, Ben. She's not like us, and she's not amón either. She's something else. Something much more fragile."

"I know," the young man groaned. "I'm sorry. I really am. I should have—agh, what was I thinking?"

He gave a shaking breath. "Thank the Flame you found her. Last night, and this morning. Especially this morning. If you hadn't...."

He trailed off with another groan. This one was more muffled, as if he'd put his hands over his face.

The young woman's voice softened. "It's not entirely your fault, Ben. None of us have dealt with an amá before. All we have to go on are the histories, and the records from back then aren't...what they should be."

"Yes," he said with a deep breath. "But she's our one chance at.... I'll take better care of her from now on, I swear."

A pause.

"Ben," she said voice somehow both soft and firm at the same time. "You don't have to save the worlds by yourself. You know that, right?"

He chuckled weakly. "Well, Yvera and Kor will help, of course."

"That's not what I meant," she said with a sigh.

There was a longer pause, for half a minute or so. By now, I was fully awake, and the memory of the past day had returned. I knew where I was—roughly, of course—and who was speaking, but I was fuzzy about what had just happened to me or why the two of them were there. I remembered a restless night...and waking up....

Svyer was speaking again. "Maybe...maybe I should come with you."

Oh, please do, I thought.

I *liked* Svyer. The thought of her being there as a buffer between me and Yvera, or me and Kor, was appealing, especially if our task to find me a way home took longer than a day.

"No," Ben said, weary but firm.

"Ben—"

"No. I appreciate the offer, Svyer, I do. And I can't thank you enough for what you've done for her. But this is something Avva has entrusted to me and my wings alone. I'm sorry."

She sighed. "So it's *that* kind of assignment. I...thought it might be."

"What else would it be?" Ben said wearily. "She's *Earthren*, Svyer. Earthren. The first in nearly a thousand years. This is the first chance we've had to redeem ourselves in *centuries*. We...can't mess this up. We just can't."

My mind was whirling now, so full of questions it felt like it might explode. Could they honestly think I was still asleep right now?

"I know, Ben," she said with a sigh. "I know."

Another pause. Now, I was deliberately holding still, trying to see how much I could glean from this raw moment between cousins.

After I put it that way in my head, I felt a squirm of guilt, but then...they were talking about me, after all, and in my bedroom. Well, guest bedroom.

I had a right to know.... Didn't I?

"Did you see her doorgem?" Svyer asked.

"How could I not?" Ben groaned. "Especially after Kor practically shoved my face into it last night."

"You think she really could be...."

Ben let out a heavy breath. "I hope so. But I *wasn't* hoping for such a flagrant display of her potential. I'm sure you've heard people talk—already."

"Maybe she should stay in my room. If...you come back."

"If we were, I'd take you up on that. But we're not, especially not now. Despite our best efforts, she's attracted too much attention here. It's time to move on. Hopefully we'll find some clue to help her get home today, but if not, we'll head to the next hold by nightfall. And hope word hasn't already spread there, too."

"You think you might have to resort to spending nights outside?" Svyer said, voice anxious.

That surprised me. Was...camping that big of a deal here?

Apparently, from Ben's grim response. "I hope not. But...maybe."

"Maybe it's better just to announce her," Svyer suggested tentatively after a moment. "Just get it over with?"

Ben snorted. "And let the dranyth of Crownhold tear her apart before she's even had a chance to prepare, let alone think about what *she* wants? No. I'll spend every night guarding her in the woods before I let 'society' get its greedy claws on her."

"You...feel passionate about that," Svyer said. Her tone seemed to imply a double meaning.

Silence settled for a few moments before Ben replied quietly. "I never had a chance to choose. She does.... And I'll be iced before I let anyone take that from her."

Another pause, but the silence wasn't complete because I heard a shuffle of movement. When Svyer spoke again, her voice came from somewhere much closer to her cousin.

"I'm sorry, Ben," she murmured.

"Thank you."

Silence.

It was about a minute before Ben said, "When do you think she'll be ready to go?"

Svyer huffed. "I can't believe I'm letting you still drag her away *today*. But, to answer your question...soon. Probably not long after she wakes up. And no, I'm not waking her. She looked like she needed the rest, on top of the healing. The fever probably didn't let her get much sleep last night."

"I feel awful I didn't notice how sick she was," Ben said with a sigh. "At least her color is looking better."

"Pretty, isn't she?" Svyer said, a hint of a teasing smile in her voice.

Ben moaned. "Not you too. Kor's pushiness about her is quite enough for me to deal with, alright?"

That statement sent my head spinning for several reasons. One, he didn't deny that he thought I was pretty, which was nothing less than jaw dropping. Two, he still wasn't interested. *Ouch*, but not surprising. I'd known that would be the case all along, and I wished Svyer hadn't brought it up. I was also fervently glad they thought I was asleep right now. Three, *KOR*?

Svyer snorted. "I don't know about *Korinth*, but all *I* want is for you to be happy, Ben."

"As I've told you and every other well-wishing person in my life, I'm *not* in a position to get involved with someone right now...." His voice lowered. "Especially not her."

Double ouch. I had a tough time suppressing a visible wince.

The hurt was confused by Svyer's next words, spoken earnestly. "What you're hoping she'll become doesn't cut her off from you. Quite the opposite."

"Doesn't it?" Ben whispered. "She's the only chance we've got. I can't risk her like that. You should know that better than most people, Svyer."

She didn't answer for several moments. Finally, she said, "What happened to *her* wasn't your fault."

"Wasn't it?" Ben said hoarsely.

I heard heavy footsteps, and when he spoke again, his voice was further away. "Thank you for what you've done for Sarah. Again. Just...let me know as soon as she's awake, please."

Svyer sighed. "I will."

I heard a door swing open and then shut.

Well, I thought faintly. *That was...interesting.*

On so many levels.

Now all I had to do was wait for a suitable period to "wake up" to prevent any awkwardness. I started counting the seconds, partly to keep track of time, partly to keep myself from thinking too deeply about everything I'd heard. Somewhere between 137 and 150, though, I realized I might not have to pretend to wake up after all. My thoughts were becoming obligingly sluggish, my body relaxing into the warm, comfortable bed.

Just as I was drifting off, though, one clear connection leaped through the synapses of my brain. In that second of clarity, it occurred to me that perhaps the "her" Svyer had mentioned to Ben in those last few moments might *not* have been me.

But then...*who?*

THE THIRD TIME I woke up that day was the swiftest, bringing razor-sharp clarity almost instantaneously. Not only that, but I felt *amazing.* As if I'd gotten the best night's sleep and was brimming over with health and vigor for the day. But I remembered how I'd felt before, and I knew what had made the difference.

As I cracked open my eyes, I was unsurprised to find Svyer sitting at my bedside, reading a book by the light of a single gem in the wall behind her. The rest of the gems were out, closing the room in cozy darkness.

"Thank you," I said, breaking the silence.

She looked up quickly, snapping the book shut.

"Sarah," she said with a relieved smile. "How do you feel?"

"Amazing," I said with a sigh, sitting up. "As I said, thank you. I know this must be your doing."

"It was nothing," she said, smile tight.

"No, it wasn't." I pushed aside the covers and set my feet on the floor. "I don't know what happened to me, but I know it wasn't *nothing*, so neither was your help."

Her face softened. "You were sick—darkfever, if I had to guess, though your symptoms were...different enough, I can't be sure."

"Darkfever." I tasted the word. "That doesn't sound good."

"It's not," she said with lips pressed thin and eyes tight with worry. "It's one of the few plagues we haven't been able to eradicate, since it's highly contagious and difficult to identify until it's almost too late. But we've also been developing our own immunity to it ever since it first broke out almost a century ago. Which is why we didn't know a strain was among us for you to catch."

"A quick, deadly disease, and I have no immunity whatsoever," I said with a grimace. "Sounds like if I hadn't had you, I would have...."

"Ben could have healed you," Svyer said hastily. I noticed, however, that she did not deny the other implications of my words. I felt a belated chill to realize I had nearly died for the second time in as many days.

Svyer continued, as if trying to distract me. "He's not a specialized healer, of course, but all drakón get enough training to save a life, and he has greater reserves to draw on than I do—more than pretty much anyone besides the King."

My heart skipped a beat while Svyer sighed. "Which is good, because it sounds like you're going to have to rely on him for healing from now on. I offered to come along, but...."

She shrugged and grimaced apologetically.

"It was kind of you to offer," I said. "Really—thank you. You've done more than enough for me already."

Svyer laughed, but the sound had a sad edge. "Once you learn what you are worth to us, Sarah, you'll understand."

My mind went back to the conversation I'd overheard between her and Ben. Putting those enigmatic hints together with the things I'd gleaned from Svyer and even Kor before, I would have been dense not to realize by now that there was a lot more going on than Ben offering to help me find my way home.

I didn't resent Ben for having another motive. The fact was relieving, since—whether or not he was what I considered a prince—he seemed far too busy as Heir to be doing me favors out of the goodness of his heart. He'd saved my life and brought me somewhere safe. If that was all there was to it, then I'd seen plenty of other drakón here who could take me where I needed to go.

Instead, I was getting not just a royal escort today but also careful protection and sheltering and healing ever since we'd met. I didn't resent or fear any of them for what they were doing. I *still* trusted Ben meant well. Maybe it was those instincts Kor was telling me to trust. But I also remembered how hotly Ben had defended my right to choose...something.

I trusted. Perhaps naively, but I did. And I still chose to go with him.

Even so, I burned to know. *Why?*

What could drakón—tall, strong people so powerful they could turn into *dragons*—need from me?

"What *am* I worth?" I asked.

I wasn't surprised when Svyer shook her head. "That's something for Ben to explain."

She sighed and stood up. "Speaking of which, he told me to tell him as soon as you woke up. Are you feeling up to traveling with him today?"

Before I could answer, she held up her hand with a stern look. "Be honest, Sarah. You don't do us any favors or get back to your home any faster by pushing yourself too hard. *We* don't know what amá limits are, so you are going to have to drop any politeness that may have been bred into you and become a vocal advocate for yourself. Ben's learned his lesson, but...I'll still worry about you out there, with only *them* to look after you. Ben and his wings—they are the best we have aside from the King and his own. They have to be. But that means they're not used to even a midspark like me trying to keep up with them, let alone...."

"Me," I finished with an understanding smile.

I gestured to myself. "I'm fine, Svyer. I can't remember feeling better.... You didn't just heal my fever, did you?"

"No," she admitted with a crooked smile. "I told you not to let Ben sneak away with you before I gave you a *proper* healing. I was coming to look for you to do just that when I found you...."

Her voice trailed off, then picked up again with forced cheerfulness. "It was an interesting experience, healing not just a human but also someone who had never been healed properly before. I could publish a paper on it once Ben determines it's safe to tell everyone about you; I know a few of my professors back in Crownhold would be eager to read about it. That is, of course, if you gave your permission."

"I'll have to think about that," I said with a nervous laugh. "Especially since it would be pretty hard to obscure my identity in it, wouldn't it?"

Svyer grimaced. "Good point. But if more amá are going to be coming here, we need to know...."

She trailed off, eyes darting away from mine as if regretting how much she'd said. "You're sure you're up to travel? And...whatever else might come today?"

"I can't imagine how I could get any better, so, yes," I said, feeling a flutter of nervousness in my stomach. "But because I have to ask...what else might come?"

"Hopefully, nothing," she said, but I could tell her smile was a tad forced. "But these are, as I said, the Heir and his wings."

"Not the safest group to be hanging out with, I get it," I said with a sigh.

"Whatever comes, they should be able to handle it," Svyer said. "Just, whatever you do, don't let yourself get separated from them. Ben especially. Stick to him as closely as you can. Korinth can take care of himself well enough to keep up with the other two, but maybe not enough to protect you as well. Yvera is lethal, but her primary focus will be protecting Ben. So, Ben is your best option."

"Got it," I said with a thick swallow.

"You'll be fine," Svyer said, her smile more genuine this time. "I'm probably scaring you for nothing. But...I'm a worrier, and I have only an inkling of what Ben is up to. He's taking your safety seriously, though, so I doubt he'll be dragging you headlong into danger."

On purpose, anyway. The unsaid truth hung in the air between us like a shadow in the dimly lit room.

She turned. "I'd better go get Ben, then."

"I can come with you, save some trouble—" I began as I stood.

"No," Svyer said. "Stay here and eat your food, please. You must be starving."

I followed her pointing finger to the tray Ben had brought me for breakfast, still sitting untouched on the desk. As soon as I had *heard* the word "food," my stomach had roared to life.

"It would seem so," I said in surprise. "How late is it?"

"Before midday. But a healing takes your own body's energy, too. You are going to need to eat twice as much as normal for the next few meals." She grimaced. "I...think, anyway."

I chuckled. "It's really bothering you that you don't know how to care for a human, isn't it?"

She groaned. "You have no idea."

CHAPTER EIGHT

INSTRUCTIONS

KORIBEN

KOR'S VOICE BROKE INTO my thoughts. "Ben? Ben!"

My head snapped toward him, and my eyes refocused on the table covered in charts and maps. I tried to recall what he had been explaining, and, failing at that, to guess, but as usual, all of Kor's materials were an unintelligible scribble of lines, notes, and diagrams with no sort of organization any sane mind could follow.

Except, of course, his.

"Did you hear *anything* I've said for the past five dek?" Kor snapped.

I hesitated a moment too long, meaning it was time to confess. "Er, no. Sorry."

Kor groaned. "Ben, the girl is *fine*. You saw that for yourself not two deken ago. All she's doing is sleeping off the healing right now."

"What makes you think I was thinking about her?" I asked stiffly, pulling over one of Kor's maps to try to make sense of the scribbles around the borders.

"Because you keep looking at the door every few seconds like it's on fire. And *not* at this," Kor said, pressing his finger firmly to the map under my hand. "Even though I'm *trying* to explain to you why I think the sungates are failing."

"What?" I asked sharply, looking up at Kor.

"Finally! *Now* you're—"

There was a knock on the study room door, and I was halfway across the room before the sound ended. I dimly heard Kor mutter behind me something about why he even bothered, but this time, I deliberately ignored him. The knock had given me the perfect distraction to put Kor off for just a bit longer until I could think of some way to dissuade him from pursuing his latest line of inquiry.

He was a good leftwing. Too good.

I pushed open the door to see Svyer standing outside the small room.

"Svyer," I greeted her in relief.

"Ben," she said with a sympathetic grin. "I thought Kor might have trapped you somewhere in the library."

Behind me, there was a thump and the hissing, fluttering sound of papers going everywhere, accompanied by a muffled curse from Kor not a second later. I turned in surprise—holding the door open wide enough so Svyer could see too—to behold Kor scrambling to pick scattered papers off the floor, cheeks darkening further with a flush that I rarely, if ever, saw on him.

"Everything alright there, Korinth?" Svyer asked wryly.

"Fine," Kor said, tersely enough that I blinked in surprise. No matter his circumstances or what he might be feeling on the inside, his default mode around females was suave. Yvera being the notable exception, of course.

And so it seemed...Svyer?

I filed *that* bit of information away for later. I was going to need it.

In the meantime, though, I took pity on my leftwing by turning back to my cousin. "She's awake?" I asked quietly.

Svyer nodded. "And fit for travel. I left her in her room, told her to eat."

"Excellent," I breathed. "*Thank* you. Kor, would you mind cleaning up and telling Yvera? I'll get Sarah, and we can meet up at the landing."

"Or *I* can bring Sarah," Kor said, straightening with as much dignity as he could muster with an armful of shuffled papers. His eyes slid over Svyer before coming back to me.

"I'd draw less attention than you would," he added, regaining something of his usual composure. Though his free hand still fidgeted with a blue stone he'd lately taken to wearing around his neck. One of his latest experiments, no doubt, since it was imbued with magic as indecipherably complex to me as his scribbles were.

"Nope," I said with a shake of my head and a smile tugging at my lips.

Kor rolled his eyes. "I promised to behave, didn't I?"

"Oh, you did, did you?" Svyer said dryly. "What did *that* kind of promise cost?"

Kor's cheeks grew darker. "I'll have you know—"

"See you at the landing in a half deken," I said, stepping outside the study room and letting the door swing shut behind me.

"I assume you're about to give me some last-dek instructions," I said to Svyer as we strode out of the hold's small library.

"You are correct," she said with mock stiffness.

I sighed. "I know pretty much all you are going to say, but you won't be happy until you do, so go ahead."

"Good. Make sure you're paying attention," she said with a grin.

"I'm listening."

Svyer sobered as she began. "Make sure she sleeps enough. She's just been healed, so her body is going to need to recuperate the energy."

"I know what it is like to get a healing, Svyer," I said with a smile.

She snorted. "Not like this one, Ben. We drakón don't get sick like that. And we've gotten healings all our lives. Aside from my superficial one last night, the one I gave her this morning was her first one *ever*. I exhausted myself going through her inch by inch, correcting everything from chemical imbalances to biome deficiencies to tooth decay to scar tissue. She almost has a new body at this point, and she's going to need deken more sleep than normal for a while to make up for it."

"I see," I said, abashed.

"Next, make sure she eats enough—same reason."

"Check. We've packed plenty of food—enough to last us for several days if necessary. And that's at the rate *Yvera* eats."

"That's another thing: watch out for intestinal issues. Most likely she's not used to our food, either; plus, it's another source of disease she has no immunity to."

"Noted," I said with a grimace of sympathy. For us both. This could get awkward fast. I was almost tempted to call Avva again and ask for an exception to let Svyer come along after all....

No. It had to be just us. I knew that.

"Which brings up the most important thing: check her *often*. I'd say at least three times a day. I know that sounds excessive, but given your lack of experience and her lack of immunity, the earlier you can catch something, the better. Darkfever probably won't give her as much trouble again, but there are other diseases that strike nearly as quickly for *us*, and I shudder to think how quickly she could succumb."

"Agreed," I said grimly.

"Remember her sensitivity to heat. I wouldn't be surprised if she's also sensitive to cold. I packed her cold-weather gear, and I'll suggest to her that she wear at least the coat before flying today."

"Good, thank you."

"When she uses the water-rooms, I recommend sending Yvera with her, if you can persuade her to help. I know Yv won't be very patient, but...."

I sighed. "I agree. Whether she'll do it is another story, but I'll try."

"Try hard," Svyer insisted. "The water-rooms are where Sarah is most vulnerable to exposure. And...other things."

I grimaced. "I know. Trust me, I know."

Silence fell between us. After about half a dek, I glanced sidelong at her.

"What, is that all?" I teased, trying to lighten the mood. "Can the mother hanna not think of another thing to instruct me about her chick?"

"Not at the moment," she said, biting her lip. "I won't try to tell you how to protect her, since you know how to do that better than I do. So...no. But I'm sure I'll think of something later—after you're gone."

Her serious reply made me realize how genuinely worried she was.

"Svyer...." I wasn't sure how to phrase my question. "You're normally the mothering type, but this...seems a little excessive, even for you."

She raised an eyebrow at me. "And you're normally the helpful, hero type, but this is a bit excessive, even for you."

"Fair point. But you know at least part of the reason I'm doing this."

"Then you know even better than I do why I'm 'mothering' her, as you're calling it."

Just then, we reached the guest wing, and Svyer's steps slowed. I matched her pace, letting her think. When we came to Sarah's door, we both stopped and looked at each other.

Svyer glanced at the door, then back at me, her emerald eyes earnest. *Do you know what I'm most worried about, Ben?*

What? I asked, my inner voice quiet.

It isn't disease or heat or monsters. I think she'll learn to handle those. She's stronger than she looks. But only if she has a friend to show her that. That's what I worry about most: that while she's stuck with just the three of you, she'll feel more alone than she's ever felt in her life.

I frowned. *She'll have—*

You know how they are, Ben, Svyer said intently. *You know what kind of friends they are to you. Imagine how they'll seem to her. Kor will push her to her breaking point out of some misguided quest to "help" her, and Yvera won't take her seriously until Sarah can hold her own. All she'll have is you. And you're already determined to push her away.*

I swallowed. *I'm not....*

Svyer glared at me while folding her arms. *You said it yourself just a few deken ago, so don't deny it. So as a friend and your kin, I'm warning you, Ben: Don't court her if that's what you think is best. Fine. But what you* really *can't afford to do is make her feel alone and worthless by pushing her away. She* might *be your only chance...but I know you are hers.*

Without giving me any time to recover from the blow of that statement, Svyer turned to Sarah's door and knocked. I only had a moment to feel a surge of inexplicable panic before Sarah pushed open the door.

Her warm brown eyes lit up when they rose to mine.

"Ben," she said, tucking a stray lock from her braid behind her ear. "Uh, hi. Again."

"Hello. Again," I managed, throat tight.

She was looking well: recovered, rested, and changed back into her white shirt from yesterday, except this time with dramá-made gray trousers and brown boots. But my relief at seeing her up, whole, and freshly dressed didn't explain the pounding in my flameheart at the sight of her.

Svyer snorted, breaking the moment of awkwardness between us. "I *knew* I was forgetting something. We have to do your hair before you leave."

Without further ado, she pushed her way into Sarah's room, shooing the girl in front of her and leaving me to catch the door before it could swing shut in my face.

"We do?" Sarah asked in confusion as I tentatively stepped into her room and let the door close behind me. Technically, I hadn't been invited, but then, neither had Svyer, and I wasn't going to just stand outside where people could stare at me and wonder what I was doing in front of the door with the bright white gem.

Curse that little thing. What had Kor been thinking?

"Of course we do," Svyer said, kindly but insistently pushing Sarah into her desk chair. She positioned herself behind Sarah and began taking apart the Earthren's braid with gentle efficiency. "You're going to be flying, remember? And maybe for longer than yesterday, too. If you don't bind that pretty hair up somehow, it's going to be a headache to untangle tonight, ferrin bristles or no."

"Did you get me a brush?" Sarah asked eagerly, then added hastily, "I mean, don't worry if you didn't—"

"Of *course* I got you a brush," Svyer said with a wink—and a pointed look in my direction. Then she leaned down and mock-whispered in Sarah's ear, "After all, *I* was the one who went shopping."

Clearly an inside joke, from the way Sarah laughed. My gut wrenched at the way her whole heart-shaped face lit up when she did so, the lines of anxiety I'd come to take for granted in the brief time I'd known her disappearing.

I realized Svyer was dead right. What Sarah needed most right now wasn't protection or healing or possessions. What she needed was a friend. Svyer's nurturing, Peacegrowth instincts had homed in on that need, perhaps from the moment they'd met. Her affection for Sarah was genuine, but it was also reflexive, an automatic response. That was why even Svyer hadn't realized what the most important thing she had been doing for Sarah was until the moment she needed to tell me what I had to do in her stead.

Which meant she was right about the other things, too. Kor and Yvera would both mean well, in their own ways, but neither of them could give Sarah what she needed most to flourish in our world: genuine, warm friendship. The kind that asked nothing of you but that you just be...you.

I was already doomed to failure in *that* regard, because I wanted something from her, and unfortunately, no need of hers, no matter how tender, could prevent me from asking for it. Too much was at stake. Her sudden arrival after a year of searching portended too much for me to deny that she was the one we needed to restore what we had lost. The one...to save Avva.

Those unhappy thoughts swirled like a slowly growing cyclone in my head as I leaned as inconspicuously as I could against the far wall of her bedroom and Svyer braided the Earthren's dark brown hair. I felt like I was intruding on something as the young women chatted like old friends, Svyer asking about how Sarah had liked the food I'd brought and Sarah asking bewildered questions about the ingredients.

Svyer finished the crown braid too quickly, even though I suspected she had dragged out the process longer than necessary by deliberately fumbling and redoing some steps.

"Think you can do that on your own?" she asked Sarah, holding out a mirror for the young woman to see her handiwork.

Sarah laughed, twirling a loose framing lock around her finger. "Definitely not. But I'll be able to manage something simpler, don't worry."

Svyer looked at me speculatively, making me throw up my hands. "Don't look at me. I never learned. I'd just make more knots."

Never mind that just the thought of touching Sarah's dark, soft-looking hair made my hands tingle alarmingly.

Sarah laughed. "I'll be fine, Svyer," she said as she stood up. Her eyes softened, expression shifting into something tender as she threw her arms around the other young woman.

"Thank you. For everything."

"This isn't goodbye," Svyer said, voice stern. No doubt to mask the tears I could see gleaming in the corners of her eyes.

"Ben is taking me home," Sarah said, pulling away.

"If he manages to send you home, that means it's because he's made a sungate connect to Earth," Svyer told her, her hand lingering on Sarah's shoulder. "And if that's the case, it can bring you back for a visit, when all is said and done."

Sarah's eyes brightened, and I felt an uplift of hope in my chest. Perhaps her time here had *not* been all terrible. Perhaps she was already inclined to want to come back....

"Really?" she asked.

"Ask Ben," Svyer said, steering her around to face me. Svyer's lips twitched, and her eyes sparkled in amusement as they met mine over Sarah's head. "Regulating the sungates is up to the Golden King and Heir, after all."

"Er, Ben?" Sarah asked, tucking her loose strands behind one ear—which ruined the framing effect to an endearing degree.

It took me a split second to realize this was my cue. "Er, of course," I said, clearing my throat. "Of course you can come back. That is. If you'd like to. And...agree to abide by certain laws...."

"Which we don't need to get into at the moment," Svyer finished, grinning at me from behind Sarah. "I doubt you'll have a problem with any of them, though."

"Makes sense," Sarah said sincerely. "Thank you, Ben."

Every time she thanked me, my gut twisted with guilt, and given Svyer's warning in the back of my mind, this time was worse than all the others.

"Thank me when I get that gate open," I said with a half-smile, half-grimace. "If you're still feeling that generous after I've explained everything, that is."

There, finally, I gave her a hint of what was to come. We'd had so few chances to talk until now, but that was about to change.

Sarah gazed up at me soberly, so I knew she'd caught at least something of my hint, but there was no trace of surprise or suspicion in those warm depths. Just...calm acceptance.

My heart pounded as I struggled against hope. Could it be that easy? Would she really be so understanding?

No—she couldn't be. Maybe it would have been different if I could have explained from the very first moment. If she'd been able to understand me. If the sun hadn't been sinking over the horizon. If I'd brought myself to just *talk* to her last night as I should have instead of making excuses to myself about how I would botch the explanation in my exhausted state—not to mention my self-consciousness after Kor's prodding.

Instead, she was thus far under the illusion that we were doing all of this because it was the right thing to do. As soon as she fully understood otherwise, she might be resentful at best, and, at worst, furious, betrayed, or outright refusing to help. Rightfully so. I *should* be doing this simply out of the goodness of my heart, when only I could help her go back to life as she knew it. I *should* be helping her to resume that life, setting her free to blissfully forget this experience as if it were nothing more than a bad dream.

I wasn't doing any of those things. Couldn't be.

Svyer startled us both out of our shared gaze with a clap on Sarah's shoulder. "Well, it's time for you two to get going, isn't it?"

"I...guess so," Sarah said, with a dart of her eyes back at me.

I belatedly cleared the remorse out of my throat. "Yes, it is. That is...if you're ready...."

"One more thing," Svyer said, going over to the two large canvas bags she had packed for Sarah. I'd nearly rolled my eyes when I'd originally seen how much Svyer had requisitioned for Sarah under my name, but that was when I'd come to see the Earthren after Svyer had sent word about her concussion and fever, so I was too full of gratitude for everything Svyer had done to protest at the excess. It wasn't like we didn't owe Sarah bags more—of whatever she wanted. If she agreed to help, I'd empty the Crown Treasury for her, Minister Thirra's protests be torched.

"Were you cold when you rode on Ben's back yesterday?" Svyer asked, giving Sarah a look that demanded nothing but the absolute truth.

"Well...." Sarah said, glancing at me again.

"What?" I asked, heart sinking. "Why didn't you...."

Say anything? When? She couldn't speak with an inner voice—she was amá. She would have had to shout over the wind and flaps of my wings. And what could I have done? Spent even more energy to have kept the air around her warm? Landed in the dark so that I could get out a coat for her?

But I should have anticipated the cold from the beginning! Not that amón usually mind it in this climate, but *still*....

Had I done *anything* right when it came to her?

Some of my devastation must have been clear on my face, because Sarah and Svyer both spoke at the same time.

"You couldn't have known—" Sarah began.

"What's done is done," Svyer said with finality.

Then she rose from where she'd been ruffling through Sarah's bags and brought out a long leather, fur-lined coat with a drawstring hood. The dark hide and white fur looked to be kallanth, so it should be able to keep even an amá warm. I was relieved and a bit impressed Svyer had found something that high quality and heavy duty here, in Elspeth Hold, near the middle of their summer. She must have bullied her way into getting access to their emergency stores and then taken the best they had to offer. I idly wondered how many Elspeth clerks were cursing my name right now. Just another reason to be glad we were leaving today, I supposed.

Even so, I sent a prayer of thanks to the Flame for my cousin and solemnly promised to forgive her for every little bit of nuisance she caused me growing up together. Even the time she'd put raidonroot in my soup so that I was sneezing uncontrollably the entire Winter Solstice feast.

"Oh," Sarah gasped appreciatively, holding up one of the front panels so that she could examine the silver-embossed pattern of fern-like swirls. I had to admit that the effect was well-done, and as Sarah bent over the coat, I noticed that the darkened leather matched her hair suspiciously well. I cast a glance at Svyer, who grinned at me.

Sarah looked up at Svyer, eyes glinting with emotion. "You got this last night? For *me*?"

"Yes, but Ben is owed some thanks, since he paid for it," Svyer said with a nod in my direction, grin still on her lips.

"No thanks are necessary," I said quickly as Sarah turned. "I had no more idea that she'd gotten that for you than you did. Besides, it's the least I can do if I'm going to put you through flying again today."

And possibly the next day. And the next.

"You got a saddle, right?" Svyer asked me as she thrust the coat into Sarah's arms.

Ah, there. The one thing I'd gotten right, it seemed.

"Yes." I smiled apologetically at Sarah. "Today is going to be a lot more comfortable than yesterday, I promise."

The relief in her expressive eyes warmed my flameheart even as it twisted my gut with guilt.

"Is that all?" I asked Svyer, since I could see thanks once again rising in Sarah's eyes.

"I think so," Svyer said with a shrug and a frown. "Was there anything else uncomfortable about flying, Sarah?"

Sarah hesitated one moment, so there was something.

"What is it?" Svyer asked gently. I made a careful mental note to do the same whenever it looked like there was something Sarah needed. Clearly this Earthren was going to need prompting.

"Nothing you can help," Sarah said with a wry chuckle. "The...height."

Svyer laughed, and I grinned ruefully.

"You're right," I said. "But the saddle should make you feel more secure."

"And," Svyer added, "if it makes you feel better, even many amón don't enjoy flying on our backs. Especially the first few times. But some of them learn to enjoy it."

"What about drakón?" Sarah asked. "Do you two enjoy flying?"

I blinked at both her knowledge and calm acceptance of our differences now—a far cry from her white-faced bewilderment when I'd first tried to explain what I was to her yesterday. I felt another twinge of gratitude as I realized Svyer must have done some explaining last night.

I had to process that for a moment before I realized that Sarah's eyes were on me, not Svyer, and that Svyer hadn't answered her.

"Of course," I said, a broad, genuine smile growing on my face for what felt like the first time in days as I just *thought* about flying. "Every drakón does. It's...incredible."

"The best feeling in the world," Svyer agreed.

Wistfulness entered Sarah's eyes for a moment, but she refocused on the coat to hide the expression.

My gut twisted again. What kind of upbringing had this Earthren had, to be so tentative about her own wants? To be so ridiculously *grateful* for every scrap of kindness shown to her?

I impulsively made a reckless and foolish vow, considering the improbability of fulfilling it: somehow, one day, I would give Sarah the slightest glimpse at the joy that came from flight. Not out of a sense of obligation to her. Not to make up for the way I was no doubt going to disappoint her.

Simply because she, Sarah of Earth, deserved to feel that kind of joy.

CHAPTER NINE

STORIES

SARAH

SVYER HOISTED ONE BAG easily in one muscular arm—even though they were nearly as large as I was and packed full—and held it out to Ben.

"Well, time to pack up."

"I can carry…" My voice trailed off as both drakón looked at me, Svyer with amusement as she *still* held out the bag with one arm and Ben with a raised eyebrow as he took it from her.

"…some of it," I finished in a mutter, flushing.

Svyer chuckled. "Let Ben handle it, Sarah. He's drakón, after all."

"That doesn't mean he's a beast of burden," I said hotly.

That startled a laugh out of him, and I was still glad of it, even if it was at my expense. A strange sadness had been lingering in his eyes ever since he'd come into my room, and I was happy to see it dispelled for a moment.

"I don't think she knows how this works, Svyer," he said with a crooked smile at his cousin. "There aren't any drakón where she's from."

"How what works?" I demanded.

He looked at me hesitantly, then at Svyer. Svyer gave him a pointed look back. Then Ben looked helplessly back at me. Something was familiar about that kind of exchange—and then I remembered when Ben and Yvera had been debating about how to get me to understand them.

"This is a drakón thing, isn't it?" I asked with a sigh. "One you think I might not like."

"Not necessarily," Svyer corrected.

Ben frowned at her. "It might frighten her. She's not used to...us."

So, Ben had noticed how nervous their dragon forms made me.

"She's going to see it happen eventually," Svyer said pragmatically. "Better right now while she's in private and braced for it."

"Svyer's right," I said, raising my chin. "Go ahead. Whatever it is you are going to do. I can handle it."

Ben looked at me dubiously, but he rolled up his sleeve and held out the arm holding my bag so I could see it clearly. For a moment, I nervously thought he was going to cut himself again, so my eyes were darting around, looking for a knife. Which was why I nearly missed when the change began.

Ben's skin...started crawling. At least, that's what it looked like at first. Then I realized it was becoming something else. Hardening. Cracking. Scaling. Turning gold and shimmery. Fingers elongating, joints rearranging, fingernails lengthening, sharpening, taking on a metallic sheen.

My stomach churned, but I swallowed the bile and kept on as blank an expression as I could manage. Ben was showing me this transformation for a reason, no matter how self-conscious his still very human face was becoming, so I tried my hardest to not react.

"And...that's it," he said bashfully, pulling his arm back as it quickly shifted into human skin and fingers again.

"Interesting," I said, proud of the neutrality of my voice. "But...what was that for?"

Both drakón stared at me.

"Didn't you see that?" Ben asked in confusion, holding out his hand. His...empty hand.

I gaped as I looked around for the bag. It wasn't anywhere to be seen. "Your...where...where did it go?"

They stared at me for a second longer, then both burst out laughing.

"Like hiding a ball from a babe," Svyer said with a grin.

"Watch the *bag* this time," Ben said, his smile more merciful as he came over and grabbed the other one.

He took a few steps back, perhaps for my comfort, and held out his arm again. Just in time, I remembered his instruction and focused my attention on the bag. My stomach was much happier that way, but I also found it difficult to ignore Ben's fingers turning into reptilian digits and his nails into talons out of the corner of my eye.

Then it happened. Whatever *it* was. One moment, the bag was clutched in his transformed hand, and the next, the bag was gone. As simple, clean, and sudden as that.

I would have thought the bag had merely turned invisible, but Ben's fingers relaxed and straightened, no longer holding anything.

"But...*how*?" I gasped as Ben withdrew his hand again. "And *why*...and *where*?"

I didn't know why this phenomenon was nearly as earth-shattering to me as the existence of dragons...but it was. This disappearing act was defying every law of the universe I'd learned, and I couldn't stop looking for either bag, sure at least one of them would turn up somewhere.

"We don't know exactly." Ben shrugged. "The answer to any of those questions. Just that when drakón change, whatever we are holding, whatever we are wearing...goes *somewhere*. Somewhere we can access when we change again."

"Surely you've wondered where our clothing comes from when we change back," Svyer quipped with a wink at Ben.

My cheeks grew hot as I realized I most certainly *hadn't*. "I've...had a lot to take in," I said in my defense.

"Understandably," Ben said.

I looked up at him, biting my lip. He didn't stand any differently, so it didn't look like he was carrying a burden, but.... "Does that...weigh you down in any way?"

"Not at all," he assured me while Svyer snorted. "I don't feel a thing. That's why it makes more sense for me to be 'carrying' them for you."

"But the bags...they are connected to you in some way? Or...can anyone access them in this...other place?"

"No, only I can," he said, and then grimaced. "Although that means I'll have to get you anything you might need. I'm sorry. I'll bring the bags out whenever we stop for the night."

"Which is why I put *this* together for you," Svyer said, bringing something out from behind her back with a flourish. I realized how she seemed to produce things out of thin air—because that was what she was doing.

I shook my head to silence the physics questions for now as I saw what was in Svyer's hands. "Oh, Svyer," I breathed.

It was a dark leather backpack, with a drawstring top and a flap with a buckle in the shape of a tree. The leather was just a shade or two lighter than the coat in my hands but embossed with the same silver swirling fronds.

Svyer shoved the pack into my arms. "That should have some essentials you'd want to keep with you," she said brusquely, eyes blinking. "No—don't open it now. I've held you up long enough, and you need to get going if you're going to have enough daylight left. If you can't figure out how to use what's in it, ask Ben or Yvera."

My eyes stung again, and I hung the coat over my arm and the bag from one hand so I could throw my arms around her again. "Thank you."

"Like I said," Svyer countered softly. "This isn't goodbye."

"No," I agreed, saying the words like a promise. "It's not."

BEN WAS RIGHT: THIS time, flying was a lot easier.

The saddle made a stark difference in my comfort level. From the more stable positioning—further up, at the juncture of Ben's dragon neck and shoulders—to the more natural hip-width saddle seat, to the straps for my legs and optional handles for my arms, I felt about as secure as was possible while being on a behemoth's back a thousand feet above the ground. I had also appreciated the hold's mounting platforms and especially Svyer's patient guidance in getting me settled, which contrasted with Yvera's scant help and blasé warning the night before. This time I could trust Svyer's hand squeeze and verbal assurance that I would be safe.

The coat was warm; the wind didn't pierce the leather, and the fur kept my body heat inside without being stuffy. With my legs close to Ben's furnace of a body, I found myself at a surprisingly comfortable temperature despite the height and buffeting wind. I even lowered the drawstring hood after a half hour to regain my peripheral vision.

That was the last thing: the view. I didn't know what the difference was. Perhaps being rested, being healed of every injury from yesterday and probably health problems I didn't even know I'd had, not being wound up with adrenaline from a near-death experience, being able to fully trust the dragon carrying me, or flying during the daylight—or perhaps a combination of all those things. All I knew for sure was that today, the view that had kept me frozen witless yesterday was breathtaking.

Trees—*enormous* trees—as far as the eye could see, and I could see pretty dang far from up here. The mountain range we had spent the night in faded quickly from view, leaving only an even canopy as the main visible feature from horizon to horizon. The leaves rustled in the wind of our passage like the hiss of the sea, a mesmerizing sight to watch and soothing to hear. I couldn't see anything below the canopy, and though I kept an eye out, I didn't see any wildlife aside from the occasional soaring bird. Maybe—considering my first encounter with the creatures of this world—that was a good thing.

The complaints I still had were the bright sun and heavy wind, which both stung my eyes and made enjoying the view more difficult. I wondered if flight goggles were a thing in this world; I would have to remember to ask Ben....

If I don't get home today, I reminded myself.

But Ben said I could come back. No doubt he would have moved on, but if Svyer, at least, wanted me to visit, then presumably this would not have to be my last flight on dragon back. That thought was satisfying. Maybe I could get used to this—maybe even look forward to it.

I was a bit in awe of Ben's open invitation. That wasn't how these things were supposed to work, was it? Once you fell into a magical world, it was all or nothing, right? I was a realist, so I knew well that you couldn't ever have the best of both worlds. You always had to choose.

There had to be a catch. Which meant it was probably in those laws I'd have to agree to, so I shouldn't get my hopes up. Svyer had said I wouldn't have a problem with any of them, but when it came right down to it, she'd only known me for less than a day, and she was another species to boot. Or...hybrid species. Or something. At least, she was from a different culture, a different world. She hadn't thought much of people who stared at me or of authoring a paper about my human anatomy with no way of obscuring my identity, so *privacy* was not as valued here as it was to me.

What would I be willing to agree to for free passage between our worlds? What would I be willing to give, or give up? I...didn't know. I'd only seen the smallest fraction—not even a day's worth—of what this world and its people offered. Part of my time here had been life-threatening, but then again, part of it had been thrilling, even magical and wondrous. If you counted the thorough healing that was making me feel better than ever, then there were even net benefits that would last me for some time to come.

They had said I was the first human being to set foot on this world for...how long? A thousand years? But if Ben was going to open a "gate" between our worlds, I wouldn't be the last. Not even close.

I knew that some people in my position wouldn't hesitate. I was riding on a *dragon*, for crying out loud. (Yes, that dragon was a sentient person who was doing me a favor, but that fact didn't lessen any of my awe, and I doubted it would for anyone else.) I'd seen architectural marvels and experimented with ingenious engineering in what everyone here had dismissed as a backwater settlement. I'd seen—I'd felt—magic. Real, powerful, unmistakable *magic*. There were people on Earth who would literally kill to come here.

I shuddered at that realization. Leave aside those people—the ones who should never be allowed to discover this place—that still left masses and masses of innocent, well-meaning humans who would not just be thrilled to come but would greatly benefit. Healing, true *healing*, could save lives—could change human society as I knew it. Never mind that there could still be plagues that resisted a magical healthcare system; millions could live who would have died from cancer, or failing organs, or accidents. Millions more could have better lives than they could have ever dreamed of. Lives could be extended, death could become a rarity....

I swallowed as the implications of what I had seen and experienced in perhaps less than twenty-four hours began spinning in my head, and those were only the ones with the most potential for good.

But even I—a normal, young, healthy human being—had nearly died in one day from exposure to the kinds of diseases that had grown among these superhuman people. If humans came here in mass, or if Ben's people went there...it could be the Black Plague all over again, except with far greater speed and even greater numbers to lose.

That was just disease. What if...*war* broke out between the humans and these people? Their drakón were, after all, terrifying to behold. If they weren't careful in how they approached us, they could get missiles sent at them first, questions asked later. If not war, at least some level of conflict was likely given humanity's track record in dealing with the other. Even if, miracle of all miracles, the two races mingled peacefully, there were other races to consider. After all, my first reception in this world didn't come from drakón.... What if unlawful, bloodthirsty creatures like the ahglen slipped through to Earth? They...they could cause a massacre.

My stomach twisted itself into knots that, this time, had nothing to do with the flight.

Regulations or no...was Ben prepared for the shockwaves he would send across Earth by doing so?

Was I?

Could *anyone* be?

I felt as if I'd been contemplating accepting an incredible present containing a golden ticket, only to discover it was Pandora's box. Except instead of being filled with all the horrible things in life, this dragon world probably had an even mix of wonderfully good and perilously terrible. There were so many, *many* things that had to be considered before any kind of permanent gate could be established between our worlds, and I was far from the kind of person to think of them all, let alone make the kinds of Earth-shattering decisions that could change humanity forever, for both good and ill.

Ben's invitation to me alone was one thing. I'd consider it, but I would warn him of the dangers I'd thought of before accepting. If it was all or nothing—if he either had to throw the gate wide open or not at all...then my responsibility was clear. *I* couldn't be that kind of catalyst for change. I couldn't bear the weight of civilizations on my shoulders. I'd have no choice but to tell him thanks, but no. Not even if that meant I could never come back.

Not even if—which was more likely in the all-or-nothing scenario—that meant I could never go home.

Not, at least, until I'd done my very inadequate best to prepare these people to control the flood of change.

My heart sank as I thought about how long those efforts could take if that impossible task fell to me, as I scrubbed my inexperienced brain raw trying to think of and then explain to Ben's people every implication, and then they debated. Weeks, possibly, but probably more like months, or even years. Maybe never, if they decided it wasn't worth the risk, as they were within their right to do. I was, after all, only one lost human; they had to weigh the good of two races against my one wish to go home. In that case, I knew which way the scales tipped.

I would accept that judgment. My heart sank and my eyes stung from more than just the wind as I contemplated that likely outcome, but I would try to be brave and accept it. In a way, it would come as a relief. I wouldn't have the deaths of millions from war or disease on my conscience. My fate would be my own, with the only others affected being my family on the other side.

My heart wrenched. That would be the worst part—abandoning them to their grief and questions forever, for the greater good. But I liked to think that, if I could explain everything to them, they would understand, too.

Ben's mental voice interrupted my morose thoughts—which, surprisingly, given his current size, wasn't "loud," but it still had a kind of depth and power to it that no other mental voice I'd heard had. No matter the gentleness of his tone, it still made me flinch and sent shivers down my spine at the same time.

Are you alright, Sarah? Yvera says you're looking...sober.

His hesitation made me think she had said a different word, and Ben was being tactful. I glanced at the purple dragon flying slightly above and to his right. It seemed his rightwing and leftwing took the directional parts of their titles seriously, because Kor was on his other side, with Ben flying point.

"I'm fine," I said with a sigh, and then realized too late that my words were just snatched away on the wind. Unless Ben had incredible hearing on top of everything else, he probably hadn't caught that.

My eyes fell on the rolled-up streamers on short wooden rods tucked in holsters within easy reach on the saddle. As Svyer was helping buckle me in, she had explained they were for amón to communicate with drakón while in flight. She'd said there was a whole signal system she couldn't get into in the time she had, so she'd instructed me to use the three colors to communicate the one-word responses *yes* and *no* and *danger*.

I was fairly sure those were the three words she told me to associate with the three flags...but for the life of me, I couldn't remember which ones meant what. There was a sky blue, a dark red, and a black, none of which seemed to correspond to the words in my mind. I *thought* I remembered being surprised that the dark red *wasn't* danger, so that narrowed down the possibilities somewhat. That meant the red was probably either *yes* or *no*.... And I didn't think it was *yes*....

That left my best guess at *yes* being the light blue.

Wait, what had he asked me again? Had it been in the negative? No, I remembered: *Are you alright?* Which meant the proper response was indeed *yes*.

I sighed as I reached for the stick with the blue streamer. This method of communication was going to get old, fast.

Not to mention I also felt a bit ridiculous unfurling the streamer and waving it as obviously as I could, like my sister Abby trying to get our parents' attention in the very back of our passenger van.

At least it seemed to work. I saw Ben turn his enormous head to the side enough to see the flag and then look straight ahead again.

Are you sure? he pressed. *I'm sorry to pry, but we can't take any chances after that darkfever. Do you feel sick at all?*

I was touched and annoyed at the same time. Never in my life had I been as fussed over as I had been in the past twenty-four hours, and it was a disconcerting experience.

Ben had asked me *two* questions, though, with different answers, which meant another flag. I reached for the dark red and unfurled it. I waved the blue first in my right hand, and then the red in my left, hoping once again that I'd remembered the correct meanings.

Belatedly, I realized that waving the flags in different hands meant Ben had to swivel his head a bit more to see them, but from his tone, he didn't seem bothered. *Alright. We're almost there, anyway. But if you ever feel even the slightest bit ill, let me know as soon as possible by waving the black one. Even if I don't see it, Kor or Yvera will, and they'll let me know.*

I didn't have a flag for *thank you*, so I simply waved the blue *yes* again in acknowledgement, and that seemed satisfactory, because after glancing at it, he said nothing more.

NOT LONG AFTER, I caught sight of a break in the trees—a clearing. *The* clearing, I soon realized, as we flew closer, and I saw the rubble that Ben and Yvera had reduced the crude stone altar to. Back to the scene of the crime, it seemed. That only made sense; it was where I had emerged, so it seemed as likely a place to send me back as any. Still, I couldn't help scanning for any sign of ahglen.

If they ran from Ben alone, then they're not going to show up when there's three of them, I told myself.

If they were smart, that is. But....

Ben touched down first, in the center of the clearing, flapping his wings hard and fast at the very end to make his landing softer. Yvera and then Kor came down next, on their respective sides of him, taking no such care with their landings, each of which caused a tremor in the ground.

Yvera, Ben said in the echoing way that I was realizing probably meant he was speaking to more than one person.

On it, Yvera said with a snort that puffed an alarming amount of smoke, and she circled the clearing with great sniffing sounds, nose low to the ground.

Kor, Ben said, golden head swinging to his much smaller friend.

I'll get started in a moment, Kor said with a laughing edge to his mental voice. *But wouldn't you like me to help Sarah down first? Or were you planning on changing with her on your back?*

Oh, right, Ben said sheepishly, and somehow his giant reptilian face managed to look chagrined. I had to bite my tongue to keep from laughing.

The laugh died quickly when Kor's enormous midnight-blue head swung near me. When I said that he was *smaller* than Ben, that didn't mean he was *small* by any measure of the word. If Ben was around the size of a Boeing 747, then Kor was the size of a medium blue whale.

In other words: still mindbogglingly huge and able to swallow me in one gulp.

Here, Sarah, why don't you try climbing onto my hand? Kor said, holding out his hand, scaly palm up, next to Ben's neck.

"Oookay," I muttered, but I couldn't think of a better idea, so I unbuckled my legs and stood up in the saddle. I grabbed one of Kor's scaled, taloned fingers (I noted with morbid interest that he only had three fingers, much like a bird or dinosaur, except one was an opposable thumb) and slowly transitioned my weight to one side of the saddle. Then I stepped over the saddle and put my foot on Kor's hand in the same motion, all while trying hard to not look at the drop that awaited me if I fell. If Kor's reflexes were fast enough, I supposed he could try catching me, but I might not like the results of the quick, crushing movement that might be required to do so. Finally, I scooted onto Kor's hand, bringing my other foot with me.

Kor lowered his hand to the ground with a gentle slowness that surprised me. The thing was, I didn't know how long this new niceness would last, so even though I might forgive, I probably shouldn't forget. I didn't think he intended me to; that had been the whole point, hadn't it?

When his hand came to a stop, I was only a few easy feet from the ground, which meant all I had to do was lower myself onto my bottom and slide off, touching down on blessedly solid ground.

"Thank you," I said with a tad too much fervor, because I heard his human chuckle a moment later.

I turned, blinking, to see him already standing a few dozen feet from me, arms folded, smirking.

"Man, you guys can change *fast*," I said.

"When we want to," Ben said, walking over to me with his hands in his pockets. "Kor *was* showing off, though. He's always been the fastest shifter among us."

"Faster than even Yvera," Kor said in the violet dragon's direction.

I heard that, you little whelp.

I winced as I heard the deep, enormous, bestial snarl that accompanied her words. I imagined it would be the sound an angry T-Rex would make. Yet Kor just stood there, as blasé as if he'd only poked fun at a teddy bear. He even had the nerve to wink at me when he caught me looking.

"Kor," Ben reminded him when he reached my side.

"Right, right—on it," Kor said with a wave as he began walking away from us toward the altar.

"What's he supposed to be doing?" I asked Ben quietly.

"He's also the arcane expert among the three of us," Ben said, then chuckled. "Well, he's pretty much our expert on *everything*. Anyway, he's going to determine, as far as he can after this much time and our destruction, what the ahglen were hoping to accomplish by sacrificing you."

I shuddered. "Any ideas?"

"A few," Ben said with a severe frown in the altar's direction. His golden eyes glowed for a moment, presumably from the echo of his fury from yesterday. The glow died before he looked back down at me. "Most of which wouldn't have worked. The only thing they could have accomplished would have been utter catastrophe."

"I assume you mean more catastrophic than my death?" I asked, surprised how casually I could speak about it now.

He grimaced. "That would have been a tragic enough loss, but yes, more than that. Far more."

"How so?"

He sighed and sat down cross-legged on the ground. Then he patted the ground next to him. "You might want to sit down. This is going to take a while."

"'This'?" I asked him uneasily, settling down next to him.

"The explanation I've owed you for a while," he said with a heavy sigh. "Since before I knocked you down in this clearing, in fact. But various things have gotten in the way of me giving it so far."

I blinked at him. "I thought you were...going to open a gate or something for me."

"Yes, but before I do *that*, there are a few things we need to discuss," Ben said, looking down at me soberly. "What the gates are, for one thing. What *we* are, for another. What I am, in particular. And what you are, most of all."

"What *I* am?" I said in surprise.

He sighed, running a hand through his golden hair, spilling it around his face like fluid sunlight for one distracting moment. "That's getting ahead of ourselves. First...how much do you already know? What are the legends you know about the Six Realms, about the Tree of Flame, about the sungates, about us?"

His expression grew increasingly concerned the longer my blank look lasted. He leaned in. "Nothing? You have been told...*nothing*?"

"*Should* I have?" I asked.

"It's only been less than a thousand years," Ben said, eyes wide.

"And that's a very long time in human history," I said. "Records weren't good back then. And I don't know how long you drakón live, but for humans now, it's only about eighty years. I don't even know what it would have been back then."

Ben stared. Then shuddered and sighed. "I guess...that would explain it."

He paused. "Wait—that can't be right. You knew *one* word without my blood to translate for you. Drakón."

"*Dragon*," I corrected. "That's what I know you as, anyway. I guess you're right about that, but dragons are the only legend I've heard that means anything to me here."

"What do you know about drakón—or 'dragons,' then?" he said with a guarded look.

I hesitated.

He grimaced. "Nothing good, I take it?"

"No, it just depends on the story," I protested.

"What do the *oldest* stories say?" he pressed, leaning forward.

I bit my lip.

"Sarah. I won't be offended, I promise. I just need to know what your preconceptions are if I'm going to explain properly."

I looked down and pulled up grass shoots with my fingers. "The oldest stories? That *I* know of? Well, for one thing, none of them change into humans. They're just how they are as...dragons."

"And?" he encouraged.

"There's not much detail in the oldest ones. Wings, scales. Breathes fire. Incredibly big, incredibly dangerous. Steals sheep and cows—uh, those are animals humans raise, livestock," I explained when his face scrunched in confusion.

"Oh," he said, face returning to a careful neutral. "Go on. What else?"

"Uh...likes treasure—sleeps on hoards of it under the mountains. Again, stolen."

Ben snorted but waved for me to continue.

I hesitated.

He sighed. "Sarah, out with it."

"Well, the human-dragon interaction never went peacefully, let's put it that way," I said tactfully.

"As in...?" he pressed.

I threw up my hands. "Why does this *matter* so much to you?"

"Because the real conflict between amá and draká is why I need your help," he shot back.

I stared at him, heart giving an extra hard thud or two. "The.... You need my help with *what*?"

"Torch it," Ben cursed, covering his eyes with one hand. "Sorry, I.... Sorry. 'Course I'm messing this up already...."

"Hey, hey, don't worry about it," I said. "I'll tell you if it's that important, but I'm just warning you, it's not pretty.... It always ends in death. Usually lots of humans first, then the dragon when they manage to...end it. And.... Yeah. That's all there is to it."

I did not mention all the damsels that were singled out and consumed in those legends. I didn't think Ben needed that detail on top of everything else.

Ben let out a heavy breath. "So, just to make sure I understand this correctly, the *only* thing the oldest legends say about us—about drakón—is that they are big, vicious, fire-breathing robbers and murderers?"

I hesitated. "The Western version, yeah."

He sighed, face set. "No *wonder* you looked at me like...."

Like he was a monster.

"I just had no idea what to expect," I said. "I *know* you now. But yesterday.... Ben, you scared those ahglen witless to drive them off, and I did not know if I was going to be next. What other kind of reaction was I supposed to have?"

"I see," he said, looking away.

I wracked my brain to come up with something to wipe the grim look off his face. "The legends about the Eastern dragons are nicer, I think. I know less about those, but I think they're more like...gods? Control the elements, are wise, sometimes help out? Those are drawn a lot differently than you look, though. They're a lot longer, almost like snakes, and I don't think they have wings."

"Well, that's...interesting," Ben said, his face getting even darker.

After a moment, he raised his head and took a deep breath. "That is...*all* you know? All the average Earthren knows?"

I bit my lip, but I nodded. "If by 'Earthren' you mean 'human from Earth'...pretty much, yeah."

"What about your Tree?" he asked, as if throwing out one final detail I *had* to know—like the sky being blue. "The Tree of Ice?"

I just blinked at him. "The what now?"

"That means *nothing* to you?" Ben said, aghast. "You don't even know your Tree *exists*?"

"I am...going to have to go with a *no* on that one." Regardless of whether such a thing did, in fact, exist on Earth, I knew nothing of it. Not even a legend.

"Well," Ben said heavily, leaning back on his hands. "When Avva told me I had my work cut out for me, he wasn't kidding."

He glanced at me sidelong for a moment, and I could swear he seemed almost...nervous. Abruptly, he said, "How about some tsha? I need some tsha. Any good story needs a fire, in any case."

"Tsha?" I asked with a blink.

Ben's face scrunched as he tried to think of an explanation. "Hot...leaf...juice?"

"Oh, you mean *tea*!" I burst out laughing and for a few moments, I couldn't stop.

Interesting that the translation magic hadn't just given me the word *tea*. Perhaps there was enough of a difference that a new term was needed.

"What?" Ben asked sheepishly.

"Nothing," I gasped, wiping my eyes. Chuckles still occasionally escaped. "But just...in the middle of the clearing where I nearly died yesterday...at the start of 'the big explanation'...and coming from *you*.... Tea. I would never have pegged you for a tea guy."

"Is that a...bad thing?" he asked tentatively.

"No, no, go right ahead," I said with a wave of my hand. I hiccupped out another chuckle. "Don't mind me. Just nerves, probably."

"You're not the only one," I heard him mutter to himself as he leaned forward.

This time, his sleeve covered most of his arm, so the transformation as he brought out each item he needed wasn't as dramatic. The speed of the change was also much faster, more fluid, leading me to think Ben had deliberately slowed down the process before to help me follow what was going on. I marveled at the *ease*, the unconsciousness of what he was doing, as if he were just pulling things out of a bag. With just a flex of his semi-reptilian fingers—not even enough change required to remove digits—he had a small brazier in his hand. Just like that—empty air one moment, brazier the next, which he set down on a clear patch of ground between us.

Next, he brought out a waxed paper bag filled with small disks of what looked like charcoal and began filling the brazier with a neat pile. He began speaking as he worked, his voice coming more naturally now that he had something to occupy his hands.

"I think it's best if I start at the very beginning, the parts that are basically myth to us, too, so I'm going to tell it to you like I first heard it—like a story. A story about the draká."

"Draká?" I asked.

"Full-blooded...." Ben frowned at the sky, struggling for the right word for a moment. Then he waved his hand vaguely. "What we can become, that creature. But the original, unmixed with human blood. One that couldn't become *this*."

He gestured at himself, his human form. Human-*like*, anyway.

"Oh," I breathed. "You mean, just like *I'm* a full-blooded human, there are full-blooded dragons—I mean...draká?"

"Exactly," he said with a relieved smile. Then the smile died. "Except, there are no more draká. Just as, before you came, there were no more humans."

"Why?" I asked quietly.

"That's what the story is about," Ben said, taking a deep breath. "This world, we call it Ykran. However, I was born on Ythra. In case that didn't translate—Old Draká often doesn't—that means 'mother.' It's the world where the draká were created."

"Created?"

Ben shrugged. "As far as the Tree has told us, yes."

I was about to ask what the Tree was when Ben continued. As he spoke, he set aside the bag of charcoal and hovered his hand over the pile.

"At the very beginning of that world, there was the Tree—the Tree of Flame."

At the same time he said the word *flame*, he touched his hand into the middle of the pile and a tongue of fire about the size of a candle flame leaped from his finger into the charcoal, setting it alight. The flare raced across all the pre-treated coals until they all were on fire.

Meanwhile, Ben began setting up a grate on top of the brazier.

His voice was soft with reverence. "The Tree of Flame is what it sounds like—an enormous Tree, one burning with everlasting fire. Legend tells us the Tree was involved in the draká's creation. At the very least, She is the source of the flameheart inside us now."

"She?"

"She always uses female avatars when She speaks to us," Ben said with another shrug. "All the Trees do, as far as we are aware."

"There are other Trees? Like the one you said was on Earth?"

"Yes, but I'll get to that," Ben said patiently. "In the beginning of this story, there was only the one."

"Sorry, I'll shut up now."

He smiled. "Don't worry about it. It's good to see that you're curious, and I'm explaining a lot of things that must be new. Although this might go a little faster if you let me just talk for now."

"I'll do that, then," I said, miming zipping my lips closed.

He cocked his head curiously at the gesture, but he didn't remark on it as he continued. "The draká were created to be the guardians of the Tree, and when they protected Her and followed Her counsel in their stewardship over the rest of Ythra, they prospered. When they ignored Her and became greedy, they faltered. And that is what led to their downfall."

As he spoke, Ben brought out a teakettle and a metal canister, took off the lids, and dumped a few scoops of leaves inside the kettle. The whiff I caught from the leaves was interesting: herbal, but also sharp, almost spicy. Then Ben capped the canister, put it "away," and "pulled out" a canteen of water, the contents of which he began dumping into the kettle.

"Draká, as you've seen, are huge creatures, requiring huge amounts of ener-gy—more than is possible without also being magical, in fact. That has never changed. But back then, draká got their energy just as any other creature does: from food. Specifically, from fresh meat, and the bloodier the better. That meant they had to keep many herds of large creatures, which meant vast fields for grazing, which required the draká to create new plains and replant vegetation in the old. It was a careful balance, but it worked for thousands of years because the draká were prudent and obedient to the Tree."

Ben set the kettle on top of the brazier grid with an ominous pause. "Then came the Great Famine."

He glanced at the sun, and then his eyes rested on me. "There's a lot more to it, but for the sake of time, let's just say that the draká began to ignore the Tree's counsel, becoming greedy and complacent—never a good combination. When the Great Famine struck, one thing led to another, and soon the draká were tangled in a cycle of hunger and bloodshed. They'd had conflicts before, but never like this. It wasn't more than a year before the entire world was affected. Things were looking dire enough...."

Ben's normally soft and warm eyes became hard, cold gold. "That was when the Devourer struck."

I felt a chill, like a whisper of a winter breeze going down my neck. Strange that such a feeling should come over me on this pleasantly warm day, sitting next to the burning coals. I had begun to get hot. But when Ben said those last words....

Ben cast a startled glance at me, as if he'd felt it too. Then he looked grimly over his shoulder at the altar Kor was still examining. I was distracted for a moment by the incredible sight of midnight-blue patterns floating in the air around the altar, turning and spinning around each other like gears in a machine. Kor's back was to me, but he appeared to be watching the patterns with folded arms, as if they were displaying data on a screen for him to interpret. Occasionally, he would raise a hand and make some motion that would send the patterns spinning in new directions. I was so overcome with fascination, I forgot about the chill.

Until Ben raised his hand, and where he pointed, a line of fire appeared on the ground—too bright and uniformly gold to be like the natural flame he'd used to light the coals. All the while, his eyes glowed, just as they had when he'd looked at the altar before. I felt a different chill—not the ominous kind of before, but one that was awe and a bit of fear.

Ben traced the fire around us in a wide circle, large enough that there was no danger of either of us accidentally touching it. When the circle was complete, he lowered his hand, and the glow in his eyes faded. The fire, however, did not. It stayed at a low level, only a foot or so at its highest, and it didn't seem to give off any extra heat, thank goodness. It also didn't seem to consume anything beneath it or spread, and yet it kept on burning.

Eerie.

"Sorry about that," Ben said with a grimace, and it took me a moment to realize he wasn't meaning the fire. "I should have set that up to begin with, but I didn't realize.... Well, I suppose that confirms one of our theories about what those ahglen were up to. Probably no more than what Kor has already discovered for himself, though."

"What?" I asked as I shifted positions, bringing my knees up and wrapping my arms around my legs.

Ben opened his mouth and then closed it. "It won't make any sense unless I keep going, sorry. But don't worry—you shouldn't feel that again, not with the ward around us."

"Then go ahead," I said, since it seemed like he was waiting for permission.

He nodded. "Some people wonder if the Devourer caused the famine in the first place. Its timing was just so perfect. But the Tree hasn't told us for sure, so it could be that it was just waiting for the right moment of weakness, caused by the draká's folly. It's that patient, after all—it isn't mortal, like we are. It can wait centuries if it needs to."

"What *is* it?" I asked, nearly in a whisper.

Ben's eyes were hard as he answered. He cast another glance at the ring of fire around us, and for a moment, the flames flickered higher. "The Devourer is...an enemy of sorts. Well, *the* enemy. The only true one in every sense. It's what its name implies: it's a force that consumes all life, leaving nothing in its place."

"When you say 'nothing.'..."

"Nothing," Ben said grimly. "Worlds consumed by the Devourer are only rock. I saw one once, in a vision from the Tree."

He shuddered. "It was not something I ever want to see again."

I swallowed. "So, it's a...*force* of some kind? That just...makes everything living vanish?"

"It's a hunger," Ben corrected seriously. "*The* hunger, the kind that only destroys, the kind that only gets hungrier the more it consumes. The Devourer. It's not just a force, either. It has a mind of some kind. It calculates. It waits when it needs to. Sometimes, it doesn't entirely consume its victim right away if it thinks it can use it to get more victims in the future. That's how it has gathered its army."

"Oh, *great*," I said under my breath. "Why am I not surprised it has an *army*?"

Ben's lips flickered with a humorless smile. "Looks like you encountered some of its more recent victims yesterday."

My jaw dropped. "The *ahglen*? I just thought those were a bunch of blood-thirsty...ogre...things."

"Unusually bloodthirsty, even for ahglen," Ben said. "Or perhaps unusually greedy, I should say. Even if they might kill an amón or a drakón if they get the chance, they rarely try to extract blood. They know that just paints a target of guilt on them from miles away. The Devourer must have consumed some of their life force, making them susceptible to its influence."

"But *why*?" I asked, flabbergasted. "Why would the Devourer want them to sacrifice *me*?"

"A very good question. One I'm hoping Kor and Yvera might have answers to by the time we're done."

"Yvera?" I realized I hadn't seen or heard her—either in human or draká-form—for some time, so I looked around the clearing and didn't see her any-where.

"She's following your trail," Ben explained. "You didn't emerge here, did you?"

"No," I said with a frown, looking around again. "It was in the jungle some-where...but I can't remember which direction."

"Wherever it was, that's where Yvera's gone. We'll want Kor to look at the spot too before we leave, just to be thorough."

He cast another glance at the sun. "But if we're going to have time for that, I'm going to need to speed this up, sorry."

"No, by all means," I said with a shudder. "Please fast forward on the dark, Devouring bits."

Ben laughed tightly. "Unfortunately, I'm just getting started. I already mentioned it has an army. Well, the only reason it needs one is because of the Trees. As long as a world's Tree remains healthy and strong, the Devourer can't enter Her world and consume its life."

"But what about the Devourer's army?" I asked.

"Exactly," Ben said, pleased at how I'd caught on. "The consumed—that's what we call still-living creatures under its sway—*can* enter a world with a Tree. That is where the Tree's children—in this case, the draká—come in. The draká were created not just to be stewards of Ythra but also to protect the Tree from the consumed—otherwise, all life on Ythra would have been doomed."

A shrill piping sound made both of us jump and look at the fire, where the kettle was cheerfully shrieking away.

"Sorry," Ben said with an abashed laugh as he took the kettle off the fire. With his other hand, he produced a mug and poured the contents of the kettle into it.

When he offered it to me, I relaxed again into a cross-legged position and reached out to take it from his hand without thinking—and then jerked my hand back with a hiss.

"What—oh, the heat," he said with a sigh. "Sorry."

"No worries," I said with a chuckle.

Still, he scowled to himself as he set the mug gingerly next to me. He produced another mug and poured the tea for himself, muttering something I couldn't hear.

As a distraction for him, I cast my mind back to what we had been discussing. "Did the draká know about all of this—the Devourer and everything?"

Ben nodded grimly as he set down the kettle. I tried not to stare as he raised his mug up to his lips and took a gulp—even with the liquid still steaming.

"They did," he said after a swallow. "But, in a way, they had known for *too* long. The Tree had warned them for ages that the Devourer was out there and that it would be keen to consume a race as full of energy as theirs. To the Devourer, Ythra was the ultimate feast, so they should have been on their guard. But like I said, the draká had become complacent. Greedy. Worst of all, they stopped listening to Her. So, first came famine. Then war. Then, when they had allowed the Tree to become weak through neglect, the Devourer could open its darkgates all over Ythra and send in its army to finish them. It nearly succeeded."

"What stopped it?" I asked quietly.

"Blood," Ben said, taking another sip. "Blood, freely given, gave the Tree the strength She needed to close the darkgates. It took seven of Her most faithful protectors sacrificing their lives, and many more died in the battle to defeat the consumed army at Her very roots. Even then, the draká weren't able to find and destroy them all. Once the Devourer has penetrated a world, it's nearly impossible to remove its influence. When the army is defeated, its creatures scatter and hide. To this day, we're still struggling to root them out of every world of ours it's infiltrated."

He grimaced. "In a way, the draká were lucky to be the way they were. Even if a Tree's world repels the initial invasion, the Devourer usually still wins through attrition. The very thing that made the draká such appealing targets also made them able to survive the first few years after. If only just. But when the dust settled, they knew they wouldn't last much longer."

"Why?"

"Two reasons," Ben said, taking another sip while holding up two fingers. "One, starvation. As I mentioned, draká needed to consume fresh meat. Famine and war had already made their herds scarce, and the full-world battle against the consumed hadn't helped. Even with the draká's drastically reduced numbers, there wasn't enough livestock left to sustain them.

"Two, fertility. There weren't enough draká left to defend themselves and the Tree from the remaining consumed. Draká lived for centuries, but they reproduced slowly—it would take lifetimes before they returned to the numbers they had before, much less had enough of them to be safe in their own world. Their victory against the Devourer was feeling hollow as they stared their extinction in the face."

"What did they do?"

"They did what they should have done in the beginning. All of them—all the ones who could be spared from guarding and herding, anyway—came to the Tree and asked what, if anything, could be done to ensure their survival. And She told them: they had to change."

"In what way?" I asked, propping my elbow on my knee and my head on my fist.

"In the most fundamental of ways," Ben answered, lowering his mug to his knee. "They needed to become something new, something not so dependent on meat, especially fresh meat. Something that could reproduce more quickly. Something that was even *more* powerful to drive back the consumed and hold the Devourer at bay. There was only one way they could do that: they needed the willing help of another Tree's children."

My eyes widened. "Humans."

"Yes," Ben said with a smile that was becoming rare in the seriousness of this conversation. "But humans were on another world, which meant the draká needed a gate to get there. The draká's first encounter with gates had been the Devourer's kind, so they were hesitant. But the Tree told them its gates were a subversion of the Creators' design. She could teach them how to create proper gates, ones the Devourer and its consumed could not use, but only on certain conditions. So the draká made the First Covenant."

Ben held up a finger with each rule he spoke. "First, to guard the gates as they guard the Tree. Second, to only use the gates to go where the Tree permitted. Third, to never take whatever lay beyond the gates by force, only by trade or gift. And fourth, to never claim a world with another Tree's children as their own."

"Sounds pretty smart of the Tree to me," I mused, thinking of humanity's poor track record with peaceful exploration.

"That's what the Tree is—the wisest being we know of, other than the Creators. And They let Her deal with us."

I didn't know how to feel about that. So far—having accepted the existence of dragons and magic and monsters by necessity—I'd also accepted Ben's word that there *was* a Tree of Flame. He sounded so certain, I got the impression he had seen Her for himself. However, any other cosmic entity was a mental stretch I wasn't quite ready to make. I wasn't going to dispute it or disrespect his belief, but neither was I going to touch on the subject until I'd had longer to grasp the *tangible* realities around me.

"So the draká promised to abide by those rules," I prompted.

"They did," Ben confirmed. "And the Tree showed them how to build the first sungate. The one that would take them to Earth."

He sighed. "It wasn't easy for them. To dedicate the draká and resources to building a gate was a sacrifice. An even greater one was the further lives it took to give it power. But they had no other choice if they wanted their race—and their world—to survive. Then the gate was open, and the Tree's chosen Seven went through."

"You're *just* at the Seven?" Kor said in amusement as he strolled back over to us. "Better hurry this up, Ben, or we'll be here past dark. And you know what that means."

He said the last words in a sing-song tone.

"I'm trying." Ben rolled his eyes and took a sip from his mug. "It's not like you would have done any better to summarize our *entire history*."

"I offered," Kor told me innocently. "He said no. Can you believe it?"

"Because *you* would have had her here until the *next* night," Ben said with a sigh.

"True enough," Kor said with a chuckle as he reached us—stepping over the line of golden flame with perfect unconcern. I winced, but his boots didn't show so much as a scorch mark. Maybe the flames were harmless after all.

Not that I—as an unproven human—was about to test that.

Kor picked up the kettle. "Ah, tsha. That's so *you*. Any left?"

Ben shrugged. "Maybe. Now be quiet and let me finish. Better yet—go find Yvera."

"Sure," Kor said with a huff as he set down the kettle. "Send me into the jungle by myself after the prickly arkukan. I see how it is."

"You'll he fine," Ben said. "If it were that dangerous right now, Yvera wouldn't have left me with just you for protection."

Kor grinned. "Ouch. Thanks for the jab *and* your concern."

"Seriously, Kor," Ben said with a pleading look. "Will you please help Yvera find the spot where Sarah emerged, if she hasn't already, and take a look at it? You know you're way better at analyzing magical traces than me, and you'll save us that much time."

"Fine, fine," Kor said with a flippant wave as he strode off again. Once again, he walked straight through the flames with no visible sign of pain or damage.

He called over his shoulder, "Just so you know, Sarah, I'm only doing this because Ben asked nicely. *Not* because I'm susceptible to flattery."

Ben snorted into his mug.

"He is, isn't he?" I whispered with a grin.

Ben flashed an answering grin back at me. *Completely. Works every time. Try it next time he's annoying you.*

"I can *feel* you talking about me, you know!" Kor shouted from across the clearing. "It had better be wonderful, complimentary things about my brilliance and selflessness!"

Ben and I held it in for as long as we could. But as soon as Kor disappeared into the trees, we burst out laughing—hard and long enough that I nearly spilled the mug sitting next to me, and Ben sloshed a few drops of his tea onto himself.

"Oh, that felt good," Ben said when he got his breath back.

"Been a while?" I asked sympathetically.

"You have no idea," Ben said, rubbing his eyes with his free hand.

Heart clenching in sympathy, I asked, "What's been the problem?"

"I'm getting to that," he said with a sigh. "Speaking of which, Kor has a point. I'd better hurry if we're going to be out of here before dark. I know you don't understand why we need to yet, but just trust me when I say that it's important."

"So I've gathered," I said. I tested my mug, discovered it was cool enough, and rested it on my knee. "So, you were saying about the...Seven?"

"Ah, yes, the Seven," Ben said, sipping his tea again. "To make a *very* long story short, the Seven representatives encountered a group of humans, got the humans to stop running away or trying to kill them—"

Ben's eyes flicked to mine with a rueful smile, no doubt thinking about my Earth legends. "—and after a long time of explaining and negotiating, the humans agreed to help."

He sighed. "It was a *lot* more complicated and painful than I just made it sound. There are *volumes* written about that time alone. It's a good thing Kor isn't here, or he would have cried."

I chuckled. "I'll bet."

"Anyway, it happened—they came to an agreement. Problem was, the humans didn't know Earth even *had* a Tree, let alone where it was. For whatever reason, their relationship with their Tree had never been as close as the draká's had been."

He glanced at me. "I guess not much has changed."

I just shrugged ruefully.

He sighed again. "The first task for the humans and draká to tackle together was to find Her. So they did—in a vast and frozen land across the sea. Then, once they found the Tree of Ice, the Seven draká and seven humans made the Second Covenant—this time, together."

"What were the terms this time?"

"We...don't know," Ben said. "It was ancient magic, we think. It was the *first* true magic. What we do know is the result: at the end, the seven humans and the seven draká became something new: fourteen drakón."

"Dragon...humans," I breathed.

"Yes," Ben agreed. "Fourteen beings able to be in an amá or a draká state. Except neither state was what it had been before. The transformation of the Second Covenant allowed them to absorb the fourteen flamehearts the Tree of Flame had sent with them. Now, the draká no longer craved meat—or any food at all. As long as they had sunlight, or barring that, any other source of light or warmth, the flameheart inside them could give them the energy they needed."

"*That's* why you all like warm things so much," I said in satisfaction. It felt *good* to figure the rules out.

"Exactly," Ben said with a smile. "Especially at night, when we can't rely on the sun. And we can change into a human and eat a variety of foods to gain energy instead, and because this form is so much smaller, we need far less food than a draká would to sustain ourselves through the night."

"And that's why you're so anxious to do things during the daytime, when you have enough energy."

"That's a big part of it, yes."

"You said both states were changed," I said. "How was the human state different?"

"Lots of ways, some of which you've discovered already," Ben said. "They all stem from one monumental change: amá weren't magical creatures, in the sense that they didn't draw on the power of the Tree to supplement their life force as the draká had to. Even the draká had never had enough energy to spare for anything other than sustaining life. But when they could become amá, all the energy of a draká compacted in the efficient form of an amá meant there was power to spare. For the first time for either race, the drakón could work magic."

"Wait," I gasped. "The only reason you can do magic is because you can become human?"

"Yep," Ben said with a crooked smile. "In fact, most of us can't do so much as light a candle while we're in drakáform. It requires all the energy we have just to *exist* that way. Even I struggle to do anything more basic than that. Kor is one of the best of us at it, and part of the reason is his smaller size."

"The smaller you are, the more powerful you are?" I asked eagerly.

He grimaced. "It's not...as simple as that. The more powerful you are, the bigger you become—because that means you have more energy to grow to and sustain a larger drakáform. The other factor in how much we can do in either form is how...*efficient* our bodies are in using the reserves we have. Someone Kor's size typically has smaller reserves than, say, Yvera, but Kor is efficient in how he uses his reserve, so he can do more magic either in draká- or amáform than she can."

"I suppose that makes sense," I said. "What about you?"

"Me?" Ben asked self-consciously, tapping the side of his mug with one finger.

"I know I haven't seen many drakón yet, but you're pretty much bigger than anyone I have. What does that say about your capacity and efficiency?"

"Efficiency is learned," Ben said, eyes flicking away from me. "Like...training to run further and faster. The more you work at it, the better you are. Kor is as good as he is because he's trained harder than pretty much anyone at using magic. Plus—now, don't tell him I said this, or he'll never let me forget it—he's a torched genius. He really is. His memory, combined with his ability to process and manage so much at once...."

Ben shrugged. "I don't have the brain he has for it, nor have I dedicated the effort he has, so I won't ever match him for mastery. I'm better than Yvera, though, if you really need some kind of measure...."

He winced. "Don't tell her I said that, either."

"I bet Yvera has spent her time on other skills," I said reasonably.

"Exactly," Ben agreed hastily. "She has. She's not lazy. She's just not as interested in the arcane...unless it involves killing things."

I chuckled. "What about your capacity? I'm just trying to get a full sense of the rules here."

"I'm not exactly the typical example," Ben said ruefully.

"Why's that?"

"I was getting to that part. If you'll let me continue...?" he asked with a crooked grin.

"Oh, right," I said sheepishly. "Where were we?"

He thought for a moment. "Right after the Second Covenant?"

"Oh, yeah."

Ben took one last swig of his tea and set the mug on the ground with a sigh. "So, now the drakón could do magic. That was good, because they only had so many of them, so sacrificing themselves for anything else wouldn't have been ideal. The group built another gate and brought through the now-drakón humans and their entire clan, and for the first time, humans and draká began living together on Ythra.

"It was a difficult but exciting time. Most of the humans became drakón, but it happened gradually for the rest of them, as the Tree of Flame chose a draká here and a human there as She saw fit. Even the ones who remained human for the rest of their lives were invaluable. The humans had an ingenuity and dexterity that the draká lacked, and combining those skills with the draká's size and strength and the drakón's magic, Ythra recovered quickly enough to save the draká.

"A couple of centuries passed, mostly peacefully. I'm not saying everything was perfect. The two—now basically three—races had a lot of work to do to understand each other, get along, and explore their new abilities. There were disagreements and some fights and tragedy, but to a large extent, the two civilizations merged and then thrived.

"It wasn't long before the growing population became too much for Ythra alone, so the Tree guided the dramá to worlds that didn't have a Tree or Tree's children and allowed each of the seven clans to settle their own world one by one."

"Seven clans?"

"Oh, right, sorry," Ben said, rubbing his forehead. "That's...important."

He took a deep breath. "So, the Tree selected each of the original Seven draká for their individual qualities. Those qualities in turn influenced or enhanced their transformation into drakón, as did the humans that paired with them for the Covenant. The first human and draká became co-leaders of their clan, and every other draká or human who wished to become drakón pledged themselves to one of those seven clans. From then on, the drakón took on the same characteristics as the clan they'd joined."

"What characteristics? Can you give me an example?"

"At the most superficial level: color," Ben said with a rueful smile. "Surely you've noticed our unusual...vibrancy."

"Oh, so the color of your hair, your eyes—that shows your clan?" I asked excitedly.

"Yes: gold, violet, blue, scarlet—you get the idea. Yvera, the violet: she's Battleblood. Kor, blue: Starkissed. Svyer, green: Peacegrowth."

"And you?" I prompted.

"Sunfilled," Ben said ruefully, holding up some of his golden hair. "But we're not supposed to focus on the colors. They're only skin deep. The qualities can be over-stereotyped, too. Scholars debate how much is inherent, how much is socialized, and so on. Especially when the clans separated into their own worlds, it became much more muddled which was which. On the other hand, it's hard to argue with the fact that some types of magic and some skills just seem to come *easier* to one clan than the other. Peacegrowth has the best healers: that's just a fact. Battlebloods are larger than pretty much anyone except Sunfilleds, which inclines them to be the best warriors, and so on. The Tree Herself says it's meant to be that way: that it's supposed to encourage us to rely on and work with each other to be stronger than we can be apart."

"Does it work?"

Ben became quiet for a moment, looking at the ground. "It has. With...one tragic exception."

He sighed and ran his hand through his hair. When his eyes flicked up to mine, they once again had that strange look of...nervousness. "That's one of the most important things I have to discuss with you, but also the hardest."

"Oh?" I prompted. My mind then made the intuitive leap. "Is this...about what you need my help with? The *real* conflict between humans and drag-ons?"

His lips pressed into a thin line before he nodded. "Yes, it does. It happened only a couple of generations after the first drakón. By that point, there were no more humans, but there were plenty of amón—descendants of drakón who didn't become drakón themselves. Amón...began to feel as if they were treated less favorably than drakón. I won't go into all the reasons, but they had good cause to feel that way. And the clan that had the most amón by far was the Moontouched."

Ben's fingers plucked absently at the moss at his feet, and he didn't meet my gaze. "The Moontouched as a whole, even the drakón among them, held the least sway at Crownhold. Their motions were often dismissed, their votes counted for little; their people struggled for positions in government, or for lands and holds of their own.

"The Tree tried to intervene. She declared the Moontouched should be the next to receive their own world, but the rest of the clans argued it should be Brightflare's, who were causing trouble to become the next. Even the Queen at the time sided with Brightflare against Moontouched, citing the need for peace. The final blow was when the Moontouched Lord died during the dispute and the Crownsmeet rejected his Heir because she was amón. When she went to Crownhold to defend her claim, she...she was killed."

Ben squeezed his eyes shut and clenched his jaw; his hands gripped his thighs until the knuckles went white. I felt a pang for him. He had nothing to do with this tragedy, one that had happened centuries ago, and yet he looked as if he felt personally responsible.

Impulsively, I touched the back of his hand. He started, and his eyes flicked open to meet mine in surprise. I smiled softly. I didn't know what he needed from me, but I tried to show that I understood, that I didn't blame him, and that neither should he.

He let out a breath, and his muscles relaxed. To my surprise, he turned his hand over slowly and gave mine an answering pressure of wordless thanks. Then he let go and gently pulled his hand back, so I withdrew mine.

"We still don't know who did it or why," Ben said heavily. "Doesn't matter—it should *never* have happened. Even though the thought that any of us could do such a thing is sickening enough, the Queen should have prevented it. But...I can also see why she was unprepared to. Murder, by one of our own, not a consumed, at such a high level.... It had never happened before and never has since. Her assassination sent a shockwave through the fabric of their society.

"Before the other clans could collect themselves and respond, the drakón mate of the murdered Moontouched Lady declared the clans were no longer worthy of their association. He gathered the Moontouched and requested that the Tree grant them leave to return to Earth, the one world where they could belong and be safe. The Tree granted his request. Almost before the rest of the clans knew what was happening, they were gone. And when they left, the original gate to Earth fell to pieces."

"Why?"

Ben stared into the trees. "Unbeknown to the other clans, the Lady Moontouched's mate made a second request to the Tree, this one in secret: that, for their safety, She allow them to destroy the gate on Earth once they were on the other side. So She did, and as a final token, She destroyed the original sungate Herself. That was how seriously the clans had wronged their Moontouched kin—the Tree allowed them to cut themselves off. The Seven Clans were no more. And so, at least partially, was the Second Covenant."

"What?" I asked with a start.

Ben glanced around, but on seeing the clearing was still empty except for us, he looked back at me, golden eyes intense. The circle of flames around us roared higher than ever before, perhaps to three feet.

"I have to admit, I had another reason to get both Kor and Yvera out of the way," Ben said grimly. "What I am about to tell you, you must swear to never speak of to another soul. *Not* even to my wings. Avva—the King—has authorized me to tell you, but you alone."

I stared at him. "Why *me*? If not even Kor...."

"Avva has his reasons about Kor," Ben said wearily. "We both trust him, but Kor—as you've discovered for yourself—is a force to be reckoned with. Let's just say that he can be a bit *too* proactive as just an Heir's leftwing. As for Yvera, well...."

"I get why with Yvera," I said with a smile.

Ben gave a tense chuckle as he rubbed the back of his neck. "Seeing as you've hardly interacted with her so far, that's saying something."

"But why *me*? Why has the King said you could tell *me*, if you can't even tell them?"

"Because you're perhaps the only one who can do anything *about* what's wrong," Ben said. I was so stunned I nearly didn't notice how his hands were clenching his knees again.

"Me?" I said, putting my hand on my chest. "You don't even know me. Not really. I haven't even told you my last name, let alone where I'm from—specifically—or what role I have in Earth's society, and I'm telling you, it's nowhere and nothing. I'm barely a legal adult who just graduated high school a few months ago. I'm a nobody. I get overlooked even in my family."

"None of that matters!" Ben exclaimed. When I winced back from the force of his words, he flinched in turn and put his head in his hands. "Torch it."

He breathed deeply for a few moments and then lifted his head. His expression when he looked at me again was controlled. "Sorry. I know I'm doing an awful job at explaining all of this. But...I'm also serious. None of those things you said or could say about yourself matter. Not so much as the fact that you are *the first human* to set foot on this planet *ever* and the first in the Six Realms—in a *thousand years*. I just explained this to you, Sarah—the original gate is destroyed. It's a ruin right now, weathered stone blocks left in a heap. The runes are so faded, they're almost gone. Any hope we had of travel to or from Earth was gone...until yesterday. Until you."

He let that sink in, gold eyes burning. "Now. What do you think that says about you?"

I swallowed, heart pounding. My reflex answer was *nothing*. Nothing at all. I just fell through a magical ice hole in my neighborhood creek and somehow ended up *here*.

Something, though, made me push aside that reflex response and that whisper of doubt. Maybe it was the distressed intensity of Ben's gaze, the tightness in his whole body, muscles all gone rigid. All his tells were adding up to one thing for me: He cared deeply about this, at a forceful and personal level, and he was trying hard not to let that desperation show.

Maybe it was that desperation that made me silence my denial to look deeper inside of myself for something, anything, to tell him that wouldn't crush him with disappointment.

Though the denial was gone, I still didn't have an answer for him. My mind was drawing one endless blank. But at least it was a listening one.

"I don't know," I said quietly. "What *does* it say about me?"

"The Tree of Flame *wants* you here," Ben responded just as quietly but with a much greater intensity. "For that matter, *your* Tree, the Tree of Ice, must want you here, too. Because our Tree of Flame would not have taken you—a human, one of Ice's full children—without Her Sister's permission."

"They can...talk to each other?" I said with a hard swallow. "Even with the gate...."

"All Trees can speak to each other. At all times, across any distance of the universe. Somehow, all of Them are connected. Maybe They're not even different Trees at all, just different aspects of—"

Ben cut off and looked sharply over his shoulder at the tree line behind him. I glanced more slowly, thinking that it must be Kor and Yvera returning and catching us in the middle of this secretive discussion.

There was no one there.

"Sarah," Ben said, a different intensity in his voice now. "Get on my back."

"Excuse me?"

He turned around toward the jungle and rolled onto his knees in the same motion, offering his back to me. This time when he spoke, it was in his mental voice, and the force of it was like the shocking snap of a rubber band across my consciousness. *I have to change—now—and I don't want to leave you defenseless on the ground when I do.*

"Defense...." Fortunately, my brain was faster than my mouth, because before I was even finished with the word, I was forgetting the bizarre awkwardness of Ben's request and stumbling to my feet.

Not a second too soon, because as I was lunging for him, I caught a glimpse of the reason for all of this.

Tall—as tall as Ben at least, even with legs bent backward midway down like a beast's. Which made sense, because, despite the whole upright thing going on, that's what they looked like: shaggy, dark fur; long, thick arms with wickedly gleaming claws; gnarled manes rising to canine heads; lips pulled back into snarls revealing yellowed teeth; bloodshot eyes that stared at us with ferocious hunger.

I didn't know what Ben called them, but I knew what they would be in my world.

My worst nightmare.

Werewolves.

Chapter Ten

WORSE

Koriben

Krathen, I cursed. Only a few were visible through the tree cover, but it was the smell that had alerted me first: a now overwhelming stench of blood and rotten meat that warned of more.

Besides, krathen hunted as a pack. See one, and you were pretty much guaranteed to be dealing with them all.

This close to sunset, too, I thought. *Lovely.*

Though I was a little surprised they hadn't waited even longer. Maybe they'd tried, but their bloodlust had overcome them, and they'd come close enough to alert me. Once I was visibly on my guard, they knew they had to close in or retreat.

Only a part of my mind was spared for speculation, though. About a fourth. Half of the remainder was watching the enemies emerge, calculating how many seconds it would take them to reach us if they charged. (Too few.) The rest of my mind and body was acutely aware of the moment Sarah scrambled onto my back and wrapped her arms around my neck.

Hold tight, I told her.

She squeezed my throat in a death grip. I could only hope that would be enough. I didn't worry her by saying that this maneuver wasn't recommended for amón to do with drakón as large as I could become, so I hadn't practiced it since I was a fifteen summerling.

But she risked *more* by staying on the ground. I didn't think it was a coincidence there was a pack of krathen here, now, even after a hunt had gone through these woods to purge the ahglen. Especially krathen: fast where the ahglen had been slow, cunning where the ahglen had been stupid. Even if I always stayed over her, they could dart under me and go for her before I could stop them, and one bite was almost certainly an excruciating death for an amón.

Let alone an amá.

I didn't know she was their objective for sure. They could have smelled *me* on the wind and closed in for some payback. But krathen were usually more sly and self-preserving than to attack me head on, even while I was on my own. However much pain they might cause me, now that I was on my guard, they knew they had little chance of *killing* me.

Which told me they were desperate for Sarah's flesh. Or driven by something even worse.

Either way, my gut told me they were here for *her*.

The frontrunners of the pack, knowing what was coming once Sarah was on my back, dropped to all fours and charged. Then it was a race of seconds as I began one of the fastest and yet most careful transformations of my life.

It was *painful*.

Normal shifts feel like stretching. Hurried ones make you achy during and tired after. This one made my joints pop, my muscles scream, and my bones spear through flesh that felt like it was barely growing fast enough to cover them. A roar of agony was breaking through my maws before they were even fully formed, and by the end, flames were licking my teeth like saliva.

I managed—just. The second the first krathen got close enough to leap for my throat, I was stable enough to bat it aside with enough force to send it into a tree with a satisfying *crack*.

Two point five seconds, I thought cheerfully to distract myself from the bone-deep ache still echoing through me.

Too bad Kor hadn't been here to see me beat his record.

Speaking of Kor, though....

Yvera, Kor, I broadcasted as far as my inner voice could carry. *If you can hear me, get back here,* now. *We've got krathen.*

I was assuming they were fine, of course, but that assumption was almost immediately confirmed by Kor's spluttered *What—?*

Which was drowned out by Yvera's flat, businesslike response. *Coming. How many?*

A full pack, I'd say.

It wasn't a pleasant sight. Krathen packs worked as a seamless whole, and this one knew how to fight a drakón. Mere seconds after the first had launched itself at me—no doubt as a sacrificial distraction—the rest had surrounded me and begun darting in, trying to get to my most vulnerable point: my wings.

They'd already effectively grounded me. There were too many that were too close for me to risk opening my wings to take off: most of them would launch themselves at the delicate membranes, and at least a few would reach them—ripping as many great, excruciating gashes as they could with their infected claws. The pain would be distracting, and the wounds would need to be healed within the deken to avoid an illness that was debilitating for even a drakón. I'd had krathenis once. It was the worst few days of my life, and I did *not* want to experience that again.

Not to mention I *really* didn't have the time for that kind of bedridden nonsense right now.

As far as Sarah's immediate safety was concerned, the tears in my wings would be the true detriment. Drakáflight involved a good deal of magic to be even feasible in the first place, especially for a drakón of my size; tear up the primary non-magical aid that I had to get into the air and remain aloft, and flight would become next to impossible for me.

So even though my scales, my size, and the height of my folded wings above the ground were all keeping Sarah and me somewhat protected for the moment, this wasn't a fight I wanted to prolong.

Yvera understood that immediately.

Sarah? she demanded. I could feel her inner voice getting closer, even in that one word. I guessed she'd forgone the time-consuming and potentially damaging effort to get aloft through the thick tree cover and was sprinting toward me on foot. Kor was no doubt making his way to me as well, but he wasn't as fast and fit a runner as she was.

My back, I answered her tersely as I spun to bowl over a whole cluster of the beasts with my tail and risked one spit of fire at another jumper.

Miraculously, I could feel Sarah was indeed on my back, and even better, lodged between a couple of my mid-sized spines somewhere around my shoulders: spines large enough to keep her at least somewhat secure between them but small enough for her to wrap her arms around. The spot was near where Yvera had put her for our flight to Elspeth Hold. How I'd managed *that* near-ideal placement while changing so rapidly, only the Flame knew.

I prayed she was holding on tight. This wasn't the time for the gentle, drawn-out movements I'd tried so hard to manage the other two times she'd been on my back. This was battle, and that required all the flexibility and power I could muster while grounded like this.

But if I knocked her off.... If she fell...from that height....

A krathen—paler than usual, an ashy gray—took advantage of my worried distraction to launch itself at one of my raised hands and clamp its jaws around the more vulnerable stretch of scaly skin between my fingers and my thumb. I slammed my hand down with a roar, pulverizing it into the dirt. From the snaps and fluids I could feel beneath my hand—not to mention the horrific stench that increased three-fold—I knew I'd killed it. But its sacrifice had not been in vain: I felt a telltale sting where its teeth had latched on.

Torch it, that thing got to my blood, I thought with a curse. If I didn't want to be bedridden for the next few days, I was going to have to look at that wound, and soon.

Don't think about Sarah, I told myself. *You've done the best you can for her for now. Now it's up to her to hold on and to you to end this.*

Me—or Yvera.

Because in that moment, I heard a roar as familiar as my own.

Violet fury burst into the clearing as Yvera transformed in a flying leap. Though the krathen had been reckless with bloodlust not a second before, more than one of them whimpered as my rightwing descended. Battlebloods were feared by all consumed across the Six Realms for good reason, but since these krathen could not have mistaken who *I* was, they no doubt knew who this violet draká must be and that Yvera was no ordinary Battleblood.

Violet fire was already spewing in great gusts from her mouth, and in seconds it was everywhere around me—far more widespread, in fact, than I liked to see with Sarah so close to the heat and smoke. There was a reason I hadn't risked much fire myself until now.

At least it provided the distraction Yvera had intended it to. The krathen that weren't already charcoal were scattering from me, giving me the safe space I needed to snap open my wings and launch into the air with one powerful leap.

Within moments, I had us safely above the fight and flames, beating my wings powerfully to put us into a slow, upward spiral around the clearing. I felt a twinge of guilt at just leaving Yvera to clean up the krathen, but she was more than capable of it, especially now that any vulnerable element was out of the way.

Besides, she'd intended me to go; even if the circle of fire around me hadn't been a clear enough sign, I had the evidence of countless experiences to go on. She'd tried to push me back from many a fight before, to no avail, so she was probably relieved I'd done what she wanted for once. Hellwinds, she was probably *enjoying* herself right now. She'd seen far too little action lately, and now all the justified destruction was hers for the unleashing. I could feel her satisfaction on the waves of heat rising from the torched clearing.

Sometimes...just sometimes, mind you...my best friend worried me. Just a little.

I had a more prominent concern in my head right now. As soon as we were in the clear, I asked Sarah anxiously, *Are you alright?*

Then I remembered she couldn't answer me. She didn't even have the signal flags right now since I hadn't been able to get out her saddle as I changed.

I cursed myself and focused as hard as I could on feeling that tiny presence clinging to my back, since until I leveled out, craning my head to look back at her might unbalance me. *I'm sorry, I forgot. You can't tell me. I really, really hope you are alright, though. If you're not, just hold on as long as you can. I'm looking for a safe place to land.*

That would be a trickier proposition than I made it sound. The tree cover in these parts of Athalin was notoriously thick, with the clearing being one of the few exceptions large enough for safe take-off and landing within sight. It was one reason consumed prospered more than they should here: finding and eliminating them all was impossible.

The most cutthroat solution was to just raze the whole jungle to the ground, and it had been proposed many times before—usually by the ever-pragmatic Brightflares. Each time, Crown biologists, the entire Peacegrowth Clan, and the Monarch all shut the motion down: as dangerous as the cover the Athalin trees provided the consumed was, the greater evil would be to destroy them all for what was our fault, not the trees'—and such extreme measures would cut us off from all the resources and reagents the jungle provided us, besides. The lesson we'd learned from Moontouched had been a hard but a thorough one: you don't know what you've lost until it is gone forever.

The only acceptable solution we had found so far was to cede most of the territory to the consumed, aside from the occasional heavily fortified hold full of Peacegrowth gatherers, Brightflare collectors, and enough Battleblood protectors to make the consumed think thrice before attacking.

It looked like there was nothing for it: I would have to fly far from the clearing, as quickly as I could while still being gentle for Sarah's sake. Yvera would hopefully be satisfied enough with her fight to forgive me for abandoning her again; when I told her that I had to find a place to heal myself, that might soothe away the last of her irritation.

This way, a familiar voice said.

Kor rose into my view, smaller wings beating hard to catch up to me. Once he saw he had my attention, he swerved to the south, and I banked to follow.

There's a mesa about a quarter of a deken from here if we fly fast, Kor explained. *We can wait there for Yvera the Ferocious to finish up. And maybe spend the night, at this rate. Did any of them get a bite in?*

One, I think, I grumbled, feeling the growing sting in my left hand as it was tucked in against my underside.

I'll handle it, Kor assured me. *I've got some spare, and we'll want you and Yvera to save yourselves for the long night ahead.*

Thanks, I said, grim at the thought of spending the night in the open. Hopefully it wouldn't come to that. But...if our bad luck continued, it probably would, and it would be better to stay on the mesa, which would offer us at least *some* protection, than to venture out too late to make it to the next gate or hold before sunset and be stranded in the middle of the jungle.

Yvera, I was bitten, so we're going to find somewhere to land so Kor can take a look.

The only response I got from her was, predictably, a string of curses. I resigned myself to the inevitable lecture that was coming while Kor quickly described to her how to find us before we got out of range.

As soon as he was done, I asked him, *How does Sarah look to you?*

Kor let me pull ahead for a moment so he could take a closer look. Then I slowed to let him take the lead again. Kor clearly remembered the minutiae of the local terrain better than I did—no surprise there; that drakón had the memory of stone—so it would be better if I followed him right then, as weird as it felt to be at *his* wing.

Tense. Pale. But she doesn't look hurt, Kor said frankly. *She's holding on well enough. Don't do any pinwheels, and she'll be fine until we get there.*

I let out a deep enough sigh that the faintest trace of smoke blew behind me on the wind. *Good.*

I was surprised at how much tension Kor's favorable report released in me. Sure, we needed Sarah alive and in one piece, but most injuries she could have incurred in that brief time we could have healed quickly and easily—no permanent damage done. It made sense for me to not want her to be upset or frightened, both because that was the right thing to feel and because we needed her to help us. But there was an added dimension to my relief that had nothing to do with those logical things, and that was...troubling.

I was still wrestling with what that meant—and fighting my urge to crane my long neck to check on her myself—when we reached the mesa.

It was a small one—hardly more than a butte at the top. But its towering height—hundreds of feet high—and sheer cliffs on every side were a wondrous sight to behold.

Kor, you are a torched miracle, I breathed.

I know, Kor said smugly. *But feel free to keep saying so. Preferably in Yvera's hearing.*

If we're undisturbed the entire night, I will, I promised fervently.

Now, I can't promise that, Kor said, voice becoming serious again. *There's still the risk of flyers, after all.*

Or a few climbers, I agreed. But only a few, from the look of those blessedly high, sheer sides.

A few, Kor allowed, echoing my thoughts.

Landing on something this high was so easy, a hatchling could have done it. It was just an instinctual adjustment of height as I approached, an easy glide over the lip of the cliff and the first hundred erds of flat stone, and a few precise wing flaps to bring myself to as gentle a stop as I could manage. I crouched as my four legs touched down to absorb as much of the impact of landing as possible, and that was that.

We made it, I told Sarah reassuringly as I straightened. Stating the obvious, but I was becoming unreasonably anxious again with the long silence between us. I still felt her small presence on my back, and I'd seen Kor look back at her to check on her, so he would have told me if her state had changed. Probably. If he thought the news wouldn't distress or distract me. So....

I realized why a bit of tension had lingered and built again: until I could get a good look at her with my own eyes, and *she* could tell me she was alright, I wouldn't be able to believe it.

Sarah didn't respond, even though now, without the wind interference, I could probably have heard her if she'd spoken at a decent volume, but she probably didn't know that. Still, I waited with hopefully concealed impatience as Kor came to my side and offered his drakáhand to her as he had before.

It's alright, Sarah, he said with unusual gentleness. *You're safe now.*

Sarah said something, but it sounded like hardly more than a whisper, so I didn't catch whatever it was.

Werewolf? Kor said in confusion. *What's that?*

She spoke again, louder, but still not loud enough for me to hear. Torch the hearing of a draká! Our sense of smell in this form was so far beyond an amón's range it was incredible, but our hearing...left a lot to be desired. There was a reason we relied so much on our inner voices.

Oh, the krathen, Kor said, back to that gentle tone. If I'd heard him use it before this moment, I couldn't remember when, but I blessed him for it. *I told you, you're safe now. They're elden away from us, they can't scale cliffs like these, and Yvera's probably slaughtered or torched any of them stupid enough to not run away by now.*

I inwardly winced, wishing Kor had left out the last bit if Sarah was in such a state of shock. Then again, maybe the graphic imagery helped stir her into motion, because a second or two later, I felt a shifting on my back. I held myself as still as possible, which unfortunately meant not moving my neck to get a look at her, for as long as it took for her to clamber over me to Kor's hand.

At one point, she must have slipped, because I heard her sudden shriek, saw Kor move swiftly, and heard him quickly say, *I've got you, I've got you. It's alright.*

I spun to see what the matter was, flameheart throbbing more rapidly for a moment. Whatever had happened, it was over, and Kor was right: she was semi-collapsed but secure in his dark blue, scaled hand as he slowly lowered it to the ground. Nonetheless, I changed back into amáform as quickly as was painless and energy-efficient to do so and began striding over to her the moment I was stable.

She turned to me as soon as she slid off Kor's hand. I got one good look at her face—skin unusually pale and dark brown eyes wide—before she started running, and to my shock, she didn't stop until she crashed into me, throwing her arms around me in what was probably the tightest grip she could manage. I tentatively put my own arms around her small, fragile, trembling body.

This was a bad idea for so many reasons, but if it was what she needed right now…I couldn't find it in me to push her away. Besides, Svyer's warning from just a few deken ago still echoed in my ears.

"Are you alright?" Sarah gasped out the words before I could say the same.

She was asking *me*?

"Fine," I said with a tired chuckle.

Now that I could see her—and, unexpectedly, hold her—for myself, I could feel my adrenaline and energy crash right around the corner. Plus, there was my torched hand, tingling warningly. The bite hadn't been healed by the transformation back, as typical injuries were, but I hadn't expected it to. Wounds infected by consumed generally required purposeful, directed healing. The stinging was almost to my elbow now.…

"What about you?" I asked, using the excuse of looking at her to push her gently away from me. Her cheeks had some color back, so perhaps the hug had done some good.

Her color increased under my scrutiny. "Fine," she said, echoing my one-word reply.

"Sarah," I said sternly, letting my hands linger on her shoulders. "If you were the slightest bit hurt, *tell me*. Did you inhale any smoke? Did any of them get near you? Did any of my scales or spines cut or bruise you? Did you get hurt in your fall just now?"

At the growing mutinous expression on her face, I sighed. "Sarah, I have to know these things. You know we can't take any chances with you."

"I know," she said, and now the color in her cheeks took on an irritated flush. "I'm *fine*, like I said. Just…shaken. Besides, I wasn't the one facing down an entire pack of *werewolves* to protect one useless human."

I ignored her strange terminology for the time being. If she had those creatures on Earth, then it would make sense for her to have her own word for them. Though the presence of that race of consumed among *her* kind did not bode well.

There was one other thing she'd said that needed to be addressed much more urgently.

"You're not useless," I said with more force than I'd intended.

"What was *one* thing that I could have done to help you, huh?" she shot back. "*One.* I just...I just.... All I could do was just *sit* there while they *surrounded* and *attacked* you, again and again and...."

Her breathing hitched, and her eyes shone at the corners in the light of the lowering sun. A second later, she ducked in to wrap her arms around me again.

For the first time, I caught a glimpse of what that fight might have looked like to her. If she knew those creatures from Earth, and if the last of her world's drakón protectors were long gone, the krathen must have been a monster of devastating lethality in her eyes, and I had never once bothered to reassure her that *I* was never in any true peril, especially with my rightwing nearby to give us a simple escape. I had been so focused on protecting *her*—the only one of us who *could* have been seriously hurt in that fight—that I hadn't thought to tell her until it was over that everything and every*one* would be alright in the end.

I had assumed that she knew what the rules of my world were, that I was at far less risk than she was. Wrongly. I had good reason to know better by now, and yet that's what I had done. Would I *ever* stop messing up this badly with her?

"You could have *died*," she said, at least partly confirming my suspicions. "Died—protecting *me*."

"Hardly," I said with a tense laugh, trying to hide how shaken I was inside by my latest failure. "I'm sorry I didn't make this clear before: you were the only one I was worried about, Sarah. It would take a lot more than just one pack of krathen to kill *me*."

Kor's voice approached us, restored to a more regular drawl. "Though he *is* going to be in quite a lot of pain if you don't let me get a look at him, Sarah. Because that bite was.... Oh, how long ago now, Ben?"

"What?" Sarah gasped, pulling back.

I felt an unwarranted flash of irritation at Kor for making her do that. Then again, when she looked me up and down, when her eyes fell on the bite mark on my left hand—nicely red and inflamed now—and her expressive eyes widened in fear, I decided that the irritation was warranted after all.

There was no need to worry her like that, I snapped silently at Kor with a quick glare. I caught just the beginning of his smirk as I looked back at Sarah.

She grabbed my hand. "You said you were fine!"

The gentleness of her touch contrasted with the anger in her expression. For some strange reason, she looked as furious as only I would have had the right to be if she'd concealed the same type of thing from me. My chest felt too tight for my flameheart.

"I am. Or will be, just as soon as Kor takes care of it."

"But a *werewolf* just *bit* you," she cried, eyes still wide with anxiousness as she examined the bite.

"Yes," I said with a sigh, reminding myself that she wouldn't know the difference. "But I'm a *drakón*. The bite is dangerous for an amón if left untreated but only painful for a drakón, and healable for both if treated in time."

I didn't mention that the "time" allotted for being able to heal an amón was counted in moments versus the dek for a drakón. If my previous experience and current pain level were any indication, perhaps a deken for me. Which was why I wasn't as worried as Kor was making Sarah to be.

"Speaking of time...." Kor said pointedly, stopping next to us.

"Please, by all means," Sarah said, stepping back with a renewed flush to her cheeks.

She looked at Kor intently as he took up the hand she'd dropped. "You can *entirely* heal that? Ben's not going to...you know...."

"Die an excruciating death?" Kor said with a chuckle. "No, not even if both of us did nothing. Like he said, he's a drakón. But he *would* get so overcome with pain for a few days that he wouldn't be able to move, and I don't think he's in the mood for that right now."

"Definitely not," I said dryly, with a pointed look at him and a silent, *Will you just stop the dramatics already and get on with it?*

Sarah's face scrunched in confusion. "*That's* how werewolf bites work here? They just...either kill you if you're an amón or cause you pain if you're a drakón?"

We both looked at her in surprise.

"Just?" I asked. "What's worse than death?"

I was sorry I said that as soon as the words were out of my mouth. Of all people, an Heir should know that there are many, many things worse than death. The soberness in Sarah's too-old, too-deep eyes confirmed she knew that, too.

"I only know the stories," Sarah said, looking away. "I've never seen one for myself before today. I didn't even think—I had *hoped*—that they weren't real. They're supposed to be just a myth."

My flameheart wavered. On the one hand, I was relieved to hear that krathen weren't as great of a danger on Earth as I'd feared. On the other hand...I'd made another of her nightmares real today.

"What do the stories say, Sarah?" I asked gently. With the worst of the damage done, perhaps it would help her to talk about it.

When she didn't speak, I tried one more time, partly to distract myself from the burning pain as Kor began healing my hand and arm. "What happens if an amá is bitten by a krathen?"

Her eyes darted to mine for one second and then away. But she spoke, even if her words came in a whisper. "They become one of them."

"They become...." I repeated dumbly for a moment before the entire horror sunk into me. Even Kor spared one look of astonishment at her before returning his focus to my arm.

Worse than death.

I remembered the fervor, the hunger in the krathen's eyes as they stared at Sarah and the abject terror in her own.

Just like that, I was so full of fury that Kor could feel the fire entering my bloodstream, and his dark blue eyes darted up to me with a hard look.

Cool it, Ben. Before I knock you out so that you'll have at least some energy to guard us tonight.

Fortunately, Sarah was still staring into the distance across the mesa, so she was oblivious to my struggle. She shuddered, rubbing her arms.

"It's why they terrify me so much. Always have, ever since Michael—that's one of my brothers—made me watch a movie about them with him when I was nine. Then I was stupid enough to think that if I just exposed myself to more stories about them, I'd get over it, but the horror book I picked up next from the library made it even *worse*.... I don't know what it is about werewolves. I mean, the same basic thing happens when a vampire bites you, right? But somehow werewolves are worse to me. Maybe it's their total lack of control, or that you can be fine one night, and then the next night, when the moon is full...."

There were many astonishing and confusing things about her elaboration, none the least of which being that was as many words as I'd ever heard come from her at one time, but at her last sentence, my gaze on her sharpened.

"Moon?" I asked intently.

She shrugged, still not meeting my eyes. "That's what most of the stories say. A werewolf is just like any other person most of the time. But then, when the full moon comes out, they...change into *that*. Then they...lose themselves. They're just bloodthirsty beasts out to infect the next person they can find."

Kor and I exchanged a look. A strange twist to the truth, but then, if krathen hadn't been seen in enough generations to make them into legends, then it made sense that some things would get mixed up. But I didn't like that fewer details appeared to have been altered so far as those about drakón had been.

"What?" Sarah demanded, noticing our exchange.

"Oh, nothing," I said with a frown. This legend of hers was proving an effective distraction from the painful healing in my arm. When I could control my temper. "It's just odd. Night is when the consumed are at their greatest advantage over us—and the darker the night, the better. That's also when the Devourer opens its gates most easily. Full moons are actually a Flamesend. They don't give us as much energy as the sun, but it's better than nothing."

Sarah's eyes widened. "*That's* why you hate being out at night so much."

"Yeah, that's why it's problematic for pretty much anyone," I agreed. "But particularly for me."

I regretted the elaboration as soon as her eyes narrowed. As Kor said, she was sharper and more determined than her timidity made her first appear. "Why?"

"Because I'm the Heir," I said with a lopsided shrug, trying not to disturb the arm in Kor's hands. He still gave me an extra sting with his power as a quick scolding.

I'd hoped she would leave it at that simple explanation, but of course, she didn't.

"What does that have to do with it, specifically?"

Kor said absently, "It means that every consumed knows who Ben is and knows that one of Ben's primary duties is to hunt and kill consumed who have broken our laws. Because being *Heir* means he's the most powerful drakón in the Six Realms, aside from the King himself."

She didn't speak. Her lips only mouthed the word "most" in her own language, and her eyes went wide again.

Torch it, Kor, I growled at him. *What are you playing at? You* promised *to behave!*

I am *behaving,* he said, not even looking up from my arm. *Have you heard me be the slightest bit rude to her today?*

Unfortunately, I couldn't think of a single moment I could call him out on. That didn't make me feel any better, though. Kor was up to something, and whatever it was, I didn't like what it was doing to Sarah. Or to the way she looked at me. Like...like I was a thing to be feared.

Again.

First, yesterday I'd been a murderous, greedy beast in her eyes. Then less than a deken ago I'd been bitten by her worst nightmare, and then she'd worried for a dek or so that I would turn into the same uncontrollable monster that would turn on her at some arbitrary time. Now....

Just...whatever it is you're doing, stop, please, I said to Kor. *I'm asking you as a friend, now.*

And I am behaving...as a friend, Kor said with the tiniest of smirks, so small Sarah might not notice.

I can't see how, I complained—and hissed as a nasty spasm of his power went through my forearm.

"Fine," I told Sarah hastily when she took an anxious step forward. Though I didn't want her to be worried, my flameheart lifted a bit as concern replaced the blank look that had been on her face before.

"Fine," I repeated for emphasis when her expression turned dubious. "Healing these things is a tricky business, that's all."

"Tricky" being euphemistic for "painful," of course. I didn't know why I'd bothered, because from Sarah's adorable scowl at me, I was sure she knew what I'd meant.

Oh, I know, Kor said to me, responding to my last silent comment as his eyes flicked to Sarah and that tiny smirk deepened. *But you will. Trust me. You will.*

When Kor talked like that, I got nervous.

Very nervous.

CHAPTER ELEVEN

QUESTIONS

SARAH

AFTER KOR FINISHED HEALING Ben, the two of them brought out cushions, and we all sat around in a circle eating a simple, late lunch while Kor and Ben pored over a map of the area, debating the pros and cons of venturing to the next hold or staying put.

I stayed quiet; I gathered that we'd been lucky in finding this mesa, but it also wasn't the most comfortable place to camp, and the longer I was around these drakón, the more I took on their anxiousness about nightfall. Especially after the werewolves today, I wasn't relishing the thought of experiencing my first night out in the open in this world. Not to mention I was a more than a little disappointed to hear no discussion anymore about trying to send me home today.

Yvera joined us not too long into their debate. As soon as she landed and turned back into a human, she produced a large, warped, crushed ball of metal and tossed it with astonishing ease in Ben's direction. It hit feet away from him with a jarring clang that made the rest of us wince.

"Sorry about your brazier, Ben," Yvera said with a smirk that made it clear she wasn't *that* sorry.

While I tried not to stare at such evidence of primal power, Ben merely looked down at the hunk of scrap metal with a sigh. "It had a good run. All of...how many sevendays?"

"Three," Kor said with a grin. "You wouldn't go through so many if you didn't feel the urge to plop down and drink tsha wherever we stop. You should look into one of those new heating disks."

"I'm sure one of those would last me so much longer," Ben said dryly. "Seeing as I'm sure Yvera didn't even find the *remnants* of my mugs."

"Nope," Yvera said cheerfully, pulling out a cushion for herself and plopping down in the space on the other side of Ben from me. "The clearing is torched."

Kor rolled his eyes. "Ha. Ha. You're so clever."

"And you're so *slow*," Yvera said, punching him in the arm.

"Hey! *Someone* had to escort Ben and Sarah to safety," Kor protested. "I didn't see you rushing from that fight to heal him, either."

"'Course not, he's capable of doing that himself," Yvera said with a dismissive wave. "But I'm glad to see that it made you feel useful. Speaking of *bites*, though...."

Ben winced as Yvera turned her sharp eyes on him. "How in Flame's name did you let *that* happen?"

"It was...an accident?" Ben said tentatively. For a moment, he looked like my brother David when he'd been caught doing something ridiculously dangerous and stupid and was hoping Mom wouldn't press him for details. The similarity had me trying to hide a laugh behind a cough, which was a mistake, because the cough only made Ben glance at me worriedly.

"Just the food," I said, holding up the last of my simple sandwich.

"Well, obviously. Sloppy, Ben," Yvera scolded, waving a finger at him to get his attention back. "*Sloppy*. Master Kressa would be ashamed of you. And letting a pack of krathen sneak up on you in the first place! Honestly, can't I leave you alone for a *half deken* without you trying to get yourself killed?"

"I don't *try* anything," Ben muttered.

"Maybe that's the problem. Try *not* to—*harder*."

"Yes, ma'am," Ben said meekly.

Yvera narrowed her eyes at him. "Rolling over won't get you out of this one, Ben. I'm *still* going to put this in my report."

"Oh, come *on*, Yvera—"

"If you don't want your father to hear about these kinds of things, then don't let them happen!"

"Now that the matter of Ben's impending grounding is out of the way," Kor said. "Why don't we make some decisions about what we're doing next? Because as you can see—"

He pointed to the lowering sun. "—daylight is wasting."

Yvera snorted, but she snatched the map from Kor and started studying it. "How far are we from Kergin Hold?"

Kor scowled at her theft. "Almost too far. I don't like it."

Yvera raised an eyebrow at him. "Do you like the thought of sleeping—excuse me, *fighting* all night—here *better*? We get close enough, and we can always call for the guard to bring us in."

Ben and Kor had been through all this before, but I resigned myself to listening to them hash out the same arguments again, this time with Yvera present. She had a few new insights, including the fact that we were too close for comfort to the scene of not just one but two consumed attacks, the latest of which having dramatic enough consequences that consumed would both scatter and gather in the area in unpredictable ways.

"If there is a plotter behind both of them, then where would they send consumed to look for us next, hmm?"

Kor scowled, but I thought it was because Yvera had pointed out something that he should have thought of first than because he disagreed with her. Plus, he seemed proud of bringing us to this mesa.

In the end, it was Kor's one vote to stay against Ben's and Yvera's to leave. I thought that meant the matter was decided, but then, to everyone's surprise—most especially mine—Ben nudged me. "Sarah?"

"What?" I asked, startled.

"What do you think? Stay or go?"

Yvera rolled her eyes, and Kor put on a polite face of interest, making Ben the only one who seemed serious about giving me an equal vote.

I could feel my cheeks growing hot with self-consciousness. "I don't think I...."

"You're new, I know," Ben said patiently. "But you've heard the arguments, some of them twice now. This is about your well-being, too. You must have some thoughts."

"Ben," Yvera complained. "If she votes with Kor, then we're tied. If you say your vote counts for the most, then voting in the first place was pointless."

"In that case, Sarah's vote should count for two."

"What?" Yvera spluttered.

"She's at least twice as in danger as the rest of us, Yvera," Ben pointed out, frowning. "As today clearly demonstrated."

I felt a strange mixture of warmth and chill. Had Ben wondered, too, what would have happened if the krathen had bitten me instead of him? Had it bothered him that much?

"What today *demonstrated*," Yvera said between clenched teeth, "is that you are unusually dis—"

"Disinclined to be a tyrannical leader," Kor interrupted smoothly, causing the rest of us to look at him in surprise.

Yvera blinked furiously at him and opened her mouth, but Kor gave her a pointed *look* that made it clear there was a silent communication going on.

"Really, Yvera," Kor said, almost without missing a beat. "Don't you want to encourage Ben to be democratic? Giving deference to the amón, upholding the oaths of the Crown and all that loveliness?"

"Fine!" Yvera said, throwing her hands up in exasperation. "Fine! Let the Earthren vote. Just whatever you do, *get on with it*. We could have been an elden away from here by now if you'd just listened to me in the first place."

"Sarah?" Ben asked me.

I looked back at him pleadingly. I *hated* making split-second decisions to begin with, but this was even worse. To vote on something I felt I knew so little about, and then to give me the deciding vote, when our very lives could be at stake? I couldn't take that kind of pressure.

Yet there was no give in Ben's eyes as he gazed back at me. For some reason, he was determined to make me do this.

I rapidly thought through the two discussions I'd heard, tallying the pros and cons as quickly as I could in my head. I wished I'd been paying better attention while they were talking instead of letting my mind wander back to home and what my parents would think of me being missing yet another night.

I realized I *did* have an opinion. Or...at least, a question.

"Why haven't you talked about trying to send me home?" I asked tentatively.

Yvera snorted, but I was getting used to her, so that didn't bother me as much as it might have before. I was focused on Ben, whose eyes tightened with regret.

"Ah, sorry," he said with a sigh. "I...did it again, didn't I? Assumed you knew how these things worked."

"It's OK, I get it," I said with a crooked smile. "But before I decide, I want to know why."

"The quick answer?" Ben said with a grimace, eyeing Yvera's fingers drumming a rhythm on her leg. "Like I told you, the Moontouched destroyed the sungate on Earth, meaning there's no direct way for us to get there. Our next best bet is for me to manipulate a sungate to take us there. Even then, we're going to have to go to the Tree of Flame first to ask Her to open the way for us. That's the only way sungates ever take you somewhere without a gate at the other end. It's how the Seven reached Earth the first time, and it's how we first reached and settled each new Realm. With you here, I'm confident the Tree will grant our request, but...She might ask something of us first, to prove our worthiness. And I do not know what that might be."

"Oh," I said, trying hard to hide my sinking heart.

Of course, he saw anyway. Was I that obvious, or was he paying that much attention? I didn't know which option to dread or hope for the most.

"Agh, Sarah," Ben said, running a hand through his hair. "I'm sorry. I should have—alright, I should have done a *lot* of things better than this, but I shouldn't have let you go this long thinking that it would be quick work to send you home. But I *promise* you, I will. I swear it. Trust me, I will pay whatever price it takes."

"I believe you," I said, mustering all my growing confidence in him into my voice as I smiled at him.

Yvera interrupted with a snort. "Alright, as touching as all of this mushy promise stuff is, we need to make a decision. As in, now."

I took a deep breath, trying to refocus my mind. "Do you have to use a gate, though? I came through without one."

"Actually, you might have, after all," Kor corrected with a raised finger. "Ben sensed a wildgate opening around the time you must have showed up. That's why he rushed to the area and found you, after all."

I scrunched my face. Would I *ever* be caught up on the way this world worked? "What's a—"

"A wildgate is one that no one has built," Ben said. "It just occurs in the middle of nowhere, for no reason we've been able to figure out. And it closes almost as quickly as it opens. They're different from darkgates, the kind the...the enemy creates. If consumed get caught up in them, it's by chance."

"But the most fascinating thing about wildgates is that they didn't use to happen," Kor said eagerly. "They've only started happening since we began *building* gates. And the more gates we build, the more often they've been recorded to occur. Scholars have argued for ages whether it's correlation, greater awareness and record-keeping, or—"

"In any case," Ben interrupted, eyeing Yvera's mutinous expression. "You might have come through *that*. It's the most plausible explanation we have right now."

"Especially after what Yvera and I found," Kor said smugly. "The lingering energies from the wildgate were right where your scent began."

"My *scent*?"

"Well, yeah," Kor said in surprise. "We tracked your scent back to where it stopped, so presumably that's where you—"

"That's not the part I'm confused about. How did you track my *scent*?"

"Drakón, remember?" Yvera said with a huff, tapping her nose. "Our ears may be ashes, but our smell...."

I stared, but Ben rolled his eyes. "We can't smell strongly enough to track someone *all* the time, Sarah. But if we at least partially transform, we can. And Yvera, I'll admit, is one of the best."

"Torch right," she said with a casual flip of her braid over her shoulder.

Of course she was. When was I ever going to hear about any skill at which at least one of these three elite drakón didn't excel? I understood the reason: Ben was powerful because he was the Heir, and Kor and Yvera had been chosen from no doubt a pool of hundreds of candidates *because* of their excellence. It was merely an unfortunate—or fortunate—coincidence that I'd been stuck with "the best of the best of the best" for my sojourn on this world.

Understanding that and *not* taking a hit to my self-esteem each time were still two different things.

Again, I made myself focus. "So if a wildgate brought me here, could one take me back? Or could you harness one, like you were planning to do with a sungate?"

Ben and Kor exchanged glances. Kor shrugged, and Ben looked back at me with a frown. "I suppose it's a possibility. I've only encountered one wildgate before, actually. The problem with them is their unpredictability. We just never know when or where one is going to show up. A much safer bet is going to an established gate and asking the Tree for aid."

"Is it, though?" I said. "An established gate hasn't connected to Earth for centuries. Whereas we have a good reason to suppose that a wildgate just *did*. Because, as you claimed, the Trees wanted me here. Why can't we try using the same method They did to bring me here to take me back?"

Ben and Kor stared at me for a moment, and then Kor turned to Ben with a chuckle. "I *like* her. Can we keep her?"

"Sarah isn't a pet, Kor," Ben said from between clenched teeth. "And even if she were, that's not the point, remember? We're sending her home."

Kor sighed dramatically. "It would be so nice to have a bit more intelligence around here, though."

"You know what would *really* be nice right about now?" Yvera began snidely.

"A bottle of violet lightspark, year 437?" Kor asked innocently. "I've wanted one for ages, but it's torched expensive—"

"Enough!" Ben snapped, having to push Yvera back to keep her from launching herself at Kor. "Both of you!"

"I guess what I'm getting at is," I said, hoping to bring the two wings back on track, "is that wildgate likely to open again soon? Because if so, then it makes the most sense to me to stay here."

They all looked at me. Then Ben and Yvera looked at Kor.

"What, suddenly I'm the expert on wildgates?" Kor protested.

"You're kind of the expert on everything, aren't you?" I asked.

That made Yvera snort and roll her eyes, but Kor straightened and looked somewhat mollified. "Well, yes, but only by default, since these two don't seem to care to pick up a book."

"I like reading," Ben protested. When Kor raised an eyebrow at him, he added grudgingly, "When I have the time."

"Precisely," Kor said with a long-suffering sigh. "Whereas most of *my* precious time before becoming a full leftwing *should* be dedicated to the pursuit of knowledge, rather than traipsing across the Six Realms on some impossible quest—"

"Kor," Ben said in a warning tone.

"Anyway, regarding the likelihood of that wildgate opening again...." Kor trailed off, thinking intently for a moment. Then he shrugged. "It's possible, I guess. Once it's happened in an area, it seems to be more likely to do so again, if memory serves me. But unless the gate is *truly* unstable, it won't be soon. Not today or tomorrow. So there's no point in waiting around just for that one. Sarah's theory is intriguing, though, so you should keep your senses peeled for another one, Ben."

"Got it," Ben said dryly. Then he softened as he looked back at me. "Does that help you make your decision, Sarah?"

"It helps," I said uneasily. "But is there nothing special about this area anymore? Nothing about it that made the wildgate deposit me *here*?"

Ben looked at Kor, and Kor looked pointedly back.

"What?" Ben asked self-consciously.

"This seems to be more your realm of expertise, don't you think?"

"Why?"

"Don't you think this sounds more like a *Tree* question? Fate, destiny, manipulation of people's lives? Any of that ring a gong?"

"The Tree doesn't manipulate," Ben said, eyes narrowing.

Kor snorted but said nothing and just continued to look at Ben.

Ben sighed and looked back at me. "You want to know if there's anything special about this area that made you appear *here*, right? Before we leave it behind for good?"

"Right," I said, relieved to articulate the unease that had been building inside of me at the thought of leaving. I knew it was probably just all in my head. This was the place where I emerged. However faint, it was the last tie I had, other than the clothing on my body, to home. Especially at the news that my journey home would be longer and more complicated than I'd naively let myself hope, I was even more loathed to cut myself adrift and wash off into a sea of the unknown. The thought of getting on Ben's back again and turning from it forever....

"Alright then, I'll ask," Ben said, getting to his feet.

"You'll...what?" I said, starting to push myself up onto my own.

"No, Sarah, please stay there," Ben said. With a surprisingly gentle touch for one so big, he put his hand on my shoulder and pushed me back down. "I'll be right back.... Maybe."

Before I could respond or demand to know what he meant by "maybe," he began walking away from us.

"Great! Fantastic!" Yvera said, throwing up her hands as she glared at me. "We might as well set up camp *now* for as long as we're going to be here for him to get an answer."

"What's he doing, though?" I asked anxiously, my eyes still on him. He was still just...walking. With no clear destination that I could see on this barren mesa.

"Getting some quiet," Kor said, propping his arms behind himself and stretching his legs out with a yawn. "Flame only knows he won't get that here with us."

"But *why*?"

"You wanted an answer, didn't you?" Kor said with a raised eyebrow. "A *why* kind of answer, having to do with why the Tree brought you *here*, in particular."

"I suppose...." That was a strange way of putting my question but was essentially the same thing.... Maybe.

"Well, he's going to go ask Her for you," Kor said with another yawn. "Ah, torch it, it's been a long day. Think I have time to take a nap, Yvera?"

"Wait," I said. "He's going to go ask...*the Tree*? The Tree of Flame?"

"There's only one," Yvera said.

"That talks to Ben, anyway," Kor corrected cheekily. Yvera swatted at him, but he dodged.

"But isn't the Tree...far away?" I said as I watched Ben shrink into only a small figure in the distance.

"Yes, but the King and the Heir don't need to be present before the Tree to commune with Her," Kor said in a bored tone. "It's part of their roles as Her primary protectors and stewards of Her children, yada yada. It's more difficult to speak with Her from a distance, and it's considered lazy and bad form to do so if they can get to Her easily, but at times like these, he can always try. Now, whether She'll *answer*, that's another story."

"Why?"

"The Tree isn't a book or a scholar you can consult on a whim," Yvera said. "She's the Tree of Flame, the greatest being in the universe except the Creators."

"*Technically*, in the Six Realms," Kor said. "Don't forget Earth, where the Tree of Ice reigns, and any other unknown worlds with other Trees."

"Point being," Yvera said with a growl and a glare in his direction. "She decides when it is wise for Her to answer, and if it is, in what manner or timing."

"In other words, dealing with the Tree is an unreliable method of finding what you want to know at best," Kor drawled.

"Unreliable?" Yvera said testily. "The Tree is wise enough to not weaken us by giving us answers we can find for ourselves—or that aren't good for us to know."

"Like I said," Kor drawled, giving me a look. "Unreliable."

"Just so I have this straight, then," I said, choosing my words with care so that hopefully Yvera wouldn't be offended. "Because I asked a question that delved into the realm of the unknowable, Ben has gone off on his own for some quiet so that he can consult the Tree from a distance, as he has the ability to do as Heir, and he may or may not come back with an answer from Her."

"Pretty much," Kor said. As I'd spoken, he had pulled out more cushions out of thin air (*How many does he* have? I wondered.) and arranged them to form a long, inclined couch. When he was done, he settled into them with a contented sigh.

"If you're going to get that comfortable, you might as well help me set up camp," Yvera grumbled.

"Done," Kor said languidly. "I can sleep on this, thanks."

"Oh, and I suppose you won't want to eat anything I prepare, then," she said.

"I might," he said, eyes open only a crack.

"You—" Yvera began, then said some words that I was rather glad didn't translate very well.

"What can I do?" I asked, both to mollify her and because I itched for something to keep my hands busy. With a large family and lots of chores needing doing, rides needing given, and younger ones needing tending, I didn't think I'd been this idle for so long in my life, and it was making me anxious.

"*You* can tell Ben I've gone to catch us some dinner," Yvera said hotly, getting to her feet. "Because by the time he gets back, *this* lazy scum will be asleep."

She kicked the highest point in his pile of cushions, knocking some of them out from under him. Ignoring his yelp of protest and curses as he tumbled, she strode away with a toss of her braid.

"Lazy," Kor muttered as he restacked his cushions and settled back down. "And *who*, may I ask, is going to be doing most of the work of keeping us safely concealed tonight? I'm being *prudent*, that's what. Because I can guarantee that I'll be getting little enough rest later."

"You could have told her that."

"Oh, she *knows*," Kor said bitterly. "But will she acknowledge that my contribution is just as important as hers? Never. She'd rather hack her way through an army of consumed first."

We were buffeted by the force of her wingbeats as she took off, and then there was silence other than the whistling of the wind over the mesa. Kor's eyes were closed, and he looked determined to be asleep by the time Ben came back. I looked back in the direction Ben had gone and saw the small shape of him in the distance. He appeared to be kneeling, but that was the only detail I could make out.

I wondered at it all for a moment. First, that Ben would go through so much effort for me, and then, at what he was doing in and of itself. Was a kind of deity really going to speak to him? If so, what would that be like?

The thought made *me* nervous. But Ben hadn't seemed concerned as he left; and before, in the clearing, he'd spoken of his Tree with respect, admiration, and even something like fondness.

Reverence, I realized. That was what reverence looked like.

Like Mom's own private devotion. She was Catholic, as her mother had been before her, and hers before her. Dad was agnostic and I figured always would be, but he'd always supported Mom in her faith, encouraging her to teach us her values. He made sure that, wherever we lived, one place was set aside for her home altar, no matter how precious that real estate was with our crowded numbers. Yet most of us kids had inherited Dad's way of thinking, and Mom never said a word of protest. She had taught us to pray and encouraged us to go to mass with her, but as soon as we discovered we had a choice in the matter, we stopped doing either.

I didn't think I'd said a prayer on my own for most of my teenage years. I didn't think I'd ever had an active *disbelief* in a higher power, but what childlike faith Mom had tried to instill in me had faded at the same time as Santa and the Tooth Fairy. The question of whether there was a being to hear and answer me had faded to insignificance in the face of the chaos of growing up, pushed aside almost as soon as I was old enough to form the question.

It seemed an unanswerable question, delving into the realm of the unknowable.

Just like...the question Ben was now bringing to his Tree, with perfect confidence that She would hear, and a strong enough possibility She would answer that he was attempting to ask, despite the cost. Because there was no other way I would get my answer.

In the same way, I supposed there was no other way of my *knowing* whether there was something out there, listening to me, except...asking.

I flinched away from that thought. Who was I to bother a divine being, should one exist? It was bad enough Ben was bringing my presumptuous question to *his* deity, but I could have hardly stopped him.

Who would I even be addressing at this point? The God Mom had taught me to pray to or this Tree of Ice that Ben had every confidence must exist on Earth? If the Tree existed, did that mean there *was* no God after all? That Mom had in fact been wrong all along, and in my childhood prayers I'd spoken to nothing and no one?

I forcefully pushed all those loaded questions aside. It was all too much, especially after everything else in the past day and a half. The unknowable had remained that way for eighteen years of my life. It could wait for a while longer.

FOR THE LACK OF anything else to distract me, I pulled over the knapsack Svyer had given me and unbuckled the top flap, intending to look at what was inside.

"Oh, that reminds me," Kor said with a reluctant sigh.

I looked back at him with a start to see him sitting up and lifting his transforming hand. A second later, an object appeared in that hand that was so heart-wrenchingly familiar, it brought tears to my eyes.

"My purse!" I said, grabbing for it gratefully. "I thought I'd lost it in the fall! But...."

"We found it near where your scent ended, but with no trace of you leading to it," Kor said grimly. "So, it probably *did* come off in your fall, but it still ended up here. However, you should look to see if anything is missing."

"Why's that?" I asked, but just then, I noticed what I'd momentarily been blind to in my gratitude.

All the zippers—and I mean every one—were torn open, teeth jagged and chipped in places and sliders broken. Tears in the faux leather were everywhere, and my little bottle of hand sanitizer had burst and soaked the contents. Every pocket had been opened, spilling the contents everywhere. A receipt I'd stuffed in there was warped and the ink bleeding, and it looked like someone had tried opening it while it was wet and sticking together and then discarded it as useless, because it was in shreds and crumpled together again.

Then there was the smell, one that had nothing to do with any of the contents· like roadkill left to ripen in the sun. A smell I had caught whiffs of while on Ben's back in the clearing while he fought for both of our lives.

Understanding came in a single, nauseating second, and I dropped the bag as if it contained the plague. For all I knew, it now did.

I regretted the simple lunch I'd eaten because it was coming back up in force. I jerked to my feet and ran to the nearest decent-sized pit in the rocky plateau, fell to my knees, and heaved.

"Ah, Sarah, I'm sorry," Kor groaned, kneeling next to me. He held my hair back as I finished, and once I was done, he offered me a handkerchief to wipe my mouth and a canteen full of water to wash it out.

"Why would they do this?" I croaked as I handed him the canteen.

"Good question. That's what Yvera and I were trying to figure out when Ben called us back, saying you were under attack. That's what was taking us so long. Your things were scattered everywhere, and we wanted to be sure we found every last item."

"That was kind of you," I said dully as I stared at nothing in the distance. I tried to ignore the smell of my vomit right next to us, but my body had only just stopped trembling and didn't feel like moving. Besides, I wasn't in a hurry to go back to my violated belongings. Bile rose again from my empty stomach at just the thought.

"It wasn't just that," Kor said darkly. "They went through your belongings for a reason, Sarah. We don't know why exactly, but if they found and took something of significance to you, we need to know what that was. Besides, anything we left there would have a stronger trace of your scent than just your passing footprints. With krathen or worse on your trail, we didn't want to leave so much as a handkerchief."

"Worse?" I asked hoarsely, looking down.

"I know it's hard for you to believe right now," Kor said. "But there's worse than krathen, Sarah. A lot worse. And despite the krathen stench all over your stuff, the 'worse' are probably the ones behind the search through your things, and the smell is the cover. Krathen are more intelligent than ahglen, but it's still a more animalistic kind of intelligence. This requires a much more troubling degree of...strategy."

"Then why leave my things behind at all?" I asked with a shiver.

"Lots of reasons. As bait, to lure you back. Or, failing at that, it was a good distraction that kept Yvera and me busy enough that krathen got a go at you and Ben. And finally, as a message."

I swallowed thickly, wincing at the bile still stinging in my throat. "What kind?"

"I don't know," Kor said with a scowl. I could tell he didn't like the feeling. "Yet. But it can't be anything good. They're interested in you, Sarah. Far too much and far too *early* for my liking. They shouldn't know what you are and what you can become, not yet. But somehow...I think they do."

"What I can become?" I said, heart speeding for a moment.

Kor gave me a long look. "If Ben didn't get to that part, then I should probably leave the explanation up to him."

He stood up and offered me a hand. "Come on, let's get you back somewhere more comfortable. Besides...as much as I know you don't want to, I really do need you to look through your stuff to see if anything's missing."

"Fine," I said with a reluctant sigh, and I let him help me to my feet.

He kept a supportive hand around my shoulders as we walked back, which was a little excessive, but I appreciated the warmth and protection a somewhat human body offered, so I didn't protest.

"Is there anything you can do about the smell?" I asked with a wrinkled nose as we reached my cushion. And the discarded purse lying nearby, looking—and smelling—like some wounded beast left to die.

"Yes, but I shouldn't until Ben has had a whiff of his own," Kor said with a grimace. His next words were a mutter. "Although I'm tempted to, since he's going to flip out as soon as he does."

"Then do it," I urged. "There's no need to worry him like that."

"I would, but he'd find out anyway when Yvera tells him, and then he'd scold me for it. I can't win either way. So, sorry."

"Ugh," I gagged, feeling bile rise in my throat again as I kneeled next to the bag.

"Hang on. What I *can* do is temporarily dampen your own sense of smell," Kor offered. "Would that help?"

"Yes, please!" I said in relief.

Kor reached toward my nose. "This might sting," he warned. Once I nodded in acknowledgement and permission, he pressed his finger to the ridge of my nose. Hot tingles spread from his finger to my skin and sunk into my nasal cavities. He was right: I felt a sharp sting, almost like a few nose hairs being plucked, and then my sense of smell vanished.

Feeling air rush into my nostrils and yet smelling nothing was disconcerting, but the relief of being free from the carrion stench more than made up for the discomfort. Now, freed from the horror, I could look at my sullied belongings with a more objective eye.

I got to work on my assigned task at once, relieved as well to have been given something useful to do. I went through every pocket, grabbed the contents, and laid my things out in a wide spread over the rocky ground. When I was sure I'd gotten everything, I stood and circled the objects, identifying every one and comparing them to the mental list I was making in my head of everything I usually had in the purse and what I had added just before taking the littles to the creek.

Mini tube of sunscreen, now with a chip in the lid, check. Hand sanitizer, burst but present. Tiny first aid kit, contents spilled and torn. That was strange. The bandages and little pill packs wouldn't have been torn from just being spilled. As for the pocket mirror that Rachel had brought back for me from her study abroad to Paris (one of her few spurts of "academic" ambition), the outer case should have protected it, but the mirror inside was cracked.

Kor watched me puzzle over the mirror, his expression unreadable. Whatever he thought of the damage, he kept it to himself. I set the mirror down with feelings of loss and irritated bafflement and moved on.

The feelings increased the longer I went through my things. I didn't mind the damage so much as the violation it represented. All for *what*? Why had they done this? What had they been intending to accomplish? What was the message here, if any? That was the part that bothered me the most: the unknown. And the pointlessness of it all; the damage might have no other aim than to cause me pain.

I was scowling by the time I stood back and did another quick tally. Which deepened my suspicions.

"It's all here," I said, looking back at Kor.

"Everything?" he asked, studying me.

"Ye—wait." Of course, after giving my declaration, I remembered one more thing. "My shoes. I was holding those."

"Ah, yes, sorry," Kor said, and he pulled them out.

My eyes watered at the sight of those sneakers—torn laces and all. "Oh, thank goodness."

I grabbed them to put them on instead of my current boots, just for the comfort, and then hesitated. "Er, could you take care of the...."

Kor chuckled and waved his hands over the shoes. I felt a stir of cool air around them, but I still smelled nothing, so I trusted that he'd done his thing.

As I put them on, Kor asked, "Anything else?"

I thought. "Just my hat. I was wearing it on a tie around my neck."

I traced my neck. "I think it came off in my fall, maybe even before I reached...whatever magic brought me here."

Kor nodded slowly. "Makes sense. In any case, Yvera and I didn't find it. But as for everything else...?"

"It's all here," I said with a scowl.

"And I gather from your expression that you have a theory why," Kor said in a neutral tone, but his dark blue eyes were fixed on me like those of a hawk.

I gestured to my things. "Nothing was untouched. Everything is affected in *some* way or another, even if they had to go to a bit of trouble to damage it. But everything is still here. Even the first aid stuff, which could have easily been scattered, is still here. Now, I don't know about you, but that seems very...deliberate."

"And what do you conclude?" Kor said.

I pressed my lips into a thin line before answering. "They're trying to scare me. Say they have some kind of stupid control over me or something. That I'm only alive right now because they *let* me be."

"And how does that make you feel?" Kor asked quietly, expression and tone saying nothing about what he thought of my theory.

I met his gaze full on. "*Mad.*"

A slow, wintry smile spread across Kor's lips. The burning in his eyes was the same as when I'd touched the gem in front of him and revealed something he'd very much wanted to know.

His reply was simple but triumphant. "Very good."

My scowl this time was just for him. "I assume that means I got it right?"

He shrugged, intensity fading. "As far as I can tell. I'd come to much the same conclusion myself, but I'm unfamiliar with your things and so had less evidence to go on."

As he spoke, he gestured, and his fingers from the angle of where I stood crossed over my small leather wallet. I realized that I'd noted the wallet's closed state and the deep scratch on its surface, but I hadn't opened it. Which was odd, considering that was the first thing any human on Earth would have checked, but I'd already categorized this as no mere theft in my mind and moved on. After all, with nothing else so far missing, what use would monsters have for scraps of green paper and bits of plastic? Its contents were useless to even me until I could get back.

Troubled, however, I walked over to my wallet and picked it up. I snapped it open...and stared at the first empty slot. I knew immediately it was empty because its slot had a clear plastic film for the front to see the contents without pulling the card out.

"No," I said to myself.

"What?" Kor asked.

I didn't respond as I pried open every other slot, pulled out every other card, every dollar, every coin. But the driver's license was nowhere to be found. I tossed the wallet aside and began going through all my things again. But my heart was sinking, because I'd already been through everything else so thoroughly that I knew I wouldn't find it anywhere. I even poked through the purse again, putting my hand through every tear to make sure the card hadn't somehow fallen in a seam.

Finally, I had to admit defeat, and I let the purse fall from my fingers as I looked back at my wallet. I didn't know why losing that one bit of plastic was troubling me so much. It would be a pain to replace, but replaceable it was.

But it didn't fit the pattern! Why, of all things to be missing.... Was identity fraud a thing here?

The idea of a few werewolves trying to counterfeit their way through a dragon version of a border crossing to get to Earth was a laughable one, and not just because there was no such thing, seeing as both the original gates were destroyed.

"Sarah, what's missing?" Kor demanded in a hard voice that made it clear he wouldn't be put off a second time.

"My driver's license," I said.

"Your...what?" Kor asked.

I blinked, refocusing on Kor. "Oh. Right. You might not have something like that. My...identification card. The thing that proves I am who I say I am."

Kor was just continuing to stare blankly at me.

"You know...surely you've got *some* way of verifying someone's identity? Some way of tying someone's name to what they look like, or something else about them...."

"To what they look like?" Kor asked, eyes narrowing.

"Yeah," I said. I held up my thumbs and pointer fingers to form a rough rectangle. "It's a card, about this big. It's got my name, my picture, my birthdate, my address...."

"Your...picture," Kor said. "Your image...is on this card?"

"Yup. That's the whole point—so people can look at me and then at my card and then know I'm who I say I am."

Kor gestured at my scattered belongings, intense gaze never leaving my face. "And among all these things, *that* is the only thing that is missing?"

"As far as I can tell," I said with a shrug.

"And it couldn't have just fallen out?"

"No, see?" I grabbed my wallet and snapped it open again, showing him the slot where I usually kept it. "If I'd lost the entire wallet, that would have been one thing. But it would *not* have fallen out all by itself."

Kor frowned severely at the empty slot, as if it had personally offended him.

"Strange...isn't it?" I said as I snapped the wallet closed again. "What could they want with *that*? They're not...going try to pretend to *be* me, are they?"

His lips cracked into a thin, humorless smile. "Is that what Earthren do when they steal each other's image? Try to pass themselves off as the one they stole from?"

"Sometimes? I think? I'm no crime expert. I just know that you're supposed to never lose your ID if you can help it."

"Yes, that's to be avoided, if at all possible," Kor said with a sigh and then a groan. He muttered to himself, "Should've known it wouldn't be as simple as a warning."

"Kor," I said uneasily. "What do *you* think they want with my ID?"

"Same thing they would want with any of your things, except worse," Kor said. "To track you. Except *now*, they have something with your *image* on it that they can just show to any old band of consumed they like, point to it, and say, 'See this girl? That's the one you're after.'"

I stepped back and sunk onto my cushion with a slight thud. I felt like my heart had dropped into my stomach. It was so *obvious*. First, I'd thought of them as simple beasts, beyond the concerns of the contents of my wallet. Then I'd been so caught up in the complex concerns of human society, I forgot the simple utility that having a dratted *picture* of me could give them.

"The krathen," I said numbly. "They were looking at *me*. They knew *me*."

"This just keeps getting better and better," Kor said darkly. "No wonder they could spare all of *this* as a warning for us to find. They may have your hat, which would be *saturated* with your scent, so they could shove that under the noses of any tracker they please. And they almost certainly have your image, which, again, they can show to anyone. So, to sum up, they know what you are and therefore have at least an inkling of what you can become, and they have pretty much every means they could want at their disposal to send hordes of consumed after you. The only thing that could make this situation worse is if they had your *blood*."

I was feeling sick again, but there was nothing left in my stomach but bile.

"I was wrong," Kor groaned, running a hand through his short curls. "Ben isn't just going to be upset; he's going to explode."

"Maybe it wasn't such a good idea to stay here," I said faintly.

"Maybe. But it's a bit late for that now. You chose it pretty much by default when you asked Ben to go off and talk to the Tree."

"I didn't know that was what he was going to do!"

Kor shrugged. "You weren't ready to leave yet. Ben wanted to do everything in his power to make sure you were ready, so he decided it was necessary. You can blame him if you want, but the result is the same in the end. If we wanted to leave, we should have done so half a deken ago."

I took a deep breath. "Kor. Just how much danger are we going to be in tonight?"

Kor looked at my things for one long moment and then back at me, face grim. "I don't know. And you don't know how much I hate that feeling."

Silence fell between us for a moment. Then Kor stretched and said in a tone of forced cheer, "Well, nothing to do about it now but rest up and soak up as much sun as we can before nightfall. Which means I have a question for you, Sarah."

"Oh?" I asked suspiciously.

He smirked. "How do you feel about a bit of skin exposure?"

CHAPTER TWELVE

PANIC

KORIBEN

IT TOOK ME A few dek to reach a spot that I felt gave me enough privacy. All the way, I knew what this decision had amounted to: however and whenever the Tree responded, this was going to take long enough that we would spend the night here. But I was at peace with that.

I wanted Sarah to feel in control of her fate. To feel a part of our little group instead of our prisoner or our liability. If this was what she needed before we left behind the area where she had emerged, then so be it. Really, this was my fault for not soliciting her opinion even before Yvera showed up, since I could have been done by now.

But I wasn't sure that was the Tree's intention. I paid closer attention to the feel of the mesa beneath my feet as I walked its length. It was a rather odd geographic feature, if you thought about it. Nothing else like it existed for elden around, not as far as my eyes could see. Its size and severity of height would have been much more common in a desert or prairie, not in the middle of one of the largest jungles in the Six Realms. Now that I was looking with *all* my senses, there was something...odd about it. Something that felt...different.

I had been working with the Tree long enough to get a feel for Her will in matters before I even asked for it. This unique mesa was, after all, a short flight from where the Trees had arranged for Sarah to appear. Strange that They would have sent her to one of the more difficult and perilous parts of the Six

Realms...unless there was something They had intended for us to learn while we were here.

Perhaps Sarah's instincts—even so raw and unconscious as they were—were more attuned than mine were in this case.

I was unsurprised when I heard and then saw Yvera taking off; Kor and Yvera would have come to the same conclusion about where we would inevitably spend the night, and Yvera would have gone to work off her impatience with me by finding something to hunt. We had plenty of food, but fresh, hot meals were always preferable, and the more we could scavenge for ourselves, the longer our supplies lasted.

Not long after, I judged I was far enough. Kor and Sarah were small figures in the distance, and I wanted to keep them in view and be close enough to get to them quickly (when transformed, of course) should they need me.

So, I stopped, turned back to face them, and kneeled on the ground where I was. The kneeling part wasn't necessary, since most of the time I spoke to the Tree face to face, standing up. But from a distance like this, it helped me become still and centered as I drifted inside myself to that place where I could hear Her.

I didn't close my eyes—again, I wanted to be alert for anything that would require me to rush to Kor and Sarah, especially with Yvera gone, but my gaze became a little unfocused. I focused on my breath and let the day's tension go. Not trying to control the flow or direction of my thoughts—just letting myself be. Feeling the last rays of the sun on my face. The cool fingers of wind as they flowed across the mesa and thus around me, stirring my hair around my cheek. (My thoughts were distracted for a moment as I sighed about how long it was getting. Maybe I should ask Kor to cut it again. When we had time....) Hearing the cry of an eagle high above. Smelling the crispness of the high air mixed with the dusty grime of the mesa.

And something...else....

A few dek into this effort, when my heart rate had slowed and my mind was still, my blood grew warm, and my chest burned as it always did when the Tree's presence rose within me.

Speak, Koriben, son of Kavarian, Heir of my chosen King. I am listening.

The whisper of the Tree's voice to my inner ear nearly startled me out of my stillness. This wasn't the longest She had ever made me wait, which was a relief. Besides, my knees were complaining about the hardness of the stone beneath me.

I thank you, my Lady, I answered. Kor and Sarah were moving around, but their motions didn't look urgent, so I tried to not be distracted. *I have come before you with a question on behalf of the Earthren you sent me to find. She wishes to know if there is anything more to be gained from lingering in this place that she was sent to.*

She was wise to ask, the Tree whispered back. *You, too, have discerned something as well.*

Yes, my Lady. There is something about this...place.... I couldn't articulate what it was yet, even to myself, much less to Her.

There is indeed something I wish you to learn here. The night will be perilous, but if you guard and heed My Sister's chosen, you will learn it, and you will all see the rise of the sun.

Well. That was...not quite the kind of news I was hoping for. But I swiftly controlled my thoughts into a more mannerly tone. *Thank you, my Lady. We will heed your counsel.*

See that you do, My son, the Tree said, and I could have sworn I heard a note of amusement in Her voice.

It was gone when She spoke next. *Remember: Guard her well. And heed her. If you fail to do so, you will lose her this night, and you will not be entrusted with another of My Sister's children.*

I understand, my Lady, I said. My hands gripped my knees at just the thought. *I will* not *lose her. That I swear to you.*

See you to it, She whispered. I felt Her presence withdraw from the sudden chill in my blood and heaviness in my chest.

I groaned, bending over as my head spun and limbs trembled. Channeling the Tree of Flame's power was invigorating in the moment but always draining when She left, like the worst kind of adrenaline crash. Mortal beings weren't designed to contain an Eternal One of the First Creation. The Monarch and

Heir, having the greatest portions of Her flame in their hearts to begin with, could manage without permanent harm, but only for short periods of time.

It was far better for our health to seek Her out in person when possible and only resort to this long-distance communication when there was no other practical way. Avva, having served as Her King for so many decades by now—nearly a century—was much more used to the strain than I was, but it was still wearying for even him. Me, on the other hand—I felt as if I'd taken a tumble in the washing bin, been wrung out, and been hung to dry in the heat vents.

Speaking of heat vents, though…that sounded rather nice. I sighed. If only. With sunset so close and such a perilous night ahead, I'd better get a fire going if Kor hadn't already (I'd have been shocked if he had) and something warm inside me. Preferably tsha. Lots of tsha….

With those thoughts and my stinging knees to motivate me, I pushed myself up and onto my feet. I wasn't quite staggering as I started back, but I wasn't far from it. Fortunately, my step steadied, and my dizziness lessened the closer I got. After all, I didn't want to worry Sarah, or make her regret….

One moment, the wind was at my back. The next, when I was only about a hundred feet away, the wind shifted, blowing toward me from them.

Just like that, I was sprinting, fire blazing in my heart and ready to transform me any second. I was confused that Kor's and Sarah's positions were so calm. Kor was stretched out, sunbathing shirtless on a makeshift inclined couch of cushions, and Sarah was sitting on her own cushion with her back to him, watching me approach. Couldn't they smell that whiff of krathen on the wind? Perhaps not Sarah, but surely Kor.

Sarah stood as soon as she saw me run. She came forward, hands up. "It's OK!" she shouted. "The smell is just coming from my stuff!"

I slowed my pace, but I was still at a steady jog by the time I drew up to her. "What do you mean? What *stuff*?"

She pointed to a small, shredded bag made of some kind of strange leather and presumably what had been its contents, which were scattered around it in no pattern I could discern.

"Where did that come from?" I asked.

She bit her lip. "It came with me, yesterday. I was wearing it when I fell. Except it somehow got separated from me before or during the transition through the gate, so I didn't even think.... Not that I had much time to look for anything. The ahglen found me almost as soon as I came to. Kor and Yvera found it when they were looking for where I emerged."

"But why does it all smell like *krathen*?"

Kor opened his eyes with a sigh, as if resigning himself to being disturbed. "Because whoever—or *whatever*—went through Sarah's things didn't want us smelling whatever they were."

I spoke slowly, part of an excruciating effort to remain calm. "Whatever...was going...through Sarah's things? *Why*?"

"As far as I can guess?" Kor said with a grunt as he sat up and turned to me. "To get under your skin."

Sarah blinked at Kor as if this were news to her. There was something odd about the way her eyes darted away from him again, though, cheeks going ever so slightly pink. "But I thought—"

Kor looked at her. "Yes, scaring you was a nice side benefit. But they're aware that you're not a threat to them *yet*. The one they're focused on right now is Ben."

He turned back to me. "That's not the worst part, though. We have good reason to suspect they have an image of her now. She had one in her belongings, and now it's gone. It's the *only* thing we know for sure is gone."

I felt a chill that went to my bones. "What? Are you sure? Could it have fallen out, or...."

Sarah was grabbing a small leather object from the ground and bringing it to me. She opened it and showed me the inside.

"See, there?" she said, pointing to a slot that had some strange clear substance on the front. "That's where I would have kept it. It wouldn't have just fallen out on its own, especially not with my wallet closed, like this."

She closed the leather folds, and I heard the snaps click together.

"Nothing else from inside here is missing, either," she said. "I think they must have taken it."

I swallowed. "This likeness of you.... How good was it?"

She hesitated, as if uncertain how to explain. "It was...small. And not in color—just black and white. But it was painfully accurate."

She scowled, as if that were a bad thing *separate* from the fact that her exact likeness was now in the hands of some of the more intelligent and deadly of the consumed.

I put my head in my hands, using all my willpower to remain calm. "Anything *else* I should know?" I growled into my palms.

The silence that followed was ominous. I lowered my hands and glared at Kor. "What is it?"

"This is just speculation," he said, rubbing his neck. "We don't have as much evidence to back it up. But she had a hat with her when she fell. Yvera and I didn't see it. That could mean it fell off her early on and drifted away, not going through the gate at all...."

"Or that *they* have it, and with it, all they need of her scent," I finished.

Perfect. Just *grand.* Simply...

...horrifying.

I began pacing, too panicked to think, let alone stay still.

Perilous was the word the Tree had used to describe tonight. Well, if I'd known all of this when we first spotted this mesa—no, when Kor had offered to bring me here—I would have ignored him and dammed myself to a few days of bedridden agony rather than risk Sarah out in the open like this. I would have flown her straight to Kergin Hold, bite be torched; sent for the rest of my elites; ridden out the pain while waiting for them to show up; ordered a hunt to sweep ahead of us; and then—*only then*—would I have ventured to carry her out of the hold to the nearest gate.

They were hunting for her. They knew—torch it—somehow, they knew what she was, and they were hunting for *her. Already.* They had *all* they needed to send countless hordes of them after her. *Already.* And now we were stranded in the middle of the *Athalin Jungle* for the entire night, and all she had for protection were two wings-in-training and a fledgling Heir.

I had known it would get to this point eventually, of course. As soon as word broke out who Sarah was, it would have spread like wildfire, and that fire would have reached the ears of the more intelligent consumed. But torch it, I'd thought I would have *time*. At least a few *days*! Enough time to get her somewhere safe—ideally, to get her all the way back to Earth and beyond their reach. And yet, from perhaps the very first day....

The Tree's warning echoed ominously in my mind, with far more force than it had before, when I'd naively believed that tonight would be just like any other night in the open.

Remember: Guard her well. And heed *her. If you fail to do so, you will lose her this night.*

I could...lose her. Tonight. I was at a real and terrible risk of *losing her tonight*.

I couldn't lose her. Not her! Not now! Not when I had *just* found her. Not when she was my *one chance*....

"Ben?" Sarah said uneasily, catching my arm to bring me to a halt. I turned reflexively to look at her but was caught when I met her wide brown eyes.

My throat choked. For a moment, I couldn't breathe. I forgot all other concerns and fears as I just looked at *her*. At *Sarah*.

All I could think was, *I can't lose her.*

Not because of what she represented to me, but because she was *her*. I barely knew her, but what I did know of her was crushing me like a vise. I knew she was good, to the core. Kind. Selfless. Patient—too patient, especially with me and my fumbled explanations and hundreds of mistakes in taking care of her. Lost, so new to this world of nightmares. Vulnerable. Just at the beginning of her potential. And so trusting. She looked up at me as if all she needed was to hear me say it would be alright, and she would believe me.

Failing to protect someone like that....

Even if the Tree let me try again, I didn't think I would be able to. Not after failing someone like *her*.

I closed my eyes, blocking out the sight of her pleading brown ones for one moment. I took a deep, deep breath. Then I let it out.

I was all she had. Torch it, but I was all she had.

I had to be enough.

When my eyes opened, I knew they had the illusion of control. I smiled thinly at her. "Sorry. I was just...thinking. But it's going to be fine. You'll see."

I left it at that, knowing that if I kept talking, I would start to babble, and she would see right through me. As it was, her expressive eyes stared up at me, studying me with minute scrutiny. I let her. She would see worry, but that was only natural—rational. The complete and utter panic I felt at the thought of failing her was buried too deep for her to find. *I* was busy burying it too deep for me to consciously feel, because if I let myself enter that spiral again, I would be rendered useless to her. It would boil there, deep in the bedrock of my soul, like a birthing volcano, but for now, it would be deep enough for me to do whatever I had to do to make sure she survived the night.

Guard her well. And heed *her.*

She nodded slowly, as if satisfied with what she saw, and she gave a weak smile of her own as she let me go. For how little warmth she gave off, my skin was surprisingly cold after her hand was gone.

"I'm sorry for being so...silly as to make us stay here," she said sheepishly. "This is all my fault."

Her fault....

I nearly lost it again but took another deep, hasty breath to keep calm. "No, it's not your fault. Don't even apologize. You are right, after all."

"What do you mean?" she asked with a start.

"The Tree says there's something special about this place—this mesa in particular. She wants us to learn what it is, and apparently, that means spending the night."

I sent some carefully worded thoughts Her way—the tone of which bordered on irreverence—about how, if this was *Her* will, She had better give us a miracle.

Kor snorted, as if echoing my thoughts. Although I was sure *his* weren't so carefully worded, nor merely bordering on irreverence.

"Really?" Sarah said, looking like she was trying hard not to be incredulous. "Like what?"

"If I could tell you, then we wouldn't have to spend the night to find out," I said as a weak joke. "That's the Tree for you. Never letting you know what you're supposed to figure out for yourself."

Even if it nearly kills you.

I tried to remind myself that it wasn't the *Tree* who had stranded us here. That was me and my cascade of failures. If anything, the Tree had given us the one clue that would help save us from them.

If only I could figure out what that was. Heed her? Sarah, obviously, but.... How?

I began rearranging the cushions to make enough space in the middle of them for a fire. I needed to get busy, that was the key. Prepare, prepare, prepare, so that my mind was too occupied to panic. But keep my ears peeled for any advice Sarah may have, because it could just save our hides. Yes, that was it. Get busy...and listen to Sarah.

Sarah caught on to what I was doing and dragged her own cushion away. Kor settled back onto his pile with his hands behind his head and closed his eyes again. I rolled my own eyes, but that was Kor for you. And because we would rely heavily on him shortly, I was going to let him soak up his rays while he could.

That was, until I settled down on my cushion to set up the fire, and I noticed Sarah uneasily sitting down on her own—once again, turned away from Kor. I was about to demand if he'd been rude to her when I caught her eyes darting to his discarded robe and shirt, her cheeks going pink.

I snorted. "Kor, for Flame's sake, put your shirt back on. You're making Sarah uncomfortable."

His eyes cracked open to look at me in annoyance. "Ben," he whined. "I need to get as much sun as I can."

"Then go sunbathe elsewhere," I said, unmoved. "There's plenty of mesa, but we were here first, so I'm setting up camp here. So put your shirt back on or find someplace else to be half naked."

Kor scowled. "I did *ask* first. Sarah said it was fine."

"It is," she said quickly. Too quickly.

I looked at her with a raised eyebrow. "Is he making you uncomfortable?"

Her cheeks flushed. "If he's right, and he needs—"

"I am looking for a *yes* or a *no*," I interrupted gently.

Caught, she admitted with burning cheeks, "Yes."

"Kor," I said, looking back at my leftwing.

"Fine!" he huffed as he got up. He stowed his cushions, grabbed his shirt and robe, and strode off, muscles rigid in irritation.

While he was still in earshot, I pulled out my other brazier—a larger one, fit for roasting whatever Yvera would bring back—and got busy filling it with charcoal, but as soon as he was far enough away, I looked back at Sarah with a sigh.

"Sarah, you have *got* to be more assertive about your needs. As you can see, I won't always be around to advocate for you."

"I handled myself just fine before you came into my life, thanks," she said hotly.

"I'm sure you did," I said, hoping my tone sounded reasonable as I continued to add coals. "I'm sure that things are different where you're from. But here, when we need something, we say it. If someone does something we don't like, we let them know. If you don't do the same with Kor and Yvera, they're going to walk all over you. Yvera will take whatever you say at face value. Kor will know better, but he'll push his luck as far as you'll let him."

Especially when he's like...this, I thought but didn't say out loud. Not even I knew what *this* was. Kor was acting pushy, even for him, in ways I couldn't make the pattern out for yet.

"But he had a point," Sarah protested. Her voice was less irritated now, though, so it seemed I'd mollified her. "He's going to be spending a lot of energy to protect us all. It seems rude to kick him out like that."

"It was rude for him to make you that uncomfortable," I pointed out. "It's nice that you're thinking of others' needs, or of our needs as a whole, but your needs are part of the collective good. You don't need to ignore them just because someone else is making theirs manifest more loudly. It's almost never just one person's good or another person's good. It's about finding the solution that gives most people most of what they need. In this case, Kor can get the same benefit—somewhere else. After just a bit of effort on his part, everyone wins."

The flush in her cheeks was dying, and her eyes were turning more sheepish than irritated. "I suppose...that makes sense. It's...hard for me to do, though. I'm not used to...."

"I'm not saying it's as easy as I make it sound," I said with a rueful smile. "It was a hard lesson for me, too. My.... Well, I'm half Peacegrowth, and they tend to be the most self-sacrificing of us all."

My voice lowered as I set aside the bag of charcoal and lit the ones in the brazier with a twitch of my fingers. "For better or for worse."

Out of the corner of my eye, I saw her looking at me, so I continued briskly. "It was an instinct I had to be trained out of early on when I started taking on responsibilities as Heir. If I'd have let everyone else's needs dictate everything I did, I would have been chained to a meeting table or running around solving problems until I was worn ragged, and I would have shriveled to a useless state. By putting everyone else first and neglecting myself, I was preventing myself from being able to serve them in the way they deserved. When I balance their needs with my own, everyone benefits the most."

"That's very...wise of you," she said.

It was my turn to feel my cheeks grow hot. "Oh, not me. I had a good teacher, that's all."

"Your father?" she asked tentatively, as if not sure she could bring him up.

"Yes, him," I said, casting her a warm smile to show it was alright. "I'd have done that shriveling I mentioned within a couple weeks if it hadn't been for him. He took me in hand right away, and from then on, he's always been careful to warn me if I lose my balance."

"It sounds like he is a good father," she said quietly.

My smile died. "The very best."

I busied myself setting up the spit for Yvera, hoping Sarah wouldn't notice the return of my soberness.

No such luck.

"You must miss him," she murmured.

"I do," I said as naturally as I could manage. "But I've taken breaks to go back and visit him."

Short ones. It was always too painful to see the changes in him in person, all the starker for me because of my absences. And the longer I stayed, the more ministers and counselors tried to pin me down to put an end to my "irresponsible wanderings." In their minds, I should be focused on learning to take over. If only I could explain to them the fault in their strategy: that I was doing the far more *responsible* task in the long run. But that would require revealing things the Tree had forbidden Avva and me to reveal. So, I avoided them as best I could, and Avva tried to ignore their complaints about his errant Heir.

"And I speak to him whenever I can," I went on. Then grimaced. "Speaking of which, I should call him as soon as Yvera gets back to stay with you. Now that we've decided...on where to spend the night, he's going to want to know."

He would not be pleased, even if I only revealed a fraction of the danger.

"You can call him?" Sarah asked in surprise.

I looked at her, blinking. "Sure. It's not that hard. Simple enough magic—we learned it in secondary."

"What's it like?" she asked, eyes bright with interest.

It was like a light had turned on inside her, illuminating her from the inside out, bringing life and vivacity where before there had been withdrawn strain. The difference was so startling and captivating that I didn't realize I was staring until her light brown cheeks started turning darker.

"What?" she asked self-consciously, the light inside shuttering.

I looked away and refocused on filling my kettle with water. "Nothing—I'm just...surprised it's that interesting. But I'm happy to show you. Sometime."

Sometime when it's safer. Sometime when I can spare the energy. Sometime when I'm not calling Avva.

Those were two beings that I did not want to meet too soon. Kor was right—Avva would adore her, and I had a good enough feel for Sarah now to suspect she would be drawn to his gentle strength like a moth to a flame.

Yet I abruptly felt the exact opposite desire: the strongest and strangest impulse to *bring* the two of them together. To just sit back and watch them meet, interact, and become close. The image brought a warmth to my flameheart that was as troubling as it was pleasurable. I dismissed the thought as being cruel as I hung my kettle over the fire; I would never do that to Avva. Sarah and Avva would inevitably meet, yes, but if *I* brought her to him like that, he would get the wrong idea and start hoping I'd changed my mind.

Which I hadn't—wouldn't. Couldn't.

Argh, could I avoid *any* of the heavy thoughts this evening? I had to get my head on straight, and fast, before night fell.

"I'd like that," Sarah said shyly, and it took me a harried moment to remember what we had been discussing.

"Then I will," I said with a quick smile in her direction before getting to my feet. "Just as soon as it's safe enough for a demonstration. Who knows? By then, I might be teaching you how to do it yourself."

"What do you mean?"

I froze in the middle of brushing off my pants when I heard the startled note in her voice. I thought through our conversations today at the speed of lightning, and I realized the krathen had interrupted us at perhaps one of the worst possible points. I'd spoken to her for what must have been nearly a deken, and yet she still knew so little. Nothing, in fact, of what I needed her to decide, and to do. To become.

I said a few choice curses in the silence of my own head and then let out a breath. I looked down at her feet, not able to even meet her eyes. "Ah, Sarah, I'm...sorry. *Again*."

"It's OK," she said with a weak chuckle. "You haven't had the time to explain yet, and I know now still isn't ideal. Don't worry about me right now. My questions can wait. You just focus on keeping us safe for tonight."

I was startled into meeting her eyes, unable to believe the understanding in her voice. It was in her gaze as well, looking at me as if *I* were the one who deserved compassion.

"That doesn't mean...." I began helplessly. Then groaned, running a hand through my hair. "I *should* have had time by now. I should have *made* time. But I...don't right now. And that's just not fair to you, in so many ways. I'm sorry."

"Hey, Ben," she said soothingly, standing to come up to me. Even though she had to crane her neck to meet my eyes, she didn't look the least bit reluctant to do so. "I'm serious. One thing at a time, right? The most important thing right now is protecting us. Everything else can wait."

I looked down at her in distress for a moment, and then I folded my arms with a sigh. "You're too good. You know that? You should be shouting at me right about now."

"Would that make you feel better?" she asked with a quirk of her pink lips.

"Maybe," I muttered.

"I think you get enough of that from Yvera," she said, with a twinkle in her eye this time.

"Speaking of whom," I said, looking up as I heard a telltale flap on the wind.

Out of the corner of my eye, I saw Sarah take a hasty step back, as if only just aware of how close she had been to me. A part of me was disappointed, a part was relieved, and a part was troubled. I ignored all such parts for now as I watched Yvera come in.

As Sarah had said: one thing at a time.

Chapter Thirteen

MOONTOUCHED

Sarah

I woke up to the smell of hot meat roasting over a fire, which sent my stomach into overdrive, reminding me forcefully of how little I had digested that day. I blinked my crusty eyes open.

I still lay on the makeshift bed Ben had made for me, suggesting I try to get some rest while he and Yvera set up some magical defenses. But now, instead of having just my coat for a covering, I found myself enveloped in a giant fur blanket, the soft edge of which brushed against my cheek. Darkness had fallen, so my eyes were drawn to the fire crackling away merrily in the brazier a couple yards away, and around it sat Kor and Yvera.

Kor sat across the fire from me, sitting cross-legged on a different kind of cushion than any of the others so far: one that appeared to have an elevated portion in the middle on which he sat, and the rest lower, where his legs crossed. In keeping with the warrior-monk image, he still was shirtless, but his arms and back were covered with his robe; his spine was straight, but his head was lowered in a relaxed position, and his eyes were closed.

Yvera sat on the bare stone at the three o'clock position and was carving off chunks of a chicken-sized animal roasting on the spit. At the sight of it, dripping juice and all, my stomach growled so loudly, Yvera must have heard, because her sharp eyes snapped to meet mine.

I winced, expecting the same irritation as before. If it was there, I couldn't see it clearly enough in just the flickering light of the fire.

Her voice wasn't friendly, but neither did it have the level of acidity I was expecting. "Ben said you'd be hungry. So come get some if you are."

I slipped reluctantly out of the shelter the bed represented: both from the cold of the wind and her gaze. I grabbed my coat and pulled it back on as I walked the short distance to the fire. I sat down on the remaining cushion that seemed to have been left out for that purpose. That was when I saw where Ben was: sprawled out in the last remaining position around the fire, lying straight on his back, with a blanket to his armpits, but his arms free—one thrown over his face, the other resting on his chest.

"He always sleeps like that," Yvera said.

I started at the dry, almost amused tone and looked back at her. Her eyes had followed mine to Ben and lingered there, her lips pulling in the corners into the smallest of smirks. "Flame only knows how he breathes, but he does. How else would he be able to snore like that if he didn't?"

I listened, and a smile of my own cracked my lips as I finally identified the rhythmic snuffling of his breath.

"Could be a lot worse," I ventured with a tentative smile, not sure how far to push this truce between us. "You should hear my dad when he sleeps. Mom has to wear earplugs."

"I pity her, then," Yvera said, her smirk growing. "*This* lug is quite enough to put up with on as infrequent a basis as I have to."

Our eyes met for a moment of shared amusement. Then the moment was gone, and Yvera looked away sharply, a scowl replacing her smile.

She handed me a plate with some meat she must have carved previously and set aside, but her eyes stayed fixed on the fire.

"Thank you," I said.

She grunted but didn't otherwise reply, turning back to her task of carving up the rest of the roasting animal.

Still...it was a start.

Maybe.

Even though I felt like I was near the starvation point, I picked at the meat as I thought of what I could say to ease even just a bit more of the tension between us.

She cast a glance at me and grunted again. "*Eat*, girl. You've just had a major healing. You're going to need all the food you can fit into your stomach for the next day or so."

I put larger chunks into my mouth after that.

After about a minute, I tried again. "This is very good."

All that got was another grunt.

I finished my plate, and Yvera took it and filled it up again without me asking. But her expression was a tad softer when she handed it back this time.

I glanced at Kor, who was still in the same position as before. "What's up with him?" I whispered.

"He's spiriting," Yvera said tersely, at a normal volume.

I took a steadying breath and then dared ask for clarification. "Which is...?"

Yvera rolled her eyes but answered in an even enough tone. "He's sending his spirit out to scout the area. To keep a lookout for anything that might be coming close enough to sense us through the wards and illusion he's put up."

"That...sounds like he's spending quite a lot of power in a short amount of time. At night."

Yvera grunted. "Well, that's what he's good for, isn't it? And why else would we risk a fire unless he needed the light and warmth to keep going? 'Course, we wouldn't need such a strong illusion if we *didn't* have the fire. But then, you get a hot meal, and Ben and I get some benefit too, so Ben decided it was a net gain."

"Speaking of Ben, I'm kind of surprised he's asleep," I said, looking back at him. "He doesn't seem the type to be out at a time like this."

"He's not," Yvera said, a wicked gleam entering her eye. "I *might* have drugged his tsha with just a sprinkle of dreamhaze."

"You did?" I asked in bemused startlement.

"Not so much that he won't wake if we need him, mind you. But Kor and I both thought he should be the most rested of all of us, just in case."

I finally understood their strategy. "Kor's wearing himself out first because his specialty lies in subtlety, and the smartest thing for us to do right now is to hide. Or, at the very least, hide long enough for you and Ben to be rested enough to defend us when we're discovered."

"Yes," Yvera said in surprise, and then scowled and looked away as if she'd accidentally given me praise.

I hesitated for a moment. Then, realizing I might not get as good an opportunity as this for a while, I took a deep breath and went for the plunge. "Yvera—"

"Don't," she said, her eyes sharp when they glared back at me. She raised the carving knife in her hand and pointed it at me like a finger. "Stop right there. I know what you're going to do. You're going to simper and smile and try to make me *like* you. Well, let me just make this one thing clear right now, Earthren: I am *never* going to like you. The more you wrap Ben around your little, frail fingers, the more I can't *afford* to like you. Because for all I know, you could be the greatest threat to him that he's ever faced. So save your breath for Ben. And Kor, if you'd like. But I've got a job to do, and it is *not* to be your friend."

I stared at her, so startled by the direction of her thoughts that I still had the audacity to blurt out, "That's not what I was trying to do at all. I was trying to say you are right."

"What?" she asked, lowering the hand holding the carving knife so that the tip almost trailed in the dirt.

"You're right. I'm a weak, useless human who has put Ben in far too much danger than I'm worth," I said emphatically. "Ben wouldn't have been in the clearing yesterday if it wasn't for me. Nor would he have been bitten by a werewolf—"

At Yvera's scrunched expression of confusion, I quickly corrected myself. "Sorry, a...krathen, today. And he wouldn't be here camping on a mesa in the dark in the middle of a jungle filled with consumed. Heck, none of you would be. You don't know how much I hate that he keeps doing all these things for me and dragging you two along with him. I *am* a threat to him, for *no good reason*. He *should* be handing me off to someone else to babysit until he can figure out how to open a gate, send me home, and get back to his life."

I caught my breath and then let out a relieved sigh. "Oh, you don't know how good it felt to get that off my chest to someone who would let me finish. Let alone agree with me. Even Kor's been all...weird about me. Seems to think I have some kind of potential to *become* something. You'd think someone as smart as Kor would wait to gather a bit more evidence than that, don't you think?"

I realized I was babbling while Yvera was staring at me with a frozen expression of incredulity, and I snapped my mouth closed. After a few seconds of awkward silence, I looked back down at my plate. "Anyway. Um. That's it. That's all I wanted to say."

That was when a different bodily need made itself manifest. I winced, but the need was as pressing as it was awkward and would not be silenced.

"Yvera?"

"What?" she exclaimed in exasperation as she turned from the roast and back to me.

I took a deep breath and raised my chin against the hostility in her gaze. "Um. What should I do if I need to...."

I stared at her helplessly, hoping against hope that she would understand without further elaboration.

She barked a laugh and then pointed with the carving knife at a string strung up between two poles about ten or so feet behind her and a couple of buckets just beyond. "The bucket is right there. Pull the curtain for some privacy. Not ideal, but with no way to dig a pit...."

She shrugged and then smirked at me, as if daring me to complain about the primitive accommodations. Instead, I just gasped, "Great, thanks!" and darted behind the rope, pulling the cloth across the string as I did so. I rolled my eyes. Who did she think I was, some pampered princess back on Earth? With my parents' fondness for camping on a low budget, I'd gone to the restroom in more awkward situations than this.

OK, not *many*, mind you. Especially not with three near-strangers on the other side of a simple curtain, one of whom had just declared she would forever despise me, the second was a genius of questionable motives, and the third was...well, someone I didn't want hearing this, so I was intensely grateful he was the one in a drug-induced slumber.

But my worst experience was still the long dash through the total darkness to an outhouse in the middle of a freezing night in the mountains of Colorado with the distant howl of probably-coyotes-but-maybe-werewolves.

"Don't go far," Yvera warned. I could see the outline of her shadow against the brightness of the fire through the cloth, so I knew she was turned toward me. "Kor's illusion doesn't extend much beyond that, and if you go through the edge, you'll dispel it."

"Got it!" I said, praying she would now return to her stoic, resentful silence so that I could relieve myself in peace.

Fortunately, she did.

I finished quickly and shoveled some sand from the second, smaller bucket into the first to absorb the liquid. I was just admiring the fact that I didn't smell a thing when I closed the main bucket's lid, when something drew my eye to the far left, toward the center of the mesa.

It was...a glowing white line, growing in midair in the darkness—originating at the ground and slowly rising. For no reason I could discern. Nothing seemed to *be* there. Nothing but the rising line.

"Yvera," I said in an uneasy whisper as I pushed the curtain open.

"What *now*?" she exclaimed, turning back to me.

I pointed as I walked back to her side.

She followed my finger with a frown, then looked back at me. "What?" she growled.

I blinked. "Can't you—"

Her eyes darted behind me, and she paled. She surged to her feet and pushed me behind her, making me stumble dangerously close to the fire. Then she turned, spinning in a circle, looking all around us.

As soon as I recovered from my stumble, I saw why.

A couple of moons were out from behind the clouds now, at least partially full, shining enough light to illuminate the mesa...and the low fog creeping toward us inch by inch from all directions.

"No," Yvera said, violet eyes wide. "It can't be—they wouldn't...."

Then her eyes fell on me and narrowed to hard slits for one second.

By the time I'd swallowed, she had already moved on, darting to Kor. "Kor!" she said in a quiet yet hard tone. "Kor, snap out of it! We need you here."

When he didn't move, she grabbed his shoulder and shook him. "Kor!"

One moment, he was rigid and straight as ever. The next—he collapsed. All muscles lost tension, and he fell to the side as limply as a bag of sand.

Yvera barely caught him before his head hit the stony ground. "Kor!" she cried in panic.

"What's happened to him?" I asked breathlessly as I rushed over.

Yvera didn't answer me. Instead, she shoved him at me, and I had to fall to my knees to bear his deadweight. I gasped as I felt his ice-cold skin.

"Hold him," she barked, acid in her voice. "Drag him closer to the fire, if you can manage that much."

As I began the painstaking effort, she darted over to her sleeping Heir. "Ben!"

My back was to them, so I didn't see what was going on, but I heard Ben's relaxed snuffling cut off in a snort and then a gasp. "Yv? Wha...." he said blearily.

"They've sent a lish," she said. "It's got Kor."

Silence reigned for one second, apart from my pants and the scrape of my and Kor's bodies as I tried to drag both of us across the short distance to the fire.

"Yvera," Ben said in a voice of deadly calm. "What did you do to me?"

He didn't wait for an answer. The moment he finished, I heard a rustle and scrape across stone, and abruptly he was in my field of vision, scooping Kor up from me without so much as a huff of effort.

"You needed rest!" Yvera said in her defense.

"We'll discuss this—*later*," Ben snapped. "Now you do your job, and I'll do mine."

She nodded sharply and picked up her claymore, striding out nearly beyond the circle of firelight. My eyes darted between her and Ben, uncertain what to do or even which one to watch. Especially after Ben held Kor out from his body over the fire as if he were about to dump him in.

"Ben," I choked, reaching out reflexively to stop him.

But Ben didn't let go of Kor. With mind-boggling strength, he held his limp leftwing over the fire, even as it roared higher. Besides, Ben already seemed past hearing. His eyes weren't just glowing now. They were *burning*, shining with a light so bright I had to look away. Every exposed inch of his hair and skin glowed gold, turning him into a human sun, until I could *feel* waves of heat roll off him from where I stood.

Ben let out a roar that sounded chillingly somewhere between that of a human and a beast. Then the light faded.

I opened my eyes and blinked rapidly, disoriented by the sudden darkness. Ben's glow was gone...and so was the fire. All I saw was Ben's dark figure holding Kor—illuminated in eerie flickers from a new source of fire: a violet wall of it that encircled us completely.

"How is he?" Yvera asked, striding back to us, sword still in hand—except now it was dripping tongues of violet flame like water.

"Nnnnngh," Kor said, head lolling.

Yvera snorted. "I take that to mean he's back."

"Yes," Ben said tiredly. "But a little worse for wear."

Kor mumbled something mostly incoherent, of which I only understood "know" and "next."

"Quiet, Kor," Ben said with a weary chuckle. "We'll handle this."

"*How?*" Yvera hissed.

She and Ben exchanged a look that chilled my blood. I could see the silent conversation taking place between them, and the results did not look good. Not wanting to interrupt, however, I looked around to see what I could discern for myself. The wall of fire was only about three feet high, so I could see beyond.

My eyes were drawn back to the white line from before, which now had blossomed into an outline of a set of arched gates with the pattern of a tree. It was, impossibly, still only a two-dimensional outline in pure white light, see-through in the negative spaces, nothing but mesa beyond.

Though that was strange enough, I understood there was a more immediate threat: the fog, which was about two-thirds across the mesa to us in every direction. Perhaps even more ominous, clouds were rolling across the moons again, and this time they looked too thick and roiling and moved too quickly to be natural. In their depths, I could see white flickers with cold blue at the end of the spectrum, like lightning except...fluid? Moving through the cloud like a serpent around a tree....

I shivered, from more than just fear. The temperature had dropped rapidly since Ben's light had faded. I watched with shock and dread to see *frost* growing on the ground ahead of the fog, crawling toward us like greedy, icy fingers. Our breaths—especially Ben's and Yvera's, and to a lesser extent Kor's—fogged in the air, and Kor shuddered, curling in toward Ben. Ben glanced down at him, eyes tight with worry.

Then Ben looked up at me. For a moment, his eyes shimmered gold in the darkness, just enough for me to see the depths of the helpless rage that lay there. I did not know what was going on and therefore nothing of how bad our situation was. But Ben did. And at the tightened look of regret in his eyes, I knew it was about as bad as it could get.

No. I couldn't accept that. I would *not* accept that. If we all died tonight—if a single *one* of us died tonight—it would be because of *me*.

And that was intolerable.

"What are we going to do?" I said with chattering teeth.

"There's nothing we *can* do, you stupid girl!" Yvera said, rounding on me. Her eyes burned with a different fire than Ben's. This fire wasn't one of regret. It was full of condemnation. "We cannot fly. We have no heat. No light. No hope of driving back that *thing* that *you*—"

"Yvera," Ben said. It was just one word, but it was a command, flat and unyielding.

She turned back to him, expression agonized. She swallowed, made her sword vanish into the ether, and held out her arms. "Ben, give him to me."

"No," Ben said harshly.

"You know what you have to do."

"No," he repeated, almost in a snarl.

"Ben, it's the only—"

"I won't abandon you all to die!" he roared.

My breath froze for a moment. "Ben...you can...you can get out?"

His eyes darted to mine. "I won't."

"He can," Yvera said, not looking away from Ben. "He can surge to a sungate at any moment at will. But he can't take anyone with him."

Then, for the first time, I heard Yvera's silent voice address only me. Her eyes flicked to mine for a second with the desperation of someone seizing on their last hope. *Sarah, tell him to leave us.* He *can still survive.*

I didn't need her urging. I tried to steady my voice as I lifted my chin and met Ben's gaze, hoping I looked calmer than I felt. "Ben, if you can escape...you should."

"If I left you all now, after getting you into this mess, I wouldn't be worthy to live," Ben said. "If you die, so will I."

He wouldn't leave. I could see it in his eyes. There was *nothing* we could do to make him leave. While Yvera continued to protest, saying something about Ben's duty as Heir, he continued to gaze at me with utter determination.

He was going to die. Because of me.

"But what about the gate?" I asked, eyes stinging with desperation.

Yvera cut off, and they both stared at me, giving me their full attention.

"What gate?" Ben asked, expression shifting from grim to focused.

I pointed at the glowing white outline in the middle of the mesa. "I'm no expert, I know. But to me, that looks like a gate. Is it one you can use?"

Both drakón looked where I pointed, but both of their eyes searched the darkness in vain, never landing on anything.

"The white doors!" I exclaimed, pointing. "Tall. Arched. With a pattern of a tree on them. Glowing like a *moon* right now. How can you be missing it?"

Yvera looked at me first incredulously and then with narrowed suspicion; she cast Ben a meaningful look, but his gaze only darted between the darkness and me, face intent.

"You...you can't see it?" I asked, deflated. "Then how come I can?"

Kor spoke to all our minds then, even his silent voice faint. *Moon...touched.*

I froze, hardly able to breathe.

That's it, Ben said silently, face set, eyes burning. He shoved Kor into Yvera's stiff arms and began moving around our makeshift camp in a blur, making things disappear left and right. *We're heading for the doors.*

The doors that don't exist? Yvera exclaimed, staggering from Kor's weight. But to my disbelief, she managed without too much difficulty otherwise.

When the Tree spoke to me today, She told me that if we listened to Sarah, all of us would survive to see the dawn, Ben declared. *So that's what we're going to do.*

"What—we—Ben, that's suicide!" Yvera said out loud. "We set *one* foot outside all the protections we've set up, and we're iced meat."

We're that if we stay here, too, Ben said. *Sarah will lead because she's the only one who can see them, but you'll be at her flank to send a spear point of fire ahead of us. I'll bring Kor in the rear and try to guard us from behind and above.*

"This is insane!" Yvera snarled at Ben's back as he snatched up the last item: Kor's meditation cushion. "You know that, right? She's either gone mad or she's leading us into a trap."

Or, Ben growled, marching back to her and standing so close he bumped against Kor, *there are doors there that can save us all. Stay here if that's your choice. But I'm taking Kor and Sarah to them.*

As if to hammer in the point, Ben took Kor back from Yvera with a yank.

Yvera's eyes flashed with violet fire. Her eyes darted to mine with a message just for me. *I don't care if this is a trap or your madness—when he dies because of you, I'll kill you myself.*

I nodded, heart pounding in anticipation of what we were about to do rather than her threat, which seemed fair to me. It wasn't like I could survive anything Ben couldn't; even if he died first, I wouldn't be far behind. Yvera might even give me a cleaner end. I wasn't looking forward to freezing to death, or facing whatever horrors lay hidden in those clouds.

Speaking of which, the clouds had almost entirely closed over the sky by now and began sprinkling tiny icy snowflakes on us in a frigid flurry. A glowing white *something*—a different white than the gate, harsher, bluer—was still circling within them, twisting like a worm through an apple but staying out of sight. The fog had nearly reached Yvera's circle of fire, but a scattered pattern of golden and violet runes, which were burning with an intense light, had slowed it. Even a few rings of dark blue were fighting the icy miasma's progress, though their light was fainter.

Message delivered to me, Yvera looked back at Ben and nodded stiffly; her claymore once again appeared in her hand. *And let you get all the glory? No thanks.*

Ben's shoulders lowered the tiniest bit in relief. *Thank you,* he said.

He glanced back at me. *Sarah, get in position. We run on my mark.*

Gulping, unable to believe Ben was resting all our fates *on me* but seeing no other choice, I walked over to and then in front of Ben.

Run as fast as you can, he instructed as I went. *And stop for nothing. Nothing, do you understand? Not even if I fall behind. I'm counting on you to get the doors open;* that's *your priority. I can catch up and speed through as long as they're open. Got it?*

I cast one desperate glance back at him. "What makes you think they'll open for *me*?" I whispered.

Because it's you, Ben said, looking at me with complete faith.

Somehow, both of us were going to have to survive so he could explain to me what he meant by that. But for now, I had a job to do. I turned back to face the gate. Unconsciously, I fell into a runner's crouch, with my eye fixed on the double doors outlined in soft white light as if it were a finish line. That was it—that's all this was. Just another race. Just another....

I breathed slowly and deeply through my belly, and my world narrowed to just those doors and the rocky surface in between me and them, hidden now beneath the fog. No icy chill, no roiling clouds with a concealed menace, no lives on the line. Just me, my worn sneakers...

...and the race.

Ben's silent whisper came more softly than any shotgun—almost more prayer than command. *Go.*

I shot forward. My speed must have startled Yvera, since it took her a moment to catch up to my side, but she kept pace easily after that, even while balancing her claymore in one hand and raising her other to send a V of violet fire to blaze the path clear just ahead. Figures I would be the slower of the two of us, but maybe that wasn't a terrible thing, since I didn't know how well Ben would be able to keep up, burdened as he was. But I didn't look back. I fixed my eyes on the double doors, only sparing darting glances to the ground to determine the placement of my next foot strike.

Mere seconds after we'd begun our headlong sprint, a blue-white flash of what looked like lightning struck just to my side. A bubble of golden light surrounded and moved with us, shielding us from the worst of the energy blast, but I still stumbled from the tremor that went through the rock. Yvera yanked me upright and shoved.

"Go," she snarled.

I was already going. Even though *things* with glowing blue-white eyes and cloudy pelts were forming from the fog, closing in around us. I didn't let myself look away from the gate, worried that if I broke concentration for one second, I would see something that would freeze me in fear. I didn't look, and I didn't stop, not even when I heard a howl. Not even when Yvera's sword flashed in my periphery and that howl broke off in a yelp.

Not even when my lungs burned, and the frigid air clawed at my throat. Not even when the icy lightning struck right overhead and hit the newly formed dome with a crash that deafened me for seconds after.

The ringing in my ears probably saved our lives. Because it meant I did not hear Ben fall.

Not five seconds later, I slammed into the doors, which—despite the see-through sections—felt as solid as stone. Thick, cool, smooth, heavy stone.

Unyielding stone.

For one horrible second, I thought I had indeed doomed us all. I glanced over my shoulder in a breathless panic and saw a sight that turned me to ice.

Ben was about a dozen yards away and just stumbling to his feet, looking dazed and exhausted, with Kor now slung across his shoulders. Yvera stood with him, grimly fending off the...*things* in the mist with her claymore.

Perhaps most dreadful of all, the lurker in the clouds emerged.

Only then did I realize that the white things I'd glimpsed in the clouds were only the glowing streaks down its sides and its eyes. Everything else, from its horns to its talons to its irises, was the blackness of the void.

So large was the dark, elongated monstrosity, it seemed to encompass a third of the sky in my field of vision, and as it sank below the clouds and snaked toward us, it moved with an impossible ease and slowness that told me it wasn't dependent on wings for flight. Or bound by any of the normal laws of nature at all.

As its burning white and black eyes fixed on me, I realized that I thought I had experienced true fear on seeing my first dragon. But that was nothing compared to seeing *this* twisted one. Never mind that the fog beasts and even the fog itself gave the gate a wide berth. I somehow knew that whatever magic was repelling them would stand no chance against the hungerer that was coming for me. My mind was a frozen wasteland of fear, unable to think or to move or to do anything except tremble and wait for my fate.

Until Ben's desperate voice shattered the ice. *Sarah, open it!*

Heaving a shaking breath, I turned back to the doors, closed my eyes, pushed against the stone with all my might, and pleaded with all the fervor of my soul.

Please open. Please. If only for them. They shouldn't have to die for me. Please. Please.

Please.

I felt a coolness blossom in my torso, somewhere near my abdomen. Not a second later, that coolness turned into an icy fire. Then the doors *pulled* the fire from me. It was like when I touched the doorgem, except a thousand times stronger. The shock went through my entire body as every last drop of energy I had to spare was sucked through me and into the doors.

For one split second of utter exhaustion, I was afraid it wasn't enough.

Then the stone gave way.

And I fell into white oblivion.

Chapter Fourteen
RESTING

Koriben

Yvera and I were only a few feet behind Sarah by the time the invisible force she had been pushing against gave way to a crack of white. I cried out as Sarah collapsed, but Yvera surged ahead and caught her, sweeping her up into her arms as we dashed one after the other through the two-foot crack.

The brilliant light dimmed as soon as we entered, revealing a plain corridor of smooth stone.

"Close them!" I told Yvera urgently, and she nodded in agreement. We both deposited our living burdens on the cool flagstones as gently as was expedient—I tried not to cast a worried glance at Sarah and failed—and dashed back around to take one door each.

If this was a gate, it was unlike any I had ever dealt with before, but I wasn't about to argue with the methods when our lives were on the line.

From behind, the arched double doors were clearly stone—completely visible and very much present. They were also perfectly balanced, otherwise it might not have been possible for even drakón to push them closed. The door moved easily with a steady push from my hands, and I thanked the Flame to the depths of my soul.

The last sound we heard as the doors came together was the lish's deafening roar of fury at losing its prey.

Then...silence.

Yvera and I stood panting for a moment with our hands braced against the stone. Then we looked at each other, both of our eyes wide, as if neither of us could believe that was it. I knew I couldn't.

Would the gate remain on the mesa, or would it vanish? If it stayed, could the lish or the frostworgs see it? Would the lish be able to force or break it open?

We waited, tense with dread, but moments ticked by with...nothing.

The lish had been close enough to have reached the doors by now, if they were still present and were (or had ever been) visible to it. Yet we heard and felt nothing through the stone. Not even the slightest tremor.

"Can you feel...a gate?" Yvera panted.

A good question. I closed my eyes and concentrated on the doors, spreading my awareness out wide like a net. I opened my eyes and shook my head. "I can't feel *anything*. But then, I couldn't feel them before, so I don't know if that means much."

"Good enough for me," Yvera gasped, and she turned around and slid against the doors all the way to the ground. I copied her a second later, and we both sat for at least a dek, staring dully at nothing as the adrenaline faded and exhaustion washed over us.

I was the more rested of the two of us, and even I was sorely tempted to just curl up where I was and not move for deken. But then my eyes fell on Sarah and Kor, sprawled on the floor a few feet away from us.

A spike of fear gave me the boost I needed to get on my hands and knees and crawl to Sarah. I knew from before that Kor would be alright once his body had time to recover from his energy drain and spirit's captivity. But Sarah....

She was frighteningly cold as I turned her over, but maybe that was just from the recent chill and the difference in our running temperatures. Still, I fretted over that as I moved on in my examination; the coldness of her body couldn't be *good* for her right now.

Fortunately, she was breathing regularly, if a bit shallowly, and I felt a pulse, if weak. I scrounged up some last few drops of energy for a quick scan of her body and found nothing particularly amiss. Her nutritional levels were depleted—no surprise there with how little food I'd gotten into her system that day—and all signs pointed to an unideal body temperature, but other than that, she just felt empty of spark.

I sighed as I ran a gentle hand over the crown of her head. Opening those doors had saved all our lives, but it must have cost every drop she had.

Then it hit me.

We were...*alive*. All four of us. More or less conscious, more or less enlivened. But *alive*.

And, so it seemed, safe. Both thanks to the young woman lying next to me.

I let out a heavy breath.

"How...is she?" Yvera asked, almost reluctantly.

"She needs warmth and food," I answered tiredly.

Yvera snorted. "Don't we all."

I looked at her with barely the energy for a raised eyebrow. "You feel like eating?"

"Flame, no," she said with an exhausted sigh, sinking into the corner. "All I want is sleep. The next century ought to do it."

"Go ahead," I said, staggering to my feet. "I'll take the next watch."

Here was as good a place for us to sleep as any. The corridor extended in a straight line as far as I could see in the dimmed lighting—provided only by strips of some pearlescent material along both edges of the ceiling. As troubling as was the thought of collapsing at the foot of the gate where the deadliest kind of foe could be waiting just on the other side, we didn't know what lay ahead in this foreign place, either, and none of us had the current capacity to find out. I was willing to bet we would be undisturbed by anything that might lie ahead if we stayed here. I could smell no trace of any recent passerby or occupants—only the staleness of abandonment, which fit the profile of an ancient Moontouched stronghold.

Given all those thoughts going through my fatigued mind, the soundest strategy I could think of was for us to rest where we were before pressing ahead. If the lish started breaking down the gate, well—at least we would have an early warning.

"Ben," Yvera protested, straightening. "I should go first."

I'd begun pulling out all our cushions, but I spared her a glare that dared her to argue. "I've already had some sleep tonight, *remember*?"

She winced. "Kor thought it was a good idea, too."

"I don't care if the *chief minister* thinks it's a good idea," I retorted. "You don't drug me again, do you understand? *Especially* when we're out in the open."

Especially when Sarah's life *is on the line,* I thought but didn't say. Yvera seemed to have taken a strange disliking to Sarah for some reason I couldn't make out, and I wasn't about to try right now.

"When it comes to your safety, you can't countermand me," she said defiantly. "I'll drug you again if I have to in order to save your stupid hide."

"I'm not trying to pin you down with a command," I said in exasperation. "I'm saying this is a matter of *trust*. Of partnership. I'm saying that I can't work with you like this if you're going to be slipping dreamhaze or whatever it was you did into my tsha on a night when I need to be on my guard, just because you and Kor 'think it's a good idea.'"

She was silent for a moment as I finished arranging all the cushions together.

"I promise not to do it again unless it is an absolute emergency and I have no alternative. How is that?" she said stubbornly.

"Good enough for now," I said as I picked Sarah gently off the floor and brought her over to the hodgepodge of cushions.

"Wait, why'd you put them all together?" Yvera demanded, just noticing the arrangement.

"We all need warmth, this corridor is too cool to be of much help there, and I don't know if we can risk a fire." I set Sarah gingerly down at one edge and put a pillow under her head. "We're sleeping together tonight."

"Ugh," Yvera said, wrinkling her nose as she glanced at Kor.

"I'm not saying you have to *snuggle* with him," I said in exasperation. I got out a blanket, unfolded it with a flap, and let it drift over Sarah. "There's room for you to have your space. If not, get out some more cushions. But it won't kill you to share the same blankets. We've done this before, remember?"

"In a blizzard," Yvera said mutinously.

"Well, we were nearly just in one."

I sighed as I went to grab Kor and saw her still-rebellious expression. "Look, Yvera, I'm not forcing you. It's just a suggestion. Sarah and Kor could use at least *one* of us to give them body heat, and since you're the less rested of the two of us, it makes sense for you to go first, but if it makes you that uncomfortable, forget it."

"Fine," she growled. She pushed up onto her feet and somehow managed an exhausted but still petty march over to the pile of cushions. She fell dramatically into the middle just as I was laying a blanket over Kor.

"Want me to tuck you in?" I teased.

"If you wouldn't mind," she said with a crooked smile and only one eye open. She'd already pulled out a pillow and was looking half asleep.

"I'll accommodate you, *this* time," I said with an exaggerated eye roll. "Seeing as you've just saved my life *again*."

"Dontchu forget it," she mumbled, other eye drifting closed as I tossed a blanket over her, letting it overlap Sarah's and Kor's. As soon as it settled, I reached over them all and tucked the blanket right under her chin, just the way I knew she liked to sleep. Her eyes blinked open, and she gave me one of her rare vulnerable smiles.

"Thanks, Ben." Her eyes drifted closed again. She yawned hugely. "I'm glad...you're not dead."

"Me too," I said with a weary chuckle. "Go to sleep, silly."

"*You're* silly," she said childishly. It was an old exchange between us, from back when we were nestlings still young enough to sleep in the same room on a regular basis. Her eyes were already closed, and I could tell she'd be out in moments.

"Love you, Yv," I said in amusement.

She mumbled something so quietly and sleepily that I wasn't sure whether the words came from her conscious self or her dreams. "Not same."

I stared at her in confusion for a moment, then shook my head and shrugged. She always started spouting nonsense when she got this tired. There was no point in trying to make sense of her words now, when most likely they meant nothing at all.

I WAS SUSPICIOUSLY CONTENT as I drifted awake at dawn. I realized why when I felt a warm breath against my chest, and an accompanying greater warmth curled trustingly against me. From the size and temperature and smell of her, I knew at once who it was, and a shot of pure alarm went through me like a lightning bolt, waking me up at once.

Torch it, I even had an *arm* slung over her torso—more just to accommodate her against me than anything, but *still*. It would not be easy to—

Too late. To my horror, I felt Sarah stirring, perhaps in reaction to my sudden stiffness. In retrospect, I should have feigned sleep; that at least would have seemed more innocent. Instead, I jerked my arm off her as if she were on fire and rolled back—onto Kor's outstretched arm and leg, which no doubt had been the initial reason for our forced closeness. Kor normally sprawled in his sleep, but torch it, right then he must have been taking up two-thirds of the cushions.

Sarah gasped at the same time that Kor grunted in protest—and shoved me back.

"Kor!" I exclaimed as I rolled back toward Sarah. Fortunately, this time I braced myself on my forearms over her, but it still did not make me look good in the slightest as our eyes met under the blankets. Her face was perhaps the most flushed I had ever seen it, and I was sure mine wasn't far behind.

"Sorry!" I blurted as I pushed myself off her and onto my heels in unoccupied territory. "Sorry! I—I wasn't—I didn't—"

Flame help me, I couldn't even finish a sentence.

Now who's snuggling? Yvera asked me darkly.

I wasn't! I shot back in alarm. *Kor—*

Seemed like you were enjoying yourself to me, she interrupted.

Meanwhile, Sarah had sat up and was laughing shakily. She cleared her throat of sleep phlegm and said, "No, I'm the one who should be apologizing. I got pretty cold last night, huh?"

"Cold," I said, cheeks still flaming. And still, apparently, unable to articulate a full sentence. "Yes. Last night. Cold. All of us. Tired and cold. Very."

Even though my back was to Yvera, I could *feel* her eye roll at my brilliant explanation.

Sarah shivered, no doubt at the sudden absence of the blankets that I'd shoved away from us both as I sat up. "It *is* chilly here."

She began looking around, eyes wide. "Wherever...here *is*."

"Where in the name of the Flame are we?" Kor grunted, squinting as he propped himself onto his elbows.

"Good question," Yvera said. I glanced back at her and saw her leaning in one corner by the gate. Her arms were folded, and one foot was propped against the wall. "Why don't we ask the one who *brought* us here?"

"Me?" Sarah asked, cheeks flushing again under her glare. "*I* have no clue. I still don't know why I even could *see* the darn thing."

"Unless my last few memories are failing me," Kor drawled as he inclined his head in her direction. "I told you why."

"All you said was...." she began hotly, but her voice trailed off, as if she couldn't even say the word.

"*Moontouched*," Kor said with careful emphasis. "I assume Ben covered at least that much for you?"

"I can't be *Moontouched*," Sarah said. "I'm *human*."

"Actually," Kor said with a yawn and a stretch as he sat up. "Though your human blood is predominant, I think a more accurate term would be a very diluted amón. You are a descendant of the Second Covenant, Sarah. You have to be."

"What proof do you have of that?" she shot back.

"You're here, aren't you?"

She jutted her chin stubbornly, eyes blazing. I should have been intervening or at the very least getting us ready for the no doubt long day ahead, but I could only stare. I'd never seen her like this before. In the...thirty-some-odd deken I'd known her.

"I don't know what you mean."

"Alright, Ben clearly hasn't covered *that*," Kor allowed with a glare in my direction, making me feel a squirm of guilt. "For now then, I rest my case on this point: your doorgem."

"What about it?"

Kor held up one finger. "One, it lit up at all. That shows you have the Blood of the Covenants right there. The gem doesn't have power of its own, Sarah. It draws from that of the user. And if our records are accurate, pure *humans* do not have power—not the kind it can draw on."

Sarah remained silent, but her face was still set. My heart didn't know whether to rise or sink at this glimpse of a stubborn streak in her. On the one hand, it was a healthy and very welcome sign: she was going to need a core of iron to stand up under the weight her Tree had called her to bear. I knew that better than anyone.

But...her clear dislike of this reality did not bode well for her willingness to bear that weight.

She had a choice, of course. The Tree did not force anyone into any role or task. The result was always better for the greater good if one did as She advised, of course, but She never forced. Sarah was within her rights to refuse, and I would be the first to admit that—when considering her needs alone—she would be happier and safer doing so.

But that would be disastrous for me, and so many others. Even if I did not fail to protect her, even if the Tree had another prepared and gave me a second chance, I simply did not have the time now to find the next one. I needed *Sarah* to be willing. I needed the help only *she* could give me now. Desperately.

Kor held up a second finger. "Two, it turned white."

"So?" Sarah asked. "Seems meaningless to me. That's not any of the colors Ben mentioned."

Yvera snorted and Kor looked like he was trying hard to be patient. "That's because *white* was the color of the Moontouched Clan."

Sarah's stubborn expression faded. For some reason, her eyes darted to mine. I don't know what she saw there, but whatever it was, it cracked her open. She clutched at her chest, sending a shot of alarm through me. Was she hurting? Was she sick? Could she not breathe?

But she spoke, if faintly. "You believe it too, don't you? You believe I'm Moontouched. That's what you meant when you said the doors would open *because of who I was*."

"Yes," I said hoarsely.

"Moontouched," she continued in that faint tone. She held her hands in front of her and stared at them as if she'd never seen them before. "I...saw...doors no one else could see. And then I *opened* them. They took something inside of me to do it, just like the gem did. Moontouched doors."

"So we think," I said gently. "It's the only thing that makes sense. Those doors...."

I trailed off for a moment as I glanced behind me at them. Although right now, they were shut so seamlessly that I almost couldn't make out the split in the stone that divided them. If I'd come upon them from this side for the first time, I might have thought it was a stone wall.

I swallowed and looked back at Sarah. "They're not a gate, Sarah. Or...at least, not like any I've ever encountered before."

"And that's saying something," Kor added. "I may be the expert on most things, but as Heir, Ben is our person for gates. Even I have studied them in depth ever since becoming leftwing."

Not to be left out, Yvera said tersely, "And all *three* of us have been through more than our fair share, especially over this past year."

"All that to say," I said. "I don't know what happened last night. By all rights, we should be dead right now...or worse. The only explanation I can think of that makes any sense is that those doors appeared...and opened...and *worked* all because of you."

"Was that what the Tree was talking about, when she spoke to you?" Sarah said, clutching herself as if to stave off freezing. "About what we would learn? That I'm...."

I had to fight an intense battle to stop myself from reaching out to pull her in to share my warmth. I settled for grabbing the blanket behind me and throwing it around her. Her grateful look up at me made it harder to breathe for a second.

Once I'd settled back a safe distance away from her, I answered. "I don't think so. All of us more or less had guessed who you were by then, and the Tree was talking about something *I* didn't know. Maybe that was about the doors themselves. Or maybe it's whatever...this place is."

I looked around, but even though it was day now and the pearlescent lights were brighter, there still wasn't anything to note other than plain, smooth, square walls, similar large flagstones that made up the floor, and those strips of light. Still going on straight ahead as far as I could see. Although...now that the lights were brighter, I could almost make something out in the distance....

"I assume from all of your expressions that you still have no clue where we are?" Sarah said. I was glad to hear her voice return to a more normal tone.

"None," Kor said with a scowl.

Sarah chuckled, as if even she knew by now how much Kor hated saying that. "Well, I know this isn't much comfort to you three, but *I'm* glad for once to not be the only one feeling lost."

"Well, now that it's daylight, and everyone's awake, let's get ready to find out, shall we?" I said, getting to my feet.

While Kor got up and Yvera came over to help arrange things, Sarah stayed where she was and looked up curiously at me. "How can you tell it's daylight?"

I blinked down at her. "You...can't?"

"Human, remember?" she said.

"Amón," Kor corrected, earning him a scowl—but not a denial—from her.

Yvera snorted. "Even *amón* can tell when it's day."

"Diluted amón," Kor allowed. With his back to Sarah and in a voice so quiet *hopefully* she didn't hear, he added, "For now."

"I get it—you can tell when it's daylight," Sarah said impatiently. She seemed to be getting bolder around us. Maybe that was her getting used to us, or maybe we were rubbing off on her. Whatever the reason, I was glad to see it. "I'm asking *how*."

"It is our energy levels," I said quickly, before either of my wings could answer in either of their unhelpful ways. "Our power returns with the dawn, no matter which sun it is or how far removed from that sun we are."

I looked ruefully at the stone ceiling. "Though being inside or underground *does* slow down our renewal. If we don't get outside soon, we won't reach our capacity before the sun passes its zenith and we fade again."

At that, Sarah got to her feet, brow pinching with worry. "Given how dangerous our lives have been, I gather that's bad."

Yvera's response was to the point. "Very."

Chapter Fifteen

DESTINY

Sarah

BEN WASN'T SATISFIED UNTIL I'd eaten so much, I protested that it would be harder for me to keep up if I stuffed any more down.

"You're depleted, and I've done a shameful job so far of giving you enough to eat," he said in grim explanation as he handed me my second plate.

"Not to mention she threw up most of what she ate for lunch yesterday," Kor said helpfully. I shot him a glare, but he only smirked.

Sure enough, Ben froze. "What?" he said, looking at Kor. "When?"

"While you were off talking to the Tree."

"Why?" Ben looked back at me, eyes tight with worry. "Why didn't you say anything? Do you feel ill—"

"No!" I said, casting Kor another glare. I looked back at Ben. "I just had...a strong reaction to the krathen smell, that's all."

"Are you sure?" Ben asked.

"Positive—I had no problem after he took away my sense of smell."

"Is it back?" Ben asked in mild alarm, shooting a glance at Kor.

"What kind of novice arcanist do you take me for?" Kor said in indignation. "I made it temporary, obviously."

Ben looked at me for confirmation, and I nodded. "It's back alright." I wrinkled my nose at the pickled...something on my plate.

"I'll eat that if you don't want it," Ben offered with an absent frown; he was looking down the corridor, so perhaps it was about the day ahead. Before I could brighten in relief, he added, "Just let me know what you'd like instead."

"Ben, I'm *full*," I protested. "Really."

"Can you eat more?" he asked, looking back at me.

"Yes," I admitted.

"Then please do. You've had a major healing, and then you drained yourself cold yesterday opening those doors—all with little nutrition in your system. It showed when I checked your vitals last night. I don't know what we're going to be facing today and especially tonight, but the one thing I *can* do right now is make sure you eat as much as you can."

I sighed. "Yes, *Dad*."

Ben winced as Yvera snorted in amusement and Kor grinned.

"I'm not *trying* to be a parental figure," Ben said with a look pleading for understanding. "I'm trying to keep you alive—and thank you for saving all of us from my stupidity yesterday."

"I get it," I said. I still sighed as I picked up the third roll I'd received that morning.

Fortunately, Ben let me stop soon after that. Part of that probably had to do with their need to clean up and get going. The three of them had already put most of their things "away" by the time Ben reached for my plate. I gave it to him with a painfully tight breath of relief.

While Ben finished putting my things away, Kor examined the doors. When I stood up with a groan, he was running his hand down the minute crack that was the only sign they had ever been divided at all.

"And you said there was the pattern of a white tree on it?" Kor asked with an absentminded glance back at me.

"For the third and hopefully last time, yes."

"*White?*"

"It was *all* white," I said in exasperation. Not for the first time, I wished I hadn't been the only one to see them. Now that all of them, even Yvera, had indisputable proof, it was so that Kor wouldn't be bothering me every minute with another question about them. I *also* wished Kor had not been the one person too out of it to see even the little Ben and Yvera had.

"And just an outline," Kor said as he stood back. He rested one elbow in the other hand and tapped his chin with his finger. "Otherwise, see-through."

"Yes, and yes."

"Curious," he said. But instead of being annoyed, his dark blue eyes were alive in a way that I'd only seen a few times since I'd met him. I was just relieved that this time, it didn't have to do with me.

Directly.

Moontouched. The word still echoed strangely in my mind. The thought that I could be related to these dragon people somehow was a laughable one. Or, at least, I wanted to laugh at it. But I had no evidence to the contrary, and my academic parents had trained me too well for me to blind myself to all the evidence I now had in *favor* of that theory.

"Can you feel anything?" Ben asked, joining his leftwing.

"Not as much as I should," Kor said, glancing at Ben. "Considering it transported us somewhere else, there should be a much greater residue of magic than there is, but I'm only feeling a trace. Can you?"

"Nothing I'm familiar with as being tied to a gate," Ben said, folding his arms.

"What I want to know is if we can open them," Yvera said, standing on Kor's other side so that the three of them formed a line facing the door. I felt isolated, left to stand alone in the now bare corridor, with nothing to contribute. Not even the proper questions to ask.

"You *want* to?" Ben asked in surprise as he looked at his rightwing.

"The lish has to be gone by now, right?" Yvera said, one hand on her hip, the other gesturing to the door. "It's long past dawn, so we should be safe enough. We don't know where we are now, but we know where we were *last night*. That's a much better starting point. Besides, this place gives me the creeps."

"But Yvera, we could be in a previously *undiscovered* Moontouched hold," Kor said, voice rising with excitement. "Do you have any idea what that means?"

"It's full of dust?" Yvera said.

"It's *undisturbed*," Kor crowed. "Perhaps as pristine as the day the Moon-touched vanished. Who knows what records they might have left, what things we could learn...."

"Like I said," Yvera said briskly, flipping her newly done braid over her shoulder. "Dust. At *best*. But also traps and poisoned air and valper. Or worse."

"Well, yes, those too," Kor allowed impatiently.

"Come on, Ben," Yvera said, knowing who she needed to convince. "I thought you were in a hurry. Do you *really* want to get bogged down with dodging traps and sneezing up centuries of dust?"

Ben hesitated. "The Tree...."

"You said yourself: maybe what the Tree wanted was for us to learn that these doors existed and to save our sorry hides. Now that's done, let's *go*."

"I don't know if we *can*, Yvera," Ben said, gesturing at the doors. "They opened inward, remember? I'm not seeing any handles to pull."

"Well, let's ask our resident Moontouched to try her hand at them, then," Yvera said dryly.

Ben frowned at her. "She has a name, you know. It's *Sarah*. And you can ask her yourself instead of speaking about her as if she's not here."

Actually, I would have rather let Yvera continue ignoring my existence—she seemed to be in a better mood when she could—but my sense of isolation lifted a bit at Ben's correction.

"Fine," she huffed, turning to me. Still, her eyes glared at my sneakers instead of me as she spoke. "*Sarah*, can or can you not open the doors again?"

"But Ben," Kor whined, gesturing down the corridor. "Surely there's something here the Tree wanted us to learn, *other* than the existence of another kind of gate. Maybe we can even learn how to get to Earth."

"Maybe," Ben allowed. "But given our most important responsibility right now is to protect Sarah, Yvera has a point. It might be wiser to send back a fully prepared expedition instead."

When Kor's expression turned mutinous, Ben sighed. "Of course, I would temporarily excuse you from your duties at my side to *lead* that expedition."

"Oh," Kor said, appearing mollified.

"In any case," Ben said, "We should know what all our options are before we commit to one path."

He turned to face me. "If you wouldn't mind, Sarah...?"

I shrugged my shoulders. "I don't even know what I'm doing, but...sure. I'll give it a try."

I walked past all three of them, feeling more than a little self-conscious. Even *presuming* I had some drop of their potential, I wasn't born to this as they were. I really had no idea how to do what they wanted me to. I still didn't know how I'd opened the doors in the first place, other than asking please and letting it take my energy.

Was that really all there was to it? Well, it was all I had to go on, since none of them were offering any helpful tips.

I hesitantly raised my hands and placed them on either side of the crack. Noting what Ben had said about them swinging inward, I didn't try pushing this time. Instead, I just rested my hands there and closed my eyes.

Um...hello? If you can hear me.... If you're something that can *hear...could you try opening, please? I'd appreciate that.*

I then willed the doors to part with all my might, scrunching my face from the mental effort.

And...nothing. No motion from the stone, and none of the stirring I remembered from before. That made me realize that I'd always had some prickling awareness of the gate the night before, from the first moment I'd seen it form, to the time I'd desperately suggested it to Ben, to when I'd pushed against it and pleaded for it to open. But that awareness of *something* was gone now. I felt no more connection to the stone under my fingers than I did to an ordinary wall.

"There's nothing there to open," I said, lowering my hands and turning around to face them. I didn't know how I knew it, but I knew it as surely as if I'd spent hours banging against the doors. "I'll never be able to get them to open. Not when they're like this. There's nothing...special about them anymore. Right now, I think they're just stone."

I'd expected some doubt, but Ben just nodded in acknowledgment of my assessment, Kor's eyes glittered with unspoken questions, and Yvera threw up her hands.

"Great. Just great. Now we're trapped."

"We're only trapped if there's no way out at the other end of that," Ben said with a cheer that was a tad forced as he thumbed over his shoulder at the corridor.

"Well then." Kor's eyes gleamed as he turned to face the other way. "Looks like our only option is to go find it."

Yvera groaned but loosened her claymore in its scabbard. "Let's get one thing straight right now, then: we are looking for the way out. Period. We're not getting sidetracked by dusty records or shiny artifacts. *Got it?*" She threw a glare at Kor. "Or if there *are* valper, I'm throwing you to them."

"Agreed," Ben said, before Kor could retort. "Aside from the valper part. We're looking for the exit, and that's it. Anything else will have to wait for an expedition. Which Kor can lead if he so chooses."

"Good riddance," Yvera said under her breath.

"Oh, fine," Kor said with a sigh and folded arms. "I won't be able to enjoy myself with a purple firebrand breathing down my neck, anyway. I might as well come back with others who will be able to *appreciate* this once-in-a-lifetime discovery."

"I appreciate the gravity of what we've discovered, Kor," Ben said seriously. "But my priority right now is to keep us alive, not admire the works of the dead. Remember, Sarah is being hunted by the consumed as we speak, and they're not above sending a *lish* after her."

"What's a lish?" I asked. The memory of what I had seen last night sent goosebumps up my arms despite the warmth of my coat, and I shivered. "I know it must be that...*thing*. But what *was* it?"

All three drakón looked at me with expressions varying from dark to grim. Ben's eyes were tight with worry. When the others looked to him to answer, he sighed. "What do you think? It's a drakón the Devourer has consumed to the point they become...that."

I gulped. "Does that happen...often?"

Yvera shuddered. "Flame, no. If it gets the chance, it can consume us to the point it can control us, but even then, it can't turn us into lish—not unless *we* want it to. Even then, most of us aren't powerful enough to survive the Devourer doing its thing. We would be extinct if every torched criminal could offer themselves to the Devourer and become one of *them*."

I breathed easier. But I didn't like the way Kor's eyes darted to Ben, or how Ben's lips pressed into a pained line.

I said, "So, there aren't many."

"There shouldn't be *any* right now," Ben said, troubled. "We thought we'd killed the last one a century ago. The Devourer must have been holding that one in reserve, and the fact that it was willing to play that card to capture or kill you...."

My heart pounded at the way all three drakón looked at me: Ben with a face tight with worry; Kor with eyes that glittered with untold theories; and Yvera with eyes narrowed to slits.

My stomach clenched—painfully, considering how full I was. Now I really wished I hadn't eaten so much. I wrapped my arms around my stomach, willing my breakfast to stay down.

"They know. Whatever it is you're hoping I can do...they know about it too."

"We already suspected they did, but I would say the evidence of that is now indisputable," Kor said. "Either they know it for a fact, or they are so afraid of what you *might* be that they're willing to risk everything on that chance."

I was abruptly infuriated that some terrifying cosmic force and its people—no, monsters—knew more about me than I did, and were willing to kill me and whoever got in their way for it.

"*What* is it? Just *what* is this mysterious thing that you need me to do? That's worth sending that *thing* after me to prevent it from happening?"

Yvera and Kor both looked at Ben. Ben looked at me with an emotion in his eyes that could be described only as agony. He swallowed and said in a quiet, strained tone, "Yvera, Kor.... Would you mind scouting ahead, please?"

Yvera snorted, but she grabbed Kor's arm. "Come on, you lug. Let's make ourselves useful."

"Let go, you oaf," Kor muttered, shaking her off. But he followed her without a backward glance.

Ben looked over his shoulder to watch Yvera and Kor until they became small in the distance—a testament to how eerily long and straight this strange corridor was.

"Ben?" I asked, anger fading to nervousness.

He looked back at me, head and shoulders sinking.

"We...." He bowed his head and took a deep breath. When he looked up again, his eyes held no less pain, but the molten ore had hardened to gold. "*I need you to become the next head of the Moontouched.*"

Chapter Sixteen

HEAD

Koriben

SARAH GAPED AT ME as if I had said the craziest thing possible. She searched my expression for a moment. I did not know what she saw there, but I presumed it was too serious for her to dismiss my words as a joke. I saw the laugh that had been bubbling in her expression dispel.

She swallowed. "*Head* of the Moontouched? As in, whatever that last person was—before she was assassinated?"

"Yes," I said.

She laughed, but it was a much more bitter sound than I imagined had built up before. "I only just found out that I *might*—might—be a very distant, diluted member of this long-lost clan, and now you want to make me the *head* of it?"

"Yes," I repeated, flameheart lowering even further. Although this was only what I had expected, given how horribly I had handled everything up to this point. That was one of the many reasons I had sent Kor and Yvera ahead: so that Sarah could yell at me without their interference or judgment.

Sarah threw up her hands. "What, just by default? Because I'm its only confirmed member? Some *clan* leader I'll make—*of no one.*"

"No," I said, flinching. "Not by default. Because you were the one the Trees of Ice and Flame *sent*. Of all the descendants of Moontouched that are in your world, they sent *you*, Sarah. That's why. And it's not a clan of no one. Yes, right now, you're the only confirmed member, but you said you had a family, didn't you? Then they must be Moontouched too—"

That was the wrong tack to take, because Sarah's flush grew deeper, and her eyes flashed. "You expect me to just go back to Earth and *lord* over my family? To declare some kind of mystical power over them and start ordering them around just because a tree told me to?"

"No, that's not what I meant at all," I said, a spark of temper of my own entering my voice. "That's not what a Lady, or Lord, or Monarch *does*. Do you think that's what I've been training to do my whole life?"

Her wrinkled nose relaxed, and her eyes cooled. She even looked somewhat abashed. "No, I don't. I'm sorry."

I took a deep breath. "Don't be sorry. I'm the only one who has anything to apologize for. I know I have done a terrible job of explaining all of this, and that I gave you the wrong impression for too long on too many things. Will you just...let me try again, for just a moment?"

Sarah didn't seem to be the type built to sustain anger. Her justified fury with me was already fading from her eyes, and her shoulders and hands were lowered and relaxed once more. She didn't speak, and her eyes looked down and away from me, but she nodded.

"It all goes back to the assassination, and then the Moontouched leaving and shattering the Earth sungate after them," I said with a sigh. "That combination *broke* the First and Second Covenant, Sarah. That's what I was trying to explain before. Ever since, the power behind the broken Covenants has been unraveling. Most people don't even know it, but it has. The Monarchs are the vessels of that power, and they've felt it. Each one after has been weaker. Even the Sunfilled—my clan, the royal clan—is fading away, as we can't seem to have enough children to replace the ones we lose. Perhaps most terrifying of all...the sungates are weakening. Avva spends too much of his energy these days making sure they don't falter and cause a general panic, because if they did...."

I shuddered. "That would be the beginning of our extinction."

Sarah looked up at me, her warm brown eyes now soft with concern. She bit her lip. When she spoke, her tone was serious, showing she wasn't taking the threat lightly, but still needing to know the answer. "Why?"

Knowing my answer could well determine her willingness to help us, I chose my next words with unusual care. "We can stand against the Devourer because we're united as a people. If the sungates, the bridges between our six worlds, fail...we'll be irretrievably scattered across the cosmos, and the Devourer and its forces will pick us off, one by one. More than that, though, the sungates are almost as much a symbol of our power as the Tree Herself. In fact, they resulted from the *First* Covenant. That's why the Moontouched's shattering of the Earth sungate broke it. After the rest of the clans broke the Second Covenant by their treatment of the Moontouched, it piled a wrong on top of a devastating wrong, but the Tree could not prevent it because the clans were not listening to Her, not even the Queen. Ever since, She has allowed us to learn from our mistake, as the consumed have increased in numbers and power and we...have not. Nor has She allowed us a chance for redemption.... Until now."

Sarah bit her lip and looked away again, folding her arms. My chest constricted. I longed to keep talking, to keep babbling, really, trying to help her see.... But some instinct held my tongue and let what I had said sink in, made me stand in silent agony while I watched her turn my words over in her bright mind.

After an eternal half-dek or so of silence, she said quietly, "And you guess that I'm this chance for redemption. Just because someone from Earth with the potential to be Moontouched stumbled into your world and across your path."

"Not just because of that," I said softly. "You didn't just stumble across my path, Sarah."

She huffed. "Right, because the Trees 'sent'—"

"Because I was *looking* for you. Because just as your Tree sent you to me, mine sent *me* to *find* you."

Her head jerked to look back at me, her eyes going wide. "Find...."

She put her hand to her forehead with a groan. "Of course. This last year you've spent 'traveling.'"

I gave a rueful smile, not sure how much others had told her and therefore what else to say or do.

She looked back up at me incredulously. "That...was you trying to find *me*?"

I sighed, feeling the full weight of that eternal, exhausting year of searching and waiting and praying and despairing settle on my shoulders. "Or, well, the one the Tree promised would come. She didn't give me any details, except to say that she...or he...would be Earthren, would be Moontouched, and would be the Tree of Ice's choice of...leader."

I chose that last word carefully, as I had chosen "head" before. No need to go into the technicalities of what it meant to be a sovereign Tree's chosen right now. Yet another good reason Kor wasn't here to blurt out the conclusion. That detail and implication, not even he and Yvera had yet guessed at. Maybe.

At least Yvera assumed I was trying to return things to the way they had been before—to make Sarah the next "Lady Moontouched." She did not understand that, once again, the order of things would have to change.

A revelation for another time. It looked like "leader" would be quite enough for Sarah to swallow in this moment. Much less anything...more.

Sarah blinked. "And so, you just...wandered around, waiting for someone like me to show up? For a *year*?"

"It could have been longer," I said grudgingly. Because, as long as that year had been, I knew even now that I'd gotten off lucky.

Even if the Tree had not warned me that I would have to seek until I found, I would have known Her ways too well to think She had only one reason for sending me off on such a journey with such vague parameters—knowing, as She must have, where and when Sarah would appear. The Tree cared far more about the growth of Her Heirs and Monarchs than She did about their comfort. She had intended me to learn many things over that year that had nothing to do with finding Sarah...on the surface.

Yet they had had everything to do with making me a better Heir and perhaps future King. And, perhaps, in giving me the skills I needed to help and protect Sarah now. As much as it had sometimes grated on me to feel as if I were wasting time I did not have, I knew that there was no rushing the purposes of a Tree, nor the work needed to be worthy of mending a nearly thousand-year-old breach in the Covenants that were the foundation of our existence. When I thought of it *that* way, I despaired the Tree would ever deem me worthy.

Sarah just shook her head in bafflement. As if echoing my thoughts about myself, she said dubiously, "I still can't believe you think this person you need is *me*."

"It is," I said earnestly. "Even if the Tree hadn't told me as much, I would have known. Sarah, I hate to keep coming back to this, because it could be the reason your life is in such danger right now, but remember the doorgem."

"White," she said with a sigh.

I hesitated, then risked one hint.

"Not just white," I said. "A white so *bright* that the only one its equal...was mine."

Her eyes widened. "What does that mean?"

I kept my answer simple. "Your potential is great, even now. Too great to be merely a member of your clan. Too great to be just a wanderer from Earth, instead of the one we so desperately need."

"Need for *what*? You still haven't said." Her voice had an edge of tension now.

I sighed and ran a hand through my hair. "I don't know. Just that...if you agree to help us, I'm supposed to go with you back to Earth and to your Tree—the Tree of Ice. She'll tell us what we need to do then. It could be that we'll be able to mend the Covenants then and there. If not, She will give us the next step."

Please, please let that be all. The steps needed to get even that far seemed monumental enough—and taking all the time left before....

Sarah relaxed. "Oh, so you don't need *me* at all. You just need me to help you get to Earth and the Tree of Ice."

I blinked. "Uh, no, I'm pretty sure—"

"How? You said you didn't know. Only that we had to get to the Tree."

"Well, yes, but Sarah—I'm almost certain we will not restore the Covenants without the Moontouched clan and their leader to represent them in the Covenants. Nothing else makes sense."

"Fine then," she said with a shrug. "Still seems to me that—*if* you are right about me being that leader—that all you need me to be is a figurehead. Someone to sign the dotted line for you so that things can go back to the way they were."

My flameheart sank. "Clan leaders...aren't figureheads."

"Well, the leader of a clan of no one is."

I had nothing to say to that. Her face had fixed in an expression that was both determined and relatively relaxed—an improvement from her anger and anxiety of before. Was it such a bad thing for now, until we had more solid instructions about what would be required of her as the "leader" of the Moontouched, to let her comfort herself by downplaying her role in her own eyes? She had received shock after life-changing shock for the past two days. Perhaps it was wise to give her space to accustom herself to the very idea...then explain what it most likely entailed.

Then give her the space for her decision.

That was what decided me. I wanted her to have the chance to *choose*, fully knowing the consequences of her choice, and she would not be able to understand those now.

"In any case," I said after a moment's pause. "You don't have to give me—or your Tree, for that matter—an answer now. Our way forward is still the same: we get you home. I made you a promise, and by the Flame, I'm going to keep it, no matter what you choose. What happens after we get to Earth...is for you to decide, when that time comes."

Further relief entered her eyes. "Thank you," she said.

I felt another twist of guilt and grimaced. "It's the only decent thing to do. I'm sorry that I'm not just doing this because it's the right thing. I just...."

"I get it," she said, taking a step toward me. "You're doing your duty—what the right thing is for everyone, not just me."

I looked down at her sadly for a moment. How could she understand my role so easily...and be so dismissive of her own?

As if reading my thoughts, she took a deep breath and said, "I feel for your people, and I want to help. I just have a tough time believing that the one you need, the one you've been looking for all this time, is *me*. I'll do what I can, but I think we're going to get to Earth and you're going to find that the real Moontouched leader you need is...someone else."

At her last words, she turned away and bit her lip, as if pained by the thought, which confused me. Wasn't that what she was hoping would be the case?

"It won't be," I said with quiet conviction. "It's you, Sarah."

She just shook her head. "You haven't met my family yet. If what you say is true and they are Moontouched too, then you'll have your pick of better leaders than me."

I had opened my mouth to retort that *I* wasn't the one doing the picking, but just at that moment, Yvera's inner voice intruded.

Ben...you're going to want to see this.

"What is it?" Sarah asked, noticing the change in my expression.

"Come on," I said, unconsciously putting a hand to her back to gently urge her forward. What I had done only registered in my mind when my hand began prickling with an awareness that was as pleasant as it was troubling. I dropped the hand as soon as I thought I could casually do so; by then Sarah was walking as quickly as she could to keep up with my longer stride.

"What have they found?" she said.

"I don't know," I said. "But it's Yvera. Which means it isn't Kor enthusing about some ancient inscription or dusty sculpture."

Sarah walked even faster, allowing me to lengthen my stride. Already, she knew what I wasn't saying out loud: that if this thing had captured *Yvera's* attention, then it was most likely significant. Or dangerous.

Or both....

Probably both.

CHAPTER SEVENTEEN

DISCOVERY

SARAH

THE CORRIDOR STRETCHED ONWARD for an eerie length. For a time, I feared Ben and I had been caught in some sort of spell or trick. Ben set a grueling pace, and I soon got a stitch in my side, helped along by my very full stomach, long before we reached Kor and Yvera.

Given how far they had gotten from us, it took us a few minutes longer for us to catch up to them. Ben slowed a bit for my sake, a puzzled look on his face as he gazed ahead at Kor and Yvera's relaxed postures. They were facing the right wall, standing in a spot of light that was far brighter than the corridor on either side of them. Since I had assumed we were underground, it took me perhaps longer than it should have to realize they were standing in *sunlight*.

"Is it the way out?" I asked Ben with relief.

He shook his head, frowning. "Yvera says no, but she won't tell me what it is, either. She says I should see for myself."

That gave me pause. "I could be wrong, but...that doesn't sound like her."

"It doesn't."

Silence fell between us again as he focused ahead. I was nervous for myself, but when I glanced at him, I felt a pang from seeing his furrowed brow and tightened eyes. I realized I hated how much I had seen him worried or pained lately. He had a mouth and eyes that seemed meant for smiling. I had to fight the sudden irrational urge to reach out and take his hand in comfort. At first for his sake, and then, at the thought of having his strong, unusually warm hand in mine, I craved it for my own.

Fortunately for my self-control, we were approaching his wings now, whose gazes were still fixed on the sunlight in front of them. Even Yvera only glanced briefly to the side as Ben came up to her. Ben stopped in his tracks and stared.

It was a window—a floor-to-ceiling pane of perfect glass set seamlessly into the outside of the corridor, without so much as a lip or border at the edges. That window showed that we *were* underground, but rather than being buried deep in the earth, we were inside the shoulder of a high mountain and thus had a spectacular view of the snowy landscape all around.

It was beautiful, in a stark, barren way; nothing was in sight but icy white, cloudless blue, and gray rock. With the sun cresting over the next range, the snow was almost too bright to look at, which explained the unusual radiance Ben and I had seen from a distance.

Neither the beauty nor the barrenness seemed explanation enough for why all three drakón stared. Yvera's and Kor's expressions were beyond the initial shock that was still on Ben's, but Kor's eyes were burning hungrily, and Yvera's mouth was pressed into a thin line.

"It can't be," Ben said, still staring.

"And yet there can be no doubt," Kor said. "It's no illusion, Ben. The glass is spelled for strength, concealment, and insulation, but that's it. Besides, no illusion could make us *feel* the difference."

I sighed. "Can someone please explain to the human what the big deal is?"

"Amón," Kor said, his eyes not leaving the view.

If I'd been standing next to him, I might have swatted him. Being furthest from him in the line of people looking at the window, I settled for a scowl that he wouldn't see and a mutter, "You know what I mean."

Ben glanced down at me. Then back at the view. Then back at me. It was a tendency of his that was becoming familiar, although there was more shock mixed in than normal. And was that...a bit of awe? And rising excitement?

He swallowed, then said, "Sarah...all dramá can feel the differences between our six suns. Especially us. Given how much we've traveled the Six Realms, each is as familiar to us as old friends. But this sun...is new."

My mouth went dry. "*New*?"

"New to us," Yvera grunted.

"But He *is* a young thing," Kor pointed out, his gaze still never leaving...the sun, I realized. That's what all of them had been staring at all along. Although how they could manage it, I did not know. "And what a thing of beauty He is...."

Yvera rolled her eyes.

"But is it Sekinek?" Ben asked urgently. At my questioning look, he clarified. "Earth's sun."

Earth's....

I inhaled, my eyes going wide as I stared back at him. Ben had turned to Kor for his answer, which was good, because that meant he didn't see the panic that was probably creeping over my face.

Reaching Earth so easily should have been a *good* thing. The best possible place we could have arrived in all the cosmos. A turn of circumstances so miraculous, it would almost be indisputable proof of the hand of fate.

And yet, given what Ben had just told me, I had expected to have days before making my decision. But if the Tree of Ice was somewhere out there...somewhere *here*, in this place...then days or even weeks I had so quickly come to count on had vanished just as rapidly.

There were many reasons to panic about that. For one thing, Ben hadn't met the rest of my family; he *still* thought I was meant to restore an extinct clan and renew the Covenants. I knew that would change the moment he had any other options, and I would be free.

And yet...was that what I wanted? If *I* became the leader, then at the least, I was someone of more importance. Someone who could remain his friend, perhaps even see him occasionally. But if I handed that burden to someone else, even one of my parents or Michael or Rachel....

Would I ever see him again?

Caught in such a fierce battle of conflicting and confusing emotions, I almost didn't hear Kor's reluctant reply. "No.... I'm sorry, Ben, but I don't think it is."

I inhaled again, this time relief and disappointment waging war inside.

"How can you be sure?" Yvera demanded. "No one living has *seen* Sekinek."

My embattled mind still somehow managed one dry thought. *And most humans of Earth haven't seen it either.* Not in the way these drakón seemed to be able to.

"But they left records," Kor said. "Scant ones, but for the sake of this harebrained quest, I've been over every one perhaps a dozen times by now. Sekinek is an older star, more white than blue, and closer than this one appears to be. Right, Sarah?"

"How should I know?" I said. "Humans can't stare at the sun."

Yvera snorted, presumably at yet another sign of human helplessness.

Ben gave her a warning glare. He sighed as he looked back at the sun, then at me, wistfulness in his eyes. "It would be too simple if this was Earth, wouldn't it?"

Too simple indeed. And too heartbreaking. For the first time, as shameful relief won out over disappointment, I realized I *wanted* more time. More time learning. More time drinking in the wonders of magic and dragons. More time to decide. More time with Ben. More time to reconcile myself to....

Ben cocked his head at me questioningly, and only then did I realize I was staring into his eyes with a hunger that was bordering on desperation.

"Don't worry," he murmured. "We'll find a way, I promise."

He put his hand on my shoulder comfortingly. The shock of heat and tingles, even through my coat, sent a stab through my heart and made me swallow thickly. Yet, somehow, I still could not look away from his soft, golden eyes. Not even when the look in them turned into something that was enough to make my stomach erupt with butterflies and my legs jellify.

Fortunately, Yvera shattered the moment by stating the next obvious question. Loudly. "But if this isn't Earth...then where *are* we?"

Ben glanced away from me hurriedly and removed his hand, leaving my shoulder feeling cold. The butterflies died in the frost, and my legs froze solid.

"An excellent question," Kor said, but he was glaring at Yvera as he said it.

"Kor...." Ben said. "If this isn't any of the Six Realms, nor is it Earth...."

"Indeed," Kor said, eyes gleaming as they met Ben's. "This is something *new*. A new world."

"But that makes no sense," Yvera protested. "The Moontouched went to Earth because a request for a world of their own was refused. If that was a Moontouched gate we just went through, leading to a new world they had discovered on their own, why would they go back to Earth?"

"One potential answer to that question is obvious," Kor said, gesturing to the frozen waste before us. "Would *you* want to live here?"

Yvera only scowled in answer, but even I knew enough about their people by now to guess that an icy mountain range was not their ideal real estate.

"The glass gives me another hint," Kor said, going up to it and stroking one finger down its surface. Ripples of midnight-blue power spread from his touch, scattering arcane runes that were meaningless to me.

"Particularly strong spells of insulation," Kor explained. "This glass isn't just intended to keep the cold *out*. It's also to keep air *in*."

"So potentially the air outside isn't breathable," Ben concluded.

I felt a flutter of anxiety. For the first time, it sank in that we were...trapped. Somewhere new in the universe. On a planet that might not have the right mixture of nitrogen and oxygen to allow us to even step outside. From Ben's and Yvera's expressions, I guessed they were thinking the same thing.

"Or at least not optimal," Kor said excitedly, showing none of the same worry as the rest of us did. "Pending further evidence, I propose the tentative hypothesis that the Moontouched had another purpose for this world than habitation. Resource extraction, for instance. Or perhaps an emergency retreat. Records do say that the Moontouched became increasingly suspicious and withdrawn in the years before Lord Orren's death."

"Lovely," Yvera said. "Care to share a hypothesis on how we are supposed to *leave*?"

"All in good time," Kor said, waving a hand. "There's a much more urgent question for us to answer."

"And what could that be?"

Kor raised an eyebrow at her. "I just told you that the air outside is probably suboptimal. Then aren't you at least beginning to wonder how, after nearly a thousand years of abandonment, the air inside still *is*?"

We all stared at him.

"Or," he said, turning to stride down the corridor again, "how long it will *stay* that way? If we want to *keep* breathing, I suggest we find out the answers to those questions first."

Ben and I shared a nervous glance, and Ben started after Kor, catching up quickly with his longer legs. Yvera followed, but she cast me a glare first. The kind that seemed to say that not only was all this my fault, but I had brought us all here on purpose.

Why I would do such a thing when *my* life was on the line just as much as everyone else's, I had no idea, but she looked away before I could even give an answering glare. I sighed and resigned myself to the half-jog that would be required to keep up with three drakón who were in a hurry.

I was really regretting that full breakfast now.

AFTER ABOUT THE SAME length of time as it took for us to get to the window, we reached a set of arched double doors. Stone again, but this time the white tree was visible, and to more than just me. After I told them that the outline of the doors and pattern of the tree were identical to the ones we had passed through to get here, Ben and Kor studied the doors: Kor with pacing fascination, Ben with a frustrated wrinkle on his brow.

"I don't feel anything like gate magic," he said to Kor. "But then, I didn't with the other, either."

"I'm coming to think you wouldn't," Kor said absently. "If the Moon-touched were circumventing the need for Royal involvement, as they must have to keep something like this secret, then it's likely they discovered a new way to construct gates, one outside your authority. Which is nothing less than *fascinating*. Do you realize how significant that revelation is?"

Ben frowned, eyes troubled. He seemed to. He also seemed distinctly less thrilled about it than Kor was.

"Here, though," Kor said, stopping before the center part of the doors, "you aren't feeling anything because there isn't anything out of the ordinary for you to feel. *These*, I believe, are simply...doors."

"Then how do we get them open?" Yvera said.

Kor frowned. "I think...by pushing. How crude."

"Oh, for the love of the Flame," Yvera drawled, striding forward.

Kor smirked at her back as she passed. Perhaps that or something else made Ben say uneasily, "Yv...."

Yvera's hands stopped an inch from the surface of the doors. She turned and glared back at Kor. "There's a trap, isn't there?"

"A relatively harmless one," Kor said with wide, innocent eyes. "You would have only been blown back, momentarily blinded, that sort of thing. It would have been funny."

"You—"

"Yv," Ben said, stepping in between her and Kor and holding out a hand to both. "Kor, from now on, you will inform us of any trap you detect, *no matter* how harmless you *think* it might be. We can't afford even minor distractions or delays—or tragedy if you're wrong."

"Very well," Kor said with a sigh. He turned to me and gestured to the doors. "If you will do the honors, Sarah?"

"Me?"

"The trap is only for non-Moontouched," Kor said, a bit impatiently. "No doubt a further measure to conceal whatever secrets they have stored in this hold. It should ignore you."

"Should?" I said.

"Kor...." Ben warned.

"I'm ninety-eight percent certain she will be fine, Ben," Kor said with exasperation. "Which is better odds than I give us for our success at finding a way out if we don't get past this door. What more do you want from me?"

I walked forward. "Alright, alright, I was just checking."

Yvera stepped aside to allow me to stand in front of the doors. I took a deep breath and placed my hands on either side of the crack. I felt a cool tingle, but it faded before I could work up the proper alarm. Then, remembering Kor's assessment about pushing, I shoved with all my might.

Though the doors must have weighed tons each, my push met none of the resistance I had expected. In fact, they swung inward so easily that I stumbled forward, and Ben—who must have come up right behind me, though I hadn't noticed—caught me by both shoulders.

"Easy," Ben said kindly. "They're balanced, just like the others."

"No kidding," I muttered. I stepped reluctantly out of his touch to push the doors open further, leaving a space wide enough for even Ben to step through. He did so first, casting a wary glance around.

"See, what did I tell you?" Kor smirked as he passed me. "*Moontouched.*"

"No need to keep rubbing it in," I snapped, still raw from the choice Ben had placed before me.

Any thoughts of that or of other revelations faded from my mind as we caught sight of the end of the corridor. Once again, the light came from a disorienting direction: ahead. The large window had been to the right. Ahead should have led further into the mountain. Then how....

And where was that roar coming from?

We came to the next opening and once again stopped and stared.

We had entered a cavernous space so large it could have held a football field. A balcony with supporting marble columns rimmed its edge in gentle curves. In the center, a large, roaring waterfall spilled down in a cascade that sent sprays of mist up for dozens of feet. Lower, I could see the tops of....

"Trees," I blurted out.

"Looks like it," Ben said, stepping warily out from the corridor and onto the balcony. Yvera followed close behind him, her hand on her claymore and eyes darting around. Then Kor, his eyes riveted to the miracle of life and water and light in front of us. I came last and joined them at the balcony edge to get a better view of what was going on.

There was indeed a veritable forest—or a lush garden, at least—growing around the pool in the center of the floor several stories below, full of trees, moss, bushes, rushes, even flowers, no doubt watered by the spray and the humidity that now cloyed us. I even saw a small, scaled creature darting under a large leaf and saw an insect buzz through the air.

The waterfall's source came from a hole in the ceiling—a painfully bright hole that shimmered strangely, making it also the primary source of light in the room, though mirrors and softly glowing white stones were placed at strategic intervals around the room to mimic open daylight.

"*Mirrors*," Kor crowed. He wasn't gazing at the ones around the room but at the bright hole. "They are passing along light from outside and, with a bit of magical help, are melting the ice along the way, thereby giving the subterranean ecosystem both light and water. Ingenious."

"Well, Kor," Ben said, gazing down at the plants. "Have we found our source of pure air?"

"That's a good part of it," Kor said absently, still studying the bright hole. "No doubt there are other wards and purification spells, but if the beautiful efficiency of *this* system is anything to go by, they would be low power and cleverly designed enough to still be viable. They designed this place to function with little maintenance. I mean, *look* at it all. A thousand years of abandonment, and it's all still functioning."

"About that," Yvera said tensely, slowly drawing her claymore. "How do we know it *is* abandoned?"

"Do *you* smell anyone?" Kor asked. "You've got the best nose of all of us, as you frequently remind us."

"No," Yvera said reluctantly. "But something about this place is giving me the creeps. It's too...perfect. Where's the ruin? The decay? The dust?"

Kor had opened his mouth to retort, then paused and looked around. "You know what...there *isn't* any dust, is there? Fascinating. That's not just clever, durable engineering."

Yvera and Ben shared a prolonged look that indicated some kind of communication. Meanwhile, I looked around. I, too, was uneasy, but for a different reason than Yvera. I realized I felt *too* comfortable. After the awe had faded, a strange sense of déjà vu had taken its place. Underneath even that, my nerves were tingling pleasantly, filling me with a sense of...energy.

"The Moontouched *were* supposed to be the strongest magic workers of the clans," Kor said thoughtfully. "Stronger than even the Starkissed. That's one reason their loss was so devastating."

"Come on," Yvera said, stepping away from the balcony edge. "Let's get moving."

She led the way to the left. Ben gestured for me to go next, then he followed, tapping his leftwing on the shoulder as he passed. "Kor."

"Fine," Kor said, tearing his gaze away from the center to follow, though when I would glance back at him, his eyes would frequently dart back.

I wished I had some way to speak to him mind to mind, as the others did. Then I could ask him about the strange things that were happening inside of me without Ben or Yvera hearing—and making Ben worry.

The cavernous room was in a giant oval, and we must have entered the southern arch (assuming the sun rose in the east here as well). As we came around the waterfall, we approached the western arch, which was dark, but as we came nearer, the lights inside lit in welcome.

At least, the light felt welcoming to *me*, but the drakón froze. After a few long seconds of standing still with no enemy bursting through to attack, I whispered, "Um.... Guys, I know this isn't my realm of expertise, but I think it's just lights."

"Yes," Yvera ground out. "But who turned them *on*?"

"Us," I said in surprise. "They're motion activated."

The drakón stared at me as if the translation magic in their blood had stopped working.

"They—the lights, I mean—sensed us coming, and they turned on."

After more blank staring, I huffed. "What, you've got freaking *wind tunnels* to dry off, and you don't have motion-activated lights?"

"We don't like being cold," Ben said, his face turning thoughtful, though he kept a wary eye on the archway.

"That..." I paused. "...explains a lot of things. Like that fire that lit as soon as I walked into my bedroom in the hold."

"*That* lit when you touched your door panel to enter," Kor pointed out. "So it was you activating the fire, albeit unknowingly in your case. Not your...motion."

"And we see well in the dark," Yvera said with a snort, gesturing to the arch. "I would have had no need for these lights."

"But the Moontouched might have," Kor mused. "They were the most human. In which case, a lighting system activated by motion is...brilliant."

He said the word with some surprise mixed with consternation, as if irritated by the fact that he hadn't thought of that first. "Such efficiency in energy usage, requiring no contact to initiate...."

"But all the rest of these lights were already *on*," Yvera pointed out impatiently, gesturing around the cavernous room.

Kor shrugged. "We don't know if they were before we came here. It could be that this part of the network lights if motion is detected in any portion and remains on as long as motion is detected. Or maybe it's not motion at all, but body heat, or heartbeat signature...."

Kor's eyes were almost glowing now. It seemed that, after I'd explained the initial concept, he could grasp and even improve on it.

"Fine, whatever. Do you think there is any danger through that entrance?" Yvera said, raising her claymore again.

Kor and Ben exchanged a look. Kor answered. "No. I don't sense anything. Even the residue from the light activation is hardly even noticeable."

His voice ended on a note of reluctant admiration.

"Good enough," Yvera said, starting forward.

"Wait," Kor drawled.

"*What?*" Yvera said, whipping back around again. Fortunately, nobody had immediately followed her, so no one met her claymore in its arc. I decided to assume Yvera was aware of and cared enough about us to have known that.

Alright, maybe not about me. I made a mental note to stay well out of range.

"It's harmless, but if you are paying enough attention as you cross, you'll feel it and blame me for not telling you: there's a minor ward over the threshold. My guess is that it's to keep creatures—" He thumbed back toward the garden. "—from getting to other parts of the hold."

"Aaagh," Yvera said, turning back around and marching forward. "I'm ready for the torched *traps* already. They're here, I know they are. I will find them, and by the Flame, I will crush them."

THERE WERE NO TRAPS. Unless there was some kind of untraceable toxic gas that was slowly killing us. We searched the hold well into the afternoon without finding anything more menacing than a rat-like creature that had either come in from outside or gotten through the wards, and Yvera made quick work of that. The acrid smoke lingering in my nostrils was more sobering to me than anything else.

To Yvera's consternation, Ben's puzzlement, and Kor's interest, the first room we encountered was, most definitely...a mess. And by that, I mean in the food definition of the word.

Despite its current barren state, the long, stone tables and benches, the serving bar, and dramá-version of cooking appliances were unmistakable. Ben and Kor oohed and awwwed over the preserved and perfectly functional state of the giant, magically powered wrought iron stove and flat out puzzled over a large, insulated chest with inactivated cooling charms that I guessed was a freezer.

Meanwhile, Yvera kept watch and tried not to pull her hair out, which became her self-appointed role for the rest of the day, since even Ben let down his guard after the stove. Which was perhaps why he was the first and only one to get injured. The stone circles on the bar had us all stumped for a bit until Ben accidentally activated one and burned his hand.

"Heating disks," Kor cried, half in enthusiasm, half in consternation—ignoring Ben's winces and hisses as he stood back to heal himself. I hovered near Ben, feeling useless, but he gave me a smile that showed he appreciated the thought, anyway.

"Those were invented *two* years ago," Kor continued, the consternation winning over. "I helped approve the patent! And even *they* aren't this big yet. Nor do they heat so fast...."

"Are we really dealing with a Moontouched hold, then?" Ben asked with a frown and a darting glance at me.

"Well, one thing's for sure, we sure aren't dealing with a human—I mean, Earthren—one," I said, eyeing the disks.

Kor's mouth looked like it wanted to twist into a scowl, but his eyes looked too alive to allow it. "What we're dealing with is something unlike anything we've ever seen before. Something that has elements of dramá magic..."

His eyes fell on me. "...and human innovation."

I blinked at him. "What does that mean?"

"It means," Kor declared, marching toward the dark arch to the south and perpendicular to the one we'd come through to enter the kitchen. "I need more information."

"Finally," Yvera moaned, marching after him.

We entered a hallway filled with an assortment of rooms that, though bare once again, clearly had a domestic function: bedrooms. Two bunkrooms, with four empty bunks each, formed right out of the stone, lining one wall in each, and four smaller ones with single, larger stone slabs and symmetrical storage cavities—meant for adults or couples, perhaps.

"Not many, for a hold," Ben said with a thoughtful frown as he came out of one of the last ones. "Eight bunks, four beds. Only twelve total. Only enough for a few families."

"Or one big one," I said, thinking of my own with a pang.

Ben stared at me. "One family of *twelve*?"

"What?" I said defensively. "Counting the mom and dad, twelve is not unheard of. Mine has that many."

Exactly that many, I realized with a start. Twelve. Eight beds, presumably for children, and four for couples or older children. That would almost be perfect for the Linds, counting my sister-in-law and nephew. We would have fit these rooms like a glove. Rachel, the second-oldest child, would no doubt claim one of the extra single rooms for herself. I could hear her argument in her favor now....

I could see it all. I could just imagine my younger siblings running around this place, excitedly exploring our new, temporary home. Now I realized one reason the bareness felt so familiar to me: I had moved too many times to be troubled by an empty house, before the chaos of possessions and people fully claimed it, and after the packing and moving began again. There was something exciting about that blank slate, as daunting as the prospect of unpacking always was.

Lost in my imaginings—so strong I could almost *hear* the twins' laughter echo from one room and Abby's screech as Noah pulled her hair or stole a toy—it took me a moment to realize Ben was still staring. And now Kor and Yvera were too.

"You are a family of *twelve*?" Yvera said, startled into addressing me.

I bristled. It was a reaction I got a lot, mostly from people who assumed my parents must have been uneducated or irresponsible, and usually both. Even when people found out they both had PhDs and were careful planners, people still judged us. We were different, and it's hard growing up feeling so different. Compound that with moving so much for our parents' work, we kids had to become even more insular, relying only on each other for whatever we needed.

"Yes. So what?"

"Ten biological children?" Kor said. "From a single set of parents?"

The intentness of his gaze, as if the detail were important, made me pause.

"Technically, no," I admitted. "My oldest brother, Michael, married Laura, and they had Tommie. So, two of those ten aren't Mom and Dad's kids. But the rest are."

"Eight, then," Kor said. "Counting you."

"Yes. So what?"

"Sarah...." The tone in Ben's voice made me glance back at him. To my shock, his eyes were tight and lips pressed thin. "Most dramá are only able to have three children *at most*. One or two is the most common. Four is almost unheard of. Eight...."

It was my turn to stare at him. "That...isn't just a preference thing?"

Ben was already shaking his head. "It's all we can manage."

"Many couples struggle for decades to bear even one," Kor said, face and tone neutral as he looked at Ben.

I knew better than to ask the obvious when Ben's face hardened. His tone was detached. "Fertility is a societal concern, across the clans."

Kor's voice intruded in my thoughts. *But particularly so for Sunfilled.*

I felt like he was trying to tell me something more significant than that Ben was a long-awaited, only child. Kor didn't drop details like that just to be chatty. But once again, the greater picture of both what he was trying to convey and what his intent was in sharing it were beyond me.

Besides, I didn't like seeing Ben's pain. Why it was such a sore subject for him, I didn't know, as dearly as I now wanted to, but I wasn't going to press him for the answer.

To change the focus from him, I offered more information than I would have otherwise. "Eight is a lot for one human mother, but not unheard of. Even more is possible, for some. I've heard of twelve, fourteen...."

The drakón were gawking again, but that meant the pain had slipped from Ben's face, so the price was worth it.

Yvera was the first to recover. She began striding further down the hall. "Yes, yes, very interesting. So, humans have to breed like kapa in order to survive—"

"Yvera," Ben said sharply as my cheeks flushed.

"What?" She looked back at him over her shoulder, nonplussed. "It only makes sense. For such a weak and defenseless race, they'd be extinct otherwise."

"Just a hint, dear rightwing," Kor drawled. "Don't compare a sentient race to rodents."

"And we're not defenseless," I snapped. "Humans are the dominant species on Earth. And capable of more devastation than anyone should be."

"Really?" Yvera said, giving me a slow and deliberate look up and down.

My cheeks burned with fury rather than self-consciousness now. "Maybe not me. But some of our militaries have weapons that can destroy entire cities, ending millions of lives in seconds, and leave the ground poisonous for years."

Yvera raised an eyebrow. I wasn't sure she believed me. "And just who do you humans use these weapons against, then?"

My heart sank, and I dropped my gaze. After a moment's hesitation, I said quietly, "I told you. More devastation than anyone should be capable of."

Ben took the few steps between us to put his hand on my shoulder. The gentleness of that touch gave me the courage to look up—all the way up—to meet his eyes. They contained none of the judgment that could have been there at my first hint of humanity's darker side. They were gentle and as warm as twin suns on an early summer day, thawing the frost that had been creeping over my heart.

"Not you," he whispered, and with a start, I realized he was echoing my words, but this time using them as a declaration of innocence.

I swallowed, not realizing until that moment how desperately I now craved his approval. That made it all the harder to continue, but it was the right thing to do. He hadn't hidden his own people's mistakes from me. For the good of both worlds, I shouldn't hide those of my own. I just wished they didn't make his pale in comparison.

"Ben...I know you promised me, but you have to think of your people's well-being before mine. Think carefully before you open a gate to Earth. You have no idea what humans are capable of."

He inhaled, and his grip on my shoulder and his eyes tightened—but only from concern. I heard his voice in my head, speaking only to me. *Did they...hurt you?*

I shook my head. "No. Not me. I was lucky."

So lucky.

Even the country I lived in and loved, that in so many ways had been good to me and my family, was becoming a place of violence and hate, greed and ambition. Many good people were trying to fix that, but it seemed as if more forces every day seemed determined to hasten its decline. Meanwhile, I watched, helpless to do anything to stop it.

Yvera was right about me. More than she knew.

Ben's grip relaxed. "I don't need all of humanity, Sarah. I only need the best it has to offer...you."

My throat choked up and my eyes stung as a warmth I had never experienced to that degree filled me from head to toe. Dimly, I heard a minor scuffle behind Ben, but the sound didn't even register in my mind, and if it did in Ben's, he ignored it.

I shook my head, too baffled by and filled with that heady heat to deflect his words. Instead, I laughed shakily. "And a clan, too. Don't think I forgot that part."

He smiled. "Fortunately, it seems you have enough for one already. *Twelve.*"

He shook his head in amazement, but his eyes still held that warmth that was melting me inside now.

"If I can persuade them to help," I said dubiously. But I knew I would try. For him. For him, for that look in his eyes alone, in that moment, I would try. Even if, as soon as I introduced him to them, he realized that Michael, Rachel, Mom, or Dad—or practically any of them, even headstrong, five-year-old Abby—were more suited to lead his new clan than I was.

A stab of ice lanced through my softened heart, but I tried my best to ignore it.

"If they are anything like you, they will," Ben said confidently. And winced. "Once I have a chance to explain. Properly, this time."

I laughed again, this time more easily. "Good thing I've given you some practice."

"That was the wisdom of the Trees for certain," he agreed with a crooked smile, one that sent butterflies once again dancing inside my stomach. I had to change the subject, before I started floating or something.

That was when I realized Kor and Yvera had been silent through our exchange. A beat later, I realized how close we were standing now, no matter the crick I was getting in my neck from craning to look up at him. With a start, I took a step back, and he just as quickly withdrew his hand. My chest constricted and another shard of ice pierced my heart to see him glance away self-consciously.

What was the cause? Regret? *Please, please let it not be regret.*

Looking for a distraction from the chilling shadows of doubt that were returning, I glanced around. To my surprise, Yvera was gone, and now Kor was on the other side of us, over where she had been. There was something a tad too innocent about his expression as he studied a lightstone with his back to us.

"Where's Yv?" Ben asked him, echoing my surprise.

"Oh, you know her," Kor said airily, waving a hand toward the arch on the opposite side of the dormitory from the kitchen. "She got impatient and went ahead."

My heart sank as I realized what Yvera must have thought of our exchange. I was certain she didn't leave just to give me some privacy.

Ben, however, seemed to accept Kor's excuse with a nod and a sigh. "Come on. We'd better get moving again before she sets something on fire."

"Good thing there's so little lying around that's flammable," Kor said.

The next room changed that. There was a small antechamber, where we found Yvera pacing the length between two more arched sets of stone double doors inlaid with faintly glowing white trees, though these were much smaller. As soon as I placed my hands on the center of the inner line of the doors on the left, I felt an energy drain and a faint *pop*, like ears adjusting to changing air pressure. This time, the doors swung outward, forcing me to stumble back, which was just as well, because a gust of frigid air surged outward. At first, I panicked, thinking I'd accidentally opened the doors to the outside, and we were all about to die from cold or oxygen deprivation. But when the lights inside flickered on, we all stared.

"Well," Kor said. "I don't think we're going to starve."

That was an understatement.

The room was like an enormous walk-in freezer, the kind I'd seen in wholesale stores like Costco, except bigger. The walls were lined with shelves, and row upon row filled the center, and every shelf was packed with crates, baskets, bins, and bags of food. Roots, tubers, giant gourds, exotic fruits of all shapes and sizes. Slabs of meat hung behind a shimmering curtain of power. Bulging bags hinted at grains or legumes, and others had a slight dusting around them that suggested flour.

Yvera snorted. "Great. Even more evidence that this hold isn't as abandoned as it appears."

"Or is it?" Kor said, stepping into the room and turning in a circle. "I felt Sarah break the seal: a powerful, costly one, one meant to keep everything inside in a stasis. And even if I hadn't, it's clear this room has not been disturbed since it was filled. It's all very...organized. Untouched. Unused. And the labels seem excessive. Not to mention simplistic."

He pointed to the pictures on some barrels. There were quite a few. Though I shivered to do so, I came up to him and studied the engravings on the bronze plate that ran down its length.

The first one at the top was of vines, loaded with berries—grapes? The next one down was of those bunches gathered into a crate. The last was of them being crushed between two great slabs, juices running down into the next image, which was a sketch of the barrel itself.

"What do you think is inside, Sarah?"

I knew better than to think it was an idle question, no matter how casually he asked it.

"Wine?"

"That it is." Kor leaned in and took a great sniff. His eyes closed in a bliss I hadn't ever seen on his face before. "And exceptionally well-aged, which is impressive considering the state of preservation of everything else. Flame.... I don't suppose...."

His eyes drifted to Ben. Ben raised an eyebrow in return. "No."

Kor sighed. "Maybe later."

He turned away with the reluctance of a pirate being forced to part with buried treasure.

"Why ask me?" I said, following him. "If you could already tell what it was?"

"Oh, no particular reason," Kor said as he walked slowly enough to read the other pictograms as he went.

Which told me that there had been a very particular reason, but before I could demand he tell me, he continued. "They're not just depictions of the contents. Some are instructions."

He pointed to a crate of spiky blue fruits with an engraved plate that showed how to handle, cut, and remove the flesh inside.

"Who would need instructions on how to eat keva?" Yvera said with a snort as she joined us.

I would, I thought irritably.

"Who indeed," Kor said mildly, moving on.

I stared after him, heart pounding, and not from fear he had read my thoughts. Because I had glimpsed the suspicion growing in his mind, and it made me dizzy to think of it.

Ben looked thoughtful. "If the Moontouched knew they had to abandon this place, they would have no way of knowing when they would be coming back. How many years or generations would intervene and what their children might have forgotten or how language or writing would change."

That theory made sense and was far more comforting than Kor's, but it still didn't quite fit.

"But they left quickly, didn't they?" I asked. "So quickly, the rest of the clans didn't realize they were going until it was too late."

I gestured to the room, to the plates. "This all would have taken careful planning and execution. That strikes me as not being possible as they are practically fleeing in the assassination's aftermath."

Kor glanced over his shoulder at me, dark sapphire eyes flashing with approval.

I shivered at that further sign of being on the right track, but Ben must have misinterpreted the cause. I didn't correct him when he put a deliciously warm arm around my shoulders.

"Come on," he said to Kor. "I think we've learned enough, and Sarah is cold."

"We're *all* cold," Yvera said, so viciously that Ben looked at her in surprise.

I flinched, but before Ben could say anything, Yvera stomped out of the room. Ben gave Kor a questioning look that probably had a silent communication behind it, but if Kor answered, it was just as silently. Outwardly, he only shrugged and followed the rightwing.

The room opposite the giant refrigerator was another storage area, but not the chilled kind. Now we discovered why the rest of the rooms had been so bare: here, the shelves were full of all the necessities of a dramá household, sealed for protection against dust, creatures, and entropy behind another stasis seal that I once again broke. Pillows, mattresses, blankets, furs, clothes, pots, pans, dishes, utensils, paper, inkwells, charcoal, wood, seeds, and tools of all sorts—far more than I knew the purpose of—and so much more. Ben didn't let Kor and me open many chests or boxes before the general theme became apparent. Not only was Yvera impatient to be going again, he seemed to be uneasy as he gazed around at the abundance.

"We shouldn't be disturbing these things," Ben said when Kor complained he wasn't finished. "They're not ours. It's bad enough that we broke the seals so that now they'll decay."

"Sorry," I said sheepishly. That had occurred to me. It seemed such a shame that, whoever these people were, their careful preparation for the future might have gone to waste. Or...not....

"Not your fault," Ben said quickly to me before returning his gaze to Kor.

As if reading my thoughts once again, Kor said dryly, "You keep insisting Sarah is meant to be the next Lady Moontouched. If this is a Moontouched hold prepared for their return, then these things are, in fact, hers to disturb as she likes."

There came the dizziness again, worse for having Kor state it out loud and so bluntly.

"We don't know for certain who built this place or for what purpose," Ben insisted. "Until we do, we respect it as guests. Not robbers."

"We weren't *robbing*," Kor grumbled, but he made to leave.

"Oh?" Ben said with a raised eyebrow as he caught Kor's arm on the way out.

With an exaggerated sigh, Kor produced the silver, shimmery rod that he had spent a solid couple of minutes drooling over while Ben and I had examined the mattresses. As both of us had judged the quality together, neither of us mentioned why we were doing so: if we were stuck here much longer, we might need them.

Apparently Kor had taken advantage of our turned backs, but either Ben was sharper than Kor gave him credit for, or he knew his leftwing too well.

Ben grabbed the rod from Kor with a pointed look and walked to the shelf where it belonged to return it.

"I was going to ask you for permission," Kor said, giving me an unabashed grin.

"When?" I asked incredulously.

"When you felt confident enough in your authority to give it," he answered, grin deepening to a smirk as he left the room.

Chapter Eighteen

CURIOSITIES

Koriben

The further we went in the hold, the more I suspected that Kor's theory was right. Not that I ever admitted that out loud. But it was hard to see why else a hold this small and yet so carefully designed for longevity and self-sufficiency existed.

Holds were the dramá way of life and had been since the Devourer's Invasion, and they had only become more necessary as the centuries passed and the Devourer infiltrated each world we claimed. Most worlds were safer than that of Battleblood's and Strongshield's, but even Peacegrowth's had its problems, as Sarah had discovered to her peril. Holds gathered us together and gave us not just safety in numbers but thick, natural walls of earth and stone that, if left intact and continually strengthened with wards, prevented any consumed from entering or darkgate from opening inside. Mountain hearts kept us safe, day or night, but most especially at night, when the consumed could reign supreme.

Even with a mountain heart to guard us, we still congregated in numbers. Holds took many hands to build in the first place, so consolidation of resources was essential, and that led to communal living. And all clans, no matter which clan claimed the world to govern for its own, were needed to keep that hold sustainable: Peacegrowth to heal and farm, Brightflare to manage and trade, Starkissed to maintain the wards and magics, Battleblood to guard....

Yet this place, as miraculous as it was...seemed designed to accommodate only a few families.

Or one as large as Sarah's. *Twelve.*

She had seemed defensive about the subject, so I didn't bring it up again, but I would look at her and marvel. I itched to ask her what it had been like, growing up with so many siblings—eight! Not just cousins or second cousins or....

What would it have been like to never have to feel alone? To never feel as if the whole fate of your race rested on your shoulders, with no one else ready to shoulder the load should you fall....

Focus, I told myself as we backtracked through the dormitory and kitchen.

On the north side of the kitchen was further evidence of the intended sparse population of the hold: the water-rooms. The hall cut through the middle, with the female's and male's portions on either side—marked, instead of the usual runes, with a white outline of a female and male body, respectively. None of the anatomy was marked in the blank figures, thank Flame, but the broader shoulders and thicker musculature of the male and smaller size and curved shape of the female distinguished the two clearly.

Small, by hold standards, the male portion when Kor and I ducked inside only had three toilets, three showerheads, and one soaking tub. Sarah confirmed the same numbers from the female side when we all emerged. I hid my trepidation when I realized she had gone in alone and Yvera had remained out in the hall. I knew Yvera had probably thought it best to keep watch out there, but it would be just our luck if the one time we left Sarah alone would be the first time we encountered a trap or ambush.

Next time, go with her, I told Yvera.

She pretended not to hear me, but I knew from the way her hands fisted that she had. Whether she would do what I asked....

I'll have to keep a better watch, I told myself with a sigh as I allowed myself one more careful look at Sarah to make sure she was fine.

I was becoming as fussy a mother hen as Svyer. And somehow, I was fine with that.

Next came the laundry room, with its vats and drying vents standing ready for nonetheless being empty and inactive. The air shafts weren't, though, even as thickly warded as they were, so we got a refreshing bit of sunlight. Not even Yvera dragged us away from that room, even though its purpose was the clearest cut.

The next portion held us for even longer as we explored the various workrooms for the crafts required to live and keep a hold running. Weaving, mending, carpentry, pottery.... I named each for Sarah and described the various uses as best as I knew them, and she listened with a rapt interest that I found dangerously encouraging. I noted how her hand ran wistfully down the great loom and thought of arranging lessons for her should she ever spend time in Crownhold, when all was said and done. That would be nice.

More than nice, in fact. I dreamed, as I hardly ever dared let myself dream, of my task complete and the weight of the worlds eased off my shoulders, and Sarah, free to come and go as she pleased as one of her rank should, *choosing* to come stay sometimes in Crownhold, where we could talk and walk and laugh and be friends. I would pay for much more than weaving lessons for that....

Yvera lingered longest over the blacksmith's area, admiring the forge and tools that had been trusted to stand the test of time outside the storage area. She left it with about as much reluctance as Kor had the wine, but at least none of his greed. I kept a sharp eye on Kor in the enchanter's area, but he knew I was watching now and didn't try anything. As far as I was aware, in any case, and that would have to be good enough.

Kor was principled...in his own way. I would never have had a bit of worry about him in the Grand Market of Crownhold, for example. He took the law as seriously as a leftwing should. He just didn't have my...sentimentality, as he would have thought of it, for the gray area where personal ethics guided. In his mind, the dead were dead. No need to respect their wishes when they probably no longer cared, if they still existed at all—and I wasn't sure Kor believed they did.

Not even my dreaming or watching Kor could distract me from the worrying passage of time, so I dragged all of us on, reminding the others of the reason for our explorations: to find a way *out*. Or, if the air wasn't breathable outside, then another gate. Or a way to reactivate the one we had come through.

I was perhaps more anxious than anyone else at this point to get back to lands and worlds we knew. After all, none of the others would have to report soon to a father who would be strained by worry if we were still stranded in parts unknown. At least I'd already discovered I could call him from here; of course, since I did that to keep myself awake during my portion of the night watch, that was before I'd known we were on a previously undisclosed planet. He had been worried even then, and he was going to be more so once I gave him all the details we had learned. He had ordered me to report back as soon as we discovered where we were, so I was on a ticking timer before he lost his nearly inexhaustible patience and tried to call me.

I was about to suggest a stop to check in when we stepped into the next room.

So far, we had been led in a curve around the oval edge of the hold, but here we had come to the northern point—and pointed it was, the far northern edge in a V shape. But the shape was not what drew the eye and made Sarah gasp and even Yvera inhale.

It was the ice. For the temperature plunged the moment we passed through the doors Sarah had opened and crossed the threshold wards.

Thick, shimmering, reflective ice covered every surface, except the floor, and even then, pillars, huge icicles, and columns ringed the room, so that it felt like we had stepped into a glacier cave. Perhaps we had, since everything had a much rawer feel. At least the floor's surface was gritty and clear.

We walked soberly into the center of the room; Yvera's, Kor's, and my breaths caused great clouds of steam that fogged up the columns around. Since even I shivered, I looked worriedly down at Sarah, but though pink was rising to her cheeks from the cold, her gaze was bright with interest, and when she looked up, she gaped.

I then did the same.

The rawness of the rest of the room contrasted with the exquisite carving taking up most of the ice above, which glowed at every line with filtered sunlight.

It was a flower I had never seen before. Whatever it was, it had many layers of thick and luscious petals that spiraled from the center.

"What is it?" I asked her, wanting to know more than I should why the sight brought such a sparkle to her eyes.

She gave me a startled look. "A rose."

"An Earth flower, then?" Kor asked.

That gave her pause. Then her eyes widened and looked back up. "Yes...."

We all looked up and stared. Well, all of us but Yvera, who kept a wary eye on the shadows and her hand on her claymore.

"The amá tribe who joined us came from Earth, after all," I offered, but my voice was strained from more than just the cold.

"Let's get out of here," Yvera said. "The cold is leeching what little spark we've gained so far."

I had to agree with her, so with a grimace of apology to Sarah, I led us to the other side of the room, and Sarah opened the doors there for us.

We drakón almost sighed as one with relief as we stepped out of the cold. Sarah rubbed her hands together for warmth, but she looked back with a strange sort of longing—a different kind than the one when she'd stroked the loom.

"What?" I asked her as we walked down the short hall and the doors ground shut behind us.

She hesitated. "I don't know, honestly. I just felt so...alive in there."

I tried not to stare. I ached down to my bones from the weariness the cold had pressed on me, and energy from the distant sun was only starting to creep back. Yvera was right: we weren't in there long, but we should have left even sooner. Anything that weakened us right now, no matter how benign in its purpose, was dangerous.

"What do you think that room was for?" Sarah asked me.

My turn to hesitate. "Honestly, I haven't a clue. Kor?"

"I'm thinking on it."

Which translated to the same thing.

We had come to the next set of doors. Sarah seemed to hardly think about her role now as she stepped forward to open them, which was a relief. The more comfortable she became with the idea of her being a Moontouched, the more she used the growing gift inside her....

The next room was dark, and this time, the lights came on only dimly. As glowing white runes danced across the rows of rectangular stone monoliths, Kor crowed, "Finally!"

Yvera groaned at me as Kor rushed in. "Now we're never getting out of here."

"What is it?" Sarah asked, peering into the dark room with wide eyes.

"A library," I answered with resigned amusement and followed Kor inside. I didn't want to lose sight of him, especially in a room as dark as this.

She blinked and followed me. "A *library*? Then where are the books?"

"Who needs *books* when you have archivals?" Kor said, spreading his hands to the stones. He tapped one of them, and ripples of light scattered from that point, illuminating words in an alphabet I didn't recognize as they went. "Books decay and can only contain so much to begin with. But these stones.... They can contain volumes upon volumes of knowledge, all preserved and just waiting to be discovered...."

Sarah met my gaze, a wry smile of her own forming on her lips. I could see the realization dawning in her own eyes of how difficult it was going to be to drag Kor from *this* room.

"Strange, though," Kor said with a sudden frown. "It doesn't appear to be activating. I feel the latent power, but...."

He tapped the stone again, sending another ripple.

"What are you talking about?" I said. "There's the glow...."

Kor stared at me. "You see a glow?"

I stared back. "You don't?"

"No." He scowled.

"Neither do I," Yvera said.

"I do."

We all looked down at Sarah in surprise. She bit her lip and touched a stone, sending out a ripple of her own, which she watched travel across the black surface. She glanced at me, eyes wide. "What does that mean?"

"Torch me if I know."

"Are they *saying* anything?" Kor asked in frustration.

I shrugged. "Yeah, sure. But I can't read it. It's in some other script."

Sarah started. "Wait, your blood doesn't translate it for you?"

"That only works for the spoken word," I explained with a grimace.

Sarah laid her hand on the stone, causing the illumination to remain rather than ripple outward. In a small voice, she said, "Then how come I *can*?"

"You can read it?" Kor asked eagerly. "It's in your language?"

"Yes," Sarah said, still in that small voice. "It's the Roman alphabet, alright. And in English."

"Well, what does it say?" Kor said impatiently. I could already tell there was going to be trouble if Kor always had to get whatever he wanted to know through Sarah. "It would be open to the last text the Moontouched were reading before they left. That could be significant."

Sarah took a deep breath. In a tremulous voice, she read out loud, "Welcome home, Sarah Lind."

Chapter Nineteen

WELCOME

Sarah

My words were met with utter silence. I didn't need to look up to know they were all staring at me again, so I didn't. I just continued to stare at the glowing words under my fingers. At the impossibility of seeing my name spelled out in such stark and utter clarity.

Welcome home, Sarah Lind.

"I take it that isn't a default greeting, and it didn't somehow magically pick my name from my head," I said.

"No," Ben said tightly. "Or if it is, it's magic unlike any I've ever heard of."

"Interesting," Kor said in a very mild tone. Given its sharp contrast from his frustration of before, I figured that meant his genius mind was whirling. "Is there anything else?"

I took a deep breath. "Yes. Not much, but a bit more. Just 'We are certain you have questions, but it is best if we answer them another way. When the moons are high tonight, go into the Oculus—the room of ice you encountered just before this library—and there we will deliver our next message. Only the Golden Heir may come with you, if he wishes. Otherwise, you must come alone.'"

Silence once again.

Just to be sure there was no more, I ran my hand down the stone, but though the ripples of light spread over its entire surface, no more words were illuminated.

"That's all," I concluded quietly.

Yvera broke the silence with the force of a battering ram. "What the—"

A string of profanities spewed from her lips that I'll not bother to relay, but for the first time, her vitriol made me feel a tad better. Listening to her curse the frightening absurdity of this situation was...cathartic.

"It's a trap," she concluded, and she began striding rapidly to the far side of the library, where another set of doors were visible. "It's a hellfrosted trap, and I'll not have us torching stick around to spring it. We're torching getting out of here this flaming instant."

Ben sighed and followed. "Come on."

I hurried to catch up. I sure as heck wasn't going to be caught alone in that library with those words glowing back at me.

"But Ben, Sarah, the archivals—" Kor protested.

"Which you can't even flaming *read*?" Yvera raged over her shoulder.

"Yet! Can't read yet!"

"Fine! Stay! Ben can find a new leftwing after you're dead for all I care!"

We'd reached the doors, and by the time I had them swinging open, Kor had caught up with us, looking about as grumpy as a cat that had been doused with a bucket of cold water.

"These stones could have the key to our escape, you know," Kor said darkly.

"Or there could be a gate in the next room to take us home," Yvera said, striding through.

There wasn't, of course. There was just a large, long room with terraced seating on either side; a gathering place of some kind, obviously, but Yvera didn't let us stop and admire but continued to lead us at the same pace all the way through.

"You're suspicious enough to think that message is setting us up for a trap, but you'll trust yourself to a gate that is conveniently placed in your path?" Kor asked sharply, keeping pace with her.

"Ben will—"

"You don't torching get it, do you?!" Kor shouted at her. "Ben doesn't have any more authority here than you or I do! Right now, we're at the mercy of the

Moontouched, who somehow have created a hold filled with powerful magics and innovations centuries ahead of their time, for an amón girl who was born almost a thousand years after they left!"

We came to the next set of doors, and Kor and Yvera halted in a burning standoff in front of them. I hesitated to break it up by walking between them to open the doors, and Ben's hand resting on my shoulder confirmed my decision to wait.

"Exactly," Yvera hissed. "We're at their mercy. And for some reason, that doesn't seem to bother you. How is it that all this flashy magic and esoteric knowledge has blinded you to the fact that all this reeks of a trap intended specifically for Ben? They just *said* so! 'Send the Golden Heir alone with her to the ice chamber in the middle of the night, where killing him will be child's play.'"

Kor spoke slowly, enunciating each word. "If they had wanted to kill us, they could have done so while we slept and at a thousand points after. But they *don't*. They built this hold with care and great sacrifice, in *secret*, for Sarah, to help her and her family restore the Moontouched to their proper place within the Seven Realms."

Yvera took one more step toward him. "Sure. Maybe they want—or wanted—Sarah alive. But how are you so *certain* they were only planning to restore her as the next Lady Moontouched and not plotting to make her *Queen*?"

My gut wrenched. I looked up at Ben, anxiously hoping he hadn't thought—didn't believe—the same thing. He looked down at me reassuringly.

It's her job to look for danger to me, he said in my mind. *Even when much of the time it's not there.*

Kor gave a hard laugh. "*Queen*? Even you know it doesn't work like that. You don't become the next Monarch by murdering the last."

"But what happens when you get rid of every eligible Sunfilled Heir?" Yvera demanded. "When the Flame doesn't descend on any other? *Well*, Kor? What then? You know the law as well as anyone."

Kor's only answer was a snort.

"What...does...happen then?" I asked, unable to believe I was shifting focus to myself, but I desperately needed to understand what a potential threat to Ben could be.

Kor answered without looking at me. "It's a contingency in the unlikely event that the Sunfilled ever are wiped out or become unworthy: the Nobles are to all gather to the Tree, and She appoints one of them to become the next Monarch and lead the clans instead."

So if Ben and his father were killed, and no other Sunfilled was worthy.... And I were one of those gathered leaders....

I felt sick.

"No, no," I said, shaking my head. "They don't mean that. They can't mean that."

"And how do you know this?" Yvera said, violet eyes burning as they met mine. She took steps toward me. "Have they spoken to you? Sent spirits to whisper in your mind, help them lead Ben into—"

"Yv," Ben said with a calm firmness that brought her to a halt. He dropped his hand from my shoulder and stepped in front of me. "I thank you for all of your hard work in protecting me. I know you are tired and stressed and most likely hungry by now, as are we all. I know you want to get back as soon as we can to somewhere you know you can let your guard down. But I am telling you that I feel no menace from the creators of this hold. Only care and sacrifice. Yes, their magics are unexplainable right now, and that's frightening, but that is no reason to take out your fears on Kor or Sarah, neither of whom want me to come to any harm."

Yvera shot me a fiery glare around Ben that conveyed her doubts about me in that regard, but she said nothing else.

Ben sighed wearily and waved a hand. "Let's...just continue, shall we? We might as well know what the rest of the hold holds for us before we decide. Sarah, if you would?"

I nodded, even though his back was to me, and stepped around him warily. Though I felt the daggers of Yvera's eyes follow me, she didn't stop me.

Wearily, I pressed my hands against the set of doors, wondering how many more I would have to open today and why there were so many to begin with. Again, I felt the greater drain required for breaking a seal, as had been on the food and storage rooms, and the doors swung outward.

At first, I thought we entered a room identical to the last, and then I realized that instead of the tiered seating along both sides, there was only seating on the left. And this room was far from bare. Equipment of all kinds was in the corners or along the sides, the floor and right wall were covered in inlaid silver patterns of overlapping circles, and the entire far, south wall was taken up with a staggering display of....

Yvera inhaled.

"Weapons," I said numbly.

Swords, glaives, and spears, clubs and rods, bows and crossbows and quivers and...far, far more than I knew the name or function of, other than it looked dangerous.

Yvera approached the wall of weapons with a slowness that bordered on reverence. Ben followed but at a much more relaxed pace, casting me a rueful smile and shrug as he passed. Kor snorted and came up to me.

If we had come to this *room* first, he said silently, *she might not be in such a touchy mood right now. Even though this is the most ominous room of them all.*

"How so?" I said under my breath.

Kor gave me a sidelong look. *What does a clan that intends to take its place peacefully need with so many weapons? And such a large and sophisticated training space?*

He gestured to the inlaid, crisscrossing circles.

What indeed.

"You said yourself that these are dangerous times."

Yes. But it was not always so. The years around Moontouched's departure were some of the most peaceful and prosperous; that was one reason the clans had the luxury for petty quarrels. So, assuming good intent, how would the creators of this hold know what conditions would be like by the time they returned?

I stiffened without looking at him. Instead, I watched Yvera take down and draw a sword from its sheath, heard the *shing* that sent a shiver down my spine. She said something to Ben, her face more excited than I had ever seen before, but I was far enough away that I didn't catch the meaning of her words.

"I thought you already came to the answer. If they knew my *name*...."

"Very good," Kor said out loud in quiet approval.

I shot him a sidelong glare. He chuckled. "Just making sure you were paying attention."

"I'm not an idiot, thank you," I muttered.

"Thank the Flame for that," Kor said, eyeing Yvera.

"And neither is she," I said tartly.

Kor just looked at me.

"She just...has her priorities in a different order."

And her number one was the golden young man to whom she was holding out the sword to admire.

Inside, I was surprised at myself by coming to her defense. Maybe it was just for the sake of disagreeing with Kor. Maybe it was to support a fellow female. But as much as Yvera scared or hurt me sometimes...I understood her. More than she realized. Watching such light come into her eyes now, I glimpsed someone I might want to be friends with someday. If only I could make her see that I wasn't the threat she thought I was to Ben...or to her.

One of us would have to *have* Ben first in order to take him from the other, and that probably wasn't ever going to happen for either of us. The sooner she could realize that, the sooner we would have peace—and the safer Ben would be as she stopped wasting her energy on a nonexistent danger.

Ben cast me a glance in the middle of Yvera's gushing monologue, probably just checking to make sure I was alright. He smiled when he caught my gaze, and my treacherous pulse quickened.

And the sooner the pounding thing in my chest could know it as well as my head....

The safer *I* would be.

MY QUESTION OF HOW many more doors I would have to open was answered soon after: one.

We didn't find another in the armory, but after coming back out into the inner circle around the waterfall and some searching, we found a small door that led down a series of steep stairs to the garden. Kor enthused over the flora to no one while Ben and Yvera searched for another door without success.

Somehow knowing they would find nothing, I stood at the edge of the pool and felt the spray from the fountain kiss my face; the coolness was a soothing contrast to the warm humidity of the garden, and the relative quiet and stillness was even more so. I'd taken my coat and backpack off almost as soon as we'd come down into the garden and left them hanging on two knobs by the passage opening. Now I stood with open arms to embrace it all.

Somehow, when I heard the crunch on the gravel path of someone approaching, I knew it was Ben.

To my relief, he said nothing at first. Instead, he just came to a stop next to me and gazed into the spray with me. The quiet lasted too long for Kor and Yvera to still be there. He must have sent them away, and for that, I was even more grateful to him. Even if they'd somehow remained silent, their forceful presences would have disturbed the solitude I needed.

I didn't let myself think about why he, as large and powerful as he was, did not.

After a few minutes, he asked quietly, "What do you feel?"

I looked up to see only soft curiosity in his eyes. It gave me the courage to be honest. "Like I'm...home."

I swallowed and looked at the point where the falling water pounded into the pool and was lost to mist. "And that terrifies me."

"I would be too, in your place. Flame, I am *now*, as *me*."

I glanced dubiously at him, but he seemed earnest. His face was too open for concealment, which worried me. Surely a future King needed to be better at hiding his emotions....

Not my problem, I reminded myself as I glanced away. Even if I remained in his life long enough to see him take on that mantle, he didn't need a third wing trying to groom him for the role. Just as I didn't need someone to soothe away or distract myself from my fears now.

What we both needed right now was...a friend. To just stand there, with us, and accept what was. And understand.

"Do you ever feel like running?" I said softly.

His answer was immediate. "Every single torched day."

"What stops you?"

He hesitated. Then sighed. "I'd like to say it's a sense of duty. Or love for the Realms. Or gratitude to my father. But when I'm honest with myself, I know that not even those things are enough for a coward like me. I stay, because...there's no one else."

"What do you mean?" I risked a glance at him.

Fortunately, he was looking into the pool now, the light in his golden eyes dim. As much as it pained me to see it, I didn't try to brighten them just then, as he hadn't tried to soothe me.

"I asked the Tree once if there was another worthy. If I could just throw it all away and the Realms would be the better for it, but...."

He let out a heavy breath and ran a hand through his dampened hair. He said no more, but he didn't need to.

There was no one else.

"Is your clan that...bad?"

"What?" He blinked and looked down at me. Then grimaced. "Oh, no, not like that. Or...not just like that. It's mostly that there's just so few of us left now. Everyone who is worthy is needed where they are. And, with times being as dangerous as they are, none of them are...strong enough...."

"Except you," I murmured.

He was silent for long enough that I thought the subject closed. But then he said quietly, "For six decades after Avva was crowned, no Heir was chosen. Sunfilled child after child was brought before the Tree, and none of them received Her fire. Avva bore the burdens of both King and Heir for that long without complaining, but secretly, he worried, and despite the Tree's assurances that She was not displeased with the Sunfilled and that an Heir *would* come, the people were afraid that our way of life was ending. As Kor mentioned, there are contingencies, but none of them are ideal. The fall of the Sunfilled, after the loss of the Moontouched, could mean the final unraveling of the Covenants, the sungates, our magic...our existence."

I stared, heart thumping. I tried imagining what that would be like on Earth. That uncertainty would have been the ruin of any human dynasty, even if the monarch lived that long.

His tone was joyless as he continued. "And then, after sixty years...I was born. When I was twelve summers, I was brought to the Tree, just as all the rest of them had been, except...."

He paused for a long moment, then repeated with heavy finality, "There's no one else. And there will not be another. Not until the Covenants are restored. That's what the Tree told me, the day I asked."

My heart clenched, and I kept my gaze fixed on the falls.

We stood there for another minute or two while I tried not to think, but finally I had to say it. "You said I had a choice."

Out of the corner of my eye, I saw him glance at me. "Of course you do."

"Then which is it, Ben?" I said tightly, my eyes moist from more than just the mist. "Either I'm like you, and there's no one else, or there is, and I have a choice—"

He turned to me. "I never said—Sarah, it's not like that for you. At least, Flame Above, I hope not. All the clans failed the Moontouched, but particularly the Sunfilled. Our decline is our own torched fault. You didn't make this mess—"

"Neither did you!" I insisted, turning to face him. "Ben, you're not to blame for what that Queen did or did not do a thousand years ago. You don't deserve to be stuck with this anymore than I do. And yet you are. And you say I have a choice, but I come here, and everything just feels so frighteningly *right*, like it's made for *me*, and then I read my own freaking *name* glowing on a rock a thousand years old."

Tears were running freely now, hurried along by the wetness that had already collected. My voice lowered, becoming choked. "They knew my *name*, Ben. Never mind *how* right now. They knew my name. They saw me. What choice do I have?"

Ben gazed down at me in distress. He closed his eyes for a moment and took a deep breath. When he opened them, there was a hardness to the gold that I had only glimpsed a few times before. "You still have a choice. After all, you chose everything up to this moment, didn't you?"

I stared at him, but my mind turned through the past seventy-two hours.

"You could have stayed safely in the hold," Ben reminded me. "I don't know what Svyer told you, but I gathered she hinted at some danger. Yet you came. And you chose to stay on the mesa. And you chose to lead us to the gate that brought us here. Some of those choices came from limited options, yes, but you still chose them, and we're alive right now because of that last one—because of you."

He put a gentle hand on my shoulder. "It could be that all they saw was that you came here. Whoever wrote that message to you on the archival said '*Welcome, Sarah Lind.*' No title, nothing else."

I inhaled as I realized he was right. Even in their frighteningly precognizant message to my future self, they had not yet set anything else in stone.

My name. But *only* my name. Only who I now was. As long as I didn't read anymore, then who I *became* could remain a mystery, could remain in my control.

As long as I didn't go to the ice cave when the moons were high....

Ben remained quiet now as he watched the decision rage inside me. He even dropped his hand.

"Would you like me to leave?" he whispered.

"No," I said with an urgency that startled even me. Even more shocking—and worrisome—I reached for one of his hands with both of mine and clenched it. I tried to tell myself the electric bolts that shot up my arm came only from the sudden contrast of our temperatures: my chilled human hands wrapped around his always warm drakón one.

"Just...give me a moment," I said in explanation, swallowing.

Far from flinching from my touch, he twined his fingers in mine. "Take all the time you need."

That was it. Just that simple touch, those simple words, coming from someone who had been weighed down for years knowing that he was alone in his burden, seeing in me his only hope...standing there and giving me every chance to walk away from my own...or offering to bear it with me.

My chest swelled with warmth so strong it was pain—and pain again to see him see the beginnings of my decision in my eyes and for his too-honest face to only show support.

I swallowed, but when I spoke, I surprised myself with the strength in my voice.

"Tonight. I'll see what they have to say, this mysterious message of theirs. And then...I'll see."

He only nodded.

I took a deep breath. "I don't think it's a trap, or I wouldn't ask this of you: will you...?"

He squeezed my hand and smiled crookedly. "Not even Yvera can stop me."

Chapter Twenty

CHORES

Koriben

She tried, of course.

My rightwing kept up a constant diatribe as soon as I told her, even as Sarah and I restocked the bedrooms. (Kor vanished after I sent him from the garden, and I thought I knew where to, but I wasn't about to drag him out twice in one day.)

Yvera's face became as flushed with fury as a simolen. I knew there was no arguing back with her in this state, so I let her have at it. Thankfully, with Yvera's anger directed at me, Sarah seemed able to ignore her and work. In fact, she seemed relieved to be given a task.

While I carried in the mattresses, she darted in and out of the storage room to carry in the other things—thoughtful things that wouldn't have occurred to me, or, if they had, I would have thought them unnecessary for our (hopefully) one night's stay. Yet she seemed so happy as she worked that I couldn't say anything, and I had to admit, she had a knack of finding just the things to make each room feel livable again: rugs and braziers, cups and pitchers, baskets for the stone hollows that were shaped so perfectly they must have been for that purpose. Even personalized touches, such as a writing set for Kor or an armor rack for Yvera. As I brought in my mattress, I was touched to see a kettle, a canister of tsha, and a hot plate. I had everything I needed for tsha with me already, of course, but having the things out was more convenient and spared me the energy of taking them out of the ether. Besides, I seemed to have torched luck with my own things....

Better to use these—and leave them safely behind when I was done.

Finally, after heaving the final mattress onto the fourth bed—mine—I gave Yvera a look and waited for her to take a breath.

"Your concerns are noted."

"Don't give me that bureaucratic hogwash Kor's been training into you—"

"Fine then," I said, folding my arms. "You want it straight? I love you, I hear you, I'm doing it anyway, and you can't stop me."

Her violet eyes blazed hot, paling to a dangerously light lavender. "Oh? I have the right to prevent you from reckless endangerment of your own life—"

"And you know who the ultimate authority is on whether it's reckless endangerment?"

She clenched her jaw and narrowed her eyes. "Your father would not approve—"

"Actually, I think he will," I said with a raised eyebrow. "And as soon as I have the privacy of my bedroom, I intend to ask him."

"Oh!"

Yvera and I both looked to see Sarah backing out of the doorway, her arms stacked high with sheets and a blanket.

"I can come back later—" she began, cheeks flushing in a way that was endearing and heartbreaking at the same time.

"No, no, come back now," I insisted, ushering her into the room. "Although it's ridiculous that you expected to make my bed *for* me while I'm standing right here."

When I tried tugging the stack away from her, her face turned adorably mutinous. I couldn't help but laugh. "Here, at least let me help you, or my mother will scorch me from the other side of the Flame."

"Alright," she said, a smile finally touching her lips as we each took two corners.

Her smile faded the moment Yvera stormed out of the room. Literally—violet sparks flew off her and hissed harmlessly against the stone, leaving tiny black scorch marks.

"Don't mind her," I said quietly as we began tucking the sheet around the mattress.

"I don't," Sarah said even more quietly. But her mouth was pursed and brow furrowed.

"Then what's the matter?"

She took a deep breath. "Ben.... Do you honestly not...."

"What?" I asked hesitantly.

She frowned suddenly. "What are these hooks for?"

She held up a corner of the sheet, a hook in each hand.

I laughed. "They're to hold the sheet in place. See?"

I held up a corner of the mattress on her end and showed her how to fold the sheet to make the two hooks at the corner come and latch together.

"Oooh," she said. "That's smart! Does it stay secure that way? I'm a tosser, and I hate it when my sheets get tangled up."

I shrugged. "Enough. The seams around the corners are also sewn with an enchantment to stick together. Between the two, it works well for me. But then, I don't toss much. In fact, I sleep like a dead, noisy log, or so Yvera tells me."

She laughed. "You're not *that* noisy."

I blinked at her. "How do you—oh, that's right. The dreamhaze."

I eyed the canister of tsha. "You didn't see Yv go near that, did you?"

Sarah was already deftly tucking and hooking her other corner. She didn't need to be shown twice. "Oh, I didn't think about that when I put it out. Sorry. For what it's worth, no, I didn't."

I shrugged. "I'll just take a good sniff before I use it, that's all."

I wasn't too worried about Yvera drugging me again—tonight. She knew what kind of trouble she would be in if she tried to prevent me from going with Sarah *after* Avva gave his permission. She might defy me sometimes if she felt justified, but we both knew she would never cross Avva, who, besides being King, was almost as much a father to her as he was to me.

"You seem pretty practiced at making your own bed, for a prince," Sarah said with a crooked smile as I cast the top sheet over the bed and tucked in the closest side.

I blinked at her. "Prince?"

She chuckled. "Heir, sorry."

I raised an eyebrow. "Who else was going to make my bed? Avvi—"

I cut off, but not from the pain—from the sudden surprise at its softness. Normally it came with hard, sharp edges that made every word about her cost dearly. Then how, with soft brown eyes gazing up at me so gently, could the words come with such relative ease, such bitter sweetness?

"It's alright," Sarah said softly, ducking her head as she focused on tucking the top sheet at the foot of the bed. "You don't have to talk about her if you don't want to."

But I *did*. It was as if the words had built up like kindling in my heart, and now that she had struck a spark, the fire was spreading.

Besides, I wanted those soft brown eyes on me again, though I did not let myself think about why.

After swallowing, I resumed as casually as I could as I tucked in the far side. "She began helping me when I was four, and then she made me do it alone after I was five, and every morning, she would inspect my work. She took it as seriously as a parade review, and so, eventually, did I. Unlike a drill instructor, though, she never yelled or even scolded. She simply would never let me do anything else until I had gotten it right."

Sarah shook her head in wonder. I could imagine why—with eight children to mind, I doubted either of her parents had the time to devote every day to such things.

"Did she ever say why?"

As we tucked the blanket (a thick arlin wool as luxurious as I had back at Crownhold), she seemed as eager to hear as I was becoming to share, and that was an intoxicating feeling. I was used to being listened to, sure—being a half a head taller than most everyone else had that kind of effect, on top of being Heir. But I wasn't...used to someone listening to me to understand *me*. To want to know *me* for no other reason than the simple pleasure it seemed to bring them by doing so.

Svyer could be that kind of listener, I thought, but she was my cousin, and practically a sister. I felt like she already knew pretty much all there was about me to know. This, coming from someone new, someone who would know none of it, yet wanted to know it all....

That was dangerous for me.

I answered more carefully now, trying to hold back. "We didn't know for certain that I would become the Heir. A Monarch's child doesn't always become one, you know. In fact, they don't more often than not; even just proximity to the Crown spoils a child if the parents aren't careful, and the Tree won't have a spoiled Heir."

Sarah smiled. "So your mom was making sure you weren't spoiled."

I laughed sadly. "That was part of it, but she would have done that for my sake. But when I would complain and ask her why, she always had this...look in her eyes."

I paused in the final act of tucking the blanket in on my side of the bed to close my own eyes and remember. My heart clenched, and I could feel the usual sharpness returning. I had forgotten all this; not deliberately, but refusing to take out and hold memories in the forefront of your mind allows them to fade. I hadn't taken out this memory in far too long, and now I understood why.

Just as the edges were slicing into my heart, unusually cool, human hands laid themselves over my own, and I opened my eyes with a start to see Sarah's own eyes astonishingly close. She kneeled on the bed in front of me, having just been tucking in the side against the wall. Those warm browns banished the pain as easily as the sun does the frost on a spring day, and the memory no longer hurt to hold. It ached. Oh, how it ached. But it was a better ache, the kind that reassured me that Avvi would always be with me, never forgotten.

Always loved.

"She knew," I said.

I shouldn't be saying these things, but I couldn't help it. The words had to be spoken, or the spell she was casting to heal me would end, and the pain would return. I didn't want that, not yet. Not before this memory had been sealed forever.

"She always knew. Her eyes, when she explained, were sad. She said I had to learn to do the little things well, then...or the big things I would have to do one day would be that much harder."

I cleared my throat and looked down. "That's when I began trying. I saw she wanted to help me, and if she said hard things were coming...then I believed her."

"Was that when *you* first knew?" she asked softly.

I shook my head. I could see why this part would matter to her. "No.... That was—"

The whiff of someone nearby registered in my distracted brain, and suddenly I realized how close Sarah's face now was to my own—her hands wrapped around mine—that look in her eyes—on *my bed*—

Kor's voice wafted ahead of him. "Sarah?"

We jumped apart as if hit by lightning. I stepped in front of her, hoping to block Kor's view as she scrambled off my bed, but too late. Kor strolled in, irritated. "Sarah, I need—"

He took in the room, particularly Sarah straightening and face darkening. I was probably blushing even more obviously and stood stiff as a stump. Then Kor leaned against the doorsill with folded arms and smirked.

"*Please* tell me I'm interrupting something."

"No!" Sarah and I said at the same time, in the same tone of mortified denial.

"I was just—"

"She was only—"

Kor chuckled. "You two are incredible. Fortunately for you both, I'm not in the tormenting mood."

He straightened. "Sarah, I have tried every single thing I can think of, but I can't get these blasted archivals to activate for me."

Sarah rolled her eyes. "And so, I suppose you want me to do that for you."

"If you would be so kind," Kor said, voice and smile dripping with charm.

Even though I was used to Kor's charisma, especially since he often used it in my behalf, I was abruptly and nonsensically irritated with him and reluctant to let Sarah go, even though Kor had just given me the perfect excuse for some privacy to talk with Avva.

"Kor, you can't just usurp her as a research assistant," I snapped.

I was a bit relieved to see Sarah appeared unaffected. She put a hand on one hip and raised an eyebrow. "Did it ever occur to you that the Moontouched could have had a good reason for hiding their secrets from you?"

"Of course not," Kor said, eyes wide with innocence. "From the foolish and unworthy, certainly. But obviously, if they could have allowed one person outside the clan, they would have made an exception for me."

Sarah rolled her eyes again. "Kor, you can't even see the words, let alone read them."

"I have a few ideas for things you could try to change that," he said flippantly. "At the very least, you can find and read me what I need to know."

"Kor," I warned.

Sarah put a hand up. "I've got this, Ben."

"Of course you do," Kor said with a brilliant smile. "So, if you would...?"

He swept his arm out to the hall.

My stomach clenched, certain this was it. Even if Sarah wasn't already kind-hearted and eager to help and please, Kor was pulling all the stops now. Flame Above, he even batted his long eyelashes at her.

I had wanted to punch Kor many, many times before, but never like this. I was imagining how satisfying it would be to hear his breath knocked from his lungs when Sarah gave her answer.

It was low and tremulous, but still not at all what either of us had been expecting. "No."

Kor's eyes flashed. "Excuse me?"

Sarah opened her mouth, hardened her face, closed it, and took a deep breath. As she spoke, my flameheart warmed with quiet relief...and a surprising amount of pride.

"I...understand why you might be so eager, Kor. The pursuit of knowledge is your passion and your duty. But with whatever small authority I hold in this place, and I guess that's my cooperation in this case, I say no. Or rather, not yet. There are so many things we don't understand—"

"Exactly!" Kor said. "That's why we need to access the archivals—"

"No," Sarah said, more comfortable in her refusal the more times she said it. "We got what we needed from the archivals. What we need now is to go get the message they promised to send."

"A message," Kor said flatly. "A drop in the bucket, when oceans of knowledge could be at our fingertips—"

"You're the one who told me to trust my instincts, Kor. You said I had good ones."

I blinked. When was this? That inexplicable mixture of irritation and possessiveness rose again.

But Sarah was still speaking. "And right now, they're telling me to wait. It doesn't feel right to pry into things that are deliberately being hidden from us, probably for good reasons."

"Yet you feel comfortable taking and using their things?" Kor retorted, gesturing to the room.

Sarah stood firm, even though her mouth pressed into a thin line for a moment.

She answered quietly. "They said this was my home. I don't know what that means, but home is a place where you can at least borrow what you need and what comforts you. That's what we're doing. Home is *not* a place where you break into and take what has been locked away. So...if I'm really this long-lost Moontouched you keep saying I am, if this is my home...then my answer is no. Not yet."

My flameheart was burning so hot with pride, I was surprised it wasn't glowing through my shirt.

Kor's reaction was different, if predictable. His face hardened. "Fine, then. Forgive me for trying to help us find a way back to *our* home."

Sarah blanched and stumbled forward even as he turned and strode away.

"Kor, that wasn't what I meant—"

I put a hand on her shoulder to stop her—and steady her when my grip brought her to a halt. "He knows. He...also knows what to say to cut deep when he gets mad."

Fortunately, that didn't happen very often. Kor got irritated as frequently as the next person. But truly, deeply angry...blessedly seldom. For all our sakes.

Sarah's shoulders slumped. It was good that Kor had left before seeing her like this, or he might have taken advantage of her moment of weakness—or tried to. I would have thrown him out before he could. Yet another good reason he left so quickly: I didn't need to add bodily insult to injury.

Sarah stared after him. "Ben, did I do the right thing? If Kor's right, and the answer is in there—"

"Don't listen to Kor," I said. Then paused. "In this. You did the right thing, and even Kor might have agreed if he wasn't so torched disappointed. But you're going to have to get used to disappointing people, Sarah. If a leader is popular, they are usually doing their job wrong. A popular leader is one who gives people what they want instead of what they need—instead of what is right."

Blessed Flame, that last bit sounded like Avva. Would I turn into him one day? Creators, I hoped so. Before the Six Realms were stuck with just *me*.

And I desperately hoped I'd have decades more before that happened.

She looked at the floor. Her voice was quiet, almost a whisper. "How do you know whether your right is *the* right?"

A good question, so I paused to be certain of my answer. "I suppose...that is what the Tree is for. She, at least, is never wrong."

Except perhaps in one thing. But even I had a hard time blaming Her. My burden wasn't Her fault, after all. Not really.

"Never?" Sarah asked skeptically as she looked up at me, as if she could sense the lone, blasphemous doubt in my heart.

I drove out the shadow at least temporarily so that I could say with finality, "Never."

It was an absolute that I had taken for granted for most of my life, but for a moment I considered what the burden of being King would be like without the

Tree to keep me on the right way. At the thought, I could hardly breathe. The Crown would either corrupt or drive me mad. I hurriedly dismissed the thought as being too terrifying to contemplate.

"That must be nice," she said dubiously, as if she still did not quite believe me. "Having an absolute authority like that to consult practically any time you'd like. Too bad I don't."

"Yet," I said with a crooked smile.

Careless of me. She was too sharp to not catch the implication—but blessedly still too ignorant and trusting to be suspicious. "Oh? So, leaders of clans can consult Her like you can?"

"Er—sort of," I said, improvising. With my usual method, one both Kor and Avva were trying to break me of: babbling. "They have their own offshoots of the Tree in their own realms that they can consult. They have to have one, to keep their world from being open to the Devourer. But since They all come from the Tree of Flame, They are all essentially Her.... Or so She tells us. Yet they seem to have their own...quirks. So, take that for what you will."

Sarah blinked. "But if the Seventh Realm is Earth, and Earth already has a Tree...."

"All great questions," I said, rubbing my neck self-consciously. Time for my second method: claiming busyness. "Which I'll help you dive into sometime. But right now, I've got a father who's worried about me...."

"Oh, right!" Sarah gasped. "I'm so sorry. I'll just get out of your way—"

"Don't be sorry," I said hastily as she backed toward the door. "I, er, appreciated your help making the bed. As I said, it's been a long time since I had any...."

I trailed off, swallowing with difficulty.

Sarah's soft, warm eyes met mine and once again dispelled the sharp cold that had crept in with the memories. "It was my pleasure. Just let me know if you need help with anything else, and I'm there."

"I will," I promised.

I felt a clench of guilt as I said it, knowing that, if it came to it, I was prepared to take far greater advantage of her eagerness to help than Kor ever would.

Chapter Twenty-One

KING

Sarah

I was half inside a chest of linens, having just made Kor's bed with ridiculously luxurious silks that I thought he might appreciate and was picking out Yvera's, when I heard Ben call my name.

"Sarah?"

"What?" I said with a start, hitting my head on the shelf above the chest. "Agh!"

"What is it?" Ben said urgently, rushing into the storage room.

I straightened, rubbing my tender scalp. "Nothing, just bonked my head. What's wrong? I thought you were talking with your father."

Ben frowned and raised his hand to the back of my head. I pulled away from his touch, which made his eyes tighten. "I'm just trying to heal you, Sarah."

"No need to waste your energy on a bruise," I insisted. "I know you haven't gotten much sunlight today—"

"Ashes," Ben said, in the tone my British gran would say "rubbish."

"I have enough to spare to heal a bruise. Besides, I don't want you to be in pain when you talk to Avva for the first time."

My heart plummeted into my stomach. "Talk to...."

"He wants to speak with you, if that's alright?" Ben said uncertainly.

I stared at him. Somehow, my heart was still managing to pound inside my stomach. "The *King of the dragons* is asking if it's 'alright' if I speak with him?"

Ben put a hand to his forehead and briefly closed his eyes. "We're not.... Never mind. Yes, he is asking. If you don't want to, just say so. He won't push. But he *did* make me at least come ask you if you would."

"He's giving me an *option*?"

"For the last time, *yes*. *Now* can I heal your head?"

"Maybe you'd better," I muttered. "Then at least I might be able to wrap my brain around this."

"Thank you." Ben reached for my head again, and this time I made myself stand still. Svyer's healing already seemed like a lifetime ago, so I waited with almost as much apprehension as if it were the first time. And it was a first—the first time for Ben to be the healer, and somehow that difference was significant.

Sure enough, I had to use all my willpower to keep from shivering when his warm fingers wound through my hair to gently touch the scalp. Then the warmth sunk from his fingers into my head, and I about went to heaven.

It felt like soaking my head in a hot bath, without having to worry about water or hair getting in my face. But even more, his magic sent electric tingles through my whole body in a way Svyer's hadn't. With so much of my self-control going to keeping myself in a state somewhere between trembling and melting into a puddle, a soft "oooh" escaped my lips. Fortunately, Ben didn't seem to hear. His gaze was distant, even though his gold eyes glowed.

All too soon, the warmth faded, but the tingles remained until Ben removed his hand and the glow in his eyes died.

He scowled. "You had a headache building, didn't you?"

"Maybe," I said, too blissed to even be sheepish.

"We overextended you." Ben sighed. "And didn't feed you."

Now that he mentioned it, my stomach felt hollow. Strange, considering I'd stuffed myself to bursting for breakfast.

"All I've done today is walk around—"

"And open how many magically sealed doors? That takes energy, Sarah—energy you've scarcely begun to build, let alone use. You're going to be powerful, that's for sure, but you have to give yourself time to work up to it."

He sighed again. "Or rather, *I* have to give you that time. Don't let any of us ask you to do anything remotely smelling of magic for *at least* the rest of the day, you hear me?"

I shrugged. "Sure, if I could even recognize what 'smells of magic.'"

Ben grimaced. "Well, talking to Avva won't. I've already got the spell going—"

"Wait," I gasped. "You mean there's a King sitting around *waiting* for me? Why didn't you *say* so?"

I hadn't realized I had made my decision until my legs were already striding as quickly as they could out of the storage room and toward Ben's room.

"It's not a big deal," Ben said, catching up to me easily. "He's patient—the most patient person I know. He's probably just reading some report to pass the time. Besides, he's the one who told me to go ask you if you'd come speak with him."

"Yes, but he didn't expect you to heal me—"

"He would have been disappointed with me if I hadn't," Ben cut in.

I would have protested some more, but we'd reached Ben's door. I didn't know how this communication spell worked, but it seemed likely that if it was still going, the King would now be within earshot. I froze there as my panic at entering the presence of royalty overshot my anxiety at keeping him waiting.

Since my gaze was fixed on the open doorway, I felt but didn't see Ben place a hand on my shoulder.

There's nothing to worry about, he said. His mental voice was half gentle reassurance, half amusement. *You're not in trouble. He only wants to talk.*

"About *what*?" I hissed.

You, of course.

I stared up at him, jaw dropping.

Ben sighed. *Somehow, I thought you might panic like this. I tried to tell him to give you more time, but he told me to ask.*

"No, it's OK," I said numbly, looking away. It was a blatant lie, of course. I was trying ridiculously hard not to hyperventilate right now. "Just, um. What do I do?"

Ben gave my shoulder a comforting squeeze. "Walk in and talk. You ready?"

If I spoke, it would probably be a squeak, so I only nodded.

Ben put an arm around my shoulder and led me into his room.

At first, nothing appeared to be different to me than when I had left. There was the bed we'd made up together. (My brain was too full of panic for a return of the mortification of when Kor had interrupted us.) There was the rug I'd placed, the tea set I'd found and put on the desk.... But there was something hanging on the wall now above the desk, set into brackets. At first, I thought it was strange that Ben had settled in enough to decorate, but then Ben slipped his arm off my shoulder to go stand in front of and look at the gold oval.

"Avva," he said to it, a warmth in his voice and a tug to his lips. "This is Sarah Lind of Earth."

I froze again, so Ben had to reach back and pull me in front of him, placing a hand on each of my shoulders—to steady me or keep me from bolting, or both.

For a moment, I thought we were looking into an oval, convex mirror, and that Ben had lost it. But I was not reflected in its surface, and the golden-haired man displayed on it had crinkles in the corners of his eyes and the slightest traces of lines in his forehead that Ben did not. His beard was also more robust—not long, but fuller than Ben's more closely trimmed version. And there was something in those eyes that Ben did not have—not yet. It was a depth—a warm, welcoming depth, but also a terrifying one in its piercing nature. As if those eyes had seen all there was to see, and more.

The King smiled, and his eyes crinkled and warmed in a way that made me feel dizzy with wonder. I'll admit, I was dazzled; without even a crown, he looked every part a King, in all the highest ideals of the role. And yet my fear vanished. No one could smile like that, could have that kind of look in their eyes, and mean me harm.

"Sarah," Ben said quietly. "This is Kavarian Sunfilled, Golden King of the Six Realms...and my father."

"Sarah," the King repeated, his eyes warming even further. His voice, too, was like Ben's, but deeper and more mature. "I do not have the words to tell you how honored I am to finally meet you."

I blinked. It was as if he had read the words straight from my mind. Except he would first have had to decipher and string them in coherent order first.

"Me?"

"Fetch her a chair, Koriben," the King said with a chuckle. He glanced back at me. "Forgive me, my dear. I can see you have had a long day. You look ready to fall over."

He wasn't wrong.

"I'll have to go look for one," Ben warned him. "All the things like that were put in storage, like I said."

"I think there's some in the back corner, by the kitchen supplies," I offered. I gripped the edge of the desk, and Ben gave my shoulders one last squeeze before letting go.

See? Nothing to worry about, he told me as he left.

I shook my head at him. Maybe not in the way I had first thought, but this interview, whatever it was for, would not be *easy*. But Ben was no doubt too used to his father to understand that.

Though I marveled again for a second at how closely they resembled each other. The King was older and wiser-looking, sure, but would Ben one day...?

Too late, I realized my thoughts had wandered, and the King was waiting for me to refocus, his head cocked and a slight smile on his face.

"Sorry," I said, embarrassment making me blurt out the truth. "It's just, you're so similar...."

"It's true," the King said fondly, looking to the side where Ben had vanished from his view. "And more so every day. He's growing so quickly."

He sighed. "Too quickly."

"He's twenty," I said in puzzlement.

Kavarian turned that fond smile to me. "And I am one hundred and forty."

I stared. I couldn't help it, no matter how rude it might be. He didn't look a day over fifty, if that: he had not a single streak of gray in his golden hair, and had perfect musculature, judging from his neck and what I could see of his broad shoulders and torso as he reclined in his chair.

"No," I said, shaking my head. "You can't be."

He laughed warmly. "I shall take that as a compliment. But I am indeed. Drakón live long—especially a Monarch if the Tree is pleased with them. Something for you to consider when making your choice."

I didn't know what he meant about that last bit, but I was more interested in asking about something else. "What does the Tree have to do with it?"

"All drakón derive their strength from the heartfire granted them by the Tree—but especially the Monarch and Heir. The greater heartfire She gives us is the source of our greater strength and power. That gift can be added to if one proves worthy of a greater trust...or taken away, if one does not."

I didn't realize I had grimaced until he gave me a compassionate smile. "I can understand how that might discomfort you, having grown without the knowledge of your Tree your entire life. I cannot speak from personal experience of the Tree of Ice, but I can say that the Tree of Flame can be trusted. She is the purest and wisest being I know; all the good that I have become, all the good that I have done, has been because of Her."

That gave me pause, but by then, Ben was returning with a simple wooden chair.

"You're right: the back right corner. How much have you been through the storage room already?" he teased.

As he set the chair behind me and pushed it in for me, I said self-consciously, "I like unpacking, settling in. It's the satisfying part of moving."

"By that, do you mean traveling?" the King asked curiously.

"No," I said in confusion. Meanwhile, Ben pried the oval off the wall and lowered it to head height for me, reattaching it with a gold glimmer of power. "Moving. Packing everything you own and taking it somewhere else, where you'll live for a while until you need to move again."

"Why would you do that?" Ben asked, looking nonplussed. "Battle? Earthquakes?"

"Those, but also lots of peaceful reasons. A different job, going to school, wanting a change.... What?"

Ben was staring. "And you've done that a lot? With *twelve* of you?"

"Well, my oldest brother and his wife and son live separately now, so no, not with twelve. But when it was the ten of us...yeah."

"Interesting," the King said sincerely. "And this is a regular thing for your people?"

I hesitated. "Maybe not as *many* times as we did. My parents have careers that...move them a lot."

Or that was the story I always gave. The truth was a bit more complicated. Both of them seemed to be on a never-ending quest to find what they needed from their work and thus far hadn't found it—or not for long, and not at the same time. Mom struggled to find a job in her field of linguistics that would give her enough flexibility to be as home as much as she wanted to be and yet earn enough to help make ends meet. Dad...was a brilliant yet highly principled engineer who kept seeking companies or colleges that would pay him what he was worth yet give him work and leadership he could sanction.

Since his field was the higher paying, some of my siblings resented him for how he never seemed to be able to compromise his standards. I was the most like him, and even I struggled to understand why he never seemed able to settle, if only for our sakes. Yet every time an ethical situation came up or toxic culture grew, he stood his ground, and if needed, he left without looking back. I admired him for his conviction as much as I struggled with its consequences.

But I had always put on the brave, loyal front for others. Even though that was harder now than usual to deceive these two, I added, "But it's common for most families to move a time or two."

"Was that difficult for you, doing this more than most?" the King asked softly.

I looked away and didn't answer right away. I struggled for a moment to say the polite, the superficial thing, but I couldn't. Even without meeting the King's gaze, I could feel his eyes on me, seeing the truth anyway and not judging me for it. "It.... Yes. It was."

Ridiculously, my eyes stung. I blinked rapidly. The King didn't need to see me cry, especially over such a simple question and my equally simple answer. But it got harder to fight back the tears when I felt Ben's warm hand rest on my shoulder again.

This was too much, being in between the two golden men. I'd grown up in a loving family, but it was a busy, loud, chaotic mess of chores and schedules and school and work and extracurriculars and mismatched socks and hand-me-down clothes and struggling to find the right shoes for everyone before rushing out the door. One in which it was so easy to feel lost and forgotten, even with the best of intentions. Never in my memory had I felt so...*seen*. So listened to. So wrapped in the warm glow of two of the best souls I had ever met. Like sitting next to a fire after a long trek through the dark on a cold winter's day, wrapped in a blanket and with a mug of cocoa in my hands.

Hard as I tried, a tear spilled over. I wiped it away furiously. "Sorry. Sorry, I didn't mean—"

Ben was leaning in to say something, but the King held up a hand. "Koriben, would you mind leaving the two of us alone?"

"Alone?" he said in surprise.

"What, why?" I asked at nearly the same time, feeling a twinge of my former stage fright return.

The King's answer fit more with Ben's question, but he looked at me. "Yes, I think that is best."

Ben hesitated as he gazed at the King, looking like he wanted to protest but knowing or respecting his father too much to do so. He looked at me, as if for confirmation that was alright. I turned to face him, hoping he would see the panic in my eyes and that the King would not.

Whatever Ben saw, it wasn't enough to defy his father. He sighed and gave my shoulder another comforting squeeze. "Call me back in when you're done."

He went to the door. Out of his father's view now, he stopped for a moment and cast me a troubled look, but then he closed the door behind him.

"Thank you for agreeing to speak with me, Sarah," the King said gently, drawing my attention back to him. He leaned back in his wooden chair—far too simple and utilitarian to be a throne—and regarded me kindly. "Especially in private. I apologize for asking so much of you so soon. I would not do so, except I fear that time is short, and I did not know when you would have another moment of such relative safety and leisure again. None of the other times in which Koriben and I have spoken since he found you have been as ideal."

"Time is short?" I asked, feeling an icy curl of dread form in my stomach. My former stage fright now seemed petty in comparison. "How?"

"Koriben told me he gave you a brief explanation of the unraveling of the Covenants, and how our magics and sungates are waning. Is that correct?"

"Yes," I admitted. "A *brief* explanation. But he didn't say we were working under a deadline. I figured that if they've held for the past thousand years, they would for at least a few more."

"And they might...if left alone," the King said heavily. He sighed, and for the first time, I saw what it looked like to bear the weight of six worlds on your shoulders. "But shadows creep over the horizon that tell me we shall not be so lucky."

I swallowed. "Why didn't Ben say so?"

The King smiled wearily. "No doubt because he has tried not to overwhelm you or influence your decision. But he...has also been fixated on one shadow in particular, thinking that in dispelling it, the others will be at least partially as well."

"And what shadow is that?"

For the first time, the King hesitated, studying me. He said quietly, "A conversation for another time, I think. Flame willing that we have it."

"Then what *did* you want to speak to me about?" I demanded. Then flinched at my rudeness. "Sorry, your majesty."

"My what?" the King said, mild amusement dispelling some of the darkness in his eyes.

I sighed. Either that hadn't translated well or dramá honestly thought differently about what it meant to be royalty. "Nothing, just something people say to address a king or queen respectfully."

"Please, call me Kavarian, my dear," the King said, shifting in his seat as a warm, fond smile returned to his face. "Even if we had such terms of respect, your rank would render them unnecessary. We speak now as equals, you and I. Or, at least, I choose to do so, until you decide to deny your birthright."

"Equals?" I stammered.

"Indeed. In fact, that is what I wished to speak with you about." He paused one moment, and his eyes grew soft. "My son confided in me that you have had difficulty accepting that your Tree could have chosen you. Is this true?"

I flushed. "Does Ben tell you *everything*?"

The King chuckled. "Blessed Flame, no. And thank the Tree for that. I have no more desire to know everything that goes on in the life and mind of a boy of twenty summers any more than Koriben wishes me to. In fact, one benefit of Koriben's travels over the past year has been his increased independence in that regard."

He gave me a confidential smile. "Although don't tell him I said that."

"I won't," I said with an uneasy smile in return. I wasn't sure if I'd ever get used to this whole "chatting as equals with a one-hundred-and-forty-year-old King of the Dragons" deal.

"I have a confession, though," the King said with a rueful smile. "And that is that I have waited for you for far longer than Koriben has been searching for you. You cannot imagine the joy and relief it brought me when Koriben said he had found you."

"For far longer.... Why?"

"I have known since becoming Heir myself well over a century ago that if my people were to survive, the Covenants would have to be restored, as have most of the Heirs and Monarchs since their breaking. The Tree promised me that I would have a hand in their restoration but only revealed to me how a little at a time. When my son was born, I knew he was part of our answer. A significant part, but the salvation of seven worlds and two peoples is too great for one mortal to bear alone. When I understood that, the Tree revealed to me the final piece we needed to begin: you."

My heart thudded, loudly enough I wondered if he could hear through the looking glass, or whatever this oval was.

"Me? Like...someone *like* me, like a Moontouched—"

"No, Sarah Lind," the King said gently. "*You*. In Her sacred fire, I saw you, just as you are now, in every detail, from your face to your voice, to your mannerisms and expressions. In fact, I have seen you many, many times before. The Tree appears to me wearing the avatars of the women of my past, with one exception. I never knew until that moment why She would sometimes choose to counsel me in the form of a good, wise, strong young woman with brown hair and eyes—the only form I could not remember having ever seen elsewhere. And that is because I had not. And would not, until the moment my son brought you into this room on this day."

I froze in my seat, ramrod straight from the effort of fighting a primordial urge to flee. After a few moments of silence, I said, "I...don't...know how to take this."

"Take it as you will, then. I only thought that you should know."

The King's eyes were soft with compassion, but somehow that only made my panic deeper. If he were flippant, charismatic, or manipulative, I could sense something was off and discard everything he said. Write him off as a madman, smash this oval, run out of the room, and tell Ben I was done.

But those soft golden eyes.... They fixed me to my seat with the crushing weight of truth and the eye-pricking warmth of understanding.

I realized what the hardest part was.

"You...." I rasped. Then swallowed. Hardly believing the words even as I said them, yet unable to contain, let alone deny them, they escaped through trembling lips. "You...love me. Don't you?"

His golden eyes warmed, and in spite of myself, I felt that warmth sinking into me, wrapping me as if in sheltering wings of that pure...love.

"Indeed, I do. More than I can express. As difficult as I know it may be for you to believe and accept, I already think of you as a daughter. I cannot help it."

"You don't *know* me."

"Yet somehow I do. I will not try to give an explanation; there is none. Yet that is the truth."

I could not help but believe him.

I sat there, stunned. "I...I don't know how to take this, either."

"Again, take it for what you will. But I hope the knowledge will give you strength as you make your decision."

"What decision?" I cried. "Everything I keep hearing seems to tell me that the decision has already been made *for* me."

"No, it has not," the King said with kind patience. "The Tree did not tell me why She spoke to me in your form. She only did, until one day She briefly assumed it to tell me that my son would not have to bear his burden alone. You have already helped him bear it. If that is all you wish to do, I do not blame you for it. I thank you for that help and wish you a safe return to your home."

He allowed the silence to rest between us. It was probably peaceable silence for him; for me, it felt like I was sitting on a thousand needles. I didn't feel like he was guilting me—there was nothing passive-aggressive about his manner. He was simply waiting with inexhaustible patience and knowing eyes for me to feel to the bone and then say out loud the conclusion we both knew I had already come to.

"That...is not all I wish to do. If Ben needs me...I want to help."

A memory of Svyer, speaking to Ben, came to me: *You don't have to save the worlds by yourself. You know that, right?*

"He needs help," I said softly. "Even if he doesn't know what that looks like yet. Even if neither of us do."

"I couldn't agree more," the King said quietly. "But that is about my son's troubles. We are here to discuss yours, and I see there is something else, something deeper, still troubling you. What is it?"

I hesitated. Took a deep breath. And, ignoring all the reasons I should have had to not trust this near-stranger, I spoke my greatest fear. "If none of us know what we need...then what makes all of you think it is me?"

The King leaned back and pondered long enough that I wondered if he was going to answer.

Finally, he said, "It appears to me, my dear—and please correct me if I have misunderstood—that you are caught in a battle between what you want and what you think you deserve. And the fear of reaching for what might be within your grasp, but being denied it, is keeping you from reaching altogether."

I felt as if I had been punched in the gut. The impact of that blinding light he had cast on the shadows of my heart made breathing a monumental task.

My arms gripped the edges of that simple wooden chair until my hands began cramping.

"Is that right?" the King asked gently.

I couldn't speak, so I only nodded. I couldn't meet his eyes, so I only looked down at the desk.

He said softly, "Are you unworthy, Sarah?"

"I...." I swallowed. "I'm not...a leader."

A hint of sternness entered the King's expression for the first time. "That is not true. I might have lost my son last night if it were not for your leadership."

"He wouldn't have been in danger at all if I hadn't made him stay!" I cried.

"If you hadn't stayed, would you ever have discovered this hold? Would you ever have discovered your birthright? Who you *are*? Who you could become? You were *meant* to stay, Sarah. Remember that the Tree asked it of you, but you felt it first. You are the reason Koriben and his wings are alive. You are the reason they are where they are now. You *will* be the reason they restore a gate to Earth and renew the Covenants to save both our peoples. You have led and will lead them to do this. You are already their compass...if not their leader."

I shook my head helplessly. Ridiculously, I was fighting tears again. No doubt proof that I wasn't made of the iron stuff needed for a leader.... Right?

"A leader is not always the person flying at the front, receiving all the glory, my dear," the King said more gently. "We need very few of those. What we need far more dearly are good people with brave hearts who see what must be done to help the ones they love, and who do it. Perhaps you may never be the former. But you are already the latter. And I am already so very, very proud of you."

There went the tears, spilling down my cheeks. I was too overwhelmed to even thank him.

He didn't appear to need thanks, however. He only inclined his head and gazed at me with lips pulled into a smile and eyes glowing with a look of pure fatherly tenderness. "You can have no idea how much I wish to embrace you."

His smile died. His voice lowered, so quiet he almost seemed to be speaking to himself. "And how difficult it is to know I may never get that chance."

"This isn't goodbye," I burst out. "Not forever, I mean."

It wouldn't—couldn't—be. Even if I hadn't already promised Svyer I'd see her again, the thought of never coming back to see him in person was unacceptable.

His smile returned, but it had lost its full strength. "I'm relieved to hear it. I think there is more we need to discuss, so...Flame willing, we *will* speak again, Sarah."

"Yes," I agreed. "And...thank you. For everything. I don't know what to do with most of it yet, but I promise I'll think about it."

"Do, please. And if I could ask a great favor, promise me one more thing, if you would."

"Anything," I said. And without alarm, I realized I meant it.

He smiled briefly before sobering.

"It is regarding the shadows I mentioned. The shadow Koriben is most fixated on is not, in fact, the most important, but I cannot convince him of that. Promise me you will keep the renewal of the Covenants and yours and Ben's safety as your greatest priorities. The Covenants are the goal, and you both are the keys. Without you both doing what only you two can, *all* will fall to shadow. Do not let Ben forget that or pull you astray. Promise me, please."

My heart thudded more quickly for a moment, but I nodded. "I promise."

CHAPTER TWENTY-TWO

SISTER

KORIBEN

I PACED OUTSIDE THE bedroom door, straining to hear anything from the muted discussion inside. It was juvenile, I knew, but I couldn't seem to help it. I had already been anxious about Sarah and Avva meeting so soon, though I'd done my best to hide my worry from Sarah, who had her own needless nerves to deal with. Little did she realize that far from disliking her, Avva was in much greater danger of becoming more attached than was good for him. I knew that as soon as he saw us together, he would not be able to stop himself from hoping.

Then Avva, on top of being so determined to request an audience, asked to speak with her alone....

What for? What could he be discussing with her that he didn't want me hearing? Was he telling her the parts that I had evaded giving so far? About her ultimate role in all of this? About his...fading?

I didn't worry about him botching any explanation he saw fit to give—this was Avva, and unlike me, he almost always knew what to say and how to say it. He had a clarity of sight and way with words that I despaired of ever matching, even if I had another hundred and twenty years to strain at it. If he had been the one sent to find Sarah, she wouldn't have been in this mess I'd brought on all of us, I was sure of that.

No, I worried about what he would convince her of, and what he would ask her to do because of it.

The only clarity Avva consistently lacked was about himself.

And yet, despite my best efforts at eavesdropping, I heard nothing except the unintelligible murmur of voices. Sarah spoke little, mostly listening. Though that fit in with what I knew of her so far, it was still worrisome. The long pauses in which I heard nothing weren't reassuring, either.

Then, much sooner than I thought it would, the door opened. I happened to be pacing in the storage room's direction, so I stumbled and hurried on another couple of steps before turning as innocently as I could manage when Sarah called my name.

"Ben."

"Oh," I said with overdone casualness. "Done already?"

I tried to examine her without being obvious about it, and my gut twisted. Her eyes glistened and looked red, as if she had been crying, and just before she answered, she sniffled.

"Yes," she said, and then laughed weakly. She smiled and continued so quietly she must have been intending Avva not to hear. "I'm not sure how much more I could take, anyway."

I knew what she meant. She had that *look* that I knew all too well: that one of wonder mixed with equal parts chagrin and adoration. Avva had that kind of effect on people, especially one on one. On anybody decent, anyway. If they weren't decent...the adoration was replaced with the opposite feeling. Avva had made quite a few enemies for no other reason than he saw through them to their black hearts.

But if they had a heart as bright as Sarah's....

Well, let's just say it was a good thing that Avva was over seven times her age and a committed widower, because she looked half in love with him already. And that bothered me more than it should have.

As I passed her in the doorway, I paused and put a hand on her shoulder in wordless comfort. She smiled up at me and put a hand over mine. "I'm fine," she whispered. "Like you said...nothing to worry about."

On the contrary, I thought with a mental groan as I passed her into the room.

At least as far as Sarah was concerned, their first meeting was every bit as bad as I'd feared it would be.

Sarah went out into the hall and back to whatever she had been doing before, no doubt to give me privacy, but I left the door open anyway. Avva had probably said all he had wanted to both of us.

"Well?" I asked him when I came into view.

"That will be all, I think, Koriben," Avva said. He was leaning back in his chair, looking wearier than he had a right to be after just sitting in conversation for a half deken. I hated that weariness, and it was only becoming more frequent over the past year.

It made my father look...old.

"Avva...." I trailed off, knowing how useless it was to scold or urge him to rest. Or ask, even circumspectly, just what had been discussed while I wasn't in the room. If Avva wanted me to know what that was, he wouldn't have asked me to leave.

As if he didn't even hear me, he gazed without focus on something else on his wall, and his lips pulled into a slight smile. "She's a rare one, son."

My gut twisted again. I said with a shrug, "She's a Tree's chosen, so of course she is."

Avva's eyes flicked to mine, and his smile deepened, letting me know he, as always, saw more than I let on. More than I admitted to even myself. My flameheart thudded.

Mercifully, he didn't press the point. Instead, he let his smile fade. "Take care of her."

"I will." This, at least, I could say with genuine feeling. "As I've said I would."

Avva sighed. "I know you will. Forgive me. I just can't help but...."

He stared wistfully in the direction Sarah had gone. His look turned the twist in my gut into a knife.

Every bit as bad.

"Avva...." I said uneasily. I inhaled deeply, trying to scent if Sarah was close enough to overhear. "You know that...."

He waved a hand, smoothing out his expression. "I know that too. I have not forgotten. But I do not need your...*intervention* to call her my daughter. At least in private."

I blinked. And felt rather stupid that the possibility hadn't occurred to me. It was just...Avva had informally adopted so many dramá by this point that I'd taken his fathering instincts for granted. His nature was to help whoever needed him—whether or not they knew it or even wanted him to. Yet none of his informal "daughters" had seemed to quite fill that void I learned was inside him, the one that I could only halfway fill as a son.

There seemed to be something different about Sarah. No other young woman that he'd taken under his wing had brought that look of wistfulness to his eyes.

Avva continued with a thin smile. "Think of her as your sister, if that's what you wish."

That...didn't sit right. At all. In fact, it kind of made my lunch sour in my already twisted and stabbed gut. And I did not appreciate Avva's chuckle at my expression.

I braced my hands on the desk and lowered my voice. "Look, Avva, we can't lose sight of—"

A hint of sternness entered Avva's eyes. "I am not the one likely to lose sight of what must be, son."

I put my face in my hands and prayed to the Tree for calm.

"Is that what you discussed with her?" I said from between clenched teeth, daring to push that far.

"Only in the briefest sense."

I lowered my hands in surprise.

He met my eyes calmly. "I didn't tell her...specifics. Today, I focused on her needs, not mine."

I let out a breath of relief. Which was strange. Avva's confession might have been the final capstone in Sarah's decision to embrace her role and help us. But perhaps that was one reason I'd delayed telling her. Because as soon as she knew....

She *would* think she had no choice.

Avva nodded slowly, as if reading my thoughts. "Don't tell her just yet. She has too much to process and decide before then. My needs can wait."

I agreed with the request but not the last sentiment, so I only nodded in grim assent.

His eyes softened, another kind of wistfulness entering them. "Take care, Koriben."

I swallowed with difficulty. "I will, Avva."

Trying to prevent any other gut-wrenching requests or looks, I reached up and touched his scale. Avva's image faded, and it once again became simple gold.

I had only a moment to sigh before I felt the itch of my own scale, and a moment later, I recognized the touch. Sighing, I brought out my own scale, swapped it with Avva's, and sat down. This would not be a restful call, either—especially since this was the third time she had tried to contact me that day. Then, with a last sigh, I touched my scale to accept the connection.

As I'd known it would, Svyer's anxious face faded into being on the surface.

"Thank the Tree!" The relief gave way to fury. "I've been—"

"I know," I said, letting my full exhaustion show as I propped my forehead on my hand. "I've been busy, Svyer."

She took a deep breath, visibly trying to calm herself. "I get that. I do. And I'm not the type to badger—"

I snorted, and she huffed.

"I mean, badger *you*."

At my raised eyebrow, she folded her arms and tapped a finger against her skin. "I mean when it isn't important. But Ben, when I heard you hadn't reached Kergin Hold.... And no one knew where you were...."

I softened my expression. "I told Avva where we were—last night and this morning. He said he would pass the message on to the elders."

"I know, and that's why there hasn't been a general panic. Still, they wouldn't say where. You can't expect me to have gotten a restful night's sleep, not knowing if all of you were out in the middle of...."

Her voice trailed off as her eyes darted around me to what she could see. Which clearly wasn't in the middle of the Athalin Jungle.

Her eyes widened. "Where *are* you?"

I hesitated. I loved my cousin, trusted her, and knew how worried she must have been about me and her new chick. And yet, Avva and I both had agreed that specifics about this hold must not be shared. Besides, this wasn't even our jurisdiction anymore—not ours to rule, and not ours to disclose. This hold was Sarah's, and here, she answered only to her own Tree.

I heard a rap on the door, and when I looked, I saw Sarah standing tentatively just outside my threshold. "Is that...Svyer? I thought I heard her voice."

Relieved, I waved her over. "Yes! It is. Come on in!"

Sarah brightened and hurried over. I tried to appear casual as Sarah put her hand on my shoulder to brace herself as she leaned into view of the scale. But her touch, even through my shirt, and the swirl of her scent coming from her hair falling in front of me, made me hot and dizzy in the best—and worst—way. I found myself thinking of doing things I should *not* think of or do. Such as gently pulling her into my lap, immersing my face in her hair, pressing my lips to her throat....

Sister! I chanted in my head, no matter how it turned my stomach.

"Svyer!" Sarah exclaimed, blessedly oblivious to what she was doing to me.

Cousin? Maybe second cousin. Three times removed.... No! Sister!

Svyer's face similarly brightened, and she grinned as if the two of them hadn't seen each other in months, rather than only a day.

"Sarah! How are you? Are you alright? You look alright, but are you? Has Ben been taking care of you?"

Sarah laughed. "What do you want me to answer first?"

Using every ounce of my willpower, I began scooting out of the chair—and away from Sarah. If my face looked as hot as it felt, I hoped they pinned it down to masculine embarrassment. "I'll just let you girls get caught up, shall I?"

Sarah readily took the chair I'd vacated, but her beaming look of thanks was another dagger to my greatly abused gut. "So sorry for hijacking another conversation."

"Please," I said, gesturing at the scale. "Svyer didn't want to talk to *me*, anyway. I was just the one she could get ahold of."

"That's not true," Svyer said, rolling her eyes. "I *was* worried about you, too, you big lug."

"And on that touching note, this lug is leaving, before he becomes irrelevant." But I winked at Sarah to show her I didn't take it amiss.

She grinned at me, grabbed my hand with both of hers (tangling my intestines in another knot), and mouthed *Thank you*.

I smiled as best as I could as I pulled away from her and left without another word—trying hard not to feel as if I were fleeing for my life. But Sarah's handprint was burned into my shoulder, and her scent followed me far longer than it had any right to.

I braced my hands on the balcony railing in the central chamber of the hold and took in great gasps of clear air. Once my head cleared and the brand faded, I looked up at the waterfall. Grimly, I suppressed every unbrotherly impulse I felt toward Sarah with a ruthlessness I hadn't ever had to use before.

Ever since my vow years ago, I'd had a lot of practice ignoring the way females made me feel—a trait that came in handy as a single Heir around plenty of skillful coquettes who wanted nothing more than to become a King's consort one day and were willing to use quite a few tricks to get to their goal. We dramá were a touchy race, so I'd had to learn how to avoid or keep those casual touches from becoming anything more—and to control myself when my guard slipped.

But never had I had as much difficulty recovering as I had just then, much less when the touch was so innocent. Perhaps that was the problem: Sarah had *no* ulterior motives. She simply was comfortable around me, trusted me. Wanted nothing from me except friendship.

Blessed Flame....

That was a heady blend I had never tasted before. And it was utterly intoxicating.

How am I going to do this? I thought. Even now, just the thought of her....

Heat rose, my flameheart thudded, and I gripped the stone railing with renewed tension.

But the waterfall only roared on, silent to my question.

Perhaps the only advice I was ever going to get came, ironically, from my father. Even if Sarah refused her title, Avva had made it clear that she was going to remain a part of our lives from now on. And that was good. That was what I wanted. Because as much as it was going to hurt to keep my distance, I knew it would hurt far worse to keep us apart. I needed Sarah now, separate from what I needed her to be, to do. Now that I'd had a taste of her friendship, I knew I couldn't go back.

But that made it even *more* necessary to do nothing to poison it, to betray her trust or ruin her comfort. So, I would take Avva's teasing advice far more to heart than he'd meant me to.

I brought Sarah's face to my mind's eye. Then I said the word—this time with grim determination. *Sister.*

I ignored the wrongness that echoed like a discordant chord through my whole being and repeated the word firmly. I don't know how long I stood there, repeating the word, but I didn't stop until I had iced the heat and numbed the wrongness to silence. Hopefully for good.

Sister.

That's what she would be to me. Even if it killed me.

Chapter Twenty-Three

DINNER

Sarah

Svyer grinned as Ben left, and after a pause to allow him to get out of earshot, she said, "Well, I can see for myself that at least one thing is going well."

"What?" I asked, baffled.

"Oh, nothing," Svyer said. Then her smile faded. "Truly, Sarah. How are you?"

"I'm well," I said with feeling. "Truly, Svyer. We're safe, for the moment. Ben's been fussing over me in your place, so don't worry about that."

"Good to hear," Svyer said with a straight face. "Is he giving you enough to eat?"

I rolled my eyes. "Rather too much."

"Good. And regularly checking you for any more surprise infections?"

I shifted. "Well, I'm sure he would have, but we've been a bit busy...."

Her eyes narrowed in worry again. "So Ben said. But when Ben says 'busy,' and doesn't answer my calls for over a day, that usually means 'in mortal peril.'"

"Does it now," I said, flushing a bit.

"Just what happened last night? And where are you? No one in the know has said—if they even know more than the fact that Ben's not dead and doesn't need a search party sent out for him—though I hear the King ordered a battlewing to be on standby all night at Kergin Hold."

I hadn't known that, but presumably Ben had. No doubt the reason he hadn't called for them when the lish struck was because they couldn't have gotten to us in time. Especially in the dark.

I hesitated, mostly because I didn't want to worry Svyer. "We...had a rough night, but we survived. We found cover, and we're safe now."

"Where, though?" Svyer said. "That's just the thing: there *isn't* any cover in that whole massive jungle, and no gate close enough for Ben to have taken you somewhere else. Are you sure you're safe?"

A quiet little something inside me held my tongue for just one second. Before I could overcome it with guilt or eagerness to soothe, it occurred to me for the first time that part of the reason for our current respite was that *no one*, except maybe the King, had any clue where we were. And even *we* knew little more than *what* we were in—not where.

But the *what* was still universe-shatteringly significant, perhaps even more so than the fact of a lish on my trail.

I trusted Svyer. But could I—*should* I—ask her to keep this kind of secret?

Was friendship—was *leadership*—sometimes more about what you didn't need to burden someone with, rather than telling all?

Oh, how I wished Ben were there to tell me.

Svyer's eyes tightened, her lips pressed, and she leaned forward earnestly. "Please, Sarah. This is my cousin. And—mind, I'm going to totally deny this if you tell him—he's my favorite one. What's more, he's our Heir, a good one—the best we could have hoped for. But, unfortunately, one who has a dangerous tendency to get himself in over his head. And I'm fond of you as well, now. So it's been driving me crazy, not knowing, wondering if I should have been there with you. And if I should come searching for you now."

"Don't!" I said, more quickly than I should have. I took a breath. "Svyer, stay, please. We're fine. And you wouldn't be able to find us, trust me."

She leaned in further, eyes soft. "Then trust *me*. Don't be like Ben, Sarah. Don't feel like you have to save all the worlds on your own."

I hesitated one more time.

Then, decision made, I took a deep breath and opened my mouth.

I jumped when I heard a suave voice in the doorway. "What a sound for sore ears. Is that Svyer's dulcet voice I hear?"

Smooth as silk, Kor strode into the room and bent down to our level, slinging an arm around my shoulders as he did so. "Svyer, darling! How good to see your beatific face."

As if to defy him, Svyer leaned back with a scowl. "Kor. How good of you to interrupt."

Kor only smirked as he fingered a smooth, shiny blue stone etched with runes and embedded with mica-like flecks, which hung on a woven black cord around his neck.

"Impeccable timing is only one of my many considerable skills. Among—"

Svyer's face vanished, only to be replaced with what had been underneath the image all along: the smooth convex surface of a gold, tear-drop oval.

Kor cursed under his breath.

"What happened?" I asked in alarm. "Is she OK?"

"Lost connection," Kor said as he straightened. He dropped the stone he'd been fingering and crossed his arms, displeased. "It happens. Not surprising in this case, considering the possible interference."

The explanation made sense (it was miraculous they had *any* communication method that worked across solar systems at all), but the timing was suspicious. I scrutinized Kor, but the scowl on his face appeared genuine—unlike the charm he had been oozing before.

That made another suspicion form in my mind.

"Kor...." I said slowly. "Is there a...history between the two of you?"

Kor looked down at me with a start. Then a slow, catlike smile came over his face. "I keep forgetting you aren't an idiot."

I snorted. He laughed. At least he seemed over his pique about both my refusal to help him with the archivals and Svyer's dropped call.

"It's less of a surprise each time, don't worry. Sorry to disappoint you, Sarah: there is no 'history' to report yet."

His eyes narrowed as he gazed at the gold oval on the wall. "But if my instincts are correct...there will be."

I raised an eyebrow. I couldn't see it working between them, but Svyer seemed aware of that. "Then just a friendly hint: you might want to tone it down. Like...*way* down."

His face darkened, and he fingered the blue stone again. "Oh, I know *exactly* what I'm doing, Sarah. Trust me."

WHEN I FOUND BEN again, he seemed jumpy around me for some reason. Still, he helped me cobble together dinner, since even Kor had made himself scarce again after Svyer's call had ended. (I decided he reminded me of nothing better than our deceased, cunning cat, Felix.) Ben had been the only one I could find when I stepped out onto the center-chamber balcony that I was beginning to think of as the Rim.

Ben showed me how to cook and prepare a few easy dramá dishes from things we found in the freezer room. We could have eaten some of the food we'd brought with us, but Ben said that would keep (apparently nothing aged in the nothing-place they put their stuff in), and it would be a shame to waste the food in the freezer, now that I'd broken the seal and restarted the entropy clock. We also could have eaten bread, vegetables, cold-cuts and the like instead of cooking something, but Ben said the cooking smell would lure his wings in better than any other method, and he was right.

Besides, the cooking seemed to settle Ben. I didn't know why it still surprised me that he seemed to know his way around a kitchen, but it did. I guess I figured that, sure, he might stay in guest rooms, clean for himself, and make his own beds, but surely cooking was the one thing that had fallen to the wayside among the many other things an Heir had to do—and especially with all the traveling he'd been doing. Yet there he was, chopping, sauteing, and flipping like he was an expert chef. The longer he was in that element, the more his stress seemed to melt off him, until he was smiling unconsciously. Then he began *singing*.

Soft and low, in a fully masculine baritone and a jaunty tune that wouldn't have been out of place in an Irish pub. And he was....

Happy. Well and truly happy, for perhaps the first time I had ever seen. With that simple contentment setting him off with a golden glow, and his smooth, rich singing voice winding through the mess's killer acoustics....

The sight and sound of him filled me with a nameless ache I'd never felt before, one so deep and yearning that I couldn't breathe.

I hadn't realized I'd stopped my vegetable chopping to stare until he glimpsed me and silenced abruptly, looking away with a blush. "What?"

I hurriedly resumed chopping. "Nothing," I said as casually as I could, though my throat was dry and heart pounding. "Please, don't stop."

But I'd popped his bubble, or let out some of the air. He didn't pick up the song again, but to my relief, his contented smile slowly returned as he flipped the vegetables in his pan with a skill I watched in sidelong envy.

"I've missed this," he said with a sigh.

"How'd you get so good?"

"At what?" Fortunately, with him concentrating on measuring some things into a bowl, the question didn't seem to make him so self-conscious this time.

"The singing. And...*this.*" I gestured with both hands at the counter spread with food, utensils, and cookware.

Though I'd helped carry things, he had selected everything with a swiftness and surety born of experience and practice, and with about as much admiration of the stock and tools as Yvera had in the armory and Kor in the library. Only now did I realize the restraint it must have taken for him to leave behind the kitchen and storage rooms without giving away his interest the first time.

"Surely an Heir doesn't have time to *cook*?"

"Ah, well, those all have the same answer," Ben said, his smile fading.

Then my heart clenched, and I knew I'd done it this time. "Your mother."

"Avvi," he agreed.

"Ben, I'm so—"

"No, don't be sorry," he said calmly as he stirred. "I need to remember. And right now...with you..."

His eyes narrowed, and something seemed telling about how hard he was concentrating, on how he was not looking at me.

"...it's easier," he concluded.

I dutifully went back to chopping. After a moment, I tentatively asked, "She taught you to cook?"

"Among many things, including singing," Ben said with a chuckle. "But cooking—and singing while cooking—were her favorite."

"So they became yours."

"So they did," he agreed. "You had a point: a Monarch, and even a Monarch's consort, doesn't always have time to cook, but Avvi did, whenever she could. It made her happy, and it showed her love for Avva and me. And it was something we could do together. So yes, it became my favorite. And remember how I was talking about balance? This was one thing Avva suggested I do for myself. So, I made the time, whenever I could. Took classes when I could. Just like she did. And it made Avva happy, too. Because what's the point of cooking just for yourself?"

"I hadn't ever thought of it that way. I...haven't ever had to. There's always so many mouths to feed in my family...."

I didn't mention that cooking in our house was often either a chaotic mess that ended in tears or was frozen pizza. Even when it was my turn, and I was left mercifully alone, and it turned out perfectly, and everyone liked it, cooking had always felt like a chore. Like scrubbing the toilet: it was a dull and thankless task which had to be done.

It occurred to me that my attitude was perhaps why, even though I'd done my fair share of cooking, I had nowhere near Ben's skill.

He paused and shook his head in wonder. "I forgot. *Twelve.*"

"Counting my sister-in-law and nephew," I reminded him.

He chuckled. "That's right, sorry. I'll get over the shock soon, I promise."

He glanced at me, then asked almost as tentatively as I had about his mother, "What was that like? Growing up with...seven siblings."

I smiled to myself at the audible pause required for him to do the math. I paused, trying to think of a neutral description, since I'd also heard the wistfulness in his voice.

"Loud," I said finally.

After another moment, I asked, "What was it like, being the only one?"

He paused. "Quiet," he said.

"I imagine it would be," I said awkwardly. Then, trying to change the subject, I inhaled deeply. "Well, if this tastes anything like it smells already, it'll be amazing. So, thank you for doing this, and showing me."

He chuckled as he dumped the contents of his skillet onto a platter. "Thanks for indulging me. Like I said, I've missed this. It's not often that I've had access to stores of food and a kitchen in the past year. Much less ones as good as what you have here."

He sighed. "It's also one thing I feel guilty about, being away from Avva. He has others to cook for him—because, believe it or not, he's hopeless—"

"No!" I said with a gasping laugh. I couldn't imagine the King I had seen being hopeless at *anything*.

Ben gave a laugh of his own as he took my tray of chopped vegetables and dumped them in the empty skillet. "I swear, it's the Fire's truth. Avvi used to tease him that he could burn water. Anyway, he has others to cook, thank the Flame."

His voice lowered. "But though he never complains, I know no one can make things as close to the way Avvi did as I can."

Hands and mind free now, I turned to look at him. I hesitated, but my loathing of that renewed tightness in his expression overcame my inhibitions.

I crossed to him and laid my hand over his, the one holding the skillet handle. He looked down at me in surprise, but not as if the touch was unwelcome. Though he started going red at my expression and glanced away. I was becoming too fond of how adorable the combination of blush and beard was on him.

"I understand the guilt," I said quietly. "But you are a good son, Ben."

He said nothing, but his hand tightened its grip on the skillet.

"You are. And your father is proud of you. Trust me. If even I could get that impression after fifteen minutes or so, then it must be true."

Ben shifted away, ostensibly to check something in the oven. I took over stirring the vegetables, but I saw him swiping at the corners of his eyes when he thought my view was blocked.

"Thanks," he said, coming back while blinking rapidly. "But—er—be careful about those elik. They're stronger than usual."

He nudged me aside, and I let him. I didn't mention that the small, red, onion-like bulbs he'd warned me about hadn't bothered my eyes, either when I was chopping them or stirring the skillet.

"Dinner ready yet?" Yvera said as she strolled in, making me jump. "I'm starving."

Her hair was wet and loose, she was dressed in loose-fitting clothing, and she wore a small towel around her shoulders, so I assumed she had worked out her frustration in the armory and showered.

Ben didn't even look up. "Almost. It would be ready sooner if you'd set the table."

"Fine," she huffed and strode over to a table.

"Sarah can show you where—"

"We have our own things, don't we?"

Without giving Ben a chance to argue, she began pulling plates, cups, and utensils out of thin air, her hand only shifting the slightest bit for each item before she set it in place on the table she chose.

Kor's timing once again proved to be impeccable. Just as I was helping Ben set the last dishes and serving utensils on the center of the table, I asked Ben if we should go looking for him, and Ben only had enough time to shake his head before Kor casually strode into the mess, hands in his pockets, looking pleasantly surprised.

"Ah, dinner, is it?"

"As if you didn't *know*," Yvera muttered just loud enough for me to hear as she served herself.

Ben rolled his eyes but answered without resentment as he dished his own plate. "It is. So, sit down and help yourself."

At least, I *thought* Ben had been serving himself, but he grabbed the empty plate in front of me and set his overflowing one down in its place.

"Ben," I groaned.

"You're hungry, aren't you?"

He'd no doubt heard my stomach growl and caught me snitching, so it wasn't as if I could deny it.

"Not *this* hungry! And I won't want to be facing...whatever it is we're facing tonight...while I'm as stuffed as a turkey."

"What is a—" Kor began, eyes alight.

Ben ignored him. "Sarah, you're still recovering from the healing, let alone everything else we've asked you to do since."

"Yes, but Ben, this binging isn't making me feel great, either. I know this may be surprising to you giants, but my stomach is only about this big at rest."

I held up a clenched fist, and all of them stared. Fortunately, I was getting somewhat used to being the human freak, and if it got my point through Ben's well-meaning head, then I'd take it.

Ben shook his head. "Fine. Just eat your fill, and we can set the rest aside for you somewhere so you can get to it without asking one of us if you get hungry again."

He frowned and eyed my torso for a moment, as if picturing that fist. "Now that I think of it.... Maybe it's better for you to eat more frequently rather than more at once, anyway."

I snorted. "You think?"

"From my research," Kor offered in a neutral tone, not looking up from his food, "humans appeared to eat less than dramá, yet more frequently."

"What do you mean, more frequently?" I asked. "I'm used to about three meals a day, and that's what you all seem to eat."

Kor was already shaking his head. "We're exceptions to the norm, given how much energy we spend normally, let alone in the past couple of days."

Ben put in, "Plus, in situations like this, we never know when we'll have the chance for another good meal, so we eat as much as we can, when we can."

"What is the norm, then?" I asked, now more fascinated than exasperated.

Ben shrugged. "About two meals. One in the morning to get the body going again before the sun can do the rest, and one very large one in the evening."

"To get through the night," I concluded thoughtfully. "The most dangerous time."

"And the time we lose our greatest source of power."

That explained the veritable Thanksgiving feast Ben had cooked up and spread out before us, which the drakón were already making quick work of. Particularly Yvera, who was *already* on her second plate. Though Ben's cooking was incredible (I already knew that from what I'd snitched), that couldn't have been the only explanation for how she was packing food away.

I realized that if she spent much of her time being *this* hungry…that explained quite a lot about her in general.

"You said humans eat three meals a day?" Ben said.

"Give or take." I shrugged. "That's my culture's norm: breakfast, lunch, dinner. But I eat smaller meals and snack in between."

Ben grimaced. I knew what was behind it, so I hastily added, "You meant well. I know you did. So don't beat yourself up about it. And I *was* starving this morning. It's just that I fill up much faster than you all do."

"She needs more sustained energy," Kor mused to Ben. "She can't draw what she needs from the sun throughout the day."

Ben sighed again and looked at me. "We'll need to find some foods that are easy for you to carry around in that pack Svyer gave you. Nuts, fruit, rolls, things like that. That way you can eat when you need to."

"And you won't immediately starve if you get separated from us," Kor said cheerfully.

Ben grew still, but his hand gripped his cup so hard that I heard the metal groan and saw it cave, and the liquid inside sloshed over the rim. I tried my best not to stare, but my heartbeat sped up.

Ben acted like a normal person (albeit a ridiculously tall and ripped one) most of the time, so it was too easy for me to forget he was so much more—that the potential for becoming a mammoth of a dragon lay just under his golden skin. Just how strong *was* he, even in this form?

"Ben!" Yvera snapped after a quick swallow. "Those are from Mysha."

Ben blinked as if waking up and released his grip sheepishly. "Sorry."

Sure enough, the sturdy, thick metal cup looked like a crushed soda can in the middle. Again, I tried not to stare.

"Shoulda grabbed the ones from the storeroom," Yvera grumbled under her breath, stabbing a sautéed elik with more force than before. And shot me a glare as if I were the one at fault here.

I might have been, indirectly. My heart was touched by the severity of Ben's reaction, and was still beating faster than normal as I imagined the same thing he had, with only a fraction of Ben's knowledge of all the horrors that awaited a helpless human like me out there.

While mopping up the spilled liquid, Ben cast me a glance with tight eyes. "Just...don't get separated from us, please."

Perhaps because my mind was on the dragon inside him, my memory flashed to the moment I'd first seen him—and ran from him as if my life depended on it. And how, in his desperation to not lose me in the jungle, he'd changed to human and tackled me to the ground.

Now I knew that my life depended on quite the opposite of my first impulse. I needed to stick to these drakón—but particularly Ben—like glue. No matter how my whole body ached when he sang while cooking us dinner, or when he looked at me like that.

I nodded. "I'll do my very best."

CHAPTER TWENTY-FOUR

SUNSET

KORIBEN

AFTER SHE WAS DONE eating, Sarah began gathering the empty dishes. To stop her, I grabbed her elbow—gently, mindful as always of her delicacy, and gingerly, all too aware of how the skin-to-skin contact woke a different hunger than the one that had just been sated.

"Oh no you don't," I said. "We cooked, so Yvera and Kor clean up. That's the rules."

"Ben—" Yvera and Kor began at the same time, in nearly the same plaintive tone. Then glared at each other. I caught Sarah covering her mouth to hide a smile.

I raised an eyebrow at the two of them. "That's the rules, and you both agreed to them. I can't think of a single excuse you could have that would get either of you out of it this time. Yv, we're safe enough for now; besides, this way, you can make sure you get your things back when they're clean. Sorry about the cup; I'll apologize to Mysha for you and ask for another one. Kor, the mysteries have waited a thousand years, and they can wait a few dek more."

"Fine," Yvera huffed, pushing to her feet. She grabbed the stack that Sarah began and glared daggers at Kor. "But *you* had better do your share this time."

As I stood and stepped over the bench, Kor grinned lazily at her. "I always do my share. *You* just consider magic to be cheating."

"Of course it's unfair if all *you* have to do is—"

"Come on," I told Sarah, putting a hand to her back to nudge her out. Silently, I added, *This usually gets ugly. Best for us to get clear before they really get started.*

"Oh, I'm all too familiar with that sort of ugliness," Sarah whispered, but she followed me out to the center chamber.

She walked to the balustrade and rested folded arms on the top rim. My heart constricted in a painfully pleasant way at the contented smile on her face as she closed her eyes, turned her face up to the fading "sun," and took a deep breath.

I should leave. She was, as I'd told Yvera, safe enough right now, and she'd get precious little time to herself once we left the shelter of this secret, isolated hold. And yet, I couldn't make my feet turn around, and for much the same reason: the peaceful time I would have to spend with her like this, let alone in such privacy, was slipping away just as quickly.

If she asked to be alone, I would go. But until then...I couldn't seem to tear myself away.

To keep things from becoming awkward, I searched desperately for something a brother might say—which, of course, would have nothing to do with how beautiful she looked with her dark hair falling back and the fading gold light illuminating her skin and delicate, exposed throat.

I quietly cleared my own throat as I joined her. "You don't look nervous."

"I'm not, which is unlike me." She opened her eyes and chuckled. "Maybe it just hasn't hit yet."

She frowned at the cavern ceiling. "How are we going to tell when both moons are high, anyway?"

"I'll know," I assured her. "It's nothing like the energy coming from the sun, but it's something. I can feel one of them rising now."

"I wish I could see it. That would be beautiful, coming up over the snow."

I concentrated, gauging the rise angle and direction. It was a bit like trying to locate a sound, that unseen source of the faintest of energy streams to my flameheart. "You know what? I think you can. I think we might be able to see it from the window in the corridor."

"Really?" she said with surprising excitement. To my shock, she grabbed my hand and pulled me in the corridor's direction. "Let's go see!"

Let's. Far from wanting to be alone, she wanted me to come. That was as plain as her cool, small hand in mine.

My flameheart surged with that same painful pleasure, yet greater than ever before.

My instincts told me I shouldn't go anywhere alone with her. In the center chamber, we were out of sight but not quite hearing of Yvera and Kor. Their faint bickering acted like a safety line for me. And yet I let that small hand lead me on until that tether faded to nothing. Worst of all, I felt none of the regret or warning I should have at its loss.

Only the thrill.

Fortunately, Sarah let go of my hand soon after we entered the corridor, and I kept just enough sense to stick my hands in my pockets and order them to remain there. The silence as we walked was companionable, and that was new, too. Unless Yvera was hunting or fighting, she hated silence. So did Kor, except if he was concentrating on some scheme or paper of his. But Sarah obviously felt no need to fill the corridor with chatter, and neither did I. It was enough to be together.

More than enough, in fact. In the focused task of walking, I didn't have to worry about giving myself away with some uncontrolled touch or word. In the silence, I could focus on breathing her in, memorizing every subtle note of her heady scent.

I tried to think what her scent reminded me of. Of course, no person's scent smelled *exactly* like a spice, a plant, or an element—we weren't made of those things. But with no other closer comparisons, the mind was drawn to describing our scents in those ways, especially with the scents of magic-invested beings.

The humanness in Sarah was unmistakable to me by now. The greatest difference between her scent and any others I had smelled before was the utter lack of the molten undertone of heartfire, which even amón had to at least some degree. In its place was only cool stillness, like bedrock after a long, chilly night. That undertone should have been unappealing to me; instead, I found something restful, something soothing in it. Something I could lay my head down on.

I hurried my contemplation along before I could follow that thought any further.

Her high note was more lively, almost sharp with clarity, yet still cool and subtle. Like glacial runoff, wind through pines, or the whirling, silent power of falling snow.

It was her middle note that was the greatest puzzle to me, even though it was the strongest. And—if my mind wasn't playing tricks on me—stronger than it had been this morning.

It was....

Just when the word was at the tip of my tongue, we reached the window. Sarah strode in front of it first and inhaled in awe, and when I came to her side, I stilled.

The sun was setting behind us, on the other side of the mountain sheltering us in its heart, but the fading rays were lighting the sky in a glorious gradient of deepening blue, and all below fell into cool shadow. All the more dramatic a backdrop for the large, white moon cresting the range in front of us, like a watchful eye beginning to open.

A beautiful sight, but I couldn't help the regret and anxiousness that came to the heart of every dramá every sunset as the source of our very lives sunk out of reach.

In stark contrast, Sarah pressed her palms to the glass, heedless of the cold, and looked up at the moon with unmistakable excitement. Her lips were parted, and her eyes were round, shining orbs of their own, the warm browns fading to—

I inhaled sharply, and Sarah looked at me in alarm. "What? What is it?"

The rings in her eyes returned so quickly to brown that I wondered if I had imagined the shift. Yet I had seen them change to that color once before, and her scent swam in the air more strongly than ever, especially that enigmatic middle note. Just as a drakón's did when....

Ignoring her question for a moment, I tentatively put a hand on her shoulder. Sure enough, I felt great stirrings within her, as biting and powerful as winter winds. Even though my first impulse was to jerk away from the icy burn, I withdrew my hand slowly to avoid alarming her or hurting her feelings.

Sarah swallowed, no doubt coming to her own conclusions as she felt the beginnings of the storm stir within her. "Ben.... What is happening to me?"

I looked at her as calmly as I could, but my flameheart was racing. I scrambled to think of a way to explain the miracle I was only just coming to understand, in a way that would not frighten her. Even though it was terrifying me.

I kneeled and took her hand, ignoring the dual chills of skin and magic, and tried to not let fear for her plummeting body temperature show in my face.

I put her hand over my heart. "Sarah, what can you feel there?"

Her eyes widened, her fingers spasmed, and she inhaled. "You're burning. Gosh, Ben, you're a furnace."

She raised her other ice-cold hand to my forehead and frowned. "You're not as hot there. Still, you're so.... Are you sure you're feeling OK?"

"I'm perfectly healthy," I hedged, and I brought down the hand on my forehead to also cover my heart. "Look past the heat and *feel*. Can you do that? Can you feel something there?"

If I had guessed right, then she should have had enough sensitivity by now to feel something else.

She furrowed her forehead in concentration for a moment, then her eyes—still warm and brown—went wide. "The heat. It...it pulses with your heartbeat. And with it pulses...."

She raised her eyes to meet mine and whispered the word. "Power."

"Yes," I said. "What you're feeling is my flameheart, the source of my power...and my existence. But right now, it's nothing like it could be, Sarah. It's fading."

She inhaled sharply before I saw understanding return to her eyes, and she let out the breath more steadily. "Because the sun is fading. Like it does every night."

I pointed at the wall across from the window. I made my face gentle and my voice soft. "Yes. It takes a tremendous amount of energy to even *exist* as I am, and the best source for me is a sun. Somewhere out there, I can feel this sun's light being eclipsed by the turning of this world. I know that sun is still out there, and because it is and it's close enough, I'll still live, but with its energy blocked from me, I'll have to rely on any heat source I can find and the meal I just ate to keep functioning until it returns."

"I can feel it," she said in distress, pressing her hands deeper into my chest. "Even in the seconds since I first felt it, I can feel the difference."

When she glanced anxiously at the darkening sky, I didn't mention that her ice-cold hands pressed to my chest weren't helping. The different warmth that her concern and touch stirred inside my flameheart might have been nullifying the negative effects, anyway.

"This happens every night, Sarah," I soothed, as one would a hatchling.

That didn't mean the loss wasn't distressing to even adults. Every night felt like a kind of death to us, especially in times of danger. The vulnerability that night brought even me—or especially me, considering how much the consumed desired my blood and my death—was usually enough to make any sleep I got full of nightmares.

I hated sleep.

Sarah took a deep breath and withdrew her hands. "Every night," she repeated to herself. "And we're safe here. For tonight."

"Exactly," I said.

She shook her head and gave a shaky laugh. "How can you live with that...fading? Every night?"

I shrugged, trying to not make it seem like a big deal. "Lots of ways."

"Like hot baths and wind tunnels, big meals and large fires," she said with a faint smile.

"Now you're getting it," I said with a crooked grin.

Her smile faded, and she looked at the rising moon. She bit her lip. "But...Ben...if you are fading right now, then why am I...."

She stared at her own two hands as if she had never seen them before. Then slowly pressed them to her heart. Her eyes widened again; then, to my shock, she grabbed my hand and placed it gingerly over her own heart. I worked hard to suppress a shudder, both from thrill and dread. Mostly dread. She was so cold—and what stirred underneath my fingers, colder still. For one moment, when her wide eyes met mine...the irises flashed an icy silver.

My flameheart thudded to a halt before restarting in a lurch.

"Ben." Her voice hitched as she repeated, "What is happening to *me*?"

I hesitated. Then decided I had cushioned my answer for long enough. Now was the time to give her the simple truth. "I don't know. The Moon-touched were *supposed* to be like us. Even their drakón strengthened and faded with the sun, just like us. And yet, while I am fading...."

"I am strengthening," she said.

I swallowed. "Yes. I don't understand how this could be happening. I'm sorry. Especially when...."

I put a hand to her forehead, and it felt like touching ice.

I could resist the impulse no longer. Whether or not this was the way things were supposed to be, I pulled her into my arms and crushed her to me, fueling my flameheart recklessly to warm her.

"Blessed Flame," I found myself whispering out loud. "What am I supposed to do?"

Don't let me lose her, I prayed. *Not her.*

She shivered, but before I could wonder if I should let go, she put her own arms around me and pressed tightly to me. "You're so warm."

"And you are so cold. So cold...." I swallowed again and closed my eyes tightly. Her scent was stronger than ever, its icy burn sliding down my throat. It drowned me.

I turned up the heat in my blood even further. It was a good thing I'd eaten so much, because I was burning through those reserves at a heedless rate, considering only the Flame knew what still lay in store for us tonight. Even more rashly, I scanned her with my power as deeply as I dared, drained and often repulsed by the frigidity of the stirring power within her. Even so, I felt enough to know it wasn't illness turning her to ice. She didn't feel ill at all.

She shivered again and echoed my thoughts. "And yet...I've...I've never felt this way before, Ben. I've never felt so...*alive*, not even when we first got here. So filled to the brim.... Your warmth is nice, but it's not...."

She released her hold on me and shifted back enough that I got the message. Yet it still was physically painful to let her go, to allow her to step out of the shelter of my arms.

She studied her hands again in awe. "Without you, I don't feel *cold*."

"Are you sure?" I asked in disbelief as I sat back on my heels.

She shook her head. "I'm sure. Not cold in the slightest. Or stiff. Or achy, or anything bad. At all. I feel...."

She curled her hands into fists, and a faint shimmer, like moonlight over the ripples of a lake, ran over her skin. Her eyes flashed silver for another half second.

"Strong," she breathed.

Her wide eyes met mine again. "Is this...what it feels like for you? After dawn?"

Slowly, hesitantly, I nodded. "Yes."

I knew what she meant: that ever-increasing aliveness, wellness, strength. That power filling you to the brim so full you thought you might burst with it. This was all so familiar. And all so wrong.

Or was it?

In my fear, had I forgotten how the Tree had told me the order of things needed to change? Forever?

But *change* meant I didn't know what she felt, or what was coming for her. And the fear that uncertainty evoked threatened to choke me.

Ahglen, krathen, even a lish were things I knew how to face and conquer, given the right circumstances.

But how could I protect her...from herself?

Chapter Twenty-Five

LIGHTS

Sarah

I KNEW BEN WAS worried: that was as plain as...well, day. But after the initial shock, I couldn't work up the same level of anxiety. This energy that was growing inside of me felt too right. Too exhilarating. For perhaps the first time in my life since I was a toddler, I had to concentrate to keep from bouncing off the walls.

The only thing that worried me was what others might say or think. My family, most importantly. But Ben's wings, most immediately.

As we walked back down the corridor, I had only one request. "Don't tell the others. Not just yet."

"Why?" Ben asked, brow furrowing even further as he looked down at me. He had probably been thinking of doing just that. "Kor might have some insight—"

"But first he'll poke and prod and treat me like some science experiment. He won't look at me like a person, Ben. Not like you."

Nothing like Ben. Nothing like that look in his golden eyes as he kneeled in front of me and held my hand to his flameheart.

Ben hesitated, then sighed. "You're right. But he's going to find out eventually, and the longer you keep something from him...."

"I get it," I said in a quiet voice as we approached the arch leading out to the Rim. "But...not tonight. I don't want to deal with that tonight. Besides, by this time tomorrow...we might have some answers."

A voice purred, "Answers to what, may I ask?"

I let out a tiny scream as Kor appeared at my side the moment Ben and I stepped through the arch. As if he had been waiting around the corner, just out of sight.

"How do you *do* that?" I cried, fisting my hands but using all my willpower to prevent myself from punching at him. Not because I didn't think he deserved it, but because I knew I'd look pathetic doing it. Even though he was smaller than Ben and Yvera, Kor was still six feet of more muscle than a scholar-politician-spymaster had any right to have.

Ignoring my question, Kor looked at my arms, propped one of his elbows in one hand, and tapped his chin with a gleam in his eyes. "Fascinating. It seems my hypothesis was correct."

I looked down just in time to see a ripple of white, like sunlight on water, shimmer over my skin. And my fists were glowing.

"Ben!" I squeaked, holding up my hands as if they had become radioactive. Which...they might have. How was I supposed to know?!

"It's OK, it's alright," Ben soothed, taking one of those hands in his without a qualm. "Breathe. Just breathe. You just need to slow your heart rate."

And try *not to think of punching Kor*, Ben added dryly to just me. *Not that he doesn't deserve it, but that will only make it worse.*

Ben's glare in Kor's direction made me feel better. As did his hand, still twined with mine. So I could focus on his advice and take slow, deep breaths, and gradually, my heartbeat slowed, and the glow faded.

"That's it, breathe," Ben encouraged.

"Very nice—" Kor began with admiration, but he wisely shut his mouth at Ben's glare and a return shimmer down my arms.

A few seconds later, the glow was gone, and I took a deep breath. "I...think I'm OK now. Thanks, Ben."

Though I hated to let go of his warmth, I extracted my fingers from Ben's. Kor was still watching, after all, and with eyes that were too bright and knowing.

"Alright, 'fess up," I said, jabbing Kor in the chest. "What's this 'hypothesis'?"

"First, is there something *you* would like to tell me?" Kor asked.

"Kor," Ben warned.

"It's fine, Ben," I said with a sigh and folded my arms. "Seems like that cat's already out of the bag. Well, Kor, all we know so far is that I seem to have...a lot more energy right now than I have any right to."

Or knew what to do with, apparently, if only being spooked and then wanting to punch Kor gave me the bioluminescence of a deep-sea squid.

"There, don't you feel better now?" Kor smirked. "You should be thanking me."

I just raised an eyebrow. "Your turn."

Kor sighed. "Did anyone else besides me think about why a *gate* of all things would appear, let alone be active, at *night*?"

Ben and I just looked at him.

Kor counted down another finger. "Or why the message left on the archival says to return to the room full of *ice* at *night*? When the *moons* are high? Assuming, of course, that it isn't to lure Ben into a trap when he is at his weakest."

At our continued nonreaction, Kor rolled his eyes. "Or I don't know—about *that*?"

He thumbed over his shoulder. At first, I didn't know what he meant. Then I gasped and pushed past him. "Ben...the waterfall."

It had been too quiet as we had approached the central chamber, and now I saw why. The waterfall had dried up: either because the mechanism had shut down or the lack of sun meant no snowmelt, I couldn't tell at first. That wasn't the most shocking thing, though.

It was as if the hold had been a sleepy hive locked in a nice, peaceful winter slumber. And now it had woken up.

The bees in this case were lights. Small, glowing, featureless white orbs with an aura so bright I couldn't tell if there was anything in the center. And they were everywhere. Hovering busily around the mouth of the waterfall, floating in and out of the tunnel, burnishing every mirror. Others zoomed through the arches and across the chamber to another arch, disappearing before I could guess their purpose. Lights skimmed along the floors like sock-sliding children, except in far too regimented formations and without the squeals, and specks of dust or bits of leaves that had collected during the day shot toward them as if by magnetism or noiseless suction and disappeared without a trace. Similar regiments of lights raced across the ceiling and around the pillars.

"No...dust," I said faintly. Just as Yvera had said.

"Yv is losing her *mind*," Kor said with a chortle. "She's tearing through the entire hold looking for you, Ben. I'm a bit surprised she hasn't found us yet."

"They're harmless?" Ben asked intently, grabbing my shoulder to bring me back to his side.

"They appear to be. They don't respond to me at all, other than going around me to get on with their task—"

"Ben!" Yvera shouted, emerging from the eastern arch. She began racing around the Rim toward us, and man, that woman could *move*.

I was distracted from watching her turn into a violet streak by the glimpse of a few lights zipping toward me. With a little yelp, I skipped to the side—needlessly, because just as Kor said, the lights gave me and Ben a perfectly circular berth before zipping back on their former trajectory.

"See," Kor shrugged. "Just like...."

The lights slowed. Then moved in the reverse direction, gaining speed. Back toward me.

"Kor!" Ben said. He only had time to shift in front of me and raise a hand before the lights halted a few feet in front of him.

The three lights floated inches off the ground for a moment, as if confused. Then they began edging around Ben in a perfect arc, but Ben once again stepped to be right in front of me, and the lights paused once more.

"Ben," Yvera cried as she reached us. "What the hellfrost is going on?!"

"No idea," Ben said, his eyes never leaving the lights in front of us. "Kor?"

"Well, this may be a long shot, but I *think* they are trying to reach Sarah," Kor drawled.

"You don't say," Ben snapped at him.

Kor looked up. "And they aren't the only ones."

Other lights were floating toward me, coming from all directions now. They approached more slowly than the others had, gravitating along paths that avoided Ben. When he noticed, he held out a hand behind him and backed us against the wall.

"Ben," Yvera hissed as she positioned herself in front of *him*. "Get away from her."

Either she didn't see or didn't care that the lights hovering over the floor parted for her, rearranging themselves in a wider semicircle as if she were oil and they water. Kor saw, because he waded into the thick of them, and they all did the same, always leaving him a three-dimensional bubble with a radius of about three feet, no matter how much they had to jostle to do so.

"You want to protect me, protect her," Ben snapped at his rightwing. His hands flexed, and I felt a stirring—like a fluctuation in pressure—that I realized was him summoning power.

Power that he didn't have to waste right now.

That thought snapped me out of my daze.

"Ben, calm down," I urged. "I don't think they mean me—or any of us—harm."

Ben said, "You can't know that—" while Yvera spat, "Of course *you* would say—"

Kor interrupted them both. "Ben, Yv, *look* at me. Just *look*."

We all looked—which was hard to do, since he was so surrounded by lights at this point that they formed an eye-watering net around him. The mystery of how he could stand it himself was solved when I glimpsed the dark goggles he was wearing.

"They're not being aggressive. See?" He reached for one, and it and all the surrounding ones retreated, creating a momentary bulge in their otherwise perfect hemisphere formation.

"Just because they aren't making contact doesn't mean they aren't doing harm," Yvera snapped.

"They're not emitting any energy toward us," Kor snapped back. "I don't detect any off-gassing, either. They aren't even trapping us."

To demonstrate, Kor waded away from us. The lights parted and spilled around his three-dimensional bubble without a single token of resistance. As they were freed from his pattern-disturbing presence, they rearranged themselves in the air in a kind of hexagonal three-dimensional grid, further reinforcing the hive analogy in my mind.

Once Kor reached the end of the lights, he stepped into the clear without a single one following him. He walked a few paces further to drive the point home and then turned around and held out his hands. "You, me, Ben—we're in the *way*, Yvera. Other than their directive to not touch us, they couldn't care less about us."

"Then what *do* they care about?"

But we all knew the answer. Kor pointed to me. "Sarah."

"What do they want with her?" Ben demanded.

Kor ran a hand through his hair in frustration. "I don't *know*. I can't read anything from these things. I can't even figure out how they're *built*, how they're powered, how they function—they might even be *alive*. Ben...."

He trailed off for a moment. When he spoke, his voice was a mix of consternation and grudging awe. "This is magic the likes of which I have never seen before. As foreign and indecipherable to me as those doors were to you."

Ben's hands clenched into fists. "Then you don't know if they mean *her* harm."

"They don't," Kor and I said at the same time. I did so earnestly, Kor in frustration.

"You just said you knew nothing about these things. Then how do you know—"

"Ben," I interrupted with a firmness that surprised even me. Especially the next words that came from my mouth. "This is my *home*. These lights—they are *mine*."

As if in confirmation, all the lights vibrated in place at the word *mine*, letting off a momentary hum as they did.

In that hum, I finally understood. It was as if they had spoken to me in a language so primal, the key was coded into my very DNA.

I was Moontouched. This place had been made for me and my family, to shelter and protect us as we restored the balance to the Covenants. These lights had been made for me, to help me. They were mine. Their vibration had been from...joy.

After nearly a thousand years of waiting, of caring meticulously for this place for me, all they wanted to do was to welcome me home.

Welcome home, Sarah Lind.

Unable to keep them waiting a second longer, I darted out from behind Ben and ran into them, too quickly for Ben to stop me, though I felt the brush of his hand at my back.

"Sarah!"

That was the last thing I heard from any of the drakón for a while as all the lights rushed to me, as quick as bees but as eager as puppies. I could see nothing else but light. Hear nothing else but joyful humming, which steadily rose to the pitch of exquisite, alien song. Feel nothing else but their welcoming touch and the air stirred by their rapid flights.

Their combined light should have been blinding, but though I was dazzled, my eyes miraculously adjusted, so that I could still make out individual orbs, even if I still couldn't see into their centers. Even with the adjustment, I was awash in a sea of lights as they crowded around me, each eager to take their turn to touch me, great me with a hum, buzz against my skin with joy. They wound around my legs and arms, danced around my torso, even spun delightedly through my hair, sending it floating everywhere. I laughed—it was impossible not to be buoyed up, surrounded by such joy. I held out my hands, and two lights settled into them, letting me examine them up close with awe—and I could have sworn their pulses as I did so were their equivalent of preening.

Kor had said they might be alive, and now I knew for certain that they were. What *kind* of life was still a complete mystery, since I also knew with equal certainty that they had been made. They told me so, over and over again, in language more subliminal than words.

We were made for you. We waited so long for you—so very, very long. We're so happy you're finally here. We love you.

Tears spilled freely from my eyes. I felt that love radiating from each one, in each brush against my cheek, in each whisper, in each hummed note in the song. To be surrounded by that welcome, to feel as if I belonged, to drown in such pure, unfathomable love....

I knew that from this moment on, I would never be the same.

Chapter Twenty-Six

TEST

Koriben

I RUSHED TO GO after Sarah, but Yvera whirled around even faster, striking the center of my chest and slamming me back against the wall.

"Yv! Let go!" I gasped, struggling to push her away. I was bigger and stronger than her, but I was dazed by the unexpected hit, not to mention winded and my focus divided, and hampered by lack of desire to hurt her; half my attention was looking to the side to see the dozens—perhaps hundreds—of glowing white lights stream as quick as akut scenting blood.

Toward Sarah.

I jerked forward. "NO!"

"Kor!" Yvera shouted over her shoulder as she strained with all her might to keep me back.

Before I could break from her, bands of sapphire magic emerged from the walls and wrapped themselves around my arms and legs, jerking my limbs back to the stone. Meanwhile, Sarah was now surrounded, buried so deep in those things that I could barely make her out.

I said a word that my mother would have smacked me for, then, "Torch it, Kor! *Let me go!* That's an order—"

Yvera shoved her face in mine and said, "Snap out of it, Ben. Let the girl risk her life if she wants; that's her choice. But if you're determined to do the same, we're authorized to restrain you."

Kor addressed her as he approached at a casual stroll. "*Technically* Regulation 10.3 doesn't apply in this situation, since I'm fairly certain that his life isn't at risk—and nor, for that matter, is Sarah's."

At Yvera's scowl, he sighed. "*But* I'm willing to help you bend the rules on this one, seeing as I'm not one-hundred-percent positive. What I'm more certain of is that Ben would only disrupt what appears to be some kind of powerful bonding ritual, and wouldn't that be a shame."

While he spoke, I pulled against my restraints, but that was only for show. I was actually focused on eroding them, hoping Kor would be too distracted to notice.

No luck, of course. Kor's head turned to mine, and the bonds not only reinforced but tightened. "Cut it out, Ben. She is *fine*. Just *look* at her."

What did he think I had been *doing* with three-quarters of my attention? If I'd been less distracted, I might have gotten away from them by now. But the lights around her were too blinding to make out details anymore. For all I knew, she could be dying.

That thought was enough to make me go cold with agony.

But Kor...was wearing lightcrafting lenses. Squarish bubbles of glass set in metal frames and rubber seals, with leather straps; enchanters used them to discern the finer details of lightworks.

"*What* can you *see*?" I demanded, straining uselessly against his bonds.

"Oh, right," Kor said, taking off his lenses. He sighed regretfully. "They're my only pair, and this is a once-in-a-lifetime observation opportunity.... But...I suppose, to keep you calm, I'll let you use them."

I just about wanted to kill him. And, the terrible thing was, I could have. I could feel the pain inside fueling the fires of my flameheart, surging me with energy as if it were broad daylight, heedless of what the cost would be to me later. I knew the spells I could use to stop both of their hearts and had more than enough blunt force to spear them through any protections they had.

My greatest restraint wasn't these bonds, Yvera's muscle, or even my distraction. It was because, even now, I loved them too much to do what it would take to break free, because that would most likely hurt or even kill them. And they knew it.

So, with great restraint, I said from between clenched teeth. "Or you could let me go. Like I *ordered* you to."

"And let you disrupt the ritual?" Kor said as he approached and began strapping them on me. "No, I'll observe what I can of the rest with the naked eye, thank you."

The second he let go, I jerked my head to look at Sarah, flameheart pounding.

The black glass dispersed the fog of the light to allow me to see the details at last. Sarah's back was to me, so I couldn't see her expression, but her posture was light and open. She had her hands up and was leaning forward, as if to study the lights that were resting in each one. As they vibrated, she leaned back, and though I couldn't hear her over the humming, her body shook as if with laughter.

Though lights were winding around her everywhere they could, I could see no sign of harm—or any sign that they touched her at all, other than the way her clothes and hair shifted in the rush of their passage. Far from aggressive, the lights' movements seemed buoyant, and she seemed welcoming of the attention. In fact, she looked...happy.

She was *fine*.

I let out a breath that I felt like I had been holding since she had slipped away from me, and I sunk back against the wall. In a sudden reversal of feeling, I was glad for Kor's restraints, since they kept me up with some semblance of dignity while the surge of power and adrenaline in my veins dried up, and I became as weak as a hatchling.

That, of course, was when Kor let me go, and I slid down the wall into an upright heap.

"See?" Kor said. "You burned yourself up for nothing, since she's perfectly alright. As I said."

I really, really wanted to punch him in the gut, to wipe that smug look off his face and see *him* gasping on the ground. And I probably would have if I'd had just a bit more left in me. He'd probably known that would happen and had timed his release accordingly. Which only made me want to punch him more.

"Can I have my lenses back now?"

"Give me...a few seconds," I said in between heavy breaths. I glanced back at Sarah, but Kor was right. And wrong. She looked more than alright.

She...looked glorious. Shining bright as a sun, with her long, dark hair billowing around her....

Blessed Flame.... This was only a glimpse of what she was to become, and even that filled my chest with a nameless ache.

After a few moments, I reluctantly slid the lenses off. More because I could feel how useless I'd be if Sarah needed my help than because I took pity on Kor.

"Here," I said as I held them out. "But only if you promise to let us know the moment she seems in trouble."

"Yes, yes, of course." Kor snatched them back and slipped them on.

I sighed and let my head sink back against the stone wall behind me. I was going to need to rest up quickly; I could already feel the other moon beginning to rise. It might be time for some emergency tsha. The good, strong kind. And...torch it, maybe a few drops of sundew.

The stuff was worth its weight in amber, and for more than just the color of its liquid. But if there was a time for me to use it, now was it. Before Sarah and I entered a chamber of ice on our own to receive a message enigmatically promised to us a thousand years ago.

My eyes were closed, so I only heard Yvera step next to me. "You shouldn't have fought us like that."

Wrong, I thought to myself. Knowing what I knew now, yes, I shouldn't have wasted my energy on fighting my wings when Sarah wasn't in danger. But I *hadn't* known that, and I was obligated by sacred oath to protect her.

Not that oaths were on my mind at the time.... Something to think (or avoid thinking) about later.

But my spent energy hadn't been for nothing, because it had taught me one important thing: when it came to Sarah's safety, not only was I ultimately on my own, but to protect her, I might have to go through my wings first. The three of us had bickered over priorities and strategies before, but never had both of them conspired so swiftly and effectively against me. Yvera thought only of me because that was *her* duty. Kor had a better inkling of how important Sarah was, but she also represented the greatest source of novel knowledge he had ever had the chance to explore, and he was too willing to take risks with her for his own ends.

Which meant that if each of our duties and desires ever ran so counter to each other again, I had to be prepared to fight not just one but both my wings at once, in a way my conscience could live with afterward.

No, the more I thought about it, the more I realized that my struggle hadn't been a waste. This had been a test, and I had failed.

But I would not fail again.

Chapter Twenty-Seven

OATHS

Sarah

The lights took their turns as politely as could be and flew off back to their duties as soon as they were done greeting me to make room for the rest. I didn't know how long I stood there, too wrapped up in the joy to notice the aura around me had dimmed from the lack of lights until the last few came for their turn. I smiled sadly as I watched and felt them spin around me, ruffling my hair one last time, and looked after them wistfully as they floated away.

Leaving me alone.

I felt empty, and not just from the absence of radiating joy. The energy that had been building inside me since sunset was gone, at least for the moment, and I sagged as the exhaustion hit. I reached for the balustrade, but it was steps away, and I stumbled.

"Easy."

Kor caught and steadied me. He had taken off the goggles he'd been using before, and now they hung around his neck.

I let out a deep breath. "Thanks. Um...I don't suppose you know why I feel like I've run a marathon?"

"Greeting hundreds of one's subjects all at once does that, I hear," Kor said with a wink. "And those usually aren't made of pure magic or bond to you at a touch."

My jaw dropped. "My *what*?"

Kor slung an arm around my shoulders to turn me to face the rest of the chamber, where all the lights were busily back at work, and gestured grandly with his other arm. "As you said yourself, this place is your dominion, and *these* are your devoted servants."

I scowled at him. "That's not what I said at all."

Kor shrugged. "Call it what you like. But whatever these things are—and I *will* figure out what they are—"

Kor's face hardened for a moment, and I felt a flicker of unease, but the look was gone in an instant, making me wonder if I'd imagined it.

"—they are the reason for this hold's miraculous state of preservation, and they have been waiting for you, and only you. That's why they wouldn't touch any of the rest of us before they greeted you. And now that you are here and they have woken, they have all acknowledged you as their mistress and sealed themselves as yours."

I wanted to protest, but I knew it was more from Kor's word choice than the reality of what he was saying. Hadn't I called them *mine*?

But what I had meant, what I had felt.... That was different, but before I could put it to words, Ben called gruffly, "That's enough, Kor. We get the picture."

I turned to look behind me and gaped to see Ben staggering to his feet. Dizziness passed, I pulled away from Kor's arm and rushed to him—which was ridiculous, since I could scarcely have supported Ben's weight for even a second, and Yvera was already at his side. She had let him struggle at first, but at the sight of me hurrying over, she shot me a glare, grasped him under his arm, and pulled him up the rest of the way herself.

I slowed, ducking my head for a moment, but I couldn't help raising my eyes back to Ben.

"Ben, what happened?"

"I could ask you the same question," he said, glaring at me. "Except Kor just explained it all enough, as I just said."

I stared at him, even deeper at sea with the added mystery of his irritation with me.

He grimaced and ran a hand through his hair. "Come on. I think we both need some good tsha after that. At least, I know I torched well do."

"And maybe a few drops of sundew, if you are still planning on accompanying Sarah," Kor said. With a kind of *I told you so* smirk.

"I am," Ben snapped at him. He fisted a hand, and for one wild moment I thought he was going to hit Kor, but instead, he jerked away from us to stride toward the kitchen.

Yvera threw up her hands and made good use of her long legs to catch up with him. "Ben—"

"Save it, Yv."

I stared wide-eyed at Kor. I couldn't remember seeing Ben in such a bad mood. Given his size and power, it was mildly frightening.

"Kor," I whispered. "What's wrong?"

Kor looked at me with such pure innocence that I knew even before he spoke that he would lie. "I haven't a clue."

"Ugh!" I turned from him to follow Ben and Yvera...if at a slower, more cautious pace.

By the time I entered the kitchen (with Kor ambling along behind me), Ben wasn't in sight, and Yvera was lounging against a counter, eating a roll from dinner. I'd half-expected her to be in an even worse temper than Ben, but she passed me over with the usual glare and looked at Kor.

"He's gone to his room. Says not to bother him, that he'll come out when it's time."

"Probably for the best," Kor mused.

"Yeah," Yvera said with a roll of her eyes. She brushed her hands together to wipe off the crumbs. "What do you think the odds are that he'll fall asleep and miss moons-high?"

Kor raised an eyebrow. "Nil, because even if he does—which I doubt—I'll wake him."

Yvera pushed up from the wall to stand straight. "Kor, don't tell me you're on board with this! It's our job to protect him—"

"In our own ways," Kor interrupted smoothly. "Which is why I'll give him some protection before he enters the chamber, whether or not he wants it. But don't forget that our primary duty isn't to Ben—it's to the Six Realms, just as Ben's is. And Ben is doing his duty by getting that torched message."

"But if it's a trap—"

Up until this point, I had faded into the background, and I was happy there. But then Kor pointed at me. "And if it is, would you have Sarah spring it alone? The Heir of the Moontouched that we have waited a thousand years for, that we have searched the Six Realms a year for, whom the Tree commanded us to find and protect? Is sending her alone *duty*, Yvera? Or is it selfishness?"

Yvera's face hardened to ice. Without answering, she strode past us—shoving Kor as she did so—and out into the Rim.

After her footsteps faded, I said quietly, "That was a bit harsh."

Kor looked after her. "But needed. One of Yvera's greatest strengths—and weaknesses—is her narrowness of focus. Sometimes she has to be reminded of the larger picture."

Especially when it comes to Ben, I thought sadly.

KOR ESTIMATED THAT IT would only be a deken or so until moons-high, so he told me to rest while I had the chance and that either he or Ben would get me when it was time. And I tried, but the more time passed, the more energy trickled back into me, until I felt like a cup starting to overflow.

How am I going to sleep anymore? I thought as I paced my room restlessly. *Am I going to become nocturnal?*

That would be annoying even under the most benign circumstances; life as I'd known it would have to change. But for the time being, I was stuck traveling with three dragons who not only were most active but also were safest during the day. Any asset I could be at night would be offset by the dead weight I might become in the day.

Or was this a onetime fluke? It had come on so suddenly.... I'd only used "magic" for the first time last night, if you could call what I did to open the doors as doing that.

No...wait. Perhaps the very first time would be when Kor had me touch the gem on my door. I'd had a restless night after that, but that could have been from the fever as much as an awakening connection to...whatever this was.

Why was I even feeling this way? Why was I the reverse of what drakón, even Moontouched, had always been? What even was the *source* of this energy, anyway? Drakón got their power from the sun, or heat or food if they had to. Did that mean I got mine from the moon, or moons? (Was the fact that this world had two moons the reason I was feeling supercharged tonight?) But moons were just reflections of the sun, weren't they? Wouldn't that mean that my power would be diluted in comparison, at best?

The questions whirled through my mind as busily as the lights were buzzing around the hold, and far less productively. And so, I paced and pondered, trying to resist the urge to run laps around the Rim to burn off the energy, and, last but hardest of all...to try not to think about Ben.

As hard as that was becoming in general, it was even harder now that my mind kept fretting about why he was out of sorts. Maybe I should knock on his door, ask him what was wrong. Apologize if I was at fault. But he told Yvera that no one was to bother him, and he *needed* to be as rested as possible before we went into the ice chamber, and he only had a "deken" or so....

However long that was, that time seemed to stretch on into infinity.

Just when I was feeling like I was going mad, a knock sounded on my door.

"Oh, thank goodness," I breathed. Then froze in a panic as I realized that if this was showtime, I was unprepared.

"Wait one second, Kor! I'm getting ready!" I called out, riffling through the bags that Ben had deposited in my room at some point. Where was my coat? You'd think I wouldn't have misplaced it already, since I had it on this morning....

Sarah? Can I come in?

I froze again. Ben's mental voice.

"S-sure?" I said, not sure why I stuttered or ended in a question mark.

Ben opened the door and stepped inside. He looked a little flushed, but that seemed from self-consciousness rather than anger, so I relaxed somewhat as I straightened.

"What's up?"

"We need to talk about something," Ben said quietly. "May I...close the door?"

My heart skipped a beat, but I kept my face straight as I nodded. He closed the door gently, but he only took a step away from it, leaving most of the room between us.

"What...do you want to talk about?" I asked, trying hard to hide how uncertain I was. And failing by folding my arms.

Bad move, I chided myself. *You know that's supposed to make you look defensive, closed off.*

But if I rearranged my arms now, wouldn't that be worse?

Ben didn't look deterred, though. All traces of self-consciousness were gone as he set his jaw and gave me a look. One that made me feel like there were ants in my pants. As a goody-two-shoes teacher's pet, as a quiet and obedient daughter, it was not a look I had gotten very often. In fact, it was that kind of look that I dreaded more than any other, the kind that just about killed me.

"Sarah Lind," Ben said slowly. "I apologize for my temper a bit ago. But don't you *ever* do that to me again."

I stared at him. "Do *what*?"

"We were in a situation full of unknowns, and you ran from me and straight into potential danger."

I gaped. "But...I knew it wasn't dangerous—"

"But I didn't!" Ben shot back. He closed his eyes and took a deep breath. When he released it, he met my eyes again. "Sorry. But that's the thing, Sarah. You ran from me, and *I didn't know you would be alright.*"

"But I told you...." I trailed off as I realized just how little I had told him. Before I'd done just as he said.

I swallowed, but my throat was tight. "I was trying to show you, to prove...."

"And if you'd been wrong?" Ben asked. "If you'd been hurt? Killed? *Taken*?"

I knew from the order he'd placed those fates which would be the worst. And I'd had enough exposure to the monsters of his worlds by now to have an inkling why.

"But Ben...I knew...I just *knew* they wouldn't hurt me. That they couldn't. They...spoke to me, in a weird way. I know it sounds crazy, but...."

"I believe you, Sarah," Ben said with a heavy breath. He ran a hand through his hair. "And I believe *now* that they don't mean you harm. But I wouldn't make a habit of believing everything you hear in your head. Or even what you feel. There are...things...out there that can speak to you, make you feel things...."

My eyes widened, and my heart pounded.

"I don't think those light things are bad," Ben said. "They aren't those monsters. Kor agrees they're benign, too, so I think we've ruled that out. But the thing is, Sarah, they *could* have been. Back up to when we knew nothing, and try to see things from my perspective. You felt something that you didn't explain fully to me, and then you ran from my protection. Then they surround you, faster than I could get to you, and suddenly I can't even *see* you anymore."

I stared, feeling my stomach twist. Of course. I'd thought to show him. Just show him and quickly brush away any misunderstandings. But of course he couldn't see....

"Not details," Ben said. "Just a white haze. For all I knew, you could have been dying. Or not there at all."

"Of course," I groaned out loud.

Ben's voice was gentler now. "Now, imagine how that made me feel."

I flinched.

He pressed on, no matter how gentle his voice was. "I just about had a heart attack. And burned through most of my reserves fighting Kor and Yvera to get to you. *That* is why you found me sitting on the ground when it all was over. That was why I was in such a temper. And not just with you, to be honest. With Kor, Yv...but most of all, myself."

"Why *you*?"

His eyes were hard gold. "Because I had failed to protect you. Both then and before by not explaining the kinds of things I'm explaining now. Sarah, I took a sacred oath not just to search for you but to protect you with my life when I found you. And oaths to the Tree aside, I promised you I'd get you home. So yes, the one I blame the most in this scenario is me."

I sunk down onto my bed and wished I could sink further. "Ben.... That wasn't your fault. At *all*. It was mine. I'm so sorry."

"I didn't come here to make you feel guilty." He paused, then grimaced. "Alright, maybe just a little bit. I'm only mortal."

I laughed shakily as I tucked some hair behind my ear. "And I don't blame you for it."

"Because you're too good," he said with a sad shake of his head. "See, that's the thing. You were too trusting. I know you've been working on following your instincts, and I'm glad to see it. But this situation had different stakes, and this time, we got lucky. From now on, in situations like that, you *have* to talk to me. To tell me what's going on inside. Or give me at least *some* kind of warning so that I can help. I want you to promise me that."

I bit my lip. "But what if I just...*know*? And you, Kor, Yvera.... What if no one is listening to me?"

I was used to no one listening to me outside my family. I was used to either suffering in silence or finding my own way. That was why I had thought that the best way was to show him. Prove it to him.

Ben nodded solemnly. "That's a good point. So, I'll make you a promise in return. I swear to always listen. And I mean the kind of listening in which I stop whatever I'm doing, hear you, and seriously consider what you have to say. I did that before, didn't I? When you said you saw the gate, and neither Yvera nor I could."

"You did," I said faintly.

Why hadn't I thought more about the significance of that? Probably because it had been one thing after the next ever since, but the full weight of it finally sunk into me. The Heir of dragonkind had stopped in the middle of a battle for his life to listen to me. And had risked all our lives on the slim chance I was right because he didn't just listen but believed.

"I'll always listen, Sarah," Ben repeated. "I swear it."

I took a deep breath for steadiness. "And I'll make that promise: I will always speak to you before I do something like that again."

Ben's shoulders lowered in relief. "Good enough."

I chuckled weakly. "Wasn't that what you asked for?"

He gave me a crooked smile. "I know enough about leadership and people and *you* to know that I can't ask for what I *really* want, which is for you to promise to always stay where it's safe."

"I'm no daredevil, Ben," I said with a weak smile. "I'm pretty cowardly."

"Ashes," Ben said, and with a spark of fire in his eyes.

"Really. The only reason I did that was because I was *sure* it was safe."

"That's only common sense—self-preservation. I'm glad you've got that much. Though there are many dangers you aren't aware of...."

I shuddered. "Clearly. What are these things? The ones that can put thoughts into my head? Make me feel?"

Ben grimaced. Then sighed. "My first reaction was that we don't need to get into that now. But one of my failures was not telling you about such things before, so you'd be on your guard...."

He sighed as he looked at the ceiling. "But we really are running short on time now...."

I stood and risked getting closer. Not so close that I had to crane my neck to meet his eyes, but close enough that I could feel the heat of him—stronger than I should have at a foot or two away. I didn't think about the reason.

"I get it, I do. Stop beating yourself up about me, Ben. For what it's worth, I think you're doing a great job. I...." I took a deep breath, then the plunge. "I don't think the Tree could have sent anyone better."

He looked away and said nothing, but his eyes were blinking rapidly.

Following those instincts again, with the King's voice whispering in my mind about reaching, I wrapped my arms around Ben to give him a brief hug of comfort.

At least, I'd meant it to be brief. But when Ben responded almost immediately by putting his own arms around me, when he held my head to his chest and pressed his other hand to the small of my back to bring me close, when his head ducked and his breath brushed the top of my hair...

...I held on.

"You scared me, Sarah," he whispered. "Forget oaths—for a few moments, I...."

"I'm sorry," I whispered back. With my ear to his chest, I could feel the heat of his flameheart as much as I could hear its beat. I wondered, again, at the miracle of it: a source of such heat and power inside his *heart*. It couldn't be a literal flame.... Could it?

Well, whatever it was...it was perhaps the most wondrous thing I would ever feel or hear.

But...should it be pounding quite so fast?

Abruptly, Ben hooked both his arms under mine to pull me up closer to his level and hold me so tightly for a moment that I couldn't breathe, and not just from the pressure.

"Don't do it again," he said tightly as his face rested on my shoulder, pressed into the curve of my neck.

I was seeing stars, and not just from oxygen deprivation.

"I promised, didn't I?" I wheezed.

"Oops." Ben let me down swiftly but gently, face flushing. "Sorry."

I just wrapped my arms around him again and grinned up at him. "No problem. That felt rather...cathartic. Feel free to give me a bear hug like that anytime."

"You might regret that offer," he said, pain in his eyes.

My smile faded. "Ben...what—"

My door opened abruptly, and Kor stuck his head in. If he was surprised at what he saw as Ben and I leaped apart, he hid it with a smirk.

"I can't tell you how sorry I am to interrupt for the second time today, but seeing as the Moontouched have been waiting a thousand years for this night...let's not keep them, shall we?"

Chapter Twenty-Eight

MESSAGE

Sarah

We fell into an informal formation as we walked through the outer oval of rooms to the ice chamber: Ben and Yvera first, Ben looking strangely at ease and Yvera as tightly wound as a spring, hand on a knife at her waist, claymore on her back; then Kor and me, Kor looking as bright-eyed as if we were going to a concert put on by his favorite band, and I....

Well, I just felt glad that Ben hadn't made me eat fit to bursting at dinner. Although he'd handed me a roll as we passed through the mess and asked me to eat it. I complied, even though it churned unpleasantly in my stomach.

Though there were arches at the three lower cardinal points of the Rim, giving easy access to most of the outer oval ring of chambers, there wasn't an arch at the northern end. Instead, the oval ended as the walls came together in a sharp point. With the southern end of the hold curving much more broadly, the whole shape of the hold was more of a tear drop rather than a perfect oval. Or perhaps a leaf, I realized.

Since the ice chamber was at the north point, with no arch leading into it from the Rim, we didn't even bother with the Rim and instead followed the outer path through the chambers, as we had the first time. Through the bedrooms, the mess, the bathrooms, the laundry, and the workrooms.

Finally, we came to the doors to the ice chamber, which were the only ones, other than the freezer room, that had closed themselves again after I'd opened them the first time. The white trees on them glowed far more brightly than before, almost too bright for me to look at.

It was time. I could feel that in my bones, even though I couldn't feel the moons as the others could. Odd, that. *Moon*touched and all, you would think I would have a stronger connection to the moons than the drakón, but no matter how I strained, I couldn't locate them, couldn't feel anything from them like they seemed to. If the moons were the source of this energy fizzling inside me, I would have felt them by now. But the energy seemed to come to me from everywhere and nowhere at once. It simply built and built....

Maybe it was this place, this hold. Maybe it was this night, which smelled so strongly of destiny by now that even my human nose caught whiffs of it. It was cold, sharp, electric. Thrilling and terrifying at the same time, two sides of the same coin. I thought about the choice before me. About what I wanted. What I needed.

And about reaching for it.

We stopped in the antechamber, standing in a rough half-circle in front of the doors.

"Ben...." Yvera said, unable to help one last plea. And it was a *plea* this time—so uncharacteristically vulnerable that I looked away out of politeness.

And guilt. Was I doing the right thing by asking Ben to come with me? If it was a trap, as Yvera was convinced it was, was that duty...or selfishness?

But I knew even before Ben spoke that there was nothing any of us could say or do to dissuade him.

"No, Yv," Ben said, but his voice was gentle this time. He pulled her into a tight hug. As I watched out of the corner of my eye, I swallowed painfully at how much easier the hugging logistics were between them. Yvera was so much more his equal—physically and otherwise—than me. Who was I to even hope, let alone reach....

But Ben let go quickly, with a calm smile, clasping her arm like a comrade or a brother. "I'll be fine. You'll see. Besides, you'll be right outside, ready in case we need you."

"If we can even get in," Yvera said darkly.

"That's where I come in, dear rightwing," Kor said. "Speaking of which, come here for a moment, Ben."

While Kor placed his hands on Ben's shoulders and a blue haze shimmered over him, Yvera sent me another of her threat-glares behind his back. I was getting tired of them. If I were the cunning, ingratiating assassin she thought me to be, I'd have gotten the job done by now.

Some of my exasperation must have showed because her glare shifted for a moment to some other expression I didn't catch before she looked away.

"Your turn, Sarah," Kor said, letting go of Ben and coming to me.

"What are you doing?" I asked warily.

He appeared amused rather than offended. "Giving you a ward of protection, just as I did for Ben. It won't make you impervious, but it might save you from a surprise blow or an explosion."

"And that's it?" I said with a raised eyebrow.

"On my honor as a leftwing," Kor said seriously.

I looked at Ben, but he just shrugged. *It's up to you.* But his eyes glinted with worry.

The worry decided me. I looked back at Kor and nodded, trusting that if Kor tried anything else, Ben would know. He placed his hands on my shoulders, just as he had on Ben's, and closed his eyes. Just as with Ben, a blue haze fell around me, tinting everything when it passed over my eyes. I felt nothing at first, not until the blue faded. Then a weight settled over me, like a heavy blanket, except coating each surface to perfection. Feeling as if I'd just been shrink-wrapped, I took several deep, cautious breaths and wiggled my fingers.

"Everything functioning?" Kor asked with a smirk.

"Fortunately for you, yes," I said with a glare.

Oh, Kor said silently, *I would love to explore what you meant by that veiled threat, but—*

"Ready, Sarah?" Ben asked, unaware he was interrupting.

"Ready," I said, passing Kor without a glance to come to his side.

Ben put a hand on my shoulder, clenched lightly in comfort, and gestured to the doors with his other hand. "After you."

I took a deep breath and looked down at my palms for one moment. As if summoned, the energy in my body surged there. My skin shimmered again, and my arms from the mid-forearm down to my fingertips began glowing white. My vision seemed to somehow sharpen, the colors becoming more vivid, everything seeming so much *more*. Yvera inhaled, but I didn't lose focus to glance at her expression.

This is me, I realized. *This is mine, like this hold, like those lights.*

Speaking of which, the lights began streaming into the antechamber through every path that avoided Kor, Yvera, and Ben. Yvera put her hand on her claymore, but Kor held out a hand to hold her back, murmuring something. I would have waited for the lights to finish entering the antechamber, but they sent me wordless encouragement to go ahead.

With that extra boost of confidence that this was meant to be, I took another deep breath and raised my hands to the brilliantly glowing doors and placed them on either side of the nearly seamless crack.

The doors swung slowly and soundlessly outward. Ben put a hand on my shoulder again as we waited for them to still. Then, with Ben's touch at my back letting me know he was right there, I walked inside.

The moonlight overhead filtered through the ice rose in the ceiling, setting each line in icy white fire—so beautiful that my breath caught, and I could stare at nothing else until Ben and I reached the center of the chamber.

Meanwhile, the lights had streamed in behind us and began arranging themselves in random patterns along the icy walls, gritty floor, columns, and air. Once in position, they waited, like audience members politely waiting for the rest of their fellows to take their places.

Once the last lights had floated through the doors and were in position, the doors I had opened slowly closed. Kor and Yvera stood in the center of the antechamber, so we could see them until the very end. Yvera seemed fit to burst with the strain of holding herself back, and Kor had a restraining hand on her arm. When the doors sealed shut, Ben let out a breath and relaxed a margin.

Then the only other light source—the moonlight through the ice above—went out. Plunging us into darkness.

Just as suddenly, we were standing among the stars.

Ben gasped. I did too, gaping at the exquisite beauty around us. It was better than the most immersive planetarium show. The darkness was astonishingly complete, with no ambient light from the stars reaching any of the walls or the floor that *should* still be there; even though I could still feel the grit under my tennis shoes, I could hardly see my hand when I raised it. We were surrounded by the stars, which speckled even the floor we could no longer see. The small lights had even dimmed themselves to varying degrees to represent distance or size or altered their pure white to different spectrums of blue or red, green or yellow.

Our hands found each other's in the darkness. Ben gripped mine tightly.

"It's beautiful," I breathed.

"It is," he agreed in awe.

But stay close, he whispered in my mind. He shifted closer to me, turning so that we were almost back to back.

I felt a flicker of sadness that he couldn't appreciate this marvelous moment. But then, his job here wasn't to marvel, or even to receive the message that was coming. It was to make sure we both walked out of here alive.

Just when I was wondering what came next, a few stars broke from their positions to float toward us. Ben gripped my hand tighter, but I couldn't see his expression well enough in the dark to know what he felt otherwise.

The stars resettled in a broad circle around us, growing larger and more distinct as they did so.

Ben inhaled sharply.

"What?"

"Kaldrir," Ben said, staring at one of the two stars in front of him. This one was larger than most, brilliant, and from what I could tell, golden.

A flicker of understanding, a rise of excitement. "Your sun?"

"The sun of Ythra," Ben said, already turning. "And that—"

He pointed at the other star that had been in front of him. "That is Kyalid."

He kept turning, and since he never let go of my hand, moved me with him. "And Ashga, Olmen. Winalken. Yedrik, the star we came from.... All the six are here. But...."

He stopped both of us in front of the lone star I had been facing in the beginning. Smallish, but bright and blue....

My heart thudded with excitement at his long pause. "My sun? Sekinek?"

Though I still couldn't see the floor, ceiling, or walls, I could see Ben well enough now in the light of all these stars that I saw him look down at me and shake his head.

"I'm sorry, Sarah," he said regretfully. "It's...*this* sun. The sun that is near us now."

I turned, and Ben turned with me to not break our grip. "But...but seven. That makes seven stars, seven worlds, right? Earth has to be the seventh, doesn't it?"

Ben said, "That's what I always thought, but...."

He pulled us back to the solitary star.

"I don't understand," I whispered.

I hated myself for it, but tears stung my eyes. Perhaps the long day had finally become too much. After I had been on the cusp of understanding something in this new universe, the rug had been yanked from under me again.

The breathtaking beauty all around me faded. All I wanted in that moment was the simple. All I wanted was to go home.

After a few moments, Ben said slowly, "The Moontouched.... They only went to Earth because they had to. They were supposed to receive their own world."

And so they shall, son of Flame.

The voice was not a voice. Not in a sense that I heard it with my ears—of that, I was certain. It was like the mental voices that the drakón used, and yet as different from those as speech was to their mental voices.

It *was*.

It was everywhere in the darkness and nowhere at once. The words were soft in volume and mild in tone, but the power and...absoluteness of them pierced my heart like an arrow and vibrated my soul like a plucked string. I put my free hand to my chest with a gasp, and for one second, Ben gripped my hand like a vise. I looked up at him in shock, asking for answers.

He just stared down at me, expression lost in the darkness. And the voice spoke again.

Even softer, even milder.

This time, I recognized the femininity.

Peace, Sarah Lind, My daughter, My precious one—the Heir I have chosen.

I gasped again, staring sightlessly into the darkness. I didn't need Ben to tell me who was speaking anymore. I knew.

The Tree of Ice.

"*Chosen?*" I said.

Indeed. But fear not. You must choose as you are chosen, and that crossroads for you is not yet.

I swallowed. "When?"

Soon. When you return to Earth and appear before Me, I will offer My gift to you, and then you must choose whether to take it—or let it pass to another.

Over the next several moments, I took slow, deep breaths and considered my next question carefully. Finally, I said, "How am I to come to you?"

Well spoken. For that is what I brought you here this night to tell you.

Ben inhaled sharply and gripped my hand more tightly for a moment. All the suns around us floated closer, grew larger, brighter, more vibrant.

As the son of Flame said, each of these suns represents each of the Seven Realms—the Seventh being the Realm that I and My Sister have given to the Moontouched, beginning with you, Sarah. Whatever you choose, My daughter, this may always be your home and your refuge. For you will have need of both in the days to come.

Another clench from Ben's hand.

Though I didn't miss the ominous meaning in Her words, I was oddly calm. The peace the Tree had offered at the beginning was settling into my heart like snow blanketing the ground, bringing a soft hush.

"Thank you," I said.

In reply, I felt a cool brush on my cheek and a tender, icy kiss pressed to my forehead. Far from being spooked by the ghostlike touch, I turned my face upward and closed my eyes. In my mind's eye, I could almost see Her standing before me, and the moment I did, I wanted to for real. Desperately.

She spoke again, and this time Her voice—though still not a voice, and still coming from nowhere and everywhere—sounded closer, more immediate somehow. I knew it wasn't just my imagination from how Ben started in surprise.

Behold the Seven worlds of the Seven Realms.

Each sun changed, turning from uniform orbs of light to colorful spheres of greens, blues, whites, and browns. Their sizes still varied, as did their continents, cloud formations, and ratios of blue, green, and brown. Each was beautiful in its own way, each teeming with life and promise. I felt with a suddenness and intensity that shocked me how precious each world was, how dear the life each held.

Ben looked behind us, at the sun he had first stared at before, which was now one of the largest of the planets around us, covered with vast swaths of browns.

Home, Ben whispered. With such raw longing, I wasn't sure he had meant to speak to me or if I had somehow heard a private thought.

Ythra. Birthplace of the dragons, Realm of the Sunfilled. Ben's home, which he had seen too little of in this past year. The year he had spent searching for me.

My heart clenched.

Before the Moontouched left the Six Realms for Earth, on each world they made a gate. Not a sungate, made of flame and light, but a moongate, made of ice and night.

I inhaled. "Like the one we found on...."

I looked up at Ben.

"Ykran," he supplied quietly, pointing at the world directly to our left, a smallish one covered with vast stretches of uninterrupted green.

Indeed. And in finding and activating, it is now unlocked to you forever.

"You mean we can go back through it?" I asked eagerly. "How? The gate seemed...dead...before."

The gate you entered is meant to receive, not to depart.

"Oh!" Ben exclaimed, as if the Ice Tree's answer not only made perfect sense, but he should have thought of it himself. When I glanced at him questioningly, he shook his head and sent silently, *I'll explain later.*

For the Tree continued. *The sister gate to the one you discovered on Ykran is now ready and waiting for you in the chamber you call the Rim. I concealed it until this moment so that you would not pass through before I could speak with you, but you may now use it at will.*

"How did you know I called it that?" I asked, a bit of unease stirring the snow settled over my heart.

The voice held a trace of amusement and tenderness. *I know all your thoughts, daughter. As I know all the thoughts of My children, wherever they may be. It is you who have not yet learned to know Mine.*

Well, that was...something to think about. Or not.

And so I must speak with you in moments like these, when both our powers are at their highest and our connection the strongest. That time now grows short, and I have not yet answered what you have asked of Me.

"Sorry!" I said. "I'll be quiet and listen now, I promise."

Then hear Me.

The worlds turned in a slow circle around us. In contrast, my mind had not only resettled, it felt crystalline, with each word the Tree then spoke carving themselves into the bedrock of my soul. I doubted I would forget a single one.

You have found one of the seven gates with a sister in this hold. Each of the five other realms under Flame's dominion holds another, with the last remaining on Earth under Mine.

A light drifted over to the space between us and the circle of planets, positioning itself lower to not block our view of the other worlds. The light expanded and changed to form a world so blessedly familiar that I gasped and reached out.

Earth, slowly turning on its axis, just in front of me. There was Asia, Europe, and Africa, the Atlantic...North America. My fingertips could nearly brush it: the globe, the continent, home. And yet, it was still just out of reach.

Find and unlock the five other gates under Flame, and My Sister and I will unlock the last here, in this hold, for you, that you may return to Earth and come, with the son of Flame and the eleven others of your kin, to Me.

At Her last words, a white dot of light shone brilliantly in the middle of Greenland. I started at first, then realized that only made sense. A Tree of Ice, in the middle of one of the most barren, icy landscapes on Earth.

I nodded, memorizing the spot as best as I could. "Got it."

Finding all five gates would probably be harder than I could even guess—not to mention convincing my entire family to go for an adventure in Greenland with me—but at least I finally understood. We finally had a goal. I finally knew my way home. My heart lifted.

Good. Then hear My warning: by the reckoning of Kaldrir, you have ten days.

"What?!" Ben spluttered, gripping my hand like a vise. He addressed the Tree for the first time. "Lady of Ice, with all due respect, You have given us the task of a lifetime, and—"

And it must be completed in ten days, the Tree said with the weight of a glacier. *Or your people will suffer a blow from which their recovery may be nigh impossible.*

Ben froze, breath catching. I was losing feeling in my fingers, but I didn't protest. My heart was clenching, the peace once again disturbed.

Shadows, the King had said. Did he know what was coming?

Did Ben?

Have faith, son of Flame, the Tree said in a kinder tone. *We would not ask this of you both if it were not possible. We will provide the way.*

"But...so soon?" Ben choked out.

The Tree's voice became the softest yet, like the feather touch of a snowflake on the cheek. *We cannot hold it back any longer.*

I felt a different chill than the one brought by the Tree of Ice. "It?"

The Devourer comes.

A tremor went through me, a terrible feeling of premonition. The turning worlds stopped where they were in the circle, with the one Ben had called *home* in front of us.

It comes for all Our children on all Our worlds, but first to Ythra, in ten of her days.

As the Tree spoke, a shadow blossomed like a sickly plant somewhere near the equator. And grew, its tendrils snaking over the entire world. Ben choked out a cry and rushed a couple of steps forward, straining uselessly with his free hand toward the globe.

To drive it back, the King of Flame must have the aid of My Heir, after My Heir has been vested with My power.

A golden globe of light surged outward from the original spot of shadow, but the darkness swiftly swallowed it up.

Or Ythra, then all the worlds—even Earth...

The shadow now blossomed over the white light in Greenland, overcoming it to spread its darkness over my world.

I couldn't help it. Even knowing this was just a vision, I reached out with my free hand as I choked, "No!"

I grasped the weightless globe loosely in my hand, ignoring the electric shocks going down my arm, but though the glowing power I summoned to my hands drove the darkness back from the areas I touched, the darkness resurged only a moment later and overcame the entire world.

...will fall.

Chapter Twenty-Nine

FAITH

Koriben

For one second, all the lights, even the stars, went out. And in that second, the only reason I did not lose my grip on sanity was because of Sarah's too-cold hand in mine. Even so, it felt like I had been plunged into my very worst nightmare—somehow made even more terrible by that small, chilly hand.

Then the light of the moons above returned, though they had crossed their apex and the light filtering at angles through the ice was dimmer. Then the hold's little denizens regained their light, some of them flying straight to Sarah and brushing against and around her comfortingly. Others—the ones who had taken part in the vision—remained where they were, hovering like light posts over the pillars we could now once again see. Though they had reduced their size, they had resumed their sun forms, with this world's sun floating now on the pillar dead ahead of us, in the northernmost position.

Reflexively, mind still lagging behind, I looked behind me until I found Kaldrir—as warm and brilliant as it had been before—above one of the two southern pillars. His comforting aura thawed part of the ice that had encased my mind.

Sarah's quiet plea shattered it open.

"Ben."

I looked down at her. Her face was twisted with pain, and she was looking down at our hands. With a wrench of guilt, I realized I was gripping her hand with a force that might have been close to crushing her bones.

"Sorry!" I gasped, letting her go. "So sorry! Are you alright?"

Please, please be alright. If I had broken her hand...I would spend every drop of what I had, until I went unconscious, to heal it.

"Fine," she said with a strained smile as she massaged the hand with her other one. "Just numb."

I let out a breath of relief, bracing my hands on my legs for a moment. Sarah sagged against me.

"I know how you feel. Why am I so...tired?"

"Communing with a Tree does that to you," I said numbly as I put an arm around her, trying hard not to think about what we had just heard. Not until I was away from Sarah. Not until I was somewhere I could break things, punch things. Scream until the urge to blaspheme against the Tree left me. "You'll get used to it."

"Ben." Her voice was too small, too uncertain. She must not have been resisting the urge to think as hard as I was.

I gulped, but I set my face as best I could and looked down at her.

My flameheart tore in two—embers and sparks flying and singeing wherever they landed—at the look she was giving me. Begging me to tell her that everything would be alright.

Not her, I thought. Not Sarah. Not my....

But the Tree's whisper echoed in my mind. *To drive it back....*

I broke.

I hated myself for how I jerked from her, for how I backed away from her, left her even more frightened and reaching for me, but I couldn't stand it another second.

"I...Avva. I have to talk to Avva," I choked out.

That was the only explanation I gave her as I turned and almost ran through the doors that were slowly opening.

Yvera rushed to my side. "Ben, what the hellfrost happened in there?"

"Ask Sarah," I shot out without pausing in my stride. "I have to go tell Avva. *Now*. Kor, I'm leaving you in charge. Neither of you are to speak a word of this to anyone or do anything about it until I get back."

One sliver of my practicality still functioning knew that once Sarah had told my wings everything, they would be sorely tempted to do the opposite, and I wouldn't be there to stop them. Hopefully Kor could keep Yvera—and himself—in line until we had our orders from Avva.

"Get *back*?" Kor demanded, hurrying to catch up. I didn't know what had tipped him off that I hadn't meant *from my room*, but he was right, as usual.

"This isn't the sort of thing I should be telling him over a distance," I said, striding through the western arch and into what I guessed was what Sarah and the Tree had called the Rim, in her language. Fitting enough, I supposed. "I'm going to Crownhold. Now. I'll be back as soon as I can."

I just had to make sure of one thing first.

There!

Just as the Tree had said. On the other side of the southern arch from us, but I began rounding the Rim toward it as quickly as I could without breaking into a run. Poor Sarah was already jogging to keep up, and even then, she was trailing behind. Yet another thing I would have to remember to apologize for later.

"But how in Flame's name are you getting there? Or *back*?" Yvera asked. "I thought we were stuck here! And surely there isn't a sungate close enough for even you to—"

"Through that," I said, pointing.

My wings both stared at the arched doors lined in white light that had appeared in the wall next to the southern arch. Except, instead of the tree motif that had appeared on all the others, the central pattern was of the Peacegrowth crest: three shafts of grain, the center straight, the other two bent to either side.

"What—how—" Yvera spluttered.

"Sarah will explain. Just as soon as...."

I stopped in front of the doors and turned to look back. Sarah met my questioning look and full-out ran the rest of the way to me, panting, and bent over to put her hands on her legs for a moment.

"Yes, of course...just...give me...a second," she gasped.

I felt another wrench of guilt.

"Take your time," I said as I put a hand on her shoulder. "I shouldn't have rushed you."

"No," she panted, straightening with a hand on her back. "You have to act quickly, I know. Every second counts now."

The fact that she understood, already...somehow made the wrenching guilt even worse.

With surprising familiarity, Sarah raised her hands, summoning her power to them as she approached the doors. She placed her hands on either side of the white divide and bowed her head.

For one breath, nothing.

Then the brightness in her hands surged into the doors, and they cracked open, swinging outward.

Sarah swayed dangerously, looking as if she wouldn't be able to move out of the way in time. I cried out and caught her just before she could fall or the door could strike her, swinging her up into my arms and backing away into the clear.

"I'm...juz...fine," Sarah mumbled, but her lidded eyes were glazed.

I'm sorry—so, so sorry, I told her silently, so that I could allow some of my agony into the words.

For more than I could say. I had the sudden, horrible premonition that this would not be the last time I held her in my arms like this, feeling her drained, icy body against mine. Since even once was hell....

Don't think.... Don't think!

I was broken inside, that was true. But I couldn't let myself fall apart. Not yet.

"That's a *gate?*" Yvera said in disbelief.

It wasn't like any gate we were used to. Neither had been the one we'd taken to get here, but Yvera and I hadn't had time to examine it in our haste to get through and close the doors behind us.

Covering the now empty doorway was a whitish-blue film, like the beginning crust of ice on a lake. I could feel and see the cold radiating from it as it steamed in the relative heat of the hold. Beyond the semi-clear surface, I could just make out the mesa where we had left. The days and nights of the two worlds must have been somewhat asynchronous, because the dawn sun was just lighting the sky.

Finally, a stroke of luck, I thought. Nighttime wouldn't have stopped me, though it would have made my surging to the nearest active sungate more taxing, perhaps requiring me to rest somewhere along the way and risk running into people I didn't want to have to explain myself to, and it might have made Yvera argue more.

Sure enough, Yvera peered close to the icy film and pulled back, giving a grunt. "Dawn."

She sounded *somewhat* mollified. Still, I knew if she would have been able to go with me, she would have insisted on it; and if she didn't know that my surging was near instantaneous and unable to be intercepted, she wouldn't have let me go.

"Ben, give Sarah to me," Kor said.

I turned and handed her to him gratefully—and reluctantly at the same time. As I cradled the back of her head one last time, I had to fight the absurd urge to lean in to kiss her forehead. Instead, I met Kor's eyes with a hard look.

"Take care of her," I ordered. "I'm holding you personally responsible for her safety while I'm gone."

"I'm fine!" Sarah protested again, this time with more strength. Her eyes were regaining focus, and, upon realizing who was holding her now, color was returning to her cheeks. That flush caused me a confusing blend of relief for her and ill-feeling toward Kor.

"Kor, put me down!" She thrashed weakly, but Kor managed her with ease.

"No can do," Kor said with a downward look and a smirk. "You heard the Heir. Personally responsible."

Don't make me regret this, I snapped silently at him. I was already beginning to.

Kor's eyes met mine, the smirk still there. *Oh, don't you worry. She'll be safe with me—my word on it.*

Kor always kept his word. Always. So that should have made me feel better.

It didn't.

But I had to go. *Now.* I had to. I had to see my father, had to hear his voice and feel his hand on my shoulder, had to convince myself that everything would be alright in the end. That he—that Sarah—

DON'T THINK.

Kor sobered. "Go, Ben."

I forced myself to turn away, to walk up to the icy film. To take a deep breath and shove my hand through.

It was as cold as hellfrost, of course, but...the paper-thin shards of ice parted around my skin seamlessly, and immediately, my fingers were free and feeling the distant touch of a familiar sun.

I looked back at my wings. "Close the doors behind me if you can—if it even works that way. I'll do the same from this side. I don't want anything or anyone finding this gate."

Or through it, finding Sarah. The hold was her home, her refuge, the Tree had said. Well, I prayed to both Trees and the Creators that meant that if we kept it secret, it would keep her safe.

My eyes rested on Sarah one last time. She gazed back at me from Kor's arms, looking more recovered by the moment.

"Just say the word, and I'll open them again for you," she said. "Don't worry about us. Go."

I nodded, not trusting myself to speak. Then I tore myself away and stepped through the ice and into the sun.

I didn't allow myself even a moment to luxuriate in the sunlight as familiar and dear to me as family. Dawn patrols could be starting out at any moment, and the open gate on top of the mesa would be obvious. I whirled around and pushed one half door, then the other closed. From the darkness on the other side of the film as I closed the second door, I guessed Kor and Yvera had already done the same.

As soon as the two doors met once more, the stone faded into nothingness, then the white outline and tree too, until there was nothing to be seen anywhere around me but mesa and the lightening sky. A bit in awe, I reached out, but my hand met nothing but thin air. I waved my hand, even walked around in the space the doors had occupied but felt nothing.

Well, that's how they haven't been discovered, even after a thousand years, I thought.

In the contrary way my riotous emotions seemed to be behaving that night (and now day), the thoroughness of the gate's disappearance made me feel more and less at ease at the same time. I simply held to the comfort that Sarah would most likely be safe while I was gone and didn't let myself wonder if I could get back to her.

Without further ado, I settled my stance, slowed my breath…and pulled in all the warmth and light I could from around me. Then I pulled up more, from deep, deep within me. Tapping into that fire that was only mine as the Golden Heir, I reached even deeper until I felt them: the sungates. The network of gates of fire and light that were the lifeblood of the Six Realms, connecting us all together, roots and branches, in the spirit of the Tree of Flame.

Only one sungate was close enough for me to pull myself to, but that was enough to get me started. Once I was in the stream of light, I could continue through the gate to any other I wished. Any other I was permitted to enter, that is. Which, again, being Heir, was most of them, but I had only conditional access to a few—akin to having to knock on the door. The one I was aiming for was built to be one such door, but it was one I had always been welcome to use before.

I just hoped Avva was home.

I traced my path through the veins of light beforehand to set my intended destination—a necessity, since even if courses could be altered at that speed, being changed into a stream of light tended to dampen one's cognition. That also meant "knocking" at my destination before I even got started.

I only had to wait one breath before the metaphorical door unlocked, which probably meant Avva was not just in his quarters but had been expecting me. I didn't let myself think about what that meant.

Then I braced myself and gathered all my strength, like drawing the string back on a bow.

And released.

I would probably never get used to the sensation of jumping to and through gates: all that I was being changed to no more than a shooting star, rocketing faster than light through the cosmos. It was both the most terrifying and exhilarating experience imaginable. All I saw was light. All I felt was a rushing so great it should have pulverized me to bits, along with a vibration as I shot through each gate. No one standing around the gate would have seen anything, but someone watching closely might have seen the flames increase in strength for one second.

Then one more vibration....

And I was stumbling out of Avva's personal gate and into his waiting room. I'd gotten used to gate travel enough by now that normally I could exit with a bit more grace, but I was beyond exhausted, and more than grateful for a nearby couch for me to collapse into.

Though I got another shot of adrenaline as Avva opened his study door and his warm golden eyes went straight to mine.

How could eyes hold so much welcome, so much love, and so much worry all at once? Yet my father's could.

"Avva," I croaked, straining to my feet.

"Koriben," he said, and crossed the room in just a few strides of his long legs and pulled me into one of his infamous, bone-crushing hugs.

What had Sarah called them? "Bear" hugs? Well, if the word in her language matched the big creature the magic in my mind evoked, then...somehow, it fit.

How long had it been? I started counting the days and then stopped. Because I could feel myself breaking down.

No, no, no. I was a man of twenty summers, Golden Heir of the Tree of Flame. I. Would. Not. Cry.

In his eerie way of seeming to know what I was thinking, Avva said in my ear, "There's no shame in tears, son. In fact, I might be touched if you shed one or two at coming home to me."

I could hear one or two in his own voice.

"Now's not the time for tears, Avva," I said wearily, pushing back to meet his gaze. "I have news. The worst kind."

Avva's eyes tightened, and he gripped my shoulder. "Your...charge is fine, I assume?"

I knew why he was speaking in generalities. Even in his sitting room, it wasn't a good idea to speak of sensitive subjects. Few people had standing permission to open the door to his suite (the regular door, not the gate), but enough did, and one of them could come in at any moment.

I swallowed. "Fine, for now. But we'd better take this into your study."

Avva slung an arm around my shoulders. "Come, then."

He ushered me inside, and while I stared stupidly at my chair next to his (he was never one for making me sit across his desk from him), trying to remember how to sit, I noticed that there was a steaming pot of tsha sitting on a tray, with two mugs ready.

Avva hated tsha. Every variety. Not even over a century of marriage to my tsha-obsessed mother had converted him.

The dam broke. At least I minimized the damage to one or two tears that hopefully escaped unnoticed into my beard.

It's getting scraggly, I thought numbly, trying to distract myself. *I should trim it. After all, Sarah....*

Not a good distraction.

"Sit, Koriben," Avva said with gentle firmness as he closed the door behind us.

I sat. And poured the tsha into my mug. I hoped the sloshing covered the sound of me clearing my throat. "You knew I was coming."

"I guessed you might," Avva said quietly as he took his seat. "No, son, pour me one as well."

I'd begun to set the kettle down. I looked at him incredulously. "You sure?"

"Yes," he said with a grim smile. "I think even I'm going to need some tsha tonight."

"It's night, isn't it?" I said wearily as I poured. "Seems fitting. It was night there as well. When Sarah and I went to get that torched 'message.' It must have only been dek ago."

I handed him his mug and leaned back to nurse mine.

"And what was that message?" Avva asked quietly.

I made myself look up from my mug and meet his gaze. Though I did not want to believe what I was about to tell him—wanted to laugh or crack a smile at the surrealness of it, the impossibility of it coming during our time, *my* time—I couldn't. I felt the truth of it frozen into my bones with a permafrost that not even Avva's roaring hearth and the steaming mug of tsha in my hands could penetrate.

"You were right, Avva. Torch it, you were right. The Devourer.... It's coming."

Avva didn't even blink at my worlds-shattering revelation as he brought his mug to his lips and took a sip. Only then did he grimace, but he swallowed. "Did the Tree of Ice say when?"

"She—wait, how did you know we talked to the Tree of Ice?"

Avva just raised an eyebrow.

"How do you *do* that?" I asked, shaking my finger at him. "Sometime, you're going to have to tell me, because I don't know if you've heard, but I'm supposed to take over your torched job one day, and I'm going to do a hellwind's job at it if you don't share your secret."

Avva looked at nothing and said, as if to no one in particular, "It is interesting the things you can learn from the Tree...our Tree, I mean...if you don't waste Her time arguing with Her."

I ground my teeth. "I don't...argue with Her."

Avva gave me a look, then repeated, "Did the Tree of Ice say when?"

I took a deep breath for calm, then said, "Ten days, by Kaldrir."

This, finally, appeared to be news to Avva. He sat back in his chair and closed his eyes, just breathing for a few moments. When he opened them, they were pools of golden calm.

"I...see. That is sooner than I'd hoped—"

"Than you'd hoped!" I choked. "Avva...Avva, ten days is...."

I set my mug on the desk and put my head in my hands, propping my elbows on my knees. I bunched my fingers through my hair and tried taking slow, deep breaths, praying to the Tree for even a fraction of the calm of the man sitting next to me.

I was supposed to be the Heir. But how was I ever going to measure up to the King?

How was I ever going to lose him?

Avva put his hand on my shoulder and clenched it.

"Ten days is nothing," I said.

I could lose my father in ten days. I could lose...*everything* in ten days. The Devourer could take it all from me. Even...Sarah.

I could feel it coming—the shattering. I'd broken when I'd met Sarah's eyes in that ice cave, and I'd held myself together as best I could until this moment. But now it was coming.

Avva put his other hand on my other shoulder. He could no doubt feel the trembling by now. "Koriben, look at me," he ordered in a voice that brooked no argument.

My mind defaulting to obedience, I looked up.

Avva's eyes were glowing with the force of his conviction, with the power he was pouring into me to ease my pulsing flameheart and still the quaking in my bones. "Life *will* go on, Koriben Sunfilled. The Trees have provided a way. We only have to trust Them enough to follow it. We *will* drive back the Devourer, and all *will* be as it should be. And you are strong enough to face whatever that is."

That was why I'd come to him, I realized. Why I knew at a level deeper than thought why I had to survive long enough to get to him. Only he could understand my burden. Only he knew how to lift it.

I couldn't lose him.

But to protect him, to save him, meant Sarah....

I turned from that thought for the time being and closed my eyes, sitting under the warming, soothing, strengthening influence of my father's power. I knew it was selfish to take this much from him now; every day, it seemed he had less to spare. And yet, I had to take it now, or collapse into a useless heap. I still had information to deliver, and a charge to get back to. Not to mention a mission to resume with increased urgency as soon as I'd gotten some torched sleep.

After a few more breaths, I found the willpower to lean back, breaking away from him. "Enough, Avva. I think...I think I'll be alright now."

"You push yourself too hard, son," Avva said, concern tightening his eyes. "It wouldn't come on so fiercely if you would just—"

"Yes, well, now the Trees have given us a deadline, haven't they?" I picked up my tsha and drank deeply. "I'll rest when we've all *not* been devoured. And when you're healed."

Avva stared into his own mug. "The Tree of Ice spoke of healing, did She?"

I took another gulp to suppress the wince. "No. But She made it clear that She intended to invest Sarah as soon as we can get to Her. That is...if Sarah accepts."

For the first time, tonight the scales had wavered inside me, tipping dangerously toward wishing Sarah would refuse. I'd always wanted her to choose for herself.... But before, I'd always wanted her to choose to accept the mantle in the end. I knew from personal experience that Trees chose Their Heirs with extreme care. Even if there was another Moontouched descendant in the wings, one of Sarah's family perhaps, the Tree of Ice would have only chosen Sarah if Sarah was the best possible candidate. I—we all—needed the best right now, didn't we? Now, more than ever?

But I remembered my greatest moment of weakness, the moment of breaking.

Not her.

"She will," Avva said with conviction, for once oblivious to my inner turmoil as he gazed at his scale brackets on the wall. "I could see it in her, though she wouldn't yet believe it herself. She is everything we need and more."

I stayed silent. Though I gripped my mug with dangerous force.

"So now you are to find the way to Earth, as quickly as may be, so that Sarah may be brought home and to her Tree," Avva said, turning back to me, so I quickly relaxed my grip.

I took a gulp of tsha to help wash down the lump in my throat. "Yes. And the Tree gave us a hint on how to do that. There's this new kind of gate—moon-gates, She called them."

I calmed somewhat as I briefly explained all I knew about our next steps. This part, I could deal with. Yes, the time constraint was nothing short of nerve-wracking, but straightforward at the same time. Yes, dangerous too; I hadn't forgotten the ahglen, krathen, or lish. But it wasn't fraught with prophe-cies of doom. And I sure as hellwinds wasn't going to camp out in the open with her anymore.

Perhaps not even if the Tree ordered me to again.

You know.... Maybe there was something to Avva's gentle advice on how I should change my attitude toward our Tree.... I thought I'd kept my occasionally rebellious thoughts from interfering, but....

Avva's question cut straight through my distracted mulling over my second mug of tsha. "And after the Tree invests Sarah? What then?"

I took three slow, deliberate breaths before I answered. "I'm to bring the Tree of Ice's Heir—" I deliberately didn't mention Sarah's name. "—back to you...so that they can help you drive off the Devourer. The Tree said you must have their help...or all is lost."

"That would make sense," Avva said quietly. "Ten days from now is the Dark Solstice."

I stared at him, aghast. "Is it?"

"It is. It cannot be a coincidence."

I slumped in my chair. "Blessed Flame. Could this night get any worse...."

A solar eclipse on the day of the winter solstice—a combination that had not occurred in hundreds of years. For months now, we had been preparing a particularly bright and jubilant Festival of Lights to counteract the existential dread it was bringing everyone. But I had lost track of the days....

Avva was right. The Devourer could not have picked a darker day to return.

"No wonder it is being so bold," I groaned.

"You saw the shadow strike the Temple first, didn't you?"

"Yes." The shadow's point of origin, even from such a distant perspective, was unmistakable. I was the Sunfilled Heir, after all.

Bold, but strategic. It would strike swiftly, savagely, straight at our greatest defense, our very heart: our Tree. If She fell....

"It will expect some preparations," Avva said, entering deep into thought. "It is the Dark Solstice, after all. But it must calculate that what it will lose in surprise, it will gain in darkness. And it thinks that even if the Tree forewarns us, even if we heed Her, we will not be strong enough to drive it back. It thinks we are at our weakest now, but it is wrong, and we will use that."

"But we're *not* strong enough, Avva. The Sunfilled are scattered—"

"Ten days is enough time to bring them in. Slowly, discreetly."

"—and depleted." In both numbers and energy. Me being the prime example.

Avva returned his gaze to mine. "We are not the only guardians of the Tree, son. Though it is our greatest duty, all the clans share that burden with us. Perhaps it is time we relied on them as we should."

Avva was too good to speak in anything but the collective "we." Even though his urging the Sunfilled to share their burdens with the rest of the clans—and for the rest of the clans to do their part—had been one of the major focuses of his reign for decades.

"Understood." I took the point with grace, hoping he would take mine more easily. "But, Avva, *you* are not ready."

Even *if* he was healed, it might not be in time. Not for a conflict of that scale. Not for the Devourer.

"Then it is a good thing I will not face the Devourer alone," Avva said evenly.

His words, his calm, felt like a stab in my back. Though we hadn't touched directly on this, the aspect I'd dreaded the most, I had expected Avva to feel as I did—that for the first time, Avva would say the Tree asked for too much. I clenched the armrests of my chair.

"How?" I choked out. "How could the Tree...how could *you*...expect Sarah to face the Devourer?"

Avva's eyes returned to mine. "We will protect Sarah as we protect our Tree—with our very lives if necessary. Nevertheless, the Trees have made it clear that without her standing with us, we will fall."

"This isn't her fight," I said with deliberate slowness.

Avva's eyes flashed. "It is as much hers as it is ours. If we fall, the Devourer will come for her next."

I flinched. But I couldn't deny it.

The Devourer was never sated. The Devourer never stopped. And never would, not even when it had consumed not just the Tree of Flame and Her Six Realms but the Tree of Ice and Earth as well. And once it got to Earth, then Sarah, bright and powerful Sarah, would draw it in like a bleeding achik in a vorpex's hunting ground.

Avva softened. "Better for her to face it with us to shield her than for her to face it alone."

"She's not a warrior," I protested. My words were almost a plea now. "She shouldn't have to fight!"

Not her.

"Perhaps she isn't, and won't, in the ways you mean—although given time and training, I think she could surprise you in that regard. But even if she doesn't fight with sword or might, she will be the key to our survival on that dark day. Even if the Trees had not said so, I feel it in my heart."

I put my head in my hands again, took several shaking breaths. "I swore to protect her. You know that. The Tree made me swear."

Avva once again put his hand on my shoulder and clenched it. "And so we shall, Koriben. This, I swear to *you*: Sarah will be well."

I raised my head to meet his eyes and finally allowed the conviction, the utter faith there, to sink into my flameheart. Giving the strength it needed to burn strong for the next ten days.

"Right," I said, setting my jaw. "Right. Of course. She'll be fine. She, and the Tree, if nothing else, will be fine."

"I swear it," Avva repeated.

"Right," I said, nodding firmly now as I sat back.

"Though I meant what I said about keeping her from the front line," Avva said in a lighter tone, "it would not hurt for you to take full advantage of the next ten days to train her as best as you and your wings can."

"You're right," I said, but with a discouraged sigh. "She needs to be able to protect herself, as much as that's possible...."

Though how, I couldn't guess.

Avva raised an eyebrow. "Don't make the Devourer's same mistake, son: don't underestimate her. Though she may not have the size and skills we associate with a warrior, the Tree would not have left her defenseless. You may find she has her own weapons that make her the greatest threat of all."

That got my mind *thinking*, in a way the panic hadn't allowed before. And remembering.

How strong, how powerful she had looked in a dark corridor with the moons rising, as my own power waned. How glorious when doing nothing more than laughing as she greeted the lights dancing around her. How brave as she stood in the darkness, surrounded by nothing but stars.

Because Avva was watching, I nodded, to show I'd taken his point. Though still my mind kept thinking.

He was right. There *would* be a reason. She *would* have a way to defend herself. Her own way.

A new way.

Now it was up to the both of us to figure out what that was.

Have faith, son of Flame.

Well, since I had torched else to go on except faith...faith in my father, in our Trees, in Sarah...then faith was what I would have.

ACKNOWLEDGEMENTS

I HAVE BEEN INCREDIBLY blessed to be helped by many people over my lifetime of writing, too many for my fallible memory. Since this is my first published book, I'll try to acknowledge as many of them as I can here, even if they didn't directly contribute to this book or series.

I have to begin at the obvious place: with my family. I have the best parents a girl could have asked for in Ken and Millie. Even if they didn't always know what to make of my super secretive writing hobby, they graciously gave me the space and means to flourish. As avid readers themselves, at least they knew I didn't fall too far from the tree. ;) And this series would not have been possible without their financial and emotional support. Their faith in me is invaluable.

In my early years, I might never have gotten beyond my first few thousand words without my initial readers: my siblings Tia, Mark, and Jenessa, and my best friend/adopted sister Katelan Tanner. Thanks, guys, for somehow genuinely enjoying my first email-serial novels. I might have kept up with wild daydreams, but you were my motivation to keep typing them out until I became a somewhat decent storyteller. You'll always be my go-to beta readers.

A few teachers had enough impact to make a mention here. First, once again, my mother, Millie, who was the one who taught me to read, write, and learn. I'll owe her forever for that. Second, Mrs. M., my favorite high school English teacher, who was *convinced* I'd be a successful writer one day and almost made me believe it too. The "successful" part remains to be seen, but at least I'm finally making the "writer" part a reality for her now. Third, my teacher for my career exploration class my senior year of high school, who helped me figure out that psychology *wasn't* my calling and let me switch my topic to English teaching; though I never became an English teacher, I'm so glad that class convinced me to stick with a writing-adjacent career!

Moving on to my college years, thanks go to *Leading Edge* for all that I learned there, from slush reading to managing as editor-in-chief; for that latter period, I'm giving all the credit to my "rightwing" Hayley Cousin and "leftwing" Adam McLain. Seriously, I'm pretty sure all three of us knew those two were the real powers behind the throne and were both far more talented and dedicated than me. Thanks for putting up with me anyway, guys. Whatever success we had that year, it was because of you, and I have waited seven long years to tell the world that.

Huge thanks to my BYU writing group: Michela Hunter, Rachael Lynn Buchanan, Brianna Martin, L.B, and (for a short time) Adam McLain. Our sessions together were some of the best fun I had in college and the best encouragement I got at that time to keep writing. Brandon Sanderson gets a mention here for his awesome lecture series at BYU, which I took twice and without which I wouldn't have found my writing group. Also, what other teacher gives all his students a pizza party at the end of the semester?

On the more "professional" side, I'd like to acknowledge my former supervisor Devan Jensen (BYU's Religious Studies Center) for giving me such good editing work while I was a student and having such patience with my youthful mistakes and budding professionalism. Devan gets another shout-out for his mentorship of me in the Latter-day Saint Publishing Professionals Association (LDSPPA, now LDSPMA) and connecting me with such great people. Likewise, Steve Piersanti (Berrett-Koehler), whom I also connected with through LDSPPA, for being such a hopeful light in the publishing industry in general and so encouraging to me.

Which rolls into my post-college editing years, with Christopher Robbins and Brooke Jorden from Familius. Christopher was a great boss and still is a great mentor, taking the time to give me advice on publishing this series, asking to read the first book, and connecting me with others in the industry. And I learned heaps from Brooke, Familius's skilled and gracious managing editor, about substantive editing, the editing and publishing process, and running it all myself when I was her maternity-leave substitute.

There's a bunch of editors, managers, and mentors I worked with in the intervening years. I hope you all know who you are. This paragraph is for you. Thank you for teaching me so much about work, life, and everything in between. You all were the best coworkers and mentors I could have asked for.

Then we finally get to the actual writing and publishing of this book. (And here I thought I'd somehow keep something short for once. ;) Thanks for bearing with me.)

I'm grateful to Stephanie H. for the use of her wonderful home as the perfect writing retreat. The height of my writing craze for the 400,000-word behemoth that was the first three books of this series was while I was house/pet-sitting for her at the beginning of 2023, when I was able to devote literally every waking hour to writing. And, well...you can see the result. Thanks again, Stephanie! Give the boys some pets for me.

Thanks also go to my family for putting up with my disappearances and my long hours of mental absence, even when I was *technically* home. Or supposed to be focusing on something else, like instructions on the proper sanding or cutting of baseboards. (Sorry, Mom.) Tia, as always, was a wonderful cheerleader and reminder of my need to eat and sleep and (*cough*) read a good book. ;) She also patiently listened to all my enigmatic exclamations of excitement or frustration before she got to read what I was rambling on about.

Thanks again to Tia and Jenessa for helping me with "research" (little did they know it at the time) by going on a trip to Iceland with me right at the end of it all. You just *thought* it was a sisters' retreat, muahahaha! Just kidding, it was totally what it seemed. It just *also* happened to be good research and the perfect time to finish up my initial review of the behemoth. What better time to make the final touches on the first draft than in the quiet, early hours of the morning, sprawled across the front seats of a campervan in Iceland, while you two were sleeping? And what better place from which to send it out to the family to finally read? (Thank goodness for Wi-Fi hotspots.) And what better way to spend our evenings after our days of Icelandic adventuring than cozy in our heated van reading and laughing about that draft? Ha, you could probably think of better things for that last one, but I'll always remember those memories with a kind of magical light. Thanks for making that such a special time for me.

I have to once again give thanks to Mom for putting up with the behemoth's length and ending. Tia might have been the first to finish (I think before we'd even left Iceland), but Mom wins the award for the most emotional investment—for good or ill when it came to her sleep and sanity. Apologies once again, Mom.

Huge thanks once again to former writing group members Michela Hunter and Rachael Lynn Buchanan for temporarily reprising their roles to give me much-needed feedback as writers on this latest project of mine. Rachael's first-fifty-pages review was prompt and superbly professional, and Michela's heroic feedback essay (after finishing the behemoth version and undergoing surgery, no less!) was exactly what I needed at the time. That was the moment that I thought I really might just have something. Sometimes when I feel like giving up, I remember a line or two of her profuse encouragement, and I find the will to keep going for just a bit longer.

Katelan Tanner gets a special mention for letting me read the third book to her while I was visiting in the summer of 2023. Besides just being just plain fun, her real-time feedback was helpful and encouraging. I'll always remember those nights with fondness. Mom, Dad, Tia, and K.M. also listened to me read some of the books as our "audiobook" on that same trip.

Other beta readers who gave feedback on this book include Zabeth Welker, A.C., Mason Stewart, She Who Must Not Be Named, Sondi, Onalisa Tanner, and S.B. Thanks for your time and valuable feedback, one and all!

Special shout-out to sensitivity reader Nadia Koncurat for helping me expound on Sarah's Latina heritage and for being such a kind and generous person. Sarah couldn't have a more apt cheerleader and model.

When it comes to the production and publishing of this series, I'd like to thank Jane Friedman for kindly pointing me toward the rapid release model and for having a blog (janefriedman.com) full of down-to-earth wisdom and encouragement for writers. Reedsy also has a fountain of free, helpful resources that answered so many of my questions. I'm truly lucky to be self-publishing at a time when so much knowledge and support is out there, and the writing community is one of the kindest and most generous I've encountered. Thanks also go to Rebecca Frank for a fantastic cover that perfectly captured my vision and for accommodating my rapid-release schedule.

Last, but not least, I'd like to thank E. and K.N. for their free office chair. They joked that if I made it big, they expected a mention in the acknowledgements, so here they are, just in case. ;) Here's hoping their inclusion will bring me the luck to make the other part come true.

ABOUT THE AUTHOR

Leah E. Welker graduated from Brigham Young University (Provo) in 2016 with a degree in English language and a minor in editing. She then edited for seven years and pivoted to writing in 2023. She is based in the DC area, where she lives with family and her rescue Australian shepherd, Wes.

You can connect with her at
   https://www.leahewelker.com

Subscribe to her newsletter for updates, cover reveals, dog pics, and more:
   https://www.leahewelker.com/follow